The Travellers' Tales

The Travellers' Tales

Alastair Cairns Hull

The manufacturer's authorised representative in the EU
for product safety is Authorised Rep Compliance Ltd,
71 Lower Baggot Street, Dublin D02 P593 Ireland (www.arccompliance.com)

This is a work of fiction. Names, characters, businesses, places, events
and incidents are either the products of the author's imagination
or used in a fictitious manner. Any resemblance to actual persons,
living or dead, or actual events is purely coincidental.

Troubador Publishing Ltd
Unit E2 Airfield Business Park,
Harrison Road, Market Harborough,
Leicestershire. LE16 7UL
Tel: 0116 2792299
Email: books@troubador.co.uk
Web: www.troubador.co.uk

ISBN 978 1836282 907

British Library Cataloguing in Publication Data.
A catalogue record for this book is available from the British Library.

Printed and bound by CPI Group (UK) Ltd, Croydon, CR0 4YY
Typeset in 11pt Minion Pro by Troubador Publishing Ltd, Leicester, UK

Thanks to my family and friends.
Happy memories to those who have travelled the trail
and good luck to those who wish to.

Chapter 1

Istanbul. March 1971

"In any moment of decision, the best thing to do is the right thing. The worst thing you can do is nothing."

Waiting. It was the waiting that was so tiring. Waiting to get a letter or postcard. Waiting to get some news. Harry was worried and now uncertain whether Lucy would come to meet them. Maybe she had changed her mind and gone back home. Or maybe she had met someone else, a holiday romance on a Greek island.

Harry now wished he had found out more about the holiday Lucy had arranged with her friend Janet. He understood her friend was flying back home after three weeks of island hopping, and that she would travel to Istanbul to meet him. But now he wasn't sure, maybe she was staying for more time in Greece on her own, going to different islands.

When Harry and Rolly first arrived in Istanbul, Harry chose to stay in a room in the Hostel Fathir, along a narrow street in the old part of the city, a short walk to the Pudding Shop, a bit further to the central Post Office where he had arranged for letters to be kept at Post Restante.

Rolly moved the camper van to a secure park on the outskirts of the city that was used by lorries and buses, and travellers passing to and from Asia. He had the better deal; it was free, and he could sleep in the camper van, cook his food on their small *gaz* stove, and sleep away from the city noises. They had heard from other travellers when crossing Europe that in big cities it was essential to stay near your vehicle. If they parked only for a short time on the streets all their valuables would disappear, including the wheels of the camper and probably some vital engine parts.

The Hostel Fathir was a ramshackled, three-story ancient building. On the ground floor there was a tiny cubby hole of a shop selling cigarettes, plastic packets of sweets and dry biscuits, and magazines with lurid colour pictures of Turkish and Indian film stars. The narrow entrance door squeezed in next to the shop had been painted green, possibly in the past century. There were steep steps up to a landing where the owner, Mustafa, had a room that also served as the reception and office. Harry had his small room down a short corridor, just big enough for a hard, single, metal bed with threadbare grey sheets. There was a tiny window, fly–spotted and covered with dust and dirt from the city. It opened directly across the narrow street, overlooking steep sloping roofs and a spaghetti of television aerials.

The walls of the room had been lime-washed, probably at the same time as the front door was painted. They were now smeared with graffiti, old grime, and red blood stains from squashed mosquitoes.

The bathroom, across the corridor, was not a bathroom as Harry was used to, but a cubicle with no ventilation, a toilet that rarely flushed, a tap at head height as a cold-water shower, and a hole in the floor as a drain. This was an entrance for numerous cockroaches.

Harry had plenty of time to reminisce on the adventures so far. Every night since arriving in Istanbul he was disturbed by the city noises. Five times every day the muezzin called the faithful to prayers from the mosque minaret close by, the call being picked up and repeated by all the adjacent mosques in the region. The cries echoed round and round the old city; some were modulated and tuneful, others distorted and cracked by poor loudspeakers. He had to keep the window open to circulate some air into his tiny room and keep the fetid, rank smell from the toilet at bay.

As he lay on the hard bed, gazing up at the maze of cracks in the ceiling plaster, he traced rivers and roads, dreaming they were maps of countries he was going to be travelling through with Lucy. New countries they had yet to discover and learn about. New people to meet and maybe make friends with.

There were so many events and adventures to recall from the past month during the trip across Europe with Rolly in the Mercedes camper van. Each country they passed through was surprisingly different. The varied landscapes, mountains, high peaks covered with snow, steep valleys with rushing rivers and thick, dense, black woodlands. Some big, noisy, crowded cities where they noticed different architecture, with different shaped houses, roofs and churches. They found different customs, traditions, languages and money in each country.

The two boys had met at the local primary school and became friends on the first day of joining. They were different in both appearance and approach to life. Rolly fitted his name; he was short and round, and his hair was dark, straight and always cut short. He had a ruddy complexion and blushed scarlet at the smallest embarrassing situation. He enjoyed his food, especially chocolate. Harry was tall for his age, and although he did not partake in any sports, he looked athletic and fit. He had a mass of curly blond hair, that was always unruly.

After school, they usually joined in the rough and tumble of football games in the cobbled street. Some days, if it was not raining, they would run up through the woods and onto the moor, past the allotments along the side of the factory to escape into worlds of their own. Harry was always wanting adventure. He led his friend Rolly to places further and further away. Sometimes they got lost, playing games of imagination as explorers, pirates and hunters, spending a long time trying to find the way home. It was at these times Harry felt happiest.

His Mum frequently said *'Our 'arry 'as these wanderin' feet. 'E's like that bloke who went to Africa. 'Wots e' called, I read bout' im' in t' shop magazine. Lord Livingstone! That's 'im. And that one 'wot climbed the tallest mountain on our Coronation Day.'*

He reflected on the small Yorkshire town they were brought up in. The house he lived in with his mum, dad and younger brother was one of the neatest in the street. The front door and window frames were painted every other year, and the front doorstep was stained red each month. His dad, Fred, worked as a foreman in the factory just up the street, a good job with wages that meant he was saving up to buy a car. His mum was large, very large, and spent most of her time cooking in the kitchen, big healthy stews with dumplings and every weekend a roast with Yorkshire puddings and dark gravy followed by apple pie and custard. She was always worrying and fussing, her hair slipping out from under a head scarf, constantly being pushed back with worn washerwoman fingers.

Rolly's house was down the street on the other side near the factory. It always looked scruffy, with peeling paintwork and dirty windows. His dad worked for the council cleaning streets, collecting rubbish, emptying bins and in winter clearing snow from the pavements. His mum worked in the general store in the market square, usually stacking shelves, occasionally working the till, and gossiping with customers. They were always short of money, with little left at the end of the week for essential clothes or special treats.

Harry regularly daydreamed about his first meeting with Lucy.

He had studied for a degree in graphic design at Sussex University. Lucy had been doing a three-year course at Art School. Now they had both successfully qualified. They were both involved in similar activities outside their studies at University and Art School. Conservation, drama, politics, archaeology, cycling and music. It was cycling that drew Harry and Lucy together. Resting, sitting on a bench overlooking the sea, at first they shyly held hands, then kissed, then she stayed for some nights in his flat.

Soon after meeting and becoming close friends, Harry and Lucy realised they both wanted to travel, to explore the world once they had finished their education. They spent hours together planning, talking, reading, and looking at maps. This was a time of great social changes. There was a freedom of choice after the end of the world war, greater financial freedom. Changes in fashion, music, and family life. Many young people, having had a good education, were yearning to go away, get away from the routine of family home life, and learn about the world before settling into a job.

During their final year, sitting close together on the sagging sofa in Harry's flat, they talked of travelling and exploring the world. It was this idea of an adventure that grew, and they had planned together over a couple of years since they had first met.

During the hours of waiting, sleeplessness, and listening to the noises of the night, Harry's imagination and thoughts ran to the future, travelling across Asia, Turkey, Iran, Afghanistan, Pakistan and India. But his main thoughts were always of Lucy. He loved her. He missed her all the time. When would she come to join them?

Is Harry the man for me?

I sometimes stay at his flat. We have great sex. He seems to have been around a bit. I know he has had several girlfriends, so he is experienced. Unlike me. I have had just a couple of brief boyfriends, nothing serious and not for long.

His flatmates are so into music. They accept me as just one of them. I enjoy what they play, and I like it when they ask my opinion.

Do we spend enough time together? It's on and off when we feel like it. But we do spend a lot of time planning this trip. How is it going to be living all the time together? Will we have rows, arguments, things like that? I hope not.

And what about the other fellow, Rolly? I haven't met him yet. What will it be like sharing everything day after day? How will we sleep and eat? Will I get on with him? Harry says he is quite different from him.

I don't know what to expect. I don't even know how long the trip will take.

Harry told me he and Rolly are great friends from their early school days. I know Rolly is a mechanic, that's good. We'll need one. We plan to drive a long way. I've paid for this camper van, but I haven't seen it yet. I hope it's going to be safe.

So many questions, so much unknown.

Friday evening. I am on the train home to see Mother and PaPa again. It is a bit boring. I am looking forward to leaving college to go travelling, to explore the world.

I lodge with Mrs. Warner during the week, so I usually go home at the weekends, unless I am sleeping over at Harry's.

My bedroom at Mrs Warner's is in their semi-detached house in a quiet cul-de-sac. It's OK. I have a single bed, (clean sheets every week), a small table to study at, bedside drawers and a wardrobe. It looks out onto the back garden. Mrs. Warner is very pleasant, but always busy. She is a cook at the local primary school. Mr. Warner is away every week in his Ford Cortina. I think he sells insurance.

Mrs. Warner goes to work before nine o'clock in the morning. She leaves me some bread, marge, and marmalade on the kitchen table, and a pot for me to make tea. In the evening, I sit down with her for afternoon tea. It is always early so she can watch her favourite soap on the TV. The food is so predictable, you can tell which day of the week it is without looking at a calendar. Monday is cold meat left over from their Sunday roast, with baked potatoes. Tuesday is usually spag-boll with mince, also from the Sunday roast. Wednesday is a Vesta curry from the Supermarket with rice. As a treat there would be an Instant Whip as a pudding. My favourite is always butterscotch flavour. Thursday is a meat stew with overcooked cabbage. On Friday, on the way home, I have a bag of fish and chips or get together with some art school friends to have a curry, Chinese or Wimpy burger.

Just had a Chinese with my friend Janet. We are going to Greece together, so exciting! First holiday without Mother and PaPa.

We are flying to Athens, then exploring lots of islands by ferry. PaPa bought my air ticket, and Janet used her savings for hers. PaPa has given me loads of spending money. I think he is just happy to get me out of the house.

Janet is a bit of a straight horse. Maybe good for me to go travelling with her. Keep me on the straight and narrow! She thinks I am quite wild. She is just waiting for Mister Right to walk round the corner. Settle down, get married (no sex before), have babies, and a nice house.

I don't know what I want. A lot of life to go through. First of all, I want to do some travelling and exploring.

I have told Mother and PaPa about going off to Asia with Harry. That will be straight after Greece. So, I'll be away for a long time. I know they think I should start a job, get a step on the job ladder, and after a while think about getting married. This is what Mother wants. To see her daughter married in church, doing it all properly. She probably has already got the hat. But they can see it won't happen yet. They know I have wandering feet and want to explore some of the world, just like Harry.

Harry's clever and going to do well. When he asked me to come across Asia with him, I didn't hesitate. I didn't even think twice. It sounds fun, but it is one hell of a commitment to stick with the same guy for such a long time. He is doing so much planning.

The posh girls' school I went to from kindergarten to 'A' levels taught us nothing about life in the big world. One of the girls in my class got pregnant. Shock, horror! She was sent home immediately. We never heard from *her again. The other girls I had as friends have just drifted apart. I don't know where most of them are.*

He says I will get along fine with Rolly. I don't know, not sure! Travelling all day, eating together, sharing everything. These things do worry me. It's a big unknown.

Harry came home with me at Christmas. That was good, though we had separate rooms. Mother and PaPa liked him, but I think they were doubtful about his Yorkshire accent, and worried his dad was not in a profession. I know he convinced them he was doing well at uni, and that he would get a good job when qualified. All that is so important to them. Good education, good qualifications, good job. That's life to them.

When Harry asked Rolly if he would like to come on this trip, he was doubtful he would say yes. Harry could recall the details of the conversation they had in the local pub. They met up regularly during holidays now they were not at school together. Inevitably they talked about the future. Girls, jobs, and what they hoped to do with their lives. They had had a couple of pints. Harry announced out of the blue, 'I want to go travelling, I want to see the world, I've never been out of England.' Rolly looked bemused like he usually looked when approached with an idea he couldn't get his head round.

'Let's have another pint and I will tell you what I have been dreaming about for the past couple of months.'

Coming back from the bar with two full pints, Rolly questioned, 'Where do you mean, travelling, France or Spain or somewhere like that?'

'No', he replied, 'I mean Kathmandu.'

Rolly, who had always failed at geography at school asked, 'Kathmandu, where on earth is that? I've never heard of it.'

'It's the capital of Nepal, north of India. I have thought about this a lot. There are buses that go from London all the way taking people to India and Nepal. I've seen posters up in our students hall saying they leave every month, and it costs only 50 pounds. They go there quickly, not stopping except overnight. That's not what I want, what I want to do is drive overland slowly, exploring all the places on the way, taking our time.'

Rolly was mystified. He went to the bar and bought two packets of crisps and a chocolate bar. 'Who are you going with? Some of your friends from uni?'

After a long sip of beer, he looked Rolly straight in the eye.

'I'm hoping it will be you and me, and Lucy, my girlfriend. Lucy and I have talked about it a lot. She is very keen. I tried to get my flatmate, Charlie to come along, but he wasn't that interested. He just wanted to get into the music business. Rocky, who is our roadie, overheard us talking about it and thought it would be a cool idea. But the prospect of living close and hanging out with Rocky for several weeks on end was not a pleasant thought. You're my oldest mate, we've known each other forever. I thought of you first but wasn't sure it was your sort of thing.

I know you didn't do much in the way of history or geography, but I have been reading up a lot about travelling overland to Asia. In olden times it was a very famous route called the Silk Road. It followed from China to Rome through many ancient cities, so many different cultures, tribes, and languages. Some of it was through remote deserts where they used caravans of camels. This was the start of world trade; famous people such as Alexander the Great, Marco Polo, and Genghis Khan had trekked through the dust of this route. Many religions have come and gone. There was always fighting to gain new countries.'

He took another drink of beer. 'And now our generation is going along this trail to explore the world, find new ideas, meet new people. We know, that after the recovery from the war, we have freedom, independence, and money. I know this is a lot to take in. It must seem a strange idea to you.'

Rolly stared at the ceiling for several long minutes. He had eaten both packets of crisps and was opening the bar of chocolate.

'We both really want you to come with us, it will be a great adventure, we will get on well, and you are a good mechanic, help to keep our camper van going. I know you will get on with Lucy, she is very easy going.'

Rolly was still staring at the ceiling. He drank down his beer in one draught, stood up, put on his coat and said, 'I don't know what it all means, but OK, I guess I'll come.'

And so the adventure began.

Chapter 2

Istanbul. March 1971

*"People were right when they say there is
no other place on earth as beautiful
looking as Istanbul"*

Harry realised he had been moping in his room for several days, just reading or looking at the ceiling. Time spent strumming on his guitar until the couple in the room next to him asked him to be quiet because they could not sleep. He had lost track of time and how many days it had been since they arrived in Turkey.

During the first week in Istanbul, he explored many of the tourist sites of the city with Rolly. There was so much that was different: the smells, the people, the language, the sounds.

They found this city unique. It spanned two continents: Asia and Europe. It was the amalgamation of very different traditions — Eastern and European — and so many different histories. The streets were filled with people either wearing traditional hijabs or western clothes.

The two boys had explored and learned the layout of the city. The Blue Mosque with its pencil shaped minarets, Hagia Sofia, originally a Greek cathedral, then a mosque and then a museum. The Topkapi Museum and further away the Galata Tower. It all became an overdose of culture.

The grand bazaar was more interesting. It was easy to get lost in the web of narrow alleyways with an infinite number of tiny stalls selling anything and everything. Brightly lit shops, illuminated by colourful lamps made of multi-coloured glass. Dark, narrow alleyways, under a low covered roof where small industries made, copied, and manufactured all the needs of a large city. Turks with stalls crowded with shining copperware, handmade gifts, leather goods, Persian carpets and imported fabrics. Afghans with elaborate embroideries, textiles and jewellery made from lapis lazuli. The Spice Bazaar, bursting with colours, fragrances and tastes, was filled with exotic scents from cones of colourful spices. Piles of nuts, dried fruits and many multiple varieties of tea. Teas mixed with fruit and herbs, tastes for every occasion.

However, it had soon became familiar, and the novelty of being in an exotic city was wearing off.

Harry went regularly to the Pudding Shop, close to where he was staying. It had grown over previous years as the meeting place for travellers coming and going between India and Europe. The two brothers, Idris and Namak, made everyone welcome with tiny cups of strong Turkish coffee, and breakfasts of fried eggs cooked in a shallow bowl of olive oil with huge hunks of freshly baked bread.

One wall of the shop was covered with letters and notices from travellers hoping to make contact with friends, asking for information on places to stay and the possibility of getting a lift. There were details of where to get an Afghan visa in Tehran and the best place to crash in Mashhad. Requests for travelling companions; *Beautiful guy looking for a hand to hold on the way to India. I have got my own VW camper, but need a female companion to help drive, to go all the way.*

He spent hours talking, over coffee, to other travellers. Some were on buses that regularly ran between London and Kathmandu, Delhi and Goa, bus trips that he had previously seen advertised in alternative magazines and on notice boards in the university bar.

He met other travellers with camper vans, VW buses, and small Deux Chevaux or VW bugs. Some were hitching, some cycling or riding on motorbikes.

They were a mixed crowd of young people from many countries in Europe and North America.

Part of Harry's Diary.

I am getting impatient, and worried. Is Lucy ever going to turn up? I never expected that we would have to wait so long in Istanbul. I want to get on the road again, get into Asia and start discovering new countries.

It has been good up till now. Rolly and I get on well, he has been learning a lot about the world and is good at looking after the van.

It is great he decided to come on this trip. Originally, I had thought of asking some of the guys I shared the flat in Brighton to come. There were four of us sharing, we had set up a band hoping to hit the big time. We went to listen to big, famous groups playing in London and at festivals. We practiced so much, we learnt how to read music scores and improvise playing along with cassettes and vinyls of blues and jazz. I got quite good on a guitar, Charlie was the lead singer, he also played the guitar and occasionally a sax, Dev was on a bass guitar and John on drums. We all enjoyed listening to psychedelic bands such as Grateful Dead, Pink Floyd and The Doors, but we could never get our heads round to playing that type of music without getting involved in heavy mind–changing drugs. I am glad I didn't ask them. The thought of spending weeks on end in a camper van with Charlie would end up in fights.

I thought we would meet more people on the road hitching. But I am sure we will further on, when we are in Turkey. There are lots of travellers here, waiting to move on.

This lying around, waiting, has made me think about the trip up till now and reflect on home, the town I was born in, my mum and dad, some of the good times I had there.

I used to love the moors. The woods were carpeted in the spring with bluebells and wild garlic. There was a smell of dampness from the brown leaves. There we hunted for blackbird nests in the thickets, collecting the blue eggs to take home and add to our collections. Higher up the moors there was the colour purple from heather and fresh green with new growth in the spring.

We played games of imagination as explorers, pirates, hunters. At each dip and valley, it was possible to find a hiding place for a tribe of feathered Indians. We would dream up adventures in rough-built forts and tree houses, always with an element of danger and bravado.

We would collect blackberries and hedgerow fruits to eat, scrumping apples and pears from Mr Braithwait's small holding next to the factory. Sometimes I really enjoyed just lying in the heather watching the clouds, finding mythical beasts in their formation. Watching Sky Larks and Lapwings soar, singing high into the sky.

Another thing I always remember is the river that ran through the town. It was a constant source of adventure. We would try catching catfish with a pair of hands, always with a splash too late, the fish would dart behind a rock into deeper water. In the summer months, when the water level was low, we would splash about with frozen feet, toes trying to get a grip on the pebbly bottom. Returning home with wet soggy shorts and rolled-up sleeves, carrying a jam jar with two or three sticklebacks already gasping for air. My Dad would demand they were returned to the river by the next day.

In the wintertime, we watched the river in flood after a week of rain, hanging over the parapet of the ancient stone bridge. The peat brown water covering boulders with tumbling surges and overfalls of white water and froth. We would search the areas where the water was still between the rocks looking for a sleek brown trout, head into the flow, swimming against the current working its way upriver to the spawning grounds.

In the school holidays, we went further afield, all day up amongst the higher peaks and valleys, with homemade fishing rods made from a broken off twig, a cotton reel fixed to the handle and a bent pin as a hook. I still have mine in the camper. We tried fishing in a lake somewhere, but it was useless. Also, we made catapults, terrorising rabbits, but never got one. They were fantastic adventure games that we dreamt up, smearing mud on our faces as camouflage, hiding amongst the heather.

Thinking about our trip across Europe, when we were in Yugoslavia, we stopped to ask about a place to camp. This guy told us to go to a site by a big lake. He bought us a couple of beers and told us about regulations in Yugoslavia and what to do if stopped by the police. He then told a long story about a group of hippies. There were five of them crammed into a car, different nationalities. They had got stopped by the police because their vehicle was in terrible condition. The police could see they were real hippies, on the way home from India. Long dirty hair, beards, beads, tie-dyed clothes. One of them tried offering a few notes as a bribe to the policeman who was booking them, whilst another of these hippies took a photo. That was it! The bloke told us: Never ever take photos of police cars, military stuff, even road signs. He warned us it is strictly forbidden.

He continued with the story. The police took the lad who had the camera and put him in jail. 'After a couple of days, authorities found me and asked if I could act as a translator. He was going in front of a judge, he only *spoke English, I think he was American. I speak English and reasonable Serbo-Croat, so I agreed to do it.'*

The judge took one look at this hippy guy who hadn't washed for days, probably not for weeks before he was locked up. He declared they had twenty-four hours to fix the vehicle to the approval of the police and then twelve hours to leave the country. 'I also think the judge fined him quite a lot of money.'

He learnt later on that the five hippies spent all night and part of the next day fixing the electrics, so they had working lights. They then carved a tread into their worn-out tyres with a razor blade.

The police were happy to let them go and get out of their region. Their passports were stamped so they should never come back to this country. They were given just twelve hours to get out. It must have been quite a journey back up to the north border that night. The police chief said the authorities were just pleased to get them out of the way, they didn't like hippies in their region.

He gave us sound advice. The moral is don't upset anyone, follow the rules. He suggested we trim our hair and beards, and wear ordinary clothes, especially if we are crossing borders going to the east. He reminded us that Yugoslavia was a communist regime. They have very different rules.

One morning, whilst describing their camper van and retelling some of the adventures they had had driving across Europe to a young couple who were hitchhiking to India, Harry thought he had better go to visit Rolly, to pass on the fact that there was still no news from Lucy.

He caught a bus to the park where Rolly was staying; it was further out of the town than he remembered. He changed over to another bus in a residential area. Sitting at the back of the bus, Harry realised he had become isolated from the local people. He spent all day talking, drinking coffee, and eating with fellow travellers, all from Europe or America. This was not what I wanted, he thought. Our plan was to meet with locals and learn some of the language and something of their culture.

The buses were packed with workers both coming home or going to their jobs. The women, who always sat in the front seats, with carrier bags of shopping and usually with one or two small children in their arms or hanging onto skirt hems.

When he finally arrived at the lorry park, Rolly was thrilled to see him. 'I've been missing you, I wondered where you had got to.'

He had spent happy days, when not trudging around the city with Harry, doing the jobs he loved, servicing the camper, changing oil, tuning the engine, and greasing the suspension. He got to know all the regular drivers, sitting outside their shed, a *pastane*, a pastry shop, in the sun drinking tiny amounts of scalding hot, extremely strong espresso, eating honey sweet almond baklava and tiny, sweet pastries. He listened to their many stories of life on the roads. He learnt a few of the tricks of the trade, when to stop for the police, how much tip to give them, and where to find the best stopping places for a night or lunch stop.

Excitedly he said, 'I've got some great news. There's

a guy here in the lorry park with a broken-down VW van. The engine is totally kaput, he can't get it fixed, too expensive so he is selling off parts, and going back to England by bus. I got a cassette recorder with radio off him for just a tenner, and a stack of cassettes, some rubbish, but some really cool ones.' He was triumphant.

'Wow! That's ace. Are you going to fix it in our van?'

'Already done, and it works a treat.'

This had kept Rolly busy for the few days they were apart. He proudly demonstrated the new fixture to Harry. They played a couple of Bob Dylan tracks and a new cassette by Joni Mitchell. They then decided to go to the local café for something to eat to celebrate. The two friends caught up with news from each other. Both were getting worried about the delay in Istanbul and how much it was costing. Harry stirred more sugar into his coffee. He had not heard anything from Lucy, he had no idea when she was coming, and he was starting to get worried that maybe she had changed her mind.

After a snack of 'lahmacun' a type of Turkish pizza, a crunchy, doughy treat topped with spicy minced lamb and lots of spices, the two boys went back to the camper.

'We must get a name for the camper van. And maybe decorate it a bit with some painted flowers, like other travellers do,' said Rolly.

'No, we have been told several times by other drivers to keep things clean and simple, cut hair and beards. It makes it easier for passing through customs.'

'Where was it we nearly got washed away in the river flood? That was so scary, the worst bit of the trip, I reckon.'

'It was in Yugoslavia. We then went to stay at that site by the lake for few days. A great place. It gave us a chance to dry stuff out and catch up a bit.'

Rolly became reflective. 'Oh yeh! That was where we came across the Scottish guy. He wanted to tell us his life story, didn't he.'

They had been for a long walk round the lake before moving on to get to Greece. He was driving a clapped out Morris Minor Post Office van. It still had the gold lettering on the side. 'I didn't reckon he was going to get far, he had no idea, and the van was clapped out.'

He said he was born and lived on the family estate in Sutherland, north Scotland.

Originally the estate and castle were owned by his grandfather or maybe great-grandfather. They were all called Hamish McCreedy, which caused endless confusion. His great-grandfather, Hamish, was a famous traveller. He explored China in the mid 1890s looking for rare plants. Many of them were planted on the estate.

When Grandfather Hamish died, the family had to pay huge death duties. So, all the antiques, paintings and collections from the Far East were sold. There were wall-hung textiles, embroideries from China and Thailand, silk rugs from Persia and Afghanistan. They were all gone. It just left a very cold, damp, empty Scottish castle. His mother was a famous concert pianist. She travelled to all the big cities in Europe, playing with national orchestras. Until one day she didn't come home, she had moved in with a violinist from Prague.

Hamish, his father, sent Arthur away to a grim school in the Western Isles. It was even colder than the castle.

When he went home, he had no interest in the outdoors. The estate declined, no repairs or maintenance were done.

As soon as he could he left school. He hitched down to Glasgow. First living on the streets of Glasgow, he moved to a squat in Paisley. He got a job for minimum wages.

Most of this wage went towards food, but he regularly stashed away a little. This was the way of life for almost two years.

One Sunday, killing time, he went walking along a posh suburban avenue in Paisley. He froze to the spot. In a driveway was the Morris van.

His surroundings disappeared into a mist. His only thoughts were driving down an endless empty road. Sunshine, mountains, sea, desert. He was in a dream world. As he stood there, transfixed, a middle-aged man stepped out of the house. He had a trim moustache and a tweed jacket with leather patches on the elbows.

'Nice, isn't it? She's a good runner.' Arthur just stared. 'Want to go for a test drive?' Arthur was struck dumb. He explained he didn't have a licence, but he then paid forty pounds in cash for the van.

And so his life changed. Sorting out a driving test, getting insurance, leaving the squat, dreaming of distant places in the world.

After several weeks, he went back to pick up his van. The controls were different from the car he took his test in. After a few kangaroo jumps and lurches, he drove to the end of the street. It was a four-way junction. He didn't know which way to turn. He wound down the window to ask a lady with a shopping trolley the way to the south and England. She ignored him. He turned to an old man going the other way. He pointed and waved his stick straight on down the road.

Arthur got to Dover. He had no money. His father loaned him a thousand pounds. He thought that maybe like his great-grandfather he would find an occupation in the Far East.

But now Arthur didn't know whether to go east through Istanbul or drive south to Cape Town. Rolly had doubts whether the Morris Minor van would even make it back onto the main road.

'We've so many memories up till now,' said Harry, 'I hope you're writing them down.'

'Yeh! You won't believe it, I have started a diary, like you have.'

Harry was impressed. After more talking, he went back to the Hotel Fathir feeling more confident and assured that Rolly was enjoying travelling and would carry on with them.

Chapter 3

Istanbul. April 1971

*"A traveller without observation is
a bird without wings."*

Because they were both getting tired of the city, for one day Harry and Rolly escaped the noise and crowds. They took the ferry for a short trip across the Bosphorus to the Princes' Islands. Here there are no cars or lorries, just donkeys carrying goods and horse-drawn carriages. They walked up to the top of the town. Had lunch — Turkish dumplings — and a bottle of Turkish beer, sitting in the sun on metal chairs on the pavement outside a small café. It was good to discover another place, not just one of the tourist spots. Harry said this was just what he and Lucy had talked about, finding places off the usual trail to the Far East. He talked to Rolly about plans he and Lucy had made back in Brighton. Where they would travel to, how they hoped the money would be shared. Would they just go as far as Kathmandu? Or travel on to Thailand, the

Far East and maybe Australia? Rolly pointed out that he thought Australia sounded a good place to go to. He had talked to several Australian travellers at the lorry park who were making their way to London. They made their home country sound like a relaxed place, even though they thought they could get a better job in England.

It was late afternoon when they then took the ferry back to the city, just in time to get to the Post Office before it closed to check once again if there was any news of Lucy. There was still nothing. Harry was worried. He continually fretted that she would not turn up. What would they do? Would he and Rolly just carry on going east or turn back to England?

During these lazy, waiting days Harry enjoyed lying in the park by the mosque, looking up at the blue sky, watching a buzzard circling on the updrafts from the hot pavements.

There were a lot of other travellers in the city. There were always plenty of people to talk to. He occasionally scored a reefer off a fellow traveller, but he never plucked up the courage to buy some hash in the street, although he was frequently accosted. *"Pssst, you want some dope."*

One warm evening, unable to read his book because the power had flickered and cut off again leaving him in the dark, he went for a walk around the small streets close to the Hotel Fathir. He soaked up the noises of the city. They were so different from those in his town in Yorkshire and Brighton. It made him lonely, and a little homesick. He heard music playing from across the square outside the Blue Mosque, the Sultanahmet Square. There was a group of six travellers sitting in a circle on the stubbly grass. Candles had been lit casting warm light over the group. He sat down with them, muttered a greeting, and mumbled a brief introduction. One of the group had a guitar, a good player but not a good voice, also he didn't have much of a repertoire to play. Harry wished he had brought his own guitar out that evening. He had not played to an audience since arriving in Istanbul. The conversation drifted around. Stories of hitching, people met, all the hassles of officialdom, border crossing, customs, and police.

A couple were on their way back home to Sweden after two months in Goa. Both had got very sick and probably still had hepatitis. They were travelling by public transport, buses, and trains. They complained it was slow unless you spent a lot of money, which they didn't have. Goa was great, they said. Cool beach parties, a good crowd of travellers and hitchhikers from all over the world, and good food, but you had to be careful of water and fresh salads. They knew that was what made them sick.

One of the other travellers, a pretty girl from Spain who was sitting cross-legged next to him announced she was on a bus from Amsterdam going directly to Goa. She just wanted to get there as quickly as possible, to join in the midnight full moon parties, to smoke some good dope without being hassled and arrested by the police. Harry thought there would be too many hippies in Goa. It would be best to keep away from areas like that, there would be little or no local culture, just a lot of other Westerners. That was not what they wanted. They wanted remote places where they could find local people and their customs.

A large spliff was rolled and passed around. The Spanish girl moved close to Harry, her bare leg touching Harry's, then twining it between his legs. She took a deep tote on the joint, holding the smoke in her lungs for as long as she could, then passing it on to Harry. Erik, one of the Swedes lit up a clay chillum and passed that around. Harry, not used to such strong hashish spluttered and coughed as he inhaled the smoke deeply. He then passed it on. The chillum was refilled again and passed round several times. The talk drifted slowly along, with discussions and opinions on psychology, spiritual matters, the best music to listen to, festivals visited, and demonstrations attended. Which religion to follow? Buddhism, Hinduism, Sadhus. The desire to find the right religious path. Travel stories were told, some disastrous, some amusing and informative. There were strong feelings expressed and for a while, the discussions became more serious. But then the group grew quiet and reflective, the strong hashish taking its effect. Anything said whether a joke or a serious statement resulted in giggles and laughter. They had all got quite stoned.

After a while, listening to the music, occasional disjointed stories of travel from across the world, and gazing up at the sky trying to find stars but failing because of the city lights, Harry realised he was very stoned, possibly more so than he had ever been.

The Spanish girl had cuddled close to him, gently massaging the back of his neck, and whispering suggestive ideas to him. He felt aroused, ideas of a quiet, clean hotel room, rolling around on a large bed. An unusual and not unpleasant feeling. Her warm breasts pressed into him. The lights looked much brighter, the sounds louder, and the smell of car exhaust mixed with scented candles became unpleasant. He was moving towards a difficult situation; he had strong feelings to stay faithful to Lucy, but the girl next to him was suggesting a night of passion. It was difficult, should he stay faithful, or have some fun? He made a muddled decision to stay faithful, so he slipped away from the party without being noticed.

He somehow found his way back to the hotel and flopped back on the lumpy mattress in his room. His mind was running tangents, chasing ideas and dreams. He once again followed a crack in the ceiling, it was his favourite. It led back across to the large stain in the corner which in his imagination he again saw as the lake they stayed by in Yugoslavia. He remembered that it was one of the best places they had stopped in Europe. It was quiet and friendly. The owner of the bar and café was generous, he gave them some food and taught them some words in his language.

His mind drifted around in a confused state. Rolly seemed very happy by the lake, fiddling with the camper and fishing. Not so sure now he had talked with him about money and food. He sounded concerned. Although he knew him well, it was difficult to know just what he thought.

When is she coming? She should have been here a week or two ago. I hope she is OK? Does she love me? I hope she loves me as much as I love her. She was so excited about the whole trip before she went off to Greece. The thoughts went round and round in circles. Racing ahead.

How will Rolly get on with Lucy? He hasn't yet met her. – What will he think of travelling across all those different countries, Turkey, Iran, Afghanistan? I am sure he will keep the camper going. I hope we all get on together. I have heard from other travellers, it can get difficult and fraught living close together. The confused thoughts crowded in him, so many questions, so much unknown. He finally fell asleep.

There was a knock on his door. Harry was still fuzzy headed, probably still stoned. He rolled over and pulled the pillow over his head. There was a louder more urgent knock. 'It's Rolly here, wake up, wake up, there's a letter for you at the post office.'

Harry fell out of bed, tripped over his clothes discarded on the floor, looked at his watch. It was ten thirty in the morning. He opened his door. 'I must have overslept, did you say there is a letter for me? Where is it, have you got it?'

'No, it's in the Post Restante box. Only you can take it 'cos it's addressed to you. Don't forget to take your passport, you'll need it for your ID. And it's Thursday, they will be closing for the weekend at lunchtime, so buck up!'

Harry threw on his clothes. The two of them dashed across the street and up Ankara Street, dodging casual shoppers strolling on the pavement. They ran into the Grand Post Office. They were just in time, the counters were drawing down their blinds when the last customer finished.

It was a brown envelope with bold lettering across the top in red, 'TELEGRAM'. Harry tore open the envelope. There was a single brown paper page with white strips of telegraphic writing. *'BUS THESSALONICA ISTANBUL TOMORROW LOVE YOU'.*

'My God, this was sent yesterday, she is coming today. Maybe she has already arrived. We must get to the bus station.' Harry was confused and excited, very excited.

'Calm down, it's a long way from Greece to here, the bus won't arrive till late afternoon or evening.'

Harry realised he was overexcited. He knew there was plenty of time to find out bus times, where the bus station was and how to get there.

It was late afternoon when Lucy stepped off the bus, a vision of beauty. She had an even dark tan and hair sun-bleached to almost white blond. It had grown long and was tied into a ponytail. She was dressed in a cheesecloth top, sleeveless and short, embroidered across the front with colourful peonies. She had on blue shorts, just above her knees. Round her neck, there were several long strings of tiny colourful beads. She had three macramé woven bracelets on each wrist. Her face lit into a radiant smile when she spotted Harry. With a flying run across the dirty, oily tarmac of the bus station, leather Greek sandals slapping down, she leapt onto Harry, arms wrapped round his neck. He soaked up the scent of her skin around her shoulders and neck and felt the texture of her hair. He twisted round to give her a long, long hard kiss on the mouth. Fellow passengers from the bus stopped and looked. They were mostly Turkish men returning after a month of hard labour on building sites in Athens. Some looked with envy, having admired the slim figure and blond hair sitting at the front of the bus. Others averted their gaze to join their rotund wife in flowery house coats, tut-tutting at this public display of affection. Lucy broke from the embrace and crossed to Rolly, who already had his right hand out to shake hands, he was caught unawares in a tight embrace. His cheeks spread with a bright red blush.

The three of them caught a taxi back to the centre of town. Rolly was enamoured by Lucy. She was warm, friendly and lively. If she noticed someone looking at her, as many men did, she tilted her chin up, and a tiny smile creased the corners of her mouth. She was thrilled to have met up with the boys, but she obviously wanted to have time with Harry on his own.

Rolly became aware he may be a bit of a gooseberry. He told Harry and Lucy he would get a bus back to the lorry park and the camper van and leave them to catch up on all the news between them. Harry and Lucy made their way back to the hotel, holding each other close. As they entered the streets of the old town, Lucy stopped. She had spotted a tiny sweet shop. She held out her hand to Harry, he dug in his pocket to give her a few coins. She came out of the shop with a decorative bag tied with a ribbon. It was a box of Turkish delight, *lokum*.

That morning, Harry had arranged with the owner of the Fathir Hotel to move them into a larger room, the next floor up, right under the roof. It had a bathroom next door, not much better than the one downstairs, maybe a little less smelly. There was even less water pressure for a shower.

Lucy looked around the room. 'This is a bit grungy, I hope we can find something a bit better soon.' Harry felt disappointed; he had got used to the facilities and thought they weren't too bad, they weren't too expensive. 'We will soon be on the road, either sleeping in the camper or under the stars,' he said, hoping it would make the situation a little better. 'We have to wait for the last call from the mosque before we will be able to sleep. It's just across the road and is very loud.'

She grasped him by the waist to hold him close, giving a long kiss on the mouth. 'I'm not going to sleep, we have other things to do.', she whispered in his ear. Harry dipped his fingers into the box of Turkish Delight. He popped the sweet square into her mouth. 'You are my Turkish Delight', she said, licking the fine sugar coating off her lips. It tasted of rosewater and lavender with a gummy, sticky texture. They dropped onto the bed. It gave a groan and a squeak in protest. They made passionate love, catching up for the weeks they had been apart. Lucy woke up early, unused to the noise of traffic and the city coming to life. She turned over to be on top of Harry. They made long, slow love again.

Eventually, after sharing a cigarette and each telling tales of their adventures, they got up. 'Breakfast time,' Harry said, even though it was mid-day. 'I'm starving.' He led her to a nearby café with a pavement sign stating, *"ENGLISH BREAKFAST"*.

'It's not really English, but it's really good, I've been here a few times.' The café owner, wearing a white tunic with some food stains across the front where he had wiped his hands greeted them. 'This is your girlfriend?' He turned to Lucy. 'Welcome, your man has talked about you every day for one month now. I make special Turkish breakfast for you.' He first brought to the table two cups of very strong coffee, followed by dishes of cheese and olives. Then came circular pieces of bread covered with sesame seeds. 'These we call *simit*. They are very common in Turkey. We eat them with just strong coffee in the morning or with a small salad.' He went to the kitchen. They could hear the noise of chopping and a pan banging. Shortly he came with two huge omelettes, at least four eggs in each with chopped tomato, onion, and spices. Finally, a bowl of yoghurt and a pot of clear honey. 'This from my father, he lives in the hills far away.'

When they had finished, Harry asked Lucy what they should do on their first day together.

She didn't want to visit the Blue Mosque or other landmarks of the city.

'I saw too many ruins in Athens, I have had enough of trudging around with a group of tourists, I want to explore other things with just you.'

They wandered through the streets to the Galata Bridge, crossing the Golden Horn. Even though they were still full of breakfast, they stopped to buy a large hunk of bread holding a freshly caught grilled sardine, dripping oil onto the pavement. They sat in the sun outside a small café, having yet another coffee.

They boarded a small wooden ferry boat that wandered up the Bosphorus, stopping at small decaying wooden jetties. Propellers thrashing the murky waters. New passengers climbed over the rocking sides of the boat, and other passengers disembarked, arms full of plastic bags overflowing with shopping. Like a town bus, a bell sounded and off they went with loud engine noise and much diesel fumes from the short funnel. Harry pointed out the domes and minarets of the ancient city, trying to remember the names and whether he and Rolly had visited them.

'This is the sea of Marmara, that river to the left is the Golden Horn, and ahead of us is the Black Sea along the Bosporus Straits. To the left of us is Europe and over to the right is Asia.'

'This is so exciting, I just want to get on the road through Asia, like now.' Lucy excitedly jumped up and down, rocking the boat.

They looked out across the waters of the Bosphorus. It was dark blue, scattered with white sails from small fishing boats and yachts. Black smoke hung over the water from old steam tugs pulling huge, long cargo ships carrying goods from the Crimea ports to Western markets.

'We will go very soon, as soon as we get the camper registered on your passport so you can help with the driving. I'm getting tired of Istanbul, been here a long time. I'm not sure if we must go to the embassy, immigration, or the police to get the correct registration. I will ask Idris and Namak at the Pudding Shop, they know all these details.'

They returned to the old city to ask Idris and Namak about getting details of the camper on Lucy's passport.

'Not so easy, it can take several days, and it is a holiday for 2 days tomorrow so offices are closed.'

A traveller Harry recognised gave them all the information they needed. Which papers for the camper were needed, passports, passport photos and which police office to go to.

'God! More delays, I really want to get on the road, get travelling, discover new places and countries.'

'So do I,' said Lucy. 'What can we do for two or three days?' She gave Harry a suggestive poke in the ribs.

'We should go to see Rolly, you haven't seen the camper van yet. You bought it, you know.'

So they went by bus to the lorry park. A route that was becoming familiar to Harry.

Rolly was sitting outside on a camping stool. He looked almost asleep, very relaxed.

Lucy was excited, 'What have you called her?'

'We haven't got a name yet. You decide.'

Lucy had obviously already thought about it. She immediately said, 'How about *Forget-me-not*?'

Harry and Rolly replied in unison, 'Perfect.'

'Then we must decorate her, with paintings of flowers. You're a graphic designer. You can do it easily.' She turned to Harry.

'No, Rolly and I have already talked about this. We have been told several times to not decorate our vehicle and to keep it tidy. The immigration makes it easier when passing through a border crossing.'

Lucy was disappointed with the camper van. She was hoping for something maybe a bit more exotic. She climbed up the steps. The inside was a mess of clothes and an unmade bed. 'My God, it looks just like your room in Brighton. You guys just like to live in a pigsty.'

She remembered Harry's room in Brighton was chaos. This was the same. There were always piles of clothes thrown into a corner. Some dirty, some fresh from the laundry. Pinned to the walls was a poster of the inevitable

Che Guevara, looking straight into your eyes, with a knowable look in the corners of his dark eyes. There were copies of his two favourite female singers pinned to the wall, Aretha Franklin and Janis Joplin, a classic concert poster from the Adelphi in Slough headlining the Who and Traffic, with psychedelic graphics by Chris Dyer. Books were scattered everywhere. His shelves groaning under a big selection of study books on graphic design, expensive coffee table books on contemporary artists and catalogues from London art galleries and museums. There was a biography of Malcolm X with corners turned down on the floor amongst the clothes, To Kill A Mockingbird open next to the bed, with the spine cracked and broken, A Clockwork Orange half read on the arm of a chair. Titles by John Updike, Ginsberg and V. S. Naipaul squeezed on the top shelf. The Prophet by Kahlil Gibran, still in perfect condition, was one of the most read, and best looked after books in the flat. Sheets of music, jazz, blues and the latest pop lyrics scattered like a paper chase across the floor.

Rolly found two more stools to sit on outside *'forget-me-not'*. It was a warm, sunny day, so he went to the local bar to get some cold drinks.

There was still plenty to talk about, about the trip across Europe, and how they managed the immigration and customs at each country's border.

'Greece was the best,' Harry said. 'We stayed in a campsite just next to the sea. The lady who owned it gave us an all-in deal, including breakfast and dinner. We paid her in pounds 'cos we hadn't done any exchange.'

'We were looking over to a little island.' Said Rolly. 'We wondered if you were on it, or if it was part of your tour.'

'No, I don't think so, I was down in the south, in the Cyclades, places like Paros, Kos and Rhodes.'

After the local holiday, which was three days long, not two, they left all the necessary documents at the main police station. They were told to come back in three days' time but first pay a fee, a large fee Harry thought. But they felt confident that the documents were safe, and so settled down to wait more time in the old city.

Chapter 4

Istanbul. April 1971

"A journey of 1000 miles begins with one step"

After two days of wandering around the old city, shopping for a few trinkets, they went to the Karakoy district of the city. Here, they found many more shops, historical buildings, and restaurants. Lucy bought an evil eye, *(Nazar Boncuk)*. 'We'll hang it in the camper van, it gives good luck, they are very traditional in Turkey'. They gorged on tasty kebabs and Baklava, crispy, sweet pastries filled with pistachio nuts and drizzled with honey, returning to the hotel to make love yet again.

Harry and Lucy decided it was time to go to find Rolly to tell him about when they had decided to leave and move on into Turkey. They walked a long way through the town, looking at ancient buildings, mosques, and churches. They took a bus to the lorry park to find Rolly and the camper van.

Lucy opened the door and was met with a horrible

smell and the sight of Rolly twisted up in bedding, asleep. He woke up, not fully aware of where he was.

He pushed himself up on his elbows, the inside of the van whirled around in a sickening fashion. He carefully counted his breathing in and out, sitting on the edge of the bed. His bladder was bursting full. He waited until he was sure he could stand up, and that he could get across to the toilet on the other side of the yard, praying hopefully it would be vacant.

He then realised Lucy and Harry were standing in the doorway. 'Hang on I must get to the can, like now.' He rushed off.

'Looks like he's had a bug. He said he had a tummy upset when we came to meet you.' Harry went round opening the windows, Lucy pulled the dirty bedding out of the door. Eventually, after a long time, Rolly returned. He sat on the step in the doorway to the camper looking grey and shaky. He told his story. 'Since I last saw you, I have been treading the path between here and the toilet every few hours. I can't believe there is anything left in my body.'

Lucy expressed concern. He looked pale and thin. 'It is a squatty, long drop. Not comfortable if you have to spend time there, and very smelly. There is always someone else banging on the door wanting to use it.'

It was at that moment Rolly finally realised that this trip was not for him. The idea had been running around in his head for several days. He was missing home, missing his mum and dad, missing his normal regular life, his work at the garage. He had a bad stomach upset, he didn't want another in the future. He loved his travelling companion, and everything seemed to be going well, but now he felt quite out of it now Lucy had joined them. He had made his decision and was going to stick by it.

'Guys, I'm going home.'

They both looked up, startled. 'What!'

'Yep, I now feel in the way of you two. I miss home. I'm tired of all this foreign food. I have had the shits big time. I have decided to catch a bus back to Holland, then to home. I have got to know one of the drivers, he is just over there, by that blue bus.' He pointed across the parking lot. 'He says I can join him, I need only to pay him ten dollars, just for food. I can help with the driving. It is normally about twenty-five dollars from here, so it is a good deal. He is a great guy, we seem to get on well. He reckons it takes only about four or five days. He is hoping to leave tomorrow.' Rolly stopped and took a deep breath.

'You can't leave us, we have so far yet to go,' said Lucy. She was worried. 'And what about keeping the camper going? I know it has been reliable up to now, but we have some pretty rough roads to travel over and many, many miles. How will Harry and I know how to fix things?'

'I have made up my mind. You'll be able to cope. There will always be other people on the road who can fix things, and garages that will help.'

Harry got up, and gave Rolly a big man hug. 'I understand, you've been ill, and if this way is not your way, then I'm with you. Obviously, we will miss you no end, you have been great, just so cool, but I can see you have made up your mind and no way will we try to convince you otherwise.'

'What about money? You've paid for lots of things.' Lucy was still worried.

'We can sort that kind of stuff when you get back.' He nodded his head across to the bus. 'Come over to meet Hans, I can see him by the bus.'

As they walked over the rough lorry park, they were all quiet. Rolly obviously thinking about travelling on his own back to Yorkshire, right across Europe back home. Lucy was worried about the practicalities of keeping the camper running, paying Rolly for his contribution, and dealing with all the problems they may encounter on the road. Harry was just trying to get his head round the different circumstances.

Rolly introduced them, 'This is Hans, he is the owner and driver of this bus'. Hans had a dark oval face, drawn longer by his neatly trimmed beard on his chin in the style of a fifteenth-century Dutch master painter. His dark hair was cut short. He was wearing a blue t-shirt, shorts and a pair of purple-tinted sunglasses.

'Hi, good to meet you, I am sad to be taking your friend away like this,' he said in perfect English. 'He will be just fine with us, the other passengers are a good bunch. I know Rolly will be useful keeping them in order.' He had an amusing twinkle in his eyes. He continued to explain that he was Dutch and when not on the road, he lived in Utrecht. He said his father and mother live in Jakarta, he was born in Indonesia and didn't travel to Holland until he was twenty. His grandmother was Malay Chinese, he didn't know who his father was, maybe Dutch or English. His grandfather disappeared during the second world war, maybe taken prisoner by the Japs and never heard of again.

'I am typically a very mixed-up person. Odd parents. Anyway, we are hoping to leave tomorrow, it is usually a quick trip across Europe. One night in Greece, one or two in Yugoslavia, one in Austria, one in Germany then home.'

'Wow, just five days, it took us three weeks or more to get here. It must be about five thousand miles.' Harry was really surprised.

'We don't hang around. The kids find it expensive in Europe after being in India, and they just want to get home.' Hans was very calm and relaxed. He continued to explain he had a 50/50 share in the business with a friend who also lived in Utrecht. He had done this driving for four years, four trips a year. So now knew the road well. 'That makes it sixteen times, thirty-two times a return trip. I know this road better than the road from my house to the local cafe.' He joked and carried on explaining how the trip works. 'I like to have ten to twelve passengers. More makes it difficult, they tend to split into two or three groups. With fewer numbers, I can persuade them to do things as one group, like cook and eat together. I now have twelve passengers including two from a stranded bus on the Iran border. So on this trip, I hope they will stick together.'

'We heard about a bus stuck in Iran, the driver was arrested for drugs. We met this guy at the Greek border who was going as the replacement driver,' Harry said.

'What an idiot! He should know better than trying to get drugs across that border, or any border.' Hans was cross. 'It must be costing the bus company a fortune, they will probably go bust. And the driver will be banged up in jail for most of his life.'

Those two who are joining us are paying me forty dollars each, which is a good profit for me. I am asking Rolly for just ten 'cos he can help with the driving.' He looked up. Rolly had disappeared off to the toilet again. 'That will soon pass, most people get ill at some stage.' He nodded his head towards the toilet. 'Here in Istanbul, they call it the *Istanbul interval*. In Tehran, it is the *Tehran trots*, in Kabul the *Kabul Craps*, in Delhi, the *Delhi Belly*. In Kathmandu the *Kathmandu end of the world,* that is because it comes from both directions, or perhaps top and bottom of the world. I think every small town between here and there probably has its own name! I know I have had an upset stomach in most of them over the time I have been using the road.'

Hans continued to talk to Harry and Lucy about taking care of travelling the road, especially at borders. 'Always dress smart and keep your hair short. I can tell you of a couple of tricks I have learnt. Ask the girls to pack their bags with their underwear on the top. The customs men open the case, get all embarrassed, and quickly close it. And take care, the police have been known to plant drugs in your bags. You just can't be too careful, I have seen parking lots filled with campers, buses and cars that have got busted. And wherever you go there are serpents. Guys who will sell you some hash, and immediately tell the police. They make a good living from doing that. And watch out for black market money changes, they do just the same.'

When Rolly returned, looking a lot healthier, Hans invited him to move his kit onto the bus. 'You use the front locker, the other ones are full of the passengers' stuff. And get your place on the back seat to sleep. I will tell everyone that it is yours, and only yours.' Once again there was the twinkle in his eyes. 'You will ride shotgun unless it's a long day and you need to get some shut eye between driving shifts. We usually do about three or four hours at a go.'

Harry said, 'We had a routine between us of doing a stretch of two hours driving on our way down here, but now he's got used to being on the wrong side, he is good and careful. He always remembers to look out when pulling out from a restaurant or filling station. It is dead easy to drift onto the wrong side of the road.'

'If Rolly is moving out of the camper into the bus, we can get out of the hotel and save some money.' Lucy said. 'We can get the dirty washing done in a laundrette, I'm sure there will be one near here. They were everywhere in Greece, we got all our washing done in them.'

'Yep, there are a couple just near the market,' Hans said.

'Ok,' said Harry, getting organised. 'Rolly you move your stuff, then go to the laundrette. Lucy and I will go to check out of the Fathir Hotel and bring all our stuff over here. We will have to get a taxi, knowing how much kit Lucy has.' He joked, 'Then we can have a good Turkish goodbye meal, all of us together.' He waved an arm to indicate Hans was included.

There was a lot of talking at the meal, simple kebabs, salad followed by fruit. Rolly did not each much, he just pushed his food around the plate. But he still had stories to tell.

'I'm sure I saw that guy we picked up hitchhiking in

the middle of nowhere. You remember he was a soldier in the army. I saw him when I went into the city. He was too far away for me to call out to him.'

'Yeh! I remember him well, he was called Chalky. He told a sad story about his life, divorce, and stuff. He was going to the South of Turkey to "twiddle his toes in the sand, get his life back again." He was a gentle, honest guy, I remember. I said I was sure we would meet him again somewhere. Maybe we will.'

'He gave us the once over, asking why we were wasting our lives travelling.'

Harry said to Lucy, 'We were somewhere in Europe, in the middle of nowhere. This well-dressed and clean-shaven guy was standing by a small track leading to a farmyard. He stepped into the road, stuck out his thumb and waved expectantly. It was our first hitchhiker.

'He told us he was trying to get to Turkey, he was hitchhiking but got dropped off by a farmer at the end of the track to his farm.

'He told us his name was Chalky, from his army days. That of course made Rolly interested. He always thought it would be a good idea to go into the army, but that was before he got the job in the garage. He wanted to know what he had done in the army.

'He was quite old, about fifty,' Harry continued, 'so he started telling us some of his life history. He had left the army many years ago, having spent a lot of the last war in North Africa, with Rommel. He was already older than most of his squad. First, they sent him to the front line, to Sidi Barrani in 1940. I think that's near Tobruk. As always in the army, he was soon moved around in Egypt, usually dealing with supplies and servicing some of the lorries. He said he was not one of the desert rats in the front line so didn't see any fighting. He was demobbed after the war and went back home to Lincolnshire where he married his childhood sweetheart. There were no jobs around then, just after the war finished. It was very difficult. His mum and dad lived in a tied cottage as part of a big farm. There was no room for the married couple, so they moved down to Aldershot where he knew a few guys there from the army days. One of them got him a job with an army equipment supplier. He said it was very boring, just checking orders from the salesperson who went round all the bases in England getting orders. He eventually took over the sales job, away travelling all the time, which although it was more money, was his downfall.

'Liz, his wife was a Lincolnshire girl, born and bred and had no friends in Aldershot. She was bringing up the two children, a boy and a girl. She couldn't get a proper job apart from part-time in a shop. She got more and more fed up, they argued all the time, about the usual things, money, house, kids' school. Finally, she went back to Lincolnshire, with the kids, and last year after almost twenty years of marriage they got divorced. She got everything: the kids, the house, and most of the savings. That's why he was hitch hiking, just to escape, and travel.

'After this tale of his life, he asked us why we were taking such a long holiday. He knew we were going to Turkey and then off to Kathmandu. But he wanted to know now we had finished our education should we be getting a job? He claimed it is never too early to start with a step on the ladder.

'I disagreed with him of course, said we have all our lives to get on the so called ladder. The best education you can have is to go travelling. You learn about people, diverse cultures, different languages, different religions. You learn how to interact with people and how to communicate. These are things you never learn at school or by stepping onto the ladder. You learn about geography and countries. One year ago, I didn't know where Nepal was, or that Kathmandu was its capital. By travelling, anyone will learn different values. You don't have to be rich and earn lots of money in a good job to have a happy life. With travelling we hope to get involved with local people. Not the way tourists do, just looking at the sights and never speaking to the local people. You have to learn a few words of their language, more than just please, thank you, how much. If you can put a sentence together people will appreciate it and will open up much more.

'I told him just be cool! Don't be uptight. I know it sounds like you have had a rough time with your divorce and things, but it was you who said you wanted to feel the sand between your toes. Just relax.'

Harry knew they all had time to get a job anytime they wished. He knew that they could earn money whenever they wished. The post-war generation was freer than any time before. It showed in the new dress fashions, the relaxed relationships you could have with a different sex, even the same sex, and the revolution in music. He realised that he was lucky to be able to do all these things. And so were his contemporaries, who also had this desire to find out about the world. It was taking an alternative approach to life.

'He left us quite happy wanting to go to the Yugoslavia coast, Dubrovnik, Split and some of the famous Venetian towns by the sea.'

When the meal was finished, Harry decided he must write a letter to his Mum and Dad for Rolly to take with him. It would be much quicker than using the regular post.

Harry's Letter

Dear Mum and Dad,

We are here in Istanbul, Lucy is now with us. We had to wait a long time for her to turn up here. I think she was having a good time in Greece, just island hopping and sun bathing. I know she has written several times to her parents telling them where she was and what she was doing.

Rolly has decided to return home by bus, he misses you all and is a bit homesick. I am missing you also, but not homesick, just really excited about travelling on. So, I am sending this note with him. It will be much quicker than the post. The journey to here was interesting, we met lots of people and found some great places. I will tell you all about it one day. I am keeping a diary.

Istanbul is a very different city. There are so many amazing old buildings here: mosques, churches and big old houses. Part of the city is ancient with tiny, narrow streets. Too small for a car or truck, so they use donkey carts. It is very crowded and noisy.

Do please ask Rolly to tell you about some of the stories, places and people that we met.

Go to the pub with him, and with his mum and dad. I know he is dying for a decent pint. He will keep talking for ages.

The camper van is running just great, no problems. Lucy has named her Forget-me-not, perfect!

You know I am no good at writing letters, and phoning from here is impossible.

This is just a quick note to say we are OK.

Love Harry and Lucy xxx

The next morning, they waved off the bus, Rolly looking happy, his stomach obviously finally settled, keen to get on the way home.

Lucy took control of organising the interior of the camper van. She delved into the food locker for cooking equipment. She finally got the *gaz* cooker lit, after a struggle, and made a pot of coffee. Sitting in the late morning sun, she asked, 'Are we leaving today? I do want to get going.'

'I think we can go, now everything is sorted. I hope we have the necessary documents for us to get through Turkey. But first, we need to plan a route for the first few days.' He pulled out a new road map of Turkey. 'First, we have to go across the Bosporus, that will take us to Asia.'

Lucy's eyes shone, 'Asia, wow, that sounds so exotic. I have wanted to go to Asia most of my life, as long as I can remember.'

'Well, now is your chance, we can be there this afternoon.'

Lucy turned to Harry with a serious look on her face. 'Harry, I've missed my period, I hope there is nothing wrong. This is the first time ever since I started at 12 or 13 years old. I was so worried about this that I called my mum from Thessalonica before catching the bus here. Mum was very calm and reassuring. She said it was most likely travelling, being in different places, different food and different climates that upset my rhythm. She said not to worry. She is not a nurse or doctor, but she seemed very sure of her information. She knows that we sleep together, she knows how long I have been away from you travelling in Greece. So presumably she had done some quick mental arithmetic. She asked me if I was behaving myself, which of course I am.'

'If she said those things, you shouldn't worry, I'm sure she knows.'

'I know.' Lucy still looked disturbed.

'OK,' Harry was never sure about these things with girls, not having had any sisters. 'Let's get on the road and get onto another continent. We can sort out which way we go from there this afternoon.'

Part of Rolly's Diary

I never knew having one of these tummy bugs would be like this. It is horrible. I can't stand it, I have to go home, back to all that I know and like. It is good of Hans to give me a lift. Maybe we will get back home very quickly.

I know Harry and me have come a long way, we get on so well and there have been plenty of adventures. I don't regret agreeing to come along that night in the pub, I know I am easily led along, I said yes without thinking. It is good to meet with Lucy, she and Harry are just made for each other. It will be better without me hanging on.

Maybe I will find a girlfriend when I get back home.

I have learnt so much in the past two months, more than I ever did at school. I never thought I would start to write a diary. I have seen others doing it, I enjoy writing now. My teacher from school would never believe it. I was a dead loss at school. Now I have been to so many countries, I know a bit of geography, I can change our pounds into foreign money. It is still confusing with all the different coins and notes. I haven't learnt any of the languages they speak, just 'hello' and 'goodbye'.

It has been no sweat keeping the van going, she is good and reliable. They need to keep up with the servicing, top up the oil, grease around, look after the tyres. They will be OK, there are other people around who can help.

It was good buying her with the help from my boss at the garage, choosing this Mercedes Delivery van rather than a VW Camper fully kitted out. Lucy's dad paid for it, we will have to sort all the money out when we all get home. My boss at the garage saved us a load off the van, and other stuff at cost. I enjoyed fitting in the sliding windows and designing the cooker and kitchen. They work well. The roof rack will come in useful to load on more fuel and water when going to remote places.

There are so many good memories, some not so good. That place where the river flooded us when we were camping right close to it. I was shit scared. I can't swim. I thought the whole camper van was a goner. I got so cold and wet, but Harry was cool and sorted the gear out to dry in the sun.

My boss at the garage said there would always be a job waiting for me. I hope, I don't want to start searching. I am looking forward to getting back into the old routine.

Chapter 5

April 1971 Turkey

*"A journey is best measured in friends,
rather than miles!"*

The ferry docked at a pier on the opposite shore.

'*Whooee!* Here is Asia, that's goodbye to Europe for many months. This is where it is all going to happen,' shrieked Lucy, so excited she was bouncing up and down in her seat. They passed a huge sign, leaning precariously into the road that read '*Welcome to Asia*'.

Harry was concentrating on the road, driving, and finding the right way. 'We have to go round an inlet from the sea, there is a ferry which will be quicker, but I would rather take the road, it'll be cheaper.'

Once they got round the gulf, through a town called Izmit, they stopped beside the road in a layby. They swapped driver seats. 'From here we have a choice. We can go a more direct route straight down the middle of Turkey to Ankara and then to Iran. Or we can do some '*wiggles*' and go to places like Izmir, the south coast by the Mediterranean for a bit, then up to the mountains and then Iran. It will be a lot further.'

'Definitely, definitely, we do the '*wiggles*'. I don't fancy going to big cities like Ankara. I just want countryside and country people, and we have all the time we want.'

'Good, I know we talked about it a lot back in Brighton, that was a long time ago, but it all seems quite different now we are here. Neither of us wants to just belt along the same road that thousands of other travellers take getting to Delhi or Kathmandu as quickly as possible. From what Hans said about the trail there are stopping places, cafes, and hostels along the road where everyone stops and eats westernised food. We don't want that.' Harry selected a cassette from the pile of them scattered on the floor and put it on to play. Dusty Springfield, *I Only Want to Be with You*.

Harry sang along to the first verse. 'It is so good to use my voice again. There haven't been any chances this last month. And this song is just for you.' He held her hand and looked at her with doe-like eyes.

'Since you mentioned Hans, I wonder how Rolly is getting on?' She was driving slowly and carefully, not yet used to driving on the right side.

'Well, he will be about three days into Europe. Probably halfway up Yugoslavia. I'm missing him. He's a good mate, but I understand why he wanted to go. He suddenly got very homesick, and I was rapidly getting the feeling this trip was not for him. I think we told you that when we were driving through the middle of Yugoslavia, somewhere near where Rolly will be about now, we met this weird Scottish guy.'

'Yep, Rolly already told me that story. You must have lots of tales to tell me about your trip across Europe, from Yorkshire to Istanbul. I want to know about some of the people you met, hitchhikers and others. What did you do in Istanbul once you arrived? I will tell you about my holiday in Greece.' She continued in a practical voice, 'Thinking about Rolly and what Hans said about tummy bugs, we haven't got any medicine for that. We must get some. Some really strong stuff.'

'We'll go to a pharmacy the next place we stop.'

The first part past Izmit was an endless industrial area and cement works, but soon the countryside opened to rolling hills, and olive and fruit groves.

'Harry, look, look.' She pulled over to the side of the road.

'What!' Immediately thinking there was some emergency.

'Look over there, at that mountain. The colours are fantastic, azure sky, the mountain a hazy purple, that field of blue flowers, I think they are lupins, and over to the left the dark green of fruit trees.' Lucy was bubbling with excitement. 'We have to stop. I must paint this. It is so beautiful. I have never seen such cool colours.'

Harry looked at the view, it was stunning. He had been in the city for a long time, with no wide vistas to look at. He could see the colours that had captivated Lucy in the foreground and the misty distance. But his mind was set on getting to the town of Bursa. He reckoned it was about one hour further on.

'No, no. We must stop for a bit. I haven't done any

drawing or painting since I got to Turkey. This view and these colours are perfect.' Lucy was already starting to get out of the camper. 'I've been waiting for colours like this ever since I finished my last project at art school. I never believed they could be real.'

'We are going to have to pull off the road. If we go along a tiny bit there must be a place. I don't know how long you are going to be, but if it is safe, maybe we could stop around here for the night.'

Lucy leaned across the front seats and gave him a big kiss.

They soon found a narrow track into some woods. Harry checked the ground first. They didn't want to get bogged down. It was a small opening in a plantation of tall slender trees. The canopy overhead was fresh pale green spring leaves. The ground was covered with last year's dead autumn leaves and a scattering of wildflowers. Lucy got her art paraphernalia and a camp stool from the back of the camper. She set off with a little gallop to a hillock where there was a view across the valley to the mountain. Harry lit a cigarette to settle down with his diary and a book.

After a couple of hours, Harry got up, crept up behind Lucy and looked over her shoulder at her canvas. 'That's fantastic. You have really caught it.'

Lucy shrugged, 'It's OK, what I really want to do is another painting in the morning, catching the light coming from the other direction, from the east. We're staying here tonight. So, I can do it first thing. We are not in a hurry to get on. You said it was only an hour to the next place?'

They set up a camp table, Harry poured two glasses of red wine he had bought in Istanbul. 'This is local, made from grapes somewhere just around here.' The wine was rough and strong. 'We also have plenty of fresh salad and some cold meat from the market back in Istanbul. I will put something together for supper.' They settled down for the evening. 'This olive oil comes from around here, as well.' Harry was reading the label on the bottle.

'We had lots of great wine in Greece, and olive oil on all the food.'

'Tell me about it, where did you get to?'

'We went straight from the airport to a ferry, it took quite a long time to our first island. It was Paros. The weather was beautiful, the sea this amazing blue. We stayed there for a few days, then went to a tiny island. We hadn't booked anywhere, but there was this old woman who took us to her house, it was tiny, in a narrow street. Everything was painted white, even the gaps in the paving stones. The colours of the flowers that hung over a wall were dazzling. I can't remember what it is called.'

'Bougainvillea,' suggested Harry.

'That's it. This woman was so lovely we stayed with her for days. She didn't speak any English so we couldn't talk to her at all. There were a couple of tavernas nearby, we ate all our food there. Breakfast, lunch and dinner and we just relaxed, read and sunbathed. The sea was still a bit too cold to go bathing. Then we took another ferry to some more islands. Tell me about your trip.'

'There is not a great deal to say. We drove across Europe, we didn't break down, thanks to Rolly. We stopped in Heidelberg for several days. You never met Jochim when he came to Brighton. He was doing Graphic Design, the same as me. He's a nice guy, we got on really well. He put us up sleeping on the floor under a snooker table in his accommodation hall. The rooms students have in that part of Germany are very posh. Much better than we had in Brighton. We ate lots of heavy German food and drank beer. Jochim had this great collection of LPs, so we sat around a lot and listened to music. His department at the uni was so well equipped, they had everything you needed for doing great drawings.' He took a long drink of wine.

'I think we mentioned Chalky, the army guy. He was the only hitchhiker we picked up, though we met lots of people. I reckon we will find many more people travelling the trail now we are in Asia.'

'If this is what the trip is going to be like from now on, I'm very happy, more than very happy,' Lucy smiled. 'I see you have been writing a diary. I'm going to do a big one with drawings and paintings of people's faces, there are so many fine beards and beautiful eyes. I'll do buildings and stuff like that, as well as writing about places we visit and people we meet. I see you haven't brought your camera with you, have you? I would have thought it was an essential bit of kit.'

'No, it was a conscious decision. I decided rather than take photos, which in years to come have just frozen a place, an image, I want to absorb all the things all around that I see. The sights with the smells and sounds into my head. That is just as important as a fixed image of a view or person. I believe it will give much better memories.'

The strong wine with the meal, even just one glass,

made them sleepy. It had been a day full of changes and some emotions. 'I think we now have a bit of Turkish Delight.' Harry said with a twinkle in his eye, as he put his arms around Lucy.

The next morning sunlight streaming onto the bed woke Harry. He reached over but Lucy was not beside him. The bed was still warm. He looked out of the door, he could see her sitting on the camp stool. She looked up at the view, then down to her canvas. Each time her ponytail slipped from one side to the other. Harry stood and watched her for several moments, a warm tingle down his spine. A niggle of worry about what she had said about her periods.

He made a pot of tea, and carefully carried two mugs up to her. Squatting down, he looked into her face. Lucy beamed at him, so full of happiness. 'I'll finish in a while then I'll show you both my paintings.' They sat together in the morning sunshine, Harry just quietly watching her painting and admiring the scenery around them.

Lucy put down her brush and turned the two canvases towards Harry. 'Wow! They are fantastic. You have really captured the light, the distance. You are brilliant. I just love them both. We can't frame them yet, I would be afraid the glass may break rattling around in the camper. We can get a portfolio in the next town for you to store all your paintings.'

After more tea, and croissants which had already gone stale, they decided to walk up to the fields where the blue lupins were growing wild. There were wafts of scent from wildflowers, oregano, thyme, and cypresses and an earthy smell from an area of cultivated soil.

Eventually, they left this idyllic spot, back onto the road towards Bursa. It was a bit disappointing after the previous night. A small provincial, industrial town. 'We do need to stop here, we have to get some fuel and provisions and find a pharmacy for some tummy bug medicine. I've checked the distances, the next place is Izmir, it is the best part of a half-day drive depending on the road conditions. Too far to reach today.'

They spent the night behind a filling station, next to what appeared to be the owner's allotment. 'He said to me that a few travellers like us stop here. He wasn't sure we would like the thermal baths in the town, too expensive. But he did recommend a restaurant where they do the best *Iskender kebab* in the whole of Turkey.'

'I don't know what *Iskender kebab* is but let's go there to find out.'

On the way out of the town the next morning, having enjoyed a traditional Turkish meal the night before, then filled the camper van with fuel and visited a mini market for a few provisions, Lucy saw a hitchhiker beside the road. 'Let's stop.'

He was tall, clean-shaven, with long, straight, dark hair. He was dressed from head to foot in blue denim. A shirt with an extra wide collar and shell buttons. A leather belt with an engraved silver buckle was holding up bell bottomed jeans. The bottom of the jeans were huge, almost as big as the waist.

'Hi, I am Jurgen. I am hoping for a lift to Marmaris.'

'We can take you as far as Izmir, we will be stopping there for a few days,' Lucy said.

'That is good, it's on my way.' He threw in his large

backpack and climbed in. 'Another guy was hitching at the same spot as me half an hour ago. He decided to move along the road. Neither of us was getting looked at, probably 'cos there were two of us standing together. I was here first, so he did the good thing, he let me take first place. He looked a nice guy, also going to Izmir. I think he was Greek.'

'If we see him, we can give him a lift, there is plenty of room,' Lucy said. 'Am I correct, from your accent, you're German?'

'Ya! I am from Stuttgart, maybe you passed there on your way.'

'We did, we stopped near there to visit a friend of mine at Heidelberg at the university.'

'I didn't go to university. I just started as a learner,' he stumbled on finding the English word, 'an apprentice. Is that how you call it? It was at my father's factory. He has a big industry in Stuttgart making metal items.'

About a kilometre further down the road they spotted the other hitchhiker.

'That's the guy, there,' exclaimed Jurgen. He was sitting on a broken plastic chair at the side of the road. They pulled over in a cloud of dust. 'Sorry, I was a bit speedy there.' She wound down her window, letting in a lot of dust. 'You want a lift? We have already picked up your mate from further back up the road.'

'That would be cool, very nice, I am making my way to Izmir.' It was quite a strong accent, Lucy could not place it initially.

'Climb in, but be quick, this is not a good place to stop, we are right on a corner and there is some fast traffic.' The hitchhiker climbed in next to Jurgen, keeping his bag on his knees.

'Hello, my name is George, George Padedimitriou.'

'That sounds Greek to me,' said Lucy, recognising the accent from her recent trip to Greece.

'My home is from near Janina, in the north of Greece. I am from a tiny village called Agios Georgios. A group of English archaeologists were coming each year to do a dig. One year I was employed as their cook, and that was when I learnt my English. When they finally finished looking for all the Neolithic bits of pottery and bone, I got a job in a taverna in the Plaka, the touristy part of Athens.'

'What was the name of the taverna? I was staying in Plaka just two weeks ago.'

'The Platanos Taverna.'

'No, I don't think we went there.' Lucy kept turning round to look at the new traveller.

'What is all this '*we*' bit?' inquired Harry, still feeling a bit green with envy from Lucy's holiday, never getting the full story of her adventures in Greece.

'Oh, it was just a crowd of us girls staying at a hostel in Athens. It was called The *Nefili*, we called it the '*no feely – no looky.*' We all met on the ferry from Mykonos. The sea was very rough, and the ferry was delayed for hours. Most of the passengers were seasick, which was pretty horrible. When we finally arrived in Piraeus we went together to Athens in this ancient taxi. It was the middle of the night, so it worked out cheaper than the bus, which probably wouldn't have come for hours.'

George looked every bit like a chef. In his early thirties, his midriff was spreading from tasting titbits from the dishes he was cooking. He had thick black hair, flicked up into an apology of a quiff, a black muscle t-shirt showing off an upper body that had regularly worked out in a gym. But he did have an ulcerous scab on his leg, which he kept picking.

'I had to do my conscription when I was 18. I had to join the army and spent most of the year on guard duty in an outpost near the border with Albania. It was on top of a hill, so freezing cold in the winter. On night duty I could see across the border to the north into Albania, there were no lights, it was always dark, but just across the sea, there were all the lights on Corfu. Tavernas open until late, parties and discos, cars driving along the coast road. It made me feel lonely but happy to be Greek.'

'I never went to Corfu. I went island hopping just down south in the Cyclades.'

'A lot of tourists go to Corfu for holidays these days,' said Harry, trying to keep in the conversation, which appeared to him just between Lucy and George.

'This is a good camper. Made in Germany I think,' Jurgen said, looking round the interior, also wanting to be part of the chatting. 'I was the wrong cow,' he hesitated as he tried to look for the right word.

'We say *black sheep*. I think that is what you mean.'

'Ya, ya! I am sorry, I am not too good with my English. I was the black sheep. I didn't fit in with my people. I like to dress in a new way and listen to the latest music from America and England. You have good music from England.'

'You want to listen to some?' Harry dug out a cassette and put it in the player.

'Ah, yes, Eric Clapton, this is very new, good guitar!'

Harry played a bit on an air guitar.

'My father is old and very strict. He did not understand my way. So, he told me to go travelling, to find the world, then come back to run the business when I had learnt about people.' He stopped for a minute to listen to the music. 'My father paid for me to go by aeroplane to India. But I am just hitching, using his money to travel like this.'

'That's far out! You hitching to India. We are taking the road slowly, going to Kathmandu. We are stopping in many places, just going to beautiful, interesting places on the way.' Lucy seemed to really get on well with this guy.

'I know of many people taking this journey now. I have read in newspapers and magazines they go for many reasons. Some like me to explore, to find new places and people. Some go just for drugs. I promised my father I would not take any drugs whilst travelling. I had met some people at my home who were hashish smokers. I have met many on the road who were just travelling to Afghanistan where they were told the best hashish was available. I think it is a little crazy.' The more Jurgen spoke the better his English became.

'I don't smoke,' Lucy said. 'Harry does a little, he finds it helps him play his music. But we are not on the road to find the best drugs, we are going so we can find the best people, the best cultures.'

'I got very stoned one night in Istanbul, I was with a crowd of other travellers,' Harry said, still feeling embarrassed about his close liaison with the Spanish girl. 'One had this huge chillum. I wasn't used to it. It wasn't a good experience.'

'I enjoy a cold beer', Jurgen said. 'It is relaxing.'

'You won't find many of those around here, alcohol is banned by Islam.'

The conversation moved back and forth, the road was good and the weather fine. They carried on towards Izmir, the road winding through small rolling hills, neat orchards of olive trees, oranges and apricots. All the time they chatted, told stories, and listened to music.

Chapter 6

Izmir. West Turkey April 1971

"We don't need objects, we need adventures."

They arrived in Izmir in the late afternoon. Jurgen and George both declared they wanted to stay for a few days in a hostel. Harry said he thought he knew where they could all go. He had met an Australian in the Pudding Shop back in Istanbul putting a leaflet on the notice board about places to stay. He made a note of this one in Izmir. The Australian was very talkative, Harry met up with him several times. He was full of information about travelling from Sydney. He said he liked to communicate with everyone. He was always giving out information, the best places to stop, the best places for food and meeting other travellers. Harry did not take much notice, he told the Australian they were most probably taking a different route. It was then the Australian explained that he was hitchhiking and taking public transport to England. That he had a friend living in Earls Court who had got a job as a barman in a hotel. That he wanted to do something like that. He thought London was a fab place, all grooving with pavements made of gold, great music at every venue.

They soon found the campsite from the rough directions Harry remembered. It was a large park shaded by big eucalyptus and pine trees. The ground was worn bare, hard sand. Attached to the camp site there was a small hostel with five or six very clean rooms and a shared bathroom. There were toilets and a shower for those camping.

Lucy was thrilled. 'Great, I desperately want to wash my hair and do some clothes. I've been going four days now without any proper facilities.' After checking in with the owner, and paying a small fee, they found a good place to park under the shade of a tree, but far enough away from the noise and music coming from the small café. Both Jurgen and George had looked over the rooms in the hostel and decided to stay there. They politely thanked Harry and Lucy for the lift.

Harry set up their awning and rigged a sheet of black plastic between two trees. They now had lots of space.

'Good place, we can explore the area, meet up with people, maybe have a party or two.' He retrieved his guitar kept securely in its case so it wouldn't get damaged. He spent time tuning it and strumming a few chords whilst Lucy went to the showers to clean up and wash.

Later in the evening, they walked over to the café for some food. A young waiter handed them a dirty, stained, creased menu. Lucy said, 'Harry, you should do them a favour and draw up a new menu for them in your best design and calligraphy. We can do it for them tomorrow.

Maybe we can find a place in town that could print a few.'

The food was great, a lamb stew with small onions and vegetables, covered with thick yoghurt. After they finished Jurgen and George joined them. Together they settled onto the two available long, comfortable seats covered in a colourful textile, exchanging news with other visitors.

A new guy joined the gathering that was taking up most of the space in the café. They made space for him to sit down. He was wearing a pop festival t-shirt promoting an event in some remote American mid-west town in 1968. He wore denim shorts and a head bandana of a rolled and folded cotton scarf of the stars and stripes on a red background. He was very thin, he did not look well. His face was red from too much sun, with an outbreak of pimples on his forehead, peeling skin on his arms and legs and sore lips. He had a straggly beard and unkempt brown hair.

He briefly introduced himself as Jack and moved to the corner on a wooden stool. The evening was lacklustre, the music from the radio and cassette player was not to anyone's taste. One of the guests tried playing his guitar which was badly out of tune, he lacked any inspiration. Harry was on the point of going to get his guitar from the camper, when the newcomer, Jack, moved into the circle, took the guitar, and strummed a chord. He then professionally tuned it in a matter of moments.

'This song by Pete Seeger. It is one of my favourite tracks.'

With a nasal voice much like early Bob Dylan he started singing *All American Boy.*

The song continued for several more minutes. Jack put down the guitar.

He announced that he was a draft dodger from the USA. 'Those words tell my story well. When I got my call up papers to go to Vietnam, I was just 18 years old. I didn't want to die. I had been in several small protests in my local town and watched some of the big ones in cities on TV. I watched some of the terrible videos shown of the war, bombing and fighting in the jungle. My Mom and Dad were quite hip, my Mom played protest songs in a small band. You will have never heard of them, *The New Philadelphia Blues Band.* They played around local towns across Ohio and up to Michigan.

I was very surprised with the reaction from my dad when he heard about my call up papers. I wasn't living at home, I shared a room with a mate from college. Dad came over to my room and gave me a bundle of money and told me to get across the border to Canada, ASAP. That same afternoon I packed up my stuff, found my passport, said goodbye to my pet crow, took the next Greyhound up to Detroit and crossed into Canada. I was scared shitless I would get picked up by the cops. I then got a flight to Sweden and here I am hitching to the east. I am hoping to get to Australia. I hear there is easy work to be had. I never realised how big the world is, and how small my bank account is.' He looked down at the ground, at the intricate patterns on the floor.

'Are you being chased by the police or army?' someone asked.

'Nope, I hope not, I reckon they don't come this far. There are many thousand guys like me draft dodging. I still must keep my head down 'cos if do get caught it will mean prison and a big fine. I have met a few travellers like me, we try to keep each other informed on what is going on.'

'What's that about your pet crow?'

'It was, hopefully still is, an unusual bird. It would sit outside my window and look at me with this beady eye, it listened to everything I said and sang. It particularly liked the folk music I played. I am sure it would have sung along if it could talk. It was strange but very therapeutic. It was good to have a friend who wasn't all messed up with drugs and stuff like lots of kids from college were. I knew it very well. It was easy to recognise because it had white feathers on one wing.'

They all absorbed this unusual story. Everyone knew about the Vietnam War, about the young kids being called up, and killed. But this was the first time many of them had met a draft dodger.

'What do you think is going to happen in Vietnam?'

'I don't want to talk politics,' he bluntly said. He picked up the guitar again.

'Joan Baez, my voice is nothing like hers,' he apologised. 'When she sings, she has a silver throat, soft, soft silver'. Jack continued for a few more verses.

The listeners all stood up and clapped. 'Carry on, we want more!' one called. Lucy went to sit beside him. 'You don't look very well. You need to look after that sunburn. I have got some cream in our camper I can give you. Are you eating enough? You look very thin and pale.'

'I am finding it a bit difficult to eat right now, nerves and a bit of a tummy bug. Stupid, I sat in the sun too long yesterday, some cream would be welcome.'

'I will get it for you later. And we've got stuff for your tummy,' Lucy said.

And so the evening went on into the small hours.

The next morning, Lucy found Jack in his room and gave him the cream. Then she took a menu from the café, and a couple of books from the swap shelf. One on Turkish food, with illustrations and one on Turkish tile designs.

'Here you are, my lovely professional, get going. I have got some sheets of drawing paper and coloured pens here for you.'

Harry, without hesitation, started drafting out his idea for a new menu.

A couple of guys in a tent next to Harry and Lucy's camper came over to share a cup of coffee. The talk drifted around. What a great singing voice Jack had. Lucy said she had seen him earlier when taking him some cream for his sore arms and face, Harry explained he was designing a new menu for the café. One of the visitors nodded over to the other side of the camp. 'Watch out for that guy over there, he's a dealer. We reckon he is a nasty piece of work. He has a list of all the drugs, powders and pills he can supply. He will give a terrible currency exchange rate and is always short. He folds a note in half, and hands you the bundle with the note in the middle, facing you. So, when you count it out it looks OK. But he will have cheated you out of a few hundred lira. It is a classic way of cheating done by money changers.'

'He is English. I think he is called Nick,' the other friend said. 'He has been seen going round all the tents and campers talking to the occupants.'

Nick was tall, his jet black hair was raked back from his forehead into a small ponytail. He had ice-blue eyes, as cold as an iceberg, too close together. He wore a smart black leather jerkin over a clean white t-shirt, a heavy gold chain round his neck, new jeans, and new trainers on his feet.

'We don't know where he lives. Not on this campsite. We think he has been here in Turkey for some time.'

Jurgen joined the group, listened in, and caught up on the discussion. 'I was woken last night very late.' He pointed over his shoulder. 'I stay in the hostel, there was knocking on my door. I thought there was some problem with the owner but it was that man over there.' He indicated across the park. 'He asked if I would like a nice Turkish girl for the night. I quickly closed the door.' He laughed nervously. 'I was told by a guest in the café this morning he has been seen dealing drugs around the campsite. He does quite well judging by the number of plastic bags passing hands. Also, he is selling money exchange, will change cash or travellers' cheques.'

'We won't have anything to do with him.' Harry said.

Part of Lucy's Diary

Now we are travelling, I am happy. It is so good to be with my Harry, it was a long time apart when I was in Greece. We each had lots of adventures and have stories to tell each other. There are some great people here, all different, each with a story and a quest. Hopefully it is going to be like this all the way to Kathmandu.

That man, Nick the snake is creepy. The others have said he is a dealer in drugs and stolen clothes. I will try to keep away from him.

I am disappointed Rolly has left and gone back home. Harry will miss him, they are such good mates. But he was worried about the food, fitting in with us, and what the future holds. He will be much happier back in Yorkshire doing the job he knows at the garage. I feel it is better for just Harry and I to be together, it would have been difficult with Rolly at night times when the weather was not good, where to sleep and sometimes just fitting in with what we wanted to do.

I am worried about my periods. I know Mother was reassuring but somehow I feel something is not right. I must be positive, think the best.

The next couple of days were warm and sunny. Harry and Lucy explored the town. They went to find a beach, but it was quite a long way away, too far to walk. They found the Konak Square in the centre of the old town. Lucy wanted to go shopping for tourist stuff in the crowded market but was disappointed, she couldn't find anything to her liking. Harry worked on his design for the menu, and Lucy did some sketching. That day they cooked their own food, buying fresh produce locally. It was cheaper and made a change from the crowd in the café.

Harry had finished his design of the menu. He decorated it with images of dishes of food copied from the book they borrowed from the book swap and some elaborate Turkish arabesques and patterns around the edge of the page. He handed it to the owner who was almost speechless with admiration. 'This is beautiful. I will sell many more dishes from this menu. I must pay you.'

'No, no! It is my profession, I have done it just for you. You must get some printed, on thick paper so they don't get spoiled.'

'I will take it to the printers immediately. If you don't want payment, I must give you a gift. It is the Turkish way.' He turned the menu over again, admiring it with a big smile on his face. 'I will give free soup, for you and your wife.' He nodded towards Lucy. 'Free soup before every meal you have here.'

He gave Harry a handshake and a big man hug.

'We don't know your name. I am Harry, this is Lucy.'

'My name in Turkish is very difficult. People just call me Omar.'

In the evening they were sitting under the awning. Lucy was finishing one of her earlier sketches, Harry was reading a magazine. It was *OZ*, he had borrowed it from a fellow camper. He was enthralled by the colourful, psychedelic front cover. He examined closely the way the colours were printed and the rhythms of the psychedelic patterns. Inside there was a controversial article about women's liberation. He thought he would give it to Lucy to read before handing it back.

Once again, his mind slipped to the thought that Lucy had missed her period. He tried to dismiss the thought that she had slept with someone in Greece, but it kept nagging at him. He loved her so much, he could not believe she would do such a thing.

As he tried to relax, lying on the ground looking up through the branches of the trees, he saw a flash of green, then another. A flock of noisy parakeets flew through the trees.

A Swedish couple from a VW camper van that was parked close by joined them as the sun was setting. The light was golden, shadows of the branches overhead patterned the ground. 'I am Casper, this is Maja. We are travelling from the north of Sweden to India.'

Maja, who was very typically Scandinavian with long blond hair to her waist, and a good, slim figure dressed in a long dress printed with an Indian design. She said, 'This weather is so good. In my town in the north of Sweden, we still have snow on the ground.'

'Yeh! We want to go to the beach tomorrow, maybe find some swimming. Would you like to come with us?'

'Oh yes! Please, we went to find a beach near here, but it was a long way, too far to walk. Do you know a good place?'

'Ya!' Casper said. 'We have a map, it shows a place called Mentes, it has a sun and shade showing on the map. We can go there in our VW.'

'That's very kind of you, we can bring some drinks, and a bit of food.'

This peaceful situation was broken by Nick, the English guy. He walked up through the shadows to join the four of them. He was dressed the same as they saw him earlier, now he had a *stubby* cooler hanging from his belt. It was printed with green marijuana leaves and contained a bottle of *Effie's* beer. He asked Harry if he would like some dope, or anything else. There was a firm 'No' in response. Maybe he would like to buy a leather coat or a pair of jeans. He had several that were top quality and the right size. Lucy jumped up. 'No, no, we don't want anything, just go away.'

Nick moved close to Lucy, he put his arm round her shoulder, he drew her close. 'You can have anything, I will give you everything,' he whispered in her ear. He stared at her cheek with unblinking cold eyes, like a snake. 'You are so beautiful, come with me. I will give you everything you want. We can go anywhere.' His tongue slithered out, he licked his lips. His expensive aftershave caught in Lucy's throat. She calmly lifted his arm from her shoulders, pushed him away, turned to Harry and took both his hands into hers. She looked into his eyes, beseechingly.

'You best go away, we want nothing to do with you,' Harry said in little more than a whisper.

'If that is what you wish, I will leave you two love birds, but I shall find you again, somewhere,' Nick walked away.

'Jesus Christ, what a snake. If I had my stiletto heels I would have put two inches right through his foot. And that would have just been for starters.' Lucy was upset, frightened and very angry.

'I suggest we go to have a meal in Omar's café. We need to calm down a bit and talk about going to the beach tomorrow and then what to do and where to go from here.' Harry said.

In the café, Omar greeted them. 'Your menu is a great success. I already sold more dishes. You sit here, I bring the soup for you as promised, then you have a good meal.'

'Omar,' Harry said, 'there is a man who comes into the campsite who is selling drugs and other illegal things. He is dressed in a leather jerkin, he has slicked back hair. Can you tell the police, and say he is not allowed to come here?'

'Yes, I have seen him. Thank you for telling me. I will deal with it immediately. I think he has upset many of my guests.'

Harry and Lucy ate their meal, starting with a delicious free vegetable soup. They talked about what to do, when to go and where. Lucy said firmly that she did not want to stay any longer at this campsite. 'It was lovely, but now it has completely lost its shine. That guy, Nick, that snake, he has really upset me. I don't know what I shall do if I see him again.'

'Ok, we'll look at the map and decide where to head for. We can leave either tomorrow after we have been swimming or the next day. Let's hope the police will stop that snake coming here again.'

It was a warm, sunny day, and the trip to Mendes was a great success. The Swedish couple were so accommodating and interesting. Lucy was fascinated by their VW camper. 'This is so comfortable compared with our old diesel van. You seem to have all the equipment you need, a little kitchen, a chemical toilet, nice big double bed and lots of headroom with the roof lifted up.'

Harry knew she was still disappointed with the looks of *Forget-me-not*.

'Ya! But it was very expensive for us to buy in Sweden. It took most of our money. And has broken several times. Your camper van must be very reliable.'

Harry wanted to talk about other subjects, he made observations about the countryside they were driving through now that they had got past the sprawl of Izmir. There was a mixture of small businesses, factories, farms and small holdings. Occasionally, set back from the road in well maintained gardens, were large expensive houses. They presumed these were holiday homes for wealthy city dwellers.

The beach at Mendes was long, sloping sand down to the azure Mediterranean. They all went into the shallows, frolicking and splashing each other. It was cold so they soon got out. Harry had found some cans of beer in a shop close to the campsite, and Lucy had made up some tasty cheese and salad sandwiches. They had a relaxing picnic sitting on a rug on the sands. It was an enjoyable and successful day. They didn't get back to the campsite until quite late, very tired.

Chapter 7

Izmir and Burdur April 1971

*"In the end, we only regret the chances
we didn't take."*

At breakfast time the next morning, they went back to Omar's café. They both ordered omelettes and coffee. The night before, Harry had listed possible routes they could take across Turkey.

Lucy said, 'We need to get to places that are not so big and touristy. Only the old bazaar was interesting here, and this campsite.'

'I totally agree. Tourist spots are not the thing for either of us, but most of the interesting places are going to attract tourists. It will be hard to find remote places that we will like. I took a guidebook off the swap shelves, I went through it last night. The book is ancient. I think it was written for the Victorian or Edwardian gentlemen on the grand tour of the Middle East. Anyway, it says Kusadasi and Ephesus are interesting, except they are just lots of ruins and museums. I know you said no more old piles of ancient stones and carvings, you had seen enough in Greece. We could go down through there and then go inland to Pamukkale. That will be going in the right direction for travelling across Turkey. The guide says Pamukkale is different, it says there are white cliffs and waterfalls. And there are swimming lakes with marble statues at the bottom. You swim over them in thermal waters. That sounds a bit different.'

'So long as it's a bit warmer than the sea we were in yesterday.'

'Or from here we could go south, along the Mediterranean coast.'

'I think that will be very touristy. When I was first looking at going to Greece, the guide books also showed the southern part of Turkey. Lots of big hotels were being built. When I was in Kos, in Greece you could see across the sea to Turkey, there appeared to be hillsides of new buildings,' Lucy said. 'All new tourist houses and hotels.'

'One place I really want to go to is Cappadocia. There was lots of information on notice boards, the guide I have got has a whole chapter on it and the Australian guy I met talked about how amazing it was. I think he said there were pixie mountains filled with caves and churches.'

'I don't understand, what do you mean by pixie mountains? Surely pixie mountains have caves filled with pixies?'

'Ha, ha! I love you so much.'

'Again I suppose there will be lots of other people there. We can't get away from them completely. But seems like a plan.'

'I agree. We should go south to Kusadasi, then east to Pamukkale, then the lake area, Konya, Kayseri, and either Van or north to Erzurum and across into Iran.'

Lucy sketched a rough map in her notebook.

At that moment George came in for breakfast. They both warmly greeted him. 'We're having an omelette each, they're fantastic. Anyway, we have just been planning our route eastwards. I think we're leaving later today, or tomorrow,' Harry said.

'It will be sad to see you leave, I also am going. I plan to go to the sea, somewhere near Marmaris. I want to get away from that English man. He is evil. The only person I don't like here.'

Lucy said, 'Yep, that's one of the reasons why we are leaving.'

After eating, they left the café to start the job of packing all their gear again. It had got very scattered and disorganised during their stay of almost a week. They were trying to find safe storage places in the camper, where they could find the most useful things again quickly.

'*Forget-me-not* is the perfect name for her. You're so clever. I will get some tiny tins of enamel paint to do a bodywork painting. Maybe blue, black and green. Possibly yellow as well. I can paint a bunch of them over each front wheel arch.' Just then Harry noticed a familiar figure running through the campground towards them. 'Hey, look what the wind has just blown in. It's Chalky.'

'Have you heard?' He was panting for breath, he obviously ran all the way from town. 'There has been a huge earthquake in a place called Burdur. Somewhere inland from here.'

'Oh my God! we were planning to pass by near there on our way east. We have just started packing up to go. Now we will probably have to find a different route to get around it.'

'At the place I am staying at in town, someone told me you were camping here. There is a real network of information here. Everyone knows what is going on, one of the guys said they had heard you were leaving soon, going east, in that direction. Anyway, as soon as we heard about this disaster, I thought of you. We started putting a plan together, to get some provisions over to this town Burdur. You have a decent sized vehicle, we could use it to transport any donations.'

'Lucy this is Chalky, we met somewhere on the way here, can't remember exactly where. I know Rolly talked about him. Chalky this is Lucy. I probably talked about her when we gave you a lift.'

'Good to meet you, Lucy. He talked about nothing else,' Chalky joked.

The news slowly sank in. 'Oh my God, let's sit down and think about this. How big a disaster is it?' Harry was thoughtful. Lucy butted in. 'We can ask people around here who are camping. Maybe they have a spare blanket, or some water bottles.'

'Yep! That is just what we thought. Whilst you are doing that, I am going to see what I can do in town. As you know, it was my job in the army. I spent twenty years sourcing equipment and stuff like that. I know how to do it. I should be able to fix something.' Chalky got up, pecked Lucy a kiss on her cheek. 'Good to meet you.' Then ran back to town.

'Ok, the four of us, let's get organised.' Jurgen had just joined the group. He also had had an omelette for breakfast. In a Germanic way he efficiently took the lead. He had picked up the news of the earthquake a few moments earlier in the cafe. He looked around. 'I will go and ask that part of the site if they have anything to spare. Maybe someone in a camper van will have a tent they don't use. You and Lucy look around the other half. And ask Omar in the hostel if he can help. He must have some bottles of water, and maybe packets of biscuits he can spare.' He paused for thought. 'I suggest we meet up again before midday, here outside your camper. There is not much time, so we must be quick. We can bring together anything we have collected. We must remember any promises that are made, better still write them down so we can go back to claim them.'

They set about their tasks. Omar was very generous. He had heard the news on the radio. He offered a case of two dozen bottles of water and promised snacks, chocolate and other provisions from his storeroom. Those staying in rooms in the hostel all claimed they were travelling light with just small rucksacks, only their necessary clothes and provisions. All they could offer was a few medicines, bandages and so on from their medical kits. Those camping donated some bedding and a few warm clothes. One family in a very large camper van said they had a small two-man tent they may be able to give, half the family were away sight-seeing, so they first needed to get permission from them.

Harry, Lucy, Jurgen and George met up again at midday. There was a small pile of donations, not as much as they had hoped. Omar came running from the hostel. 'Quick, quick, 'Arry, 'Arry, there is a telephone for you, a telephone call from a man. He said it was urgent. Follow me. The telephone is in my office.'

'Harry, it is me, Chalky. Fantastic news. I have talked to the mayor of the town, a really nice guy. He is called Yusuf. He is pulling out all the stops to help us. I am meeting him in a short while. But first of all, he has got something on the local radio, appealing for help. For bedding, medical stuff and so on.'

Lucy, who had just caught up with Harry, interrupted and took the telephone from Harry. 'Ask for children's, baby's, and women's stuff. Like nappies, feeding bottles, and baby's beds. Things like that.'

'Great idea, I must go to meet with Yusuf. You listen to the radio and local station. Bye.' Chalky cut the telephone conversation.

The radio commentary was in Turkish. Omar translated some of it, but there was not much information. A little while later Chalky drove up in a car. It was loaned to him by the mayor, Yusuf. 'Saves time in running from town to campsite,' said Chalky. 'Yusuf is coming to visit and meet you two. He has really got the bit between his teeth and doing so much.' A black shiny car pulled up, it was Yusuf. Chalky made introductions. Yusuf had an unexpected, relaxed look, not what they expected for the mayor of a large town. He wore an open shirt, no tie, chinos, and very shiny black shoes. He had thinning black hair and was getting rotund around his waist. He didn't stop moving around, hopping from one foot to the other with a nervous energy. 'It is fantastic what you are doing.

I have mobilized lots of officials from the council, they are going around to get loads of stuff. I have organised three 7-ton lorries from our fleet if needed.'

Yusuf claimed he knew the mayor of Burdur, he had met him at some official meetings. 'I haven't been able to contact him because all the electric and telephone wires are down. We have no idea how bad the situation is, but it seems it is very bad. The radio reports are not good. Our two towns have a lot of contacts, some wealthy residents of Burdur have holiday houses here, near the beach.'

Lucy wrote a list of things he should ask for including women's and babies' stuff. Yusuf made a few calls from the telephone in the office of the hostel. 'We need to get to the damaged area quickly. I have spoken to my office, they reported that emergency equipment is coming from Istanbul and Ankara, but it will take a long time, as they are far away. There is very little equipment close by. Probably builders, constructors and farmers will have some equipment, if it is not destroyed, for moving rubble. They must get doctors, fire engines and ambulances there.' It was obvious Yusuf was efficient at organising people, he could not stop talking, planning, jumping from foot to foot. 'There will be international help eventually, maybe not for a couple of days. It is the first thing needed to find people buried in rubble and give medical help. I understand you are taking items in your camper. Thank you, it is so good of you. I will organise any of the lorries to go as quickly as possible. Now I must go back into town with your friend to organise collecting the right equipment.'

Yusuf and Chalky drove away to do so in their separate cars. Those at the campsite gathered together a few more things that had been promised, including a small tent.

The telephone went again in the hostel, it was Chalky again, very excited. 'Guess what, a television crew are coming to see you soon, Yusuf has organised it. You had better do your hair and smarten up.' Before he had finished the call a big truck, with a TV logo and adverts on the side pulled into the campsite. The producer, director, camera, and sound engineers introduced themselves. Lights and cameras were unloaded. A make-up girl made Lucy and Harry sit on stools whilst she dabbed their faces with powder. 'So you don't shine in the lights,' was her only comment.

A small crowd had gathered round, speculating on the events in low voices. The director took control. He told Harry to stand in front of the camper, then added that Lucy should stand next to him. 'A beautiful couple, perfect for my TV show, helping the people of Turkey during their visit and tour,' he said. The interview was short, the producer described the horror of an earthquake. The fact that any communication with Burdur was not working, so there was little information on damage, injuries, and possible deaths. He continued with what the travellers were doing to help. The cameras had swung onto Harry and Lucy standing in front of the camper. He explained that they were changing their itinerary of travelling and exploring Turkey to make a special rescue mission. Harry and Lucy did not understand any of the rapid Turkish dialogue. They simply smiled towards the camera. As quickly as they came, the cameras and equipment were packed away, off to another interview. Omar told them as far as he knew it was going to be on the evening news, and maybe some foreign companies will pick it up. The news of the earthquake was spreading around Europe.

Exhausted by all this excitement the travellers collapsed onto the rug in front of the camper. Omar brought a big pot of tea for them and sat with them. He also had done a short interview for the TV and was thrilled because it showed the signs outside his hostel and café.

It took them a while to gather their wits and energy to collect together the remaining donations and carefully pack the camper. They decided to leave very early in the morning, at first light rather than leave immediately and have to drive in the dark along unmade roads. Harry had checked on the map, he worked out it was about five hour's drive. 'Maybe we should go earlier, whilst it is still dark. The first bit of the road looks easy. If we leave here at three o' clock, we could be there at nine,' he said. They had a very early supper whilst watching the news on television in the café. Their interview was shown. 'Good job they didn't ask us anything, it would have been lots of 'um's and er's,' said Harry. There was a lot of news about the earthquake, maps of the region were shown, and a few library pictures of the centre of Burdur, but there was no update about the disaster.

Later they gathered together with Jurgen and George, sitting next to the camper. Their two friends had decided to follow them to Burdur and changed their plans to take a lift from one of the lorries organised by the mayor. They had been told there would be room for them in the cab if they could be ready by the road outside the campsite at five o'clock in the morning.

Out of the gathering dusk, a grey shadow emerged. It was Nick. 'Ah! The beautiful people, the stars of the screen, so popular and famous now, the talk of the town.' Lucy jumped up, intending to move away as quickly as possible, but Nick reached out to grab her by the arm.

'My gorgeous, you must have decided by now. To stay with me. You are so beautiful, absolute perfection.'

'Leave her alone,' shouted Harry, as he scrambled up. 'Lucy, get away from him.' He was too far away to reach her. She struggled out of his clasp.

'Ah! Lucy, that's your name. Yes, the name is perfect. *Lucy in the Sky with Diamonds*, together we can fill the sky with shining diamonds. Just float away with me above the clouds into the beyond, into the sky.'

Harry grabbed Nick, viciously pulling him away. 'Leave immediately, we have already called the police.' Lucy turned and once again took Harry by both hands and as before looked beseechingly into his eyes. She held on tightly to him. George had got up off the ground, he looked strong, powerful and threatening in a black t-shirt. Nick turned away and walked off into the dark evening light.

'Did you see his eyes? They were like a snake. They were just black pinpricks in the ice cold blue.' Lucy said, quivering.

'Yes, I saw them, he was obviously stoned on something,' said Harry. 'You are shaking like a leaf. Go and lie down, I'll go to tell Omar to call the police. I won't be a moment.'

'No, you stay with her, I will go to Omar.' George said.

So they settled down in the camper, gradually quietening down, talking softly, reassuring each other that the incident had passed.

Chapter 8

Burdur. Central Turkey May 1971

"Even if you are on the right track,
you will get run over if you just sit there!"

It was very dark when they set off. There was no moon, but fortunately very little traffic. The road was good blacktop, with recently installed road and direction signs. Whenever a truck approached them, Harry, who was driving slowed right down. It was a habit of truck drivers to flash their headlight onto full beam, making it very difficult to see the road ahead, especially when the truck moved into the centre of the road. Lucy supplied cups of strong black coffee from a flask to ensure they both stayed wide awake. There was very little conversation between them, they were concentrating on making good time. Lucy regretted not seeing any of the passing countryside. In the dark it appeared relatively flat farmlands of olive and fruit groves. They passed small villages, just groups of houses either side of the road, dark, sleeping, and unlit. The few small towns had occasional streetlights, a flashing green neon light outside a pharmacy, a dull light over the door of a police station but no other illuminations.

As dawn approached the traffic on the road increased. Tractors towing empty trailers on the way to farm fields to collect fruit and vegetables for the market. The occasional old and decrepit car taking workers to local industrial areas, usually with just one, sometimes no lights working. They passed more lorries transporting goods from city to city. The daylight came quickly. The couple swapped seats, Lucy was confident driving in daylight. After about three hours on the road, they were getting hungry, the flask of coffee was empty. Harry spotted a small wayside stall in one of the towns they passed through, so they stopped to buy some sweet pastries and refill their flask with strong black coffee.

They made such good time, it surprised them when they passed a road sign indicating Burdur was only ten kilometres ahead. As they approached the outskirts of the city, they were stopped by a soldier waving down all the traffic. They were directed into an industrial area and a large factory storeroom. On the hard standing in front were parked several army lorries, other vehicles painted in matt green or camouflage colours, two or three red fire engines, many police cars and several tractors with heavy duty lifting buckets on the front and articulated grabbing gear on the back. The area was teaming with men, moving in all directions, but with obvious purpose. A uniformed policeman approached them enquiring what they were doing there. He soon realised he could not understand what they were saying, so he called over an officer who could understand English. They established they were delivering useful items collected in Izmir, and very soon there would be one or two loaded lorries arriving. The office instructed a team to unload the camper van, then for the couple to park out of the way at the side of the hard area.

Once done, there was nothing Harry and Lucy could do except sit watching the organised chaos in front of them. They both wanted to help somehow, but there was no one obviously in charge to ask. They ate the pastries and drank the remaining coffee.

The sun shone through a cloud of dust in the near distance. 'All that dust is obviously from collapsed buildings,' observed Harry. 'I don't know what we can do now. I know we both want to help somehow, having got here.' Their adrenaline was dropping after the rapid and stressful drive through the early hours of the day. 'I'll go and find someone who speaks English and ask where we can help.' As Harry walked across the parking area two lorries pulled in, they had the crest and logo of the city council of Izmir. Jurgen and George jumped down from the second lorry. 'You got here safely?' George said.

'Yes, we were unloaded over there, then told to wait here,' Harry replied. 'I'm on my way to ask if we can help anywhere.'

The officer Harry had met before when they first arrived directed the two lorries to back up to the warehouse. He then strode over to the three boys. 'You can't stay around here. You can see it is very busy.'

'We want to help,' Jurgen said. 'What can we do, can we go further into the town and help rescue people?'

The officer was standing to attention, he looked them over. 'No, it is specialist work. We have many people here who are experienced and equipped to deal with the situation. I must ask you to leave, not to interfere with any rescue. It is very dangerous, you have no equipment and no training. You need special clothing, Hi-Vis vests and hard hats. We don't want even more casualties or injuries, please.' He paused. 'Thank you for your help, but please leave the region. Either return to Izmir or travel east. The road out of the town is clear.'

These abrupt instructions took the three boys aback. They were surprised. 'Please go now to make more space for this work,' the officer concluded and marched away to help unload the lorries.

'Ok, it seems as if we have our marching orders.' Harry was disappointed. 'You two can come with us, we will find a nice place to go and relax.'

As they were leaving, a shiny black car pulled in, it was Chalky and Yusuf. The mayor was driving. They stepped out after the long drive. 'All OK?' asked Chalky. 'I see the two council lorries have arrived. We've a doctor and a nurse with us to help with injuries.'

'Yes, we're fine,' said Harry, 'we have delivered the donations, we've now been asked to leave. The officer in charge says we may get injured helping in anyway.' He sounded disappointed.

Yusuf looked around the yard at the heavy machinery and all the people rushing around. He paused. 'That is probably the best, this is very special work. Thank you for all your help, and the ideas how we can help. You have done the best help there is. Don't worry, the experts are here and know what to do. You go now and continue your journey through our country. We know what all this means to you, and the people of Burdur and Izmir are forever grateful.' It was a speech from a politician, a mayor.

He continued, 'The good news is the English man you complained about has been in front of the judge. He didn't put him in prison but deported him immediately to his home country. As we speak, he will be on a plane to England.'

'That's great,' was the reply in unison. Harry thought for a moment or two. 'The problem is, someone like that will just move onto Morocco or Ibiza and continue his nasty trade. I hope the judge of the town where he moves to will put him away immediately for a long time.'

'I see your point,' Yusuf considered. 'I will ask the international police to take a note of it.' He moved away to administer the unloading of the council lorries.

They chatted some more, gave big hugs all round, talked about the next steps they would take.

Chalky had already decided to return to Izmir with Yusuf. 'You guys have been amazing, thank you from my heart, you have changed my outlook, I've now finally sorted out my head. I am going south to the coast, put my feet in hot sand and start my life over again. Thank you again.' He wiped tears from his eyes.

The others moved back into the camper to set off on the road away from town.

Jurgen selected a cassette from the collection scattered around the front of the camper. *The Times They are*

A-Changin'. Bob Dylan singing his famous protest song from a decade before.

'Maybe that is very appropriate,' Lucy remarked from the back seat of the camper. She had withdrawn into herself. Harry noticed a concern and worry in her expression. He hoped it was for the victims in the town they were just leaving, not for her own condition.

After a short time, and only a mile in the direction they wanted to go, a policeman stopped them to indicate the road ahead was blocked, so they must go round on small roads to get further east. The road was very small, just unmade gravel, single lane with passing places. The surroundings were wild steep mountains and gorges.

Even though the going was slow, they eventually arrived at the small town of Egirdir, beside a large lake. The decision with all of them was that they should stop here. Jurgen and George booked into a small hostel, Harry and Lucy discovered they could park and stay in a playground beside the lake.

It was time to relax. After a light lunch they all went to sleep for the afternoon, exhausted after the early morning drive and the long day.

The next day, after eating, sleeping, and walking on the shores of the lake, Lucy took George to the local pharmacy to show the nasty scab on his leg to an expert. It was obviously infected, surrounded by raw, red skin. Having done this duty, she bought a tube of strong medicine and persuaded him to take care and to look after himself. Then Harry and Lucy wished a fond farewell to their new friends and drove north a short way into the mountains. They stopped at a tiny village, a long way up a narrow track. Running past the central square was a small, clear river with waterfalls and a weir. The few houses were a checkerboard of white with red roofs climbing up the hill. The narrow, cobbled streets led to lush greenery, sweet gum trees, cherry orchards and small terraced fields for grain and salad crops.

As soon as they stopped in the village square, a young man approached them, he wore grey suit trousers and a white shirt with button down collar. He looked smart and educated. He spoke perfect English. 'I see you are probably from England.' He pointed to the registration plates on the camper. 'You are welcome here, we hardly ever have any visitors. I am the teacher, *ogretmen*,' he pronounced in Turkish, 'at the small school in the village.'

Whilst standing by the camper he explained he had lived in London for 4 years working in his uncle's restaurant, so he had learnt English. His family had always lived in this village, for many generations. When he left England, he moved back to the village to marry his wife. He had known her since school days.

Lucy explained they were travelling east, always looking for interesting places to stop, away from the main roads. They were trying to learn about the culture and language of the places they were passing through.

'Then you must come to my house, come this evening for food. We eat early, long before the dark nighttime. I must go now to the school to give classes to the pupils.' They gratefully accepted the invitation.

In the afternoon they explored the village and surrounding orchards. They ventured a short way up into the hills behind the village, admiring the view across the rooftops, over woods and down to the lake in the distance.

Sitting on a low stone wall in the sunshine, Lucy took both Harry's hands into hers. She looked over his face and into his eyes. 'I have missed another period.'

Harry said, 'Are you OK, you're not ill or anything?' Slowly the situation dawned upon him. 'Jesus, that is over two months now. It means you could be pregnant, doesn't it?'

Lucy held onto his hands, tightly. 'It is not possible, I always take my pill, and I haven't slept with anyone. Only you.'

Harry dropped Lucy's hands, he stood up. Looking down at her he said in a loud voice, 'You must be pregnant, you have missed two periods since you went to Greece. You must have slept with someone whilst you were there, I don't believe you.'

His fists were closed tight, so tight that white skin was showing at his knuckles, his whole body was shaking. 'You met up with some other bloke on holiday on one of those little islands, or god forbid, you made it off with some greasy Greek waiter.'

He was losing control of himself, his voice raised to shouting. 'Fuck! we planned all this trip together, all our lives together, and now you have totally screwed it up.' He turned away, gazing up to the top of the hills, fists tightly bunched, his body still shaking.

He swung round and pointed his finger at her. 'I love

you so much, how could you do this to me?' He turned away again and started marching up the hill.

Lucy, pleading, called after him. 'Please Harry, don't walk away. We must talk. I promise you I've not done anything with anyone.' She was on the point of tears, Harry just carried on, striding up the hill away from her without looking back.

Lucy slumped back down onto the wall, she covered her face with her hands and let out a long wail.

How could it have come to this? I know I have been faithful to him, well almost. What are we going to do now? What will my dad say to me? These thoughts crashed and tumbled through her mind. She got up, screamed an obscenity at the sky and went back to the camper, climbed into the bed, curled up into a tight ball. The tears flowed, she was unable to think of anything.

Harry walked for miles through woods and over hills, clenching his fists tight, then opening them up, clenching them again until they burned. He talked to himself, sometimes just muttering under his breath, sometimes out loud. On a few occasions he stopped and screamed as loud as he could at a rock or a tree. His thoughts sunk deep into an abyss of despair. What should he do? Just abandon her, catch a bus back to Yorkshire and work for the rest of his life as a designer? Should he drive her back in the camper, hand her over to her mum and dad? That would be grim, sharing the same space as her for several weeks. Should he just leave her with the camper? It was hers, she had paid for it. Just let her sort it out herself whilst he goes on to India and Nepal. Why oh why has she done this? Whose baby was it? We were in so much love with each other, how can she have been so deceitful and horrible to have slept with someone else? She should know, she is a grown woman.

He paused, thoughts went back to that night in Istanbul. Getting stoned and cuddling up with that Spanish girl. But then, as he strode on, thinking that he had resisted any temptation, he didn't do anything. But he was tempted, very tempted at one point. Maybe he should go back to the camper and talk to Lucy. How could love be destroyed so quickly? He realised that he still loved her, somewhere in his heart, somehow. Maybe the whole thing is a huge mistake. He swung round and marched down the hill.

It was midafternoon when he returned. The sun was still warm. The village was quiet, it was the afternoon siesta. He tapped on the door of the camper and went in. Lucy was curled up, clasping a pillow that was soaking wet from her tears. They looked at each other, unable to say a word.

Harry just did not know what to do, he just stood in the doorway to the camper, ridged, looking at Lucy. She looked a complete mess, hair tousled, her eyes puffed and red from crying, her face drawn and pale.

'I know I'm not pregnant, I feel it in my heart, my mind and my body.' She said in a small pleading whisper.

Harry turned on his heel, both fists clenched, his mouth set in a firm grim line. He could not believe her. He strode up another path away from the village, along the river valley then towards the woods and hills. He walked without looking up, not even at the stone path he was following. Soon he came over the brow of a hill, unsure of where to go. He looked around. He noticed a small shepherds hut off to the side, down a narrow, overgrown path. He went over to it. It was deserted, rough stone walls, black from a century of smoky fires. The roof was constructed from large, twisted olive branches, holding the flat roof of leaky compressed mud. There was just one window, the wood rotten, the glass a long time shattered, now just a gaping hole in the wall.

Harry collapsed into the broken doorway. Unable to think, unable to understand. His life as he believed now destroyed. Close to tears he buried his head into his folded arms. His world seemed to come to an end. The only road ahead was either without end, an empty eternity, or a dead end. He sat there in the warm sun with just a cold feeling in his heart. His mind jumping from complete blank, through memories of times with Lucy over the past few years, unable to imagine any time in the future without her.

He had no sense of time passing, the sun was setting behind the high hills, it was getting cooler. He was dressed in just a t-shirt and shorts. He moved into the hut, hoping it was a little warmer.

His mind then seemed to jump into gear. Maybe he could live here, all on his own. He could clean the goat and horse shit off the stone floor, fix the window and rehang the door on new hinges. The crude fireplace could be rebuilt with a proper chimney up to the roof. Maybe he could grow a few herbs and vegetables in the small flat pasture behind the hut, just going down to the village occasionally to get provisions.

Maybe he should now go down to the camper to rescue his guitar. He could learn to play it properly, in the quiet on his own, he could write music, lyrics and poetry. His mind drifted around uselessly, not touching on any reality.

Lucy was still curled up on the bed, she could not think straight, her mind raced through the times she had with Harry. Their first meeting, the first time they slept together. The joy of meeting him in Istanbul after several weeks apart. The feeling of complete loss when he walked away from her, up the hill. What could she do? She had lost him. Her mind slipped back to the small white room in Greece. She had woken up in the narrow metal bed. She still had her t-shirt and knickers on. Her shorts and bag were on a small chair against the wall. She knew they had just cuddled, nothing more.

She decided she should do something, not just cry and feel sorry for herself. She splashed cold water on her face, brushed her hair, tried to get some colour back into her cheeks. Then she remembered the teacher had invited them both to his house for a meal. She knew he said they eat early but didn't know what time. She could see the sun was setting, so it was already getting a bit late. She realised she didn't know his name, but remembered his house, next to the school. She went across the street and timidly tapped on the door. The school master opened the door. 'Come in, come in.' He ushered her into a small living room. 'Where is your friend, Harry? He is coming, isn't he?' Lucy's eyes filled with tears, she wiped them away with her sleeve, she hadn't brought a hanky. The teacher immediately looked deeply concerned. 'What has happened? I heard you having a loud talk earlier this afternoon. Is everything alright?' Lucy just managed to hold back her tears. 'He's gone off up the mountain, I don't know where.'

He gently took her by the elbow. 'Come and talk with my wife, she doesn't speak English, but I can translate.' He led her to the kitchen, 'This is Yildiz, my name is Hasad. Are you able to talk to us about your problem?' Lucy took a couple of deep breaths, wiped her eyes again and said, 'It is very difficult, and personal.' She paused, looked at Yildiz, and back at Hasad.'Please, maybe your wife will understand, it is a woman thing. I have missed two of my periods, I know I'm not pregnant, I haven't done anything. But Harry doesn't believe me, he thinks I have slept with someone whilst I was on holiday in Greece. Now he has gone off up the mountain.' Yildiz came up next to Lucy, she did not need any translation, she understood, one woman to another. She looked at her in the face, a spoke a few sentences in Turkish, glancing at her husband to translate. 'She says, she understands, these things happen, and men don't understand, you must talk again to your man.' Yildiz took Lucy by her hand, led her to a small seat and sat next to her. She continued talking in Turkish. Hasad said, 'she just wants to sit with you, and you each talk in your own languages, I am going to go to find Harry.'

Very quickly, after just a few words on the telephone, three large men gathered by the front door. They looked rough with several weeks' growth of stubble on their faces, heavy boots, baggy trousers and traditional jerkins. They were obviously farmers and sheep herders. Two of them carried long staffs, their thumbs hooked through the 'v' notch at the top. These were men used to climbing through the hills, searching. Without hesitation and with few words they set off along the path up the valley.

It did not take long for the men to find Harry, they knew he would be hiding in one of the huts in the local hills. Hasad went up to him and gently said 'Come along, Lucy is down in the village, in our house waiting for you. You remember we invited you both to a meal this evening, my wife has been busying cooking.' They led Harry back down to the schoolhouse. Lucy was sitting in the kitchen, with her hand stroking her stomach, a movement Harry had seen expectant mothers doing. He didn't say anything, but one look at her confirmed he still loved her so much.

Chapter 9

Central Turkey. April 1971

"Not all who wander are lost"

Hasad broke the silence by formally introducing his household to Harry. 'My name is Hasad, my wife, who is cooking in the kitchen is called Yildiz. She only speaks Turkish, but I can translate, it is good practice. We have a baby son called Hamza who is now asleep.' Harry nodded acceptance, he was unable to express any words. They were invited to sit on a carpet laid out on the terrace.

Hasad continued explaining, filling in the difficult silence. 'This is a very traditional village, most people who live here have done so all their lives. As I said before I am the *ogretmen* at the school. We have our priest, *papaz*. Many of the other villagers grow crops and fruit which they sell in the town, we are all quite poor.'

There were wonderful smells of cooked food emanating from the kitchen. Yildiz joined them. She looked young and beautiful. She had changed into a traditional Turkish dress. A *salvar kameez*, Hasad explained, a very traditional outfit, worn now only in the country. It was colourful with prints of flowers and with an embroidered felt waistcoat over the top. She wore an exotic necklace and a silver hair piece that came over her forehead. She pressed her hands together, bowed from the waist and greeted her guests'. '*Merhaba, Nasilsiniz, Asalamu alaykum.*'

'That is a polite and traditional greeting,' Hasad again explained.

Lucy whispered quietly, directing her voice towards Harry, hoping to break into his silence. 'We are learning more language here than ever before.' He nodded. Hasad continued telling them the history of the village. It used to be much higher up the mountain, that was centuries ago, but the water from the wells ran out, so they moved the whole village down to here. 'As I have said most villagers were born here, as were their parents and grandparents. Just like Yildiz and myself.'

Yildiz went back to the kitchen to return with a large metal tray, she set it on the ground in front of their guests.

'If you are happy with this we eat in the traditional Turkish way, with our fingers. If you want, we have knives and forks.' Lucy quickly agreed she was happy to eat with her fingers. Harry still had not spoken, nodded agreement. Hasid got up to wash their hands with warm water from a jug, and a small towel to dry them. The meal he explained, was soup which they ate with a spoon, then pitta bread with which they pick up the BarBQ lamb with their hands, dipping it into the yogurt and mint sauce, tzatziki, and a spicy chilli sauce. The food was delicious, followed by dishes of pomegranate and figs. The evening was finished with small cups of very strong coffee, and more talk. Harry was still silent, he felt lost in this normal world of a married couple with a baby.

Hasad announced that in the following days there was going to be a wedding of a friend of his in the village, they were very welcome to come.

Lucy's eyes sparkled. 'A wedding, wow! That would be lovely. That is so kind of you. We would love to come.' She looked at Harry, hopefully he would also agree, it was obvious there was still a huge divide that somehow needed to be bridged.

Hasad continued to explain how a Turkish wedding worked. It was almost the same as a wedding in England, except it starts the day before with the bride having her hands painted with henna, some sad songs are sung, the bride often cries. At the ceremony it is the groom who comes in to the bride. She will be sitting on a chair with a long veil covering her head and face, the veil is usually red. The groom arrives with all the men, traditionally on a horse, but not for this wedding. To hire a good horse for a wedding was very expensive. The *papaz* reads from the *Koran,* usually in a sing-song voice.

After the ceremony all the guests sit down to a huge meal. It always starts with soup, there are traditionally hundreds of different recipes for soup, in Turkish cuisine it is very important. Hasad knows, because his wife has been involved in the making, that the base of tomorrow's soup is noodles made in the village.

Harry reflected on the soup they had in Izmir. He had not realised how important it was for Omar, the café owner, to offer free soup for the work he had done on the menu. He found it hard not to reflect back over the previous weeks, in fact the previous years.

Hasad continued explaining, 'The wedding meal continues with a whole roasted lamb, couscous, naan bread and other extras. The oldest man, the 'Uncle' offers prayers, and finally, coffee. Then the drinking and dancing starts.

'It is usual that many traditional Arabesque songs are played. These are the highly embellished and agonizing depictions of love and yearning, along with unrequited love, grief, and pain.

'The couple,' Hasad adds, 'are both from this village, they will go away for a honeymoon, then return to the parents' house. This always is the case provided the house is big enough. Be prepared, the celebrations go on for a long time, sometimes for days, so there will be a lot of noise into the night.' He continued that many things had changed from the old traditions. 'In the olden times the couple would have been chosen by the parents, an arranged marriage, but my friend met his bride at school, as Yildiz and I did. But even so, both families must agree to the union, in a formal ceremony with traditional sayings and agreements.'

Lucy was very excited by the prospect of witnessing these traditions. Harry remained guarded, silent and distant.

Hasad then said to them both, with a serious look, 'I know you are not married, I can see you are very much in love,' he looked at each in turn, hopefully, 'but to respect the people of the village please say you are husband and wife, and if possible put a ring on a finger on your right hand.'

Lucy looked across and said, 'Of course my husband and I will do that.' They laughed, even Harry smiled.

That night, when the meal was finished Lucy thanked the family and returned to the camper. Harry spoke to Lucy for the first time saying he would sleep under the awning again, she could use the bed.

They both knew the following days and perhaps weeks were going to be very difficult, if not impossible.

It was a sleepless night for Harry, the ground was hard and stoney, he was one minute too hot in his sleeping bag, then too cold. He got up at sunrise and wandered around the village. It was very quiet, most of the villagers were sleeping. Lucy insisted they stay to witness the wedding, it was a very kind invitation. Harry made no comment. He spent the day on his own, in the hills, thinking and dreaming. When he returned in late afternoon, Lucy had put on her best clothes, a little makeup and had dressed her hair. She told Harry to get ready. They were made most welcome by all the guests at the wedding, which followed all the traditions that Hasad had described.

It was another sleepless night for Harry, the ground was even harder. He again woke up at sunrise and wandered around the village. Most of the locals were sleeping off the wedding party from the night before. Eventually he sat down outside the camper, he had decided that they should leave the village straight away, drive back to Istanbul, put Lucy on a plane back to London and then he would take the camper van back across Europe. Maybe he could meet up with a couple of travellers to join him and help pay for fuel.

Not before long he heard Lucy moving around inside the camper. He tapped on the door, then shyly opened it. He told Lucy, in a soulless voice what he had decided.

Lucy immediately sat down and turned towards him. 'I am not pregnant, I know, I think women know these things, Yildiz told me yesterday when she was talking to me, it was in Turkish, but I could understand some of it. She said she knew I was not pregnant just by looking at me. She said it was difficult, but that she could see that we loved each other so much, we must just wait.'

Harry muttered he just didn't believe her, that she had slept with someone when on holiday in Greece. He had made up his mind to go back to Istanbul.

Lucy looked at the ground, then directly at his face and finally confessed. 'Yes, I did go to bed with someone, but we just cuddled, nothing else, we didn't have sex. I feel ashamed of it, but I know when we first met you had lots of experience. You bragged about all the girlfriends you had had. Can we just try for a few days, before you rush off, then it will be too late?'

'No, I've made up my mind, I don't believe you. Who did you go to bed with?'

'I can't tell you, I'm so ashamed, it was just silly. Please try and believe me.'

'No, we're going now.' He started packing up his sleeping things and folding away the awning. They set off back down the track to the road away from the village. 'We haven't even said goodbye to Hasad and Yildiz,' exclaimed Lucy.

'They'll understand,' grunted Harry. He had worked out they could make it almost to Istanbul that day. A long drive, but they could stop before crossing the Bosphorus for the night. Then go to the airport the next morning.

Lucy curled up on the back seat under a blanket with her legs tucked under. She knew she was not pregnant. She knew what happened that night in Mykonos. She could remember the tiny white room with a neat single bed. The window that looked onto a cobbled lane barely wide enough for a donkey to pass through. The white paint round each paving stone and step. But she had had a lot to drink, the waiter bought them tots of Metaxa. It was very strong. In fact, she knocked back Janet's, who didn't like it. Then the waiter bought her another one and sat down close to her. That was probably when it all started, she summarised. She didn't remember her friend Janet leaving to go back to their hotel. It was possible she was a lot more drunk than she realised. But Tassos, the waiter was very handsome, she was so relaxed, in holiday mode, she must have just followed him. Was she too drunk to know whether or not they had sex? No, she was certain, they just had cuddles.

She was on her own, he had left to go to work. She still had her t-shirt and knickers on, she knew she had never taken them off.

Harry gripped the steering wheel tightly, his white knuckles showing through the tan, driving very carefully. He didn't feel like playing any music, nothing seemed appropriate. He longed for a large joint, maybe two, to distance his thoughts away from the realities of what was going on, to what was going to happen. He didn't have any dope, the marijuana he could see growing along the roadside was not ready for picking. He only had the remains of a pack of rough Turkish cigarettes that scraped his throat to start fits of coughing. They drove on in silence, the road was in good condition and not too many large, slow lorries to pass. He stopped briefly in the middle of the day to stretch his muscles, take a bit of bread and a drink of water. Lucy did not move. They had to stop again in the midafternoon for fuel. Harry bought a couple of bars of chocolate. He tossed one on the back seat for Lucy.

She remained on the back seat, her mind not fully understanding why Harry was being so difficult. She knew she was not pregnant, in fact she had a dull aching pain in her lower stomach since the middle of the day. It was a familiar pain she had experienced regularly since she was a young teenager. She hoped and prayed it was her period coming. That would settle everything. They could get on with their adventure.

It was late afternoon when Harry stopped in a commercial camping site, still some miles from the ferry crossing, but he was feeling extremely tired after sleepless nights and unending tension. Lucy appeared asleep under the blanket, so he walked to the small town nearby, collected two take-away doner kababs and two soft drinks. When he got back, she was sitting under the awning, writing notes and making a small pencil sketch of the camper van. She had written 'Forget-me-not' in curly script under the drawing.

All Harry could say when he handed her the meal was that they still had a few miles to go before the ferry, but they probably could get to the airport by about mid-day. He made no further comment to her appealing look.

It was another sleepless, uncomfortable night for him on the hard ground under the awning. The only decision he made in the whole night long was to buy a folding camp bed to use in the future if he had to sleep outside.

He was woken before daybreak by whoops and cries from Lucy inside the camper. She called out through the door, in a very excited voice, 'I've got it, I've got my period, it's all going to be OK.' She jumped down the steps, fell down next to Harry, wrapped her arms round his neck to give him a great big kiss. Harry, who had finally gone off to sleep said, 'What do you mean?' He woke, he was befuddled and confused. 'What do you mean, what's happened?'

'I'm not pregnant, I've got my period, it's flooding.' She gave him another big hug.

They sat for a long time just looking at each other, looking into each other's eyes. Then Lucy started chattering, hardly taking a breath, talking about what they should do next, hoping Harry understood now what she had felt, hoping he had learned a bit about how women work and feel. He soon held up his hand for her to stop, 'I'm sorry I was grumpy and difficult. I just didn't understand. I could only think of the worst.'

He gave her a big kiss, then got up to make a special pot of coffee for them to share.

Harry started planning which way to go now. 'The shortest and quickest way to the east, the border with Iran is to go through Ankara, we could get visas and permission for the camper there at the Iran embassy.'

'No, as I've said before. I don't want to go the big cities, I want to carry on taking the *wiggly* route, as we decided some time ago, before all this diversion.' Deliberately making a dig at Harry for being difficult and grumpy.

'Ok, then we'll head East towards Konya.'

'No, we first must stop to say goodbye and thank you to Hasad and Yildiz. That is the most important thing we must do. They were so good to us, the talk I had with Yildiz was fantastic, she was so helpful. And I must see the baby, Hamza. He has always been asleep when we were there before.'

'OK, we will do that, follow the route back we took yesterday. But it will take two days, the drive to here was too exhausting, I don't want to do that again.'

'Nor do I,' said Lucy. The sun rose over the hills to the east, they sat together on the steps of *Forget-me-not*, sipping their hot coffee. Harry was deep in thought. 'I've got an idea, why don't we go south to Pamukkali. That was the place we were planning to go to before we diverted to help with the earthquake. If you remember I told you about it before, it's the place with white cliffs and thermal pools for swimming in.

'We can have a few days trying to get back to normal, relax a bit, then go on to see Hasad and Yildiz. I'll have a look at the map. I think it is quite a long way, so we maybe need to take a couple of days to get there.'

'That sounds perfect. As I keep saying we are in no hurry, all the time we want. We will see more of the countryside, and maybe meet more people.'

The journey south, through the middle of Turkey went without incident. The road was good in most places, but as with all roads in this area there were disorganised repairs and improvements being constructed. In the middle of the afternoon, they reached the town of Kutahya. On the road into the centre, they passed many kebab stalls, and small factories making coloured tiles and pottery. They soon learnt that this was the centre for the tiles that were used everywhere in Turkey, on building facades, floors and walls. The surrounding countryside was hilly and dominated by an imposing Byzantine castle. They parked in the central square and soon found the busy local bazaar. There were rows and rows of stalls selling colourful tiles and pottery, clay water pipes and industrial and domestic ceramics. To one side was the fruit and vegetable market, where they bought provisions for their supper, and at least one meal for the next day. They found, just outside the city, a quiet pasture by a small river for their first restful night for some time.

They were awake and on the road again early the next morning, following road signs to Afyon and Pamukkali. They had plenty of time, so stopped for a long break in the middle of the day, reading, smoking and catching up on writing diaries.

Part of Harry's Diary.

That was a terrible two days. I cannot believe it all happened. I was so confused, I did not understand these women's problems. I don't have any sisters, only my brother. Back in Yorkshire you didn't talk about things like that.

I was desperate, and so angry. I really believed Lucy was pregnant, and not by me. I had this picture of her with some bloke in Greece.

The school master and his wife were fantastic. What a calm couple they are. I have sort of forgotten all that happened before that. The collection of stuff for earthquake victims. The long drive through the night to Burdur, then not being allowed to help. We really thought we could be useful. Lucy, me, George and Jurgen, but no, we were sent packing.

The place by the lake was peaceful, then at the village it all went wrong.

My mind was in turmoil, believing I was taking Lucy back to Istanbul, to go home, have a baby fathered by someone else. Our lives and dreams destroyed. God! It was shit! But then I suppose we learn by things like that happening.

I am sure we will make it up, and we will get going as before again. Just take a bit of time to catch up.

It was a bummer. At the time I thought the end of the world had come. I could see myself in a grey suit with baggy knees and elbows designing washing soap adverts on the telly for the rest of my life in a grotty little office.

Then the sun came out from behind a cloud, I thought of myself living alone in the little stone shed I had found, growing lettuces, radishes and potatoes. Sitting by a big log fire at night playing my guitar and writing poetry. That didn't happen, reality set in. I drove Lucy towards the airport to go home. Then it all changed again. She got her period. Such a relief. Now we can carry on as before.

Pamukkali looked very boring when they first arrived. Lots of tourist hotels and the usual gift shops. It was not until they drove up to the top of the hill overlooking the valley and river that they could see the stunning natural phenomena that this place was famous for. From the terrace they could see the landscape was made up of mineral forests, petrified waterfalls and a series of terraced semi-circle pools in a step-like arrangement down the slope. Fresh deposits of calcium carbonate gave the edges of the pools a dazzling white coating, like snow or ice. The waterfalls between each pool were petrified as a static white cliff overhanging the pool below. The water in each pool, that is held by an ever increasing higher dam was a wonderful baby blue colour. There was no wind, so a thin mist hung over the hot thermal waters.

The travellers stood transfixed. 'This is the most amazing sight I have ever seen,' Lucy said. 'Thanks for bringing me here.' She took hold of Harry's arm. 'Look there are people swimming in that pool down there. Let's go now, get your swimmers on, or go bottom bare, I don't mind.'

They walked back to where *Forget-me-not* was parked. A beat-up car pulled in behind them. Three people piled out, went to the edge of the terrace, and stared at the view.

After a few minutes, the girl amongst them turned to Lucy. 'This is amazing, never seen anything like it before, except perhaps in the middle of Afghanistan, at Band-e-Amir. But there everything was brown sand and dust.' She was a talkative person.

'Hi, I'm Catherine, also known as Cath the cat, this is Richard, also known as Rich the dick, and that is Wayne, also known as Wayne.' She had a sense of humour.

'You are English, but have a car with foreign plates?' said Lucy.

'Yes, the dick and I are from England, Wayne is from the States. We are going back to Europe in our car, also known as Alexi. We bought Alexi in Kabul from a German drug dealer.'

'Wow! From Kabul, how did you know he was a dealer?'

Rich had obviously told the story several times before. 'He was imprisoned in Iran for a few months for running into a girl on the road in Tehran. But then the parents of the girl got a huge payment from somewhere, probably from Germany, so forgave him and had him released. Wayne bought the car from him for $50 in Kabul as a possible cheap way of getting back to Europe.'

Catherine continued the story. 'Wayne was in the Peace Corps in Nepal, we were also working there for a year or so. I had met Wayne a couple of times in Kathmandu, but finally met again at the Green Hotel in Kabul rushing to the toilet in the middle of the night. He got there first, but I elbowed him to one side. I reckoned my needs were more urgent.

'We met up later, talked about the trip back to Europe, and together bought Alexi. We didn't trust the German guy one tiny bit, he looked and talked like a drug dealer. So, we took all the seats out, stripped and checked everything for a stash, but didn't find anything.'

'What were you working on in Kathmandu?' asked Harry.

'Oh! We were just travelling around, like all you lot, arrived in KTM and that afternoon loved it so much, we wanted to stay. Then, back in those days, you only got a two week visa, unless you worked. The next day I got a job as a Nepalese secretary-cum-typist and Dick got a job as an architect. We were both on minimum Nepalese wages, about one rupee an hour, so we learnt to live like the locals on next to nothing.'

'That's so cool, it's a great story, I guess it is what we want to do. What did you do in the Peace Corps?' Lucy turned to Wayne. 'I was in the Terrai, the south, it was hot and humid. I didn't do much. I sat on the long drop can for many days with the shits, then I would wait for my food parcels. Cheerios and Fruity Loops for breakfast, and Hershey's Kisses and M&M's for the rest of the time. Better than rice, more rice and dhal.'

'Your car looks pretty beaten up. Is it going to get you back to Europe? And what are all those bags and sacks in the back?'

'That's stuff we bought in Afghanistan to take home to sell on a market stall. It's knitted wool socks, hats, sheep skin coats, embroideries, jewellery. It is so easy to buy stuff there. But it is a real pain on the back seat and in the boot. When we have a flat tyre, and we have lots, we have to unload everything to get to the spare. Alexi is big enough for us three to sit together on the bench front seat. But we may have problems in Germany as there are no seat belts.'

'Are you stopping here in Pamukkali?' Asked Lucy.

'Yep, we have a place in a camp site just on the edge of town, on the road from Denizli. It's great. Got a good eating place next door.'

'No sweat, we will have to move there, I can see a sign here saying no parking overnight. But first we are going swimming in that pool down there, we'll meet you later, probably at the café you mentioned.'

The swimming was above all expectations, the water

was warm from thermal springs and had a soft feel from the natural chemicals in it. It was like an infinity pool on the very edge of the cliff over the valley. As the sun set, Harry got out his guitar, sat next to one of the pools, and strummed the tune of *Windmills of your Mind*. 'I know it was sung by Noel Harrison, I saw it on Top of the Pops, really liked it, but I've never learnt the words.'

In the evening, having moved to the camp site, they met with their new friends. Their talk moved quickly, each one with stories to tell. A waiter in a smart clean uniform, and a huge turban that almost reached the ground behind him, told them that the speciality of this place was *Circassian Chicken*, chicken pounded together with paprika, garlic and walnuts. They all ordered it.

They found the town and swimming in hot pools so relaxing they stayed for three days.

The two English travellers and the American in the car Alexi had left the day before.

It was a long drive back to the village where Hasad and his family lived. They had to bypass Burdur, not knowing how the rescue operations were progressing. They did not get back to the village with the little white houses, the stream through the village square, and the familiar schoolhouse until the afternoon of the next day. They knocked on the schoolhouse door, it was opened by Yildiz. She gave a squeal of delight and gave Lucy a big hug and a kiss on each cheek. She explained with waving arms that Hasad was still in the school, teaching, but they must come in and take some tea.

Very soon Hasad came home, he greeted them as old friends. Yildiz had already led Lucy into the kitchen, and in a mixture of English and Turkish they explained to each other and understood what had happened. Harry then explained it all again to Hasad. His only comment, which he said with all sincerity, was that he thanked God, and that he knew all would be good in the end.

Chapter 10

Konya, Central Turkey. April 1971

"It's not what you look at that matters.
It's what you see."

They stayed the night in the camper parked in the village square. The next morning, they were invited to the school with Hasad. He introduced them to the two classes full of children, and then asked Harry and Lucy to talk, in English, about England and their journey to Turkey. At break time, the children went into the playground. Immediately they gathered around the couple demanding in broken English and Turkish, for them to join in some games.

They were first shown an area in the playground that was divided up into six small pits. It was explained that this was a traditional game called *Mangala*. Lucy and Harry never quite understood all the rules, so Lucy started a hop, skip and jump competition. As soon as she drew out the squares in chalk on the ground, the girls knew the game well. Lucy thought they called it *Çok, Kisa, Mesafe,* but wasn't sure until Hasad explained the English name to the children, and how to pronounce it in Turkish. With much laughter, and some falling over they all joined Lucy in an energetic game, whilst Harry was told by the boys they often play the Five Stone Game –*Beş Taş*. He knew this game well from his school days, often playing it on the cobbled street outside their houses with Rolly.

After an energetic morning at the school, Hasad and Yildiz invited them to a simple lunch at the schoolhouse. They then left after a warm and long farewell from the family they had got to know. It was obvious that life would just continue in the village as it had done for years. Yildiz returned to the schoolhouse to feed the baby, and start preparing food, Hasad went back to the school. As they drove down the lane to the main road, they both expressed what a great experience it had been in this little, rural village, what wonderful people they were, just what they had hoped for since planning the trip back in Brighton. Harry hoped their lives would move on away from the struggles they had had the previous week.

The road to Konya was good in places. There was some new construction being worked on, with diversions of rough sand and gravel at random across fields. They followed a flat valley, the surrounding fields planted with crops, fruit trees and in one area fields of commercially grown lavender. The smell in the warm midday sun was almost overpowering. Around the fields were disorganised rows of beehives, some like miniature cottages with three or four floors, others traditional cone shapes constructed of bound straw.

They arrived in Konya in the mid-afternoon, and soon found a park on the outskirts to camp in. There was already a group of travellers settled in. They had a psychedelic painted bus parked on the grass. Around the bus there was a circle of four tepees and a yurt, the canvas sides painted with two large all-seeing eyes, a third eye painted on the roof and several ban-the bomb symbols. Soon after they parked and were pulling out the awning, a large man with a big bushy beard going grey in places approached them, he introduced himself as Glenn. He invited Harry and Lucy to start a circle by moving *Forget-me-not* close to their bus and then join their group sitting around a smoking fire on rugs and blankets. Glenn said one of his group had found more travellers parked on the other side of town and he had asked them to come over to join them. He explained they were stuck here in Konya because their bus was using massive amounts of fuel, which they could not afford. They were waiting for a new pump to be delivered.

He then pointed out some of the other members of the group that were sitting around. 'Over there in the embroidered skull cap is Henri. He keeps the bus going when he can. The guy next to him is Jacque, he organises concerts and gigs for us.' He waved Jacque over to join them. He politely greeted them with his hands pressed together, raised to under his face. He uttered the greeting, *Namaste.*

Jacque started to tell a little of his recent life story to Lucy whilst Harry manoeuvred the camper into a new position. Jacque explained he was jailed after the riots in Paris in 1968 for leading a group of university students to throw street cobbles at the police. He had only recently been released from jail and joined the bus as it passed through north France. 'I am planning a bit of a concert here in this park tomorrow night. We do some protest songs, it is better than demonstrating in the streets, they are all anti-war, anti-Vietnam.'

Glenn added that they hadn't done many concerts recently. 'We always try to contact the local officials to get permission, they usually say no. The top brass in this town were cool and helpful. They told us we could go ahead provided there were no drugs, and the music was not loud. So tomorrow before it gets dark, we will put on a short gig, try to get some local kids to come along. As Jacque says we do some protest songs, ballads, but mainly country blues and blue grass, all very relaxed.' Harry told Glen and Jacque he could pluck a few chords on his guitar.

'That's cool,' replied Jacque, in a strong French accent, 'we jam everything, everyone joins in.'

Glenn added they have other musicians in the group, he liked to blow a trumpet, sax and other wind instruments. 'Lola, over there,' he indicated a tall woman with dark hair plaited down to her waist, dressed in a colourful kaftan, 'is our singer, fab voice.

'We're all desperately in love with her, so beautiful. She is Mexican but sadly for us is married to a Native American. He is called Running Feet, or something like that. We cut short most names here, we call him just '*Feet*'. He is probably in his tepee now smoking his peace pipe, the bowl filled with about half a pound of dope.'

Harry looked over to their bus. 'How do you get through immigration with a bus painted like that? We have been told several times by bus and van drivers who run this road back and forth, keep it simple, don't write slogans or decorate your van, and keep your hair short.'

Glenn explained, 'You obviously don't know about us. We are the Hog Farm, or rather part of it. The Hog Farm was started as a commune in California some years ago, early 1960s I guess, by a guy called Wavy Gravy. A great character. With him we got into setting up and looking after festivals. We had a big break at Woodstock looking after all the gear, kids and setting stages. I am from San Fran. I joined the Hog Farm there.' He had a soft West Coast accent.

'Wow, you were at Woodstock,' exclaimed Lucy.

'Yeh, that is what really got us started. We also did a gig with Pink Floyd in England.'

'I tried to get tickets for that but was too late,' said Harry.

'So after the Pink Floyd gig, a crowd of us who had come over from the States just carried along the trail. We were planning to travel to Bangladesh with two buses filled with food and medical supplies for the victims of recent flooding. There were 42 of us in the two buses from almost every country in the free world. I got left behind in London trying to get passes and visas, collecting more supplies and medicines, junk like that. I spent weeks contacting top *honchos* in lots of governments. Got some neat replies with the right signatures from various presidents. Sent them on to Istanbul post office where the two buses had reached, it was just in time, they were about to leave. When they got on the trail to the east, all they had to do was flash these letters at the immigration to pass through. We had all the documents sent back to London, so we have them now, and they work. That's why we have this psychedelic décor on our bus. And get no hassle from the big wigs.'

Another traveller joined the group sitting round the fire. 'This is P-, he is from Denmark. He has a name that is unpronounceable, so we call him P-, that is because he is a poet. He is brilliant at putting together words. A lot of his words are anti-Vietnam and anti-drugs, which is not right 'cos he smokes dope like a chimney. Anyways, he will want to quiz you. He is getting ideas from other travellers, places they have been, people met, other travellers, locals. He is looking for a rich collection of experiences, people, events, cops, sex, drugs and rock and roll. Maybe write a book,' Glenn finished with deep laugh. 'I now need to get on, do stuff, always stuff to do.'

Before P- could ask about their story, a couple walked across the park. They joined the fringe of the group. They looked exhausted and wasted. P- stood up and went over to them. 'Wait here, I will get you a mug of tea each and some biscuits. You look knackered, all in. Sit down here next to these two dudes'. He was back in a couple of minutes to hand them a packet of biscuits, and hot mugs of sweet tea.

The couple explained, after scoffing the biscuits that they had been robbed of all their possessions, their bags, passports, and money. They were hitching, but just now had to walk over twenty kilometres back into this town after the robbery by a lorry driver. They said they often found hitching very difficult. Lorry drivers would pick them up because of their blond hair and blue eyes. First, they would try to get off with the girl, with no luck, and then try with him. This had happened several times, but they always refused. They would then be dumped in the middle of nowhere as the lorry drove off. The previous night this had happened, they had lost everything, so had walked to this town. A couple of Hog Farmers sitting near heard this story, went to find Glenn to organise a sleeping place for them and some healthy food.

For a short while Harry and Lucy were left on their own, Harry went back to the camper to check it was properly locked up.

Lucy looked around at all the travellers. So many bright colourful clothes and hats, and so many hairy faces. She whispered to Harry when he returned. 'They seem very nice people, really together and helpful. And they seem to have loads of fun.'

P-, the poet returned to sit with them, he tried to get some stories from them, but Harry interrupted. He wanted to know more about The Hog Farm. P- told them they were travelling quickly to join the main party who had left about a year before. They originally were going to Bangladesh, but a war was going on so were redirected to Nepal. 'Cool idea, I guess, neat place I've heard,' he remarked, raising his eyebrows. 'They are now helping Tibetan refugees, and are enjoying the wonders of Kathmandu, the Himalayas, and the best dope in the word. So, what about you guys. You look very together and enjoying yourselves. Why are you on the trail and where are you going?'

'We are going to Kathmandu, in our camper, over there. We call her 'Forget-me-not'. Harry nodded his head over his shoulder.

'Why?' P- demanded.

'What do you mean, why?' Harry then realised he wanted to know why they were travelling the trail this way. He explained that a year before they just thought it was a cool idea, they had friends who had travelled a bit in Europe and Morocco and had heard stories of India. 'We had just finished university, got qualifications, knew we could get jobs when we got back.' He looked over to Lucy.

'I think our ideas have grown some since then,' she said 'We have already learned so much, and want to learn more. We don't want to follow the trail, get to India as quickly as possible. We want to learn about people, cultures, traditions, language, something of their religion. So, we are trying to divert off the trail, as it seems to be called, to go to remote places that don't see travellers and tourists. We have just spent almost a week in a tiny village in the mountains. They made us so welcome. We ate in their houses, met all the relations and babies, and were even invited to a wedding in the village.'

Harry added, 'Yeh! Before that we collected a whole load of food and blankets for the victims of an earthquake. We were helped by a nice guy we met hitching in Yugoslavia, he got together two big lorry loads. He knew what he was doing. He was in the army doing that kind of stuff.'

'I heard about this earthquake. It wasn't too far from here?'

Together they described their events around the earthquake, Izmir and Burdur. The people they had met, the countryside they had driven through. *P-* scribbling notes on a scrap of paper, was impressed by some of their stories.

Lucy spent the afternoon drawing faces and beards, Harry caught up on writing his diary, one of the Hog Farmers joined him, together they smoked a spliff, the first one Harry had had for almost a week.

The evening was spent sitting round the fire, eating, talking, playing music, smoking dope, they got to know the Hog Farmers, learnt many new stories, and repeated some of their adventures. A young woman with two kids joined them. Her hair was a mess of curls, spot dyed in yellow and purple. She was wearing a bright green, flowing full skirt down to the ground, colourful sandals. The back of her hands were decorated with intricate patterns in henna. Lucy related to her quickly, she had the image and fashion she hoped for, but not yet achieved. The kids were a boy of six years old and a girl aged four. The boy, called Mist, had long hair, down to his shoulders, denim dungarees and bare feet. The girl, Swallow, wore a short skirt obviously homemade from scraps of fabric. They both had grubby faces, feet and scratches on their knees, their mother explained they could just run wild, so long as they didn't go too far away.

The following morning Lucy demanded that she needed to wash her hair and clean some clothes. They soon learned from Glenn that there was an ancient Haman in town, it was a must go to place and make a visit.

So, they walked into town. The Haman was an ancient building on the central square. On the outside it was built of rough stone, there was little to indicate its purpose. But inside there was a wealth of colourful tiles, a domed roof with small areas of coloured glass letting in shafts of light. There were two very distinct areas for men and women.

Separately they soaked and sweated, wrapped in large crisp towels, and were given a deep massage. Fully revived and clean the two visited the market to get supplies of fruit, grapes, pears, and pomegranates.

The afternoon was spent leisurely arranging for the gig that evening. Lucy went round some of the travellers who had just arrived, introducing herself, enquiring about their journeys, and hoped for destinations.

Just before sunset the police turned up. They were checking all the documents, passports, vehicle documents and insurance. Harry and Lucy had to go to the camper to get their folder. Whist police were examining them, the head officer, wearing a large cap with an ornate gold badge on the peak was looking at them intently. He came over, took the passports to examine them carefully. Lucy's heart dropped, thinking there was a problem. The chief said 'I have seen you two before, you have been on TV. I saw you last night, during a programme on the earthquake.' Harry looked embarrassed, Lucy looked relieved. 'The programme was how they are getting on with recovery, I heard they have found some people alive in ruins after one week. The interviewer on television was talking about you getting help from Izmir.'

'Yes, we got together two lorries full of helpful clothing and supplies, we took them to Burdur,' said Harry.

The chief gave them each a firm handshake, thanked them and congratulated them. He told his police force to leave, not bother anymore examining documents and to return to their station.

The performance put on by the Hog Farm that evening was very much as expected. Plenty of talk by individual musicians about their next number, with slow tuning of instruments. It was a convivial group of travellers and locals in the audience, sharing smokes, food and drinks.

Glen got up onto the temporary stage to greet everyone. 'If we were in a huge stadium in Europe or the States, we would have a screen behind me showing a black and white film of B52 bombers flying in formation, dropping napalm bombs across virgin forests in Vietnam. We would show the classic, horrible film of a small, young Vietnamese girl, naked, screaming, running from her burnt village. You just need to visualise it as we have no big screen or projector. Use your imagination. And now join in. We like to play anti-war songs, some you may know well, and great jazz and folk stuff.'

He welcomed some newcomers, they were young locals from the town, who had heard there was some music going to be played.

As it was getting dark, candles were lit in glass jam jars hanging in the trees. A small van pulled up next to the field. It had pictures of kebabs on the side panels, the owner opened up the side and prepared to serve fresh kababs and wraps.

'Cool, we now have everything. Real street food,' someone remarked.

The music started. Harry felt he was out of his depth, the musicians were very good and used to playing together. He sat on the ground outside *Forget-me-not*. He had never played to an audience as big as this, only with a few friends and his fellow flat mates in Brighton.

Glenn vigorously waved him over to join them on the stage. He found a place between the other guitarist,

Sid and Glenn. He joined in the best he could following the lead from Sid, first with *Eve of Destruction* written by Barry McGuire, then *I Ain't Marching Anymore* by Phil Ochs. Old numbers that were well known by the audience.

Glen then introduced him. 'Here we have Harry, who is so famous he can shake the police off our tails.' There was a cheer from the midst of the audience.

Harry strummed a couple of chords to get his fingers loose, he then moved into a fast key change that sounded good, sweet, and precise. He looked across to Glen enquiring what number they should play. The unspoken reply, by a look, was *you choose.* He thought through his repertoire, strummed a few more chords then gently moved into a number by BB King, *Lucille.* He had been working on this in his mind for the past week, beating out the rhythm on the steering wheel of *Forget-me-not,* the tabletop and back of chairs. His fingers moved over the frets with practiced agility, stretching his whole hand to span from top string to bottom. The guy on the harmonica, Henri, joined in at the chorus, then the violin, played by Luke, then others. Luke looked interesting and different. He had long dark hair back combed into a bouffant and was wearing a paisley patterned, short skirt, with a frilly blouse. Obviously an individual, thought Harry.

They worked from chorus to solo, each player taking it in turns to elaborate the theme on their individual instrument. The clarinet sobbed, there were sweet golden sounds from the cornet, and thumping deep rhythm from the double bass with the tabla drum player. Harry worked rapid key changes on his guitar, finding places he never knew in his skills. Each time the chorus became faster and faster still. Soon all the audience were on their feet, arms in the air, swinging, swaying, and moving to the music. Some were playing on their version of air guitars. The set went on, then morphed into a fast jazz rhythm that seemed to go on without end.

Lola, the singer took the stage. After a heart breaking, soulful ballad the audience was stilled, enamoured by her voice and the words of the ballad.

Harry finally stopped playing, he was exhausted and was sweating profusely. He couldn't see Lucy amongst the crowd, so he went back to *Forget-me-not*. He found a reefer, lit it, and walked away from the gathering to the edge of the park. When he had finished his smoke, he lay on the bed. He heard Lucy return later but turned away and ignored her.

The music had finished, the lamps and candles put out, Glenn had announced they had to leave early in the morning, now their bus was fixed. Some of the crowd stayed sitting on blankets by the fire, talking and smoking.

Chapter 11

Konya April 1971

"We have nothing to lose and a world to see."

Harry and Lucy were woken up early by the noise of their neighbours packing up their yurt and tepees. Harry opened the door and stepped out. It was a beautiful morning, clear blue sky, gentle breeze. The early morning sun light glinting through the branches and leaves of the trees, casting moving shadows on the grass. He thought he might help the Hog Farmers pack up, but soon realised they were working in an organised and coordinated way, from many previous attempts. The poles were gathered together, the canvases neatly rolled and passed up to be stored and tied down on the roof of the bus. Glenn spotted Harry and came over. 'We've a long drive today, to try to catch up on our missed time fixing the bus. Today we'll try to make four hundred, even five hundred kilometres. Take care, stay safe, be cool, it has been good meeting you. Maybe again, some time, some place.'

'We are going leisurely, maybe to Cappadocia for a few days. We'll catch you in Kathmandu.'

Harry sat on the grass, his legs tightly crossed. He could do that now, he was wearing the light cotton pantaloons he bought in Istanbul, and he had been practicing sitting in the lotus position. Lucy came down the steps to be beside him. She gave Glenn a big goodbye hug. 'We will see you in KTM, in a few weeks' time.'

She turned to Harry. 'My lover, I really want to go to the Haman again and have another wash. It's such a beautiful place, and lovely experience. My hair needs another wash now it has got longer.'

Harry thought for a moment, considered the options. 'We've quite a long way to go today, but if you go now, and are back by, say, ten o'clock it will be OK. Get your hair clean and shiny, it will be sprinkled with fairy dust tonight.'

'What do you mean?'

'Wait and see, we are going to the land of fairy castles.' Lucy shook her head, not understanding. She picked up her wash bag and went off at a quick jog.

Sometime later, still sitting in the sun, not bothered to get up to make any coffee, he saw a diminutive figure walking towards him.

'Hi, I am Saki, is this your van? I am looking for a lift going east. Can I come with you?' She jumped from foot to foot, never stopping moving. 'You are very handsome, you are travelling alone?' She came closer, looked suggestively at Harry.

'No, I have my partner, she has gone to the Haman and will be back soon. We have space if you want to come with us, we are going to Cappadocia today. We hope you can offer us a bit of money towards fuel.' He looked at Saki, 'Where are you from? You look oriental.'

'I am from Japan, not Tokyo, but another place.' Saki was wearing a brief sleeveless tee- shirt, and very short pair of shorts. Harry could anticipate that local men would be disturbed by the way she showed off a lot of flesh. Saki sat down next to Harry, still fiddling, moving her feet, rubbing her hands together, always moving. She had a very small rucksack with her. Her closeness disturbed Harry, he got up to make them both a coffee.

It was not long before Lucy returned, her hair still wet from washing. 'Hello, who are you?'

Saki jumped up. 'My name is Saki, I am from Japan. Your beautiful husband has said I can travel with you today.' Lucy gave Harry an understanding glance, maybe he had understood a few things the past weeks, she thought, *'my husband now!'*

Harry whispered to Lucy as she passed him to get a coffee that she must tell Saki to get dressed properly, cover her limbs and have a scarf to put over her hair if necessary, so as to not upset the local people.

It did not take long to get on the road, to join the trail. Harry remembered some of the facts he found in the old guidebook he had taken from Omar's café. 'This is possibly the oldest road that is still used today. It was a part of the Silk Road, that was the route taken by travellers and merchants from the far east, China, probably Japan to Europe.' He glanced back at Saki. 'They would bring spices and silks, precious stones, and tea. They were exchanged for horses, glassware and manufactured goods. But most of all they exchanged knowledge. I think it started about 1,500 years ago.'

'Any other useful historical facts in that brain of yours?' joked Lucy.

'There are plenty. Just you wait, I'll be your tour guide for the next 1000 miles. I'll tell you all about Genghis Khan, Marco Polo, stuff like that.'

'Only as bedtime stories, so I can go to sleep.'

Saki fidgeted on the back seat. She didn't understand English well enough to note that they were just joking in a happy, good humoured way. She suddenly jumped up, making Harry swerve into the middle of the road. 'That lady beside the road, she is my friend, she wants a lift, stop, stop. I will ask where she is going.'

The lady in question was sitting on the other side of the road, she looked as if she was asleep.

Saki jumped out, she helped the lady to stand up by pulling on each elbow. She was skeletal thin, her clothes just hung on her shoulders. Saki guided her to the camper and helped sit her down on the back seat. She explained that they lived together, that she was often very ill, but now she looked after her. She said she was probably from Ireland, she had a very strong accent, she was impossible to understand.

Lucy looked across at Harry, who just shrugged his shoulders, put the camper into gear and continued down the road. She turned to look at the new hitchhiker, she looked deadly pale, her head dropped down and eyes closed. 'What's your friend called?'

'I don't know, I can never understand what she says. We have been living together as lovers for some weeks now. She wants to go to the east, as I do, so we go together.'

Harry said, 'we must give her a name, we can't just call her the Irish Lady.'

Lucy replied, 'You can't just give her any name, she is not a pet dog.'

Harry thought for a while. 'Most Irish names are impossible to spell, and even harder to pronounce. We had an Irish family living in the same street as us when I was little. The girl was called Orla, I think we can all pronounce that.'

Harry put a cassette of blues music in the player, John Mayall. 'I've put this on, very quiet, so we can talk without the other two hearing. I think her Irish friend, Orla, is completely stoned out of her head. I think she is shooting up opium. Look at the inside of her arm, all pin pricks.'

Lucy turned to look, the two girls were in a tight embrace. 'Yes, I see what you mean. Will they be alright?'

'I dunno, we'll take them to Goreme or Cappadocia and leave them somewhere safe before we find a place for us to stay.'

The road was good, but with a lot of traffic. 'What did you mean "Going to the land of fairy castles"?' Lucy was curious, thinking back to a comment Harry made earlier.

'All around Goreme and Cappadocia are these weird pillars of rock, bright white and over the centuries people have dug caves in them. There is a whole city underground, houses, passages, even some churches. When I was waiting for you, back in Istanbul, some guy told me he had been living in one of the caves for several weeks.'

'Sounds different, not too many tourists, I hope. Maybe we can spend a couple of days exploring. Is it like those other lakes we swam in?'

'A bit, except there is no water, no lakes. I think it is just another geological freak.'

The road passed through rolling countryside, fields of salad crops, potatoes and orchards of peaches and almonds. Harry swapped cassettes in the player. "*Western Man*." Van Morrison 'In our band in Brighton we called him '*Van the Man*''

'Maybe an Irish singer will wake our Irish friend up!' Lucy looked back again, no change. She rapidly became very concerned for her. 'I think Orla has taken a huge dose of opium, she is in a coma, we must stop and check her over. Her friend, Saki, looks as if she has just gone to sleep in her arms.'

'I've seen a tourist sign for a place ahead, I think it is called Sultan Han, we'll stop there.'

When they arrived at Sultan Han, they were surprised at the size, and ornate details of the buildings, intricate carved archways, and immense, fortified walls. A tourist information board described it as a Seljuk caravanserai, about seven hundred years old. Sited on the main caravan route, it had provided accommodation for travellers, merchants and their animals for centuries.

Lucy climbed into the back seat, she gently woke Saki. 'We have stopped because we are worried about your friend, she does not look well, is she just sleeping, or is she in a drug coma?'

'I think she has taken too much drug.' Saki climbed out of the camper. At that moment Orla appeared to come out of the coma, she muttered something Lucy did not understand. 'She wants to go pee-pee, quickly.' Saki started helping her out of the seat.

'That is something you girls must sort out. There is a sign for a toilet over there.' Harry pointed to the entrance to the caravanserai. As he waited, leaning against the camper van, a distinguished looking older woman walked across to him. She was dressed in a colourful kaftan, and at least six scarves and shawls round her shoulder, and tied round her waist. In the light breeze they appeared as sails being set. 'Hi, is your friend OK, I saw her being helped to the toilet.'

'No. We picked up the two of them hitching out of Konya. We reckon the tall skinny one has taken a drug overdose. She has been in a coma all the way, Lucy, my girlfriend is very worried, but we don't know what to do.'

'Wait till they come back. I was a nurse a long time ago when I was young. I might be able to help. I worked in a clinic for a short while.' She was reassuring. 'I live in Goreme. Every now and then I like to come here for a different view, and different light,' she explained. 'I stay in one of the ancient cells around the back of the caravanserai. I dream of all the travellers who have passed through here over the centuries.'

Harry took a moment to look at the new visitor. He observed she was probably old enough to be his mother. Her eyes were startling, green irises encircled by grey. She was tall, standing with authority, with wavy dark hair, turning grey. 'My name is Donna, and you are?'

'I am Harry, Lucy is my girlfriend, Saki is the little Japanese hitchhiker, we don't know the name of the skinny one. She is Irish, she hasn't said anything. We have christened her, Orla.'

The two girls returned, supporting the third one between them. Donna immediately took charge. She looked into her eyes, at her forearms and said. 'OK, I am coming with you to Goreme, we have to keep you awake all the way, otherwise you will be dead. Dead from an overdose of some narcotic.'

The four of them climbed into the back seat, supporting Orla upright. Harry declared he would continue driving so Lucy could help the other girls.

It was almost a two hour drive, but with a lot of talking, some singing and a lot of wiggling and moving, they kept Orla conscious. As they approached Goreme, Donna gave directions. 'Go into the main square, there will be a *domus* or taxi who can take her to Cappadocia. I have the address of a clinic there who hopefully will be able to help her.'

When they had secured a taxi, with clear instructions to Saki to keep her friend awake and the address to take her to, Donna breathed a big sigh of relief. 'God, stupid idiot, I don't know why I take time out to look after people like that.' Lucy thanked her, saying that a life is worth saving, any life.

Donna briefly said, 'You should park your camper in the Dilek Campsite, down this road. It is the safest place to park it. Then come to find me in my cave, up that narrow lane there. I will find you somewhere to stay.'

'We can't afford any hotels or guest houses, we like to live in *Forget-me-not*', Lucy said.

'That's fine, if you want to, but it is best when here to try out living in one of the ancient caves.'

'Ok, we will look into it as an idea.'

Part of Lucy's Diary

Are we getting blinkered – just looking ahead and not seeing anything on the sides? What is it ahead that we see? Jut a trail to a destination, and what is there at that destination? Are we doing the right thing? I have asked myself so many questions this past week. I am sure Harry loves me, really loves me. Do I return it? I could see his love in his reaction to my delayed period. He was lost, devastated. He did not know what to do, how to react.

Do I really love him that much? Love him more than just having good sex? Love him more than just a great friend? How do I find out? Maybe just carry on and wait and see.

Maybe that is what love is? A roller coaster of ups and downs, that eventually everything just drops back into place, then carries on.

I think of what Yildiz said to me, such reassuring words. That family is so sound, lovely people. I should learn from them, and from some of the other beautiful people we have met.

I have got some quite good sketches of it now. I must remember to get some more white and silver paint. I've used it all up.

Donna is such a good person, I know we will become close friends, it inspired us to bond with someone who has the same approach to life as we do. She was very helpful with that silly Irish girl. She was in such a mess, I hope the clinic sorts her out.

Chapter 12

Geome, Cappridocia, central Turkey. April 1971

*"Never go on trips with anyone
you do not love!"*

The couple stood in the centre of the town, stunned by the surrounding pillars of soft rocks towering above them. They could see niches, doorways, arches and balconies carved into the tufa. There were narrow, twisting passageways running off the main road, cobbled and far too small for any vehicle. In the far distance the peak of a volcano, snow-capped, floated above a layer of cloud.

'I need a joint or something stronger,' said Harry, 'maybe a line of coke or some magic mushrooms. After today's happenings, all this is just too much for me.'

'No! No way. You will have nothing of the sort. We will sit in that bar just over there to have a couple of cold beers.' He realised he was quite dehydrated, they had not stopped all day for even a sip of water. A cold beer seemed a great idea. They took two seats overlooking the square and an extraordinary pinnacle. 'It looks as if there is a Roman castle carved into that one,' said Lucy. 'There is going to be so much to explore and see here. I'm totally confused, I don't know whether this is from a Hans Anderson Fairy Tale, maybe a silver unicorn with a tail of glittering stars will gallop round the corner, or is it a Grimm's Tale, a horrible gruesome beast, stoned out of its mind will drop down on us.'

'We have had enough of stoned beasts or anything like that. I'm waiting for the unicorn to come.'

They drank down their beers and ordered two more.

Before they realised it was late afternoon, they needed to park *Forget-me-not* and find Donna. They drove to the edge of the town. The owner of the campsite assured them it was perfectly safe to park there. He said most travellers liked to go to find a cave. They walked back to the passageway they believed Donna had told them to follow. It was so narrow Harry could feel his shoulders touching the rocky sides. They came to a dead end. They tried another side passage, that was also a dead end. Almost giving up, they stopped for a moment, Lucy said she thought she could hear someone singing quietly to themselves. They looked up, high above them was a balcony and an arched opening in a cliff of white rock. Lucy called up. Donna's face appeared. 'Come on up. You see that tiny doorway to your left, just go in there and climb up the passage.' With Harry leading, they squeezed up the passage. It was barely big enough to pass through. At the top, it opened into a high, arched cave, flooded with light. Donna stood in the middle, she had changed her dress, and now wore a loose full length creation covered in purple sequins that glinted and caught the light.

There was the scent of patchouli and musk from joss sticks held in the twisted trunks of tiny green ceramic elephants. Next to a passage leading to another room there was a large glass eye, a *'Nazar Boncuk'*. There were knotted macramé hangings dropping from hooks in the high ceiling, holding pots of exotic house plants. And there were cats everywhere.

'I am home to many, many cats, cockroaches, and the occasional bat.' Donna picked up a large tabby.

Harry walked to one of the arched openings, the view across the forest of fairy chimneys was awe inspiring. 'How big is it all. Do you have a bedroom and bathroom?' Donna led them through a passageway to another cave. In the centre was a huge double bed, draped in layers of textiles. Hanging from wooden rails were dozens of colourful scarves. An arched opening faced towards the east. 'I get wonderful light in here from the rising sun. The toilet and a place to wash is downstairs, just along the passage outside. But first, we have some mint and apple tea, then we can find you a cave to live in, there are several just near here.' She poured the tea into small, ornate glasses. 'I think I am about one quarter Turkish, not sure what else. I was born in London, I came here with a boyfriend about fifteen years ago, been living here ever since. This is my home.' A ginger cat climbed onto her lap, purring like an engine. 'I don't go away from here much, sometimes to Sultan Hani, where we met this morning. I stay just here, unlike you travellers who cross continents to find what you want. I have found it here.'

The light in the room slowly changed, it was no longer bright white reflecting off the rocks, it was turning a golden colour. Harry and Lucy sat, looking around at the extraordinary room. Donna tidied up the tea glasses, singing quietly under her voice. 'I do a lot of meditation, and to earn a little money, twice a week I run yoga and mindfulness classes in a school just near here. You must join me tomorrow or the next morning. But first, we will find you a place to stay.'

They climbed down to the street level. Donna led them a short way along the passage. 'This is a nice place, I had some Turkish friends staying here for several months.' There was a narrow, rough flight of stairs going up, round a sharp bend to an arched doorway. It was so low they had to crawl through it. The cave was not as big as the one Donna lived in, but it was high, cool and airy. Just one room with an arched and decorated window opening. It was perfect. Lucy climbed down the steps again. Donna had gone. She went to under her window and called up. 'It is perfect, we love it and will move in right away. Who owns it? And how much does it cost?'

'Oh, silly! It's nothing, we all stay in these places for free. I think a Byzantine family probably owned it, but that was several thousand years ago.'

Lucy returned to their new home, she related the news to Harry. They sat side by side, close to each other, in the window opening. The view was towards a small valley of apple trees and vines, and a forest of fairy chimneys, glowing in the last of the sun. It was magical. There were so many details to discover, they could see openings and arches in the towers. Some appeared lived in, some were ancient churches, decorated with Byzantine religious frescos.

Lucy said, 'We must go to get some of our stuff from *Forget-me-not,* we need some bedding, a cooking pot, plates, stuff like that, and a few clothes.'

'Yeh! But it is already getting quite late, maybe we should stay in *Forget-me-not* tonight and sort it in the morning.'

Early the next morning they carried bundles of stuff up to their cave, including Harry's guitar. Then went back into town to buy a few essentials. The town was already busy, a mixture of traditional locals and travellers. Veiled women dressed from head to foot in black buying vegetables in the market alongside backpackers in shorts and tie-dyed t-shirts. There were small, dark, chaotic shops selling seeds, tools and clothing for farmers and market gardeners, next to new, chic shops filled with joss sticks, bells and banners. They filled their shopping bag with some food, a sharp knife and some decorative hanging items.

'We must treat Donna to lunch, let's get some tomatoes, cucumber and coriander to make a salad.' Harry reached up to pick a fresh lemon off a tree beside the marketplace. They carried it all back to their cave.

'I must go and find where Donna does her yoga classes. I really want to do some yoga. You should come as well, Harry, it will do you loads of good.'

Harry shook his head. 'I'll see you later then.' Lucy ran off to find the school.

It was already getting hot, so Harry collapsed onto their bedding. Later, Lucy returned full of enthusiasm from her class. She told Harry that she was going that evening, with

Donna, to a full moon party just a short distance away in Love Valley. 'Just us two girls, to have some time together away from you blokes. I haven't had *"girly"* time since I was in Greece.' Harry could not make any comment, it was obviously a fixed decision. They took the bowl of salad round to Donna's. She was once again singing happily to herself, cradling two of her cats. She was thrilled to share the salad they had made.

When it was starting to get dark, Lucy went off with Donna, to go to the party.

Harry tuned his guitar, he started strumming some chords from a tune that had been running round in his head for several days. He was happy with the way it came together. The first phrase was reflected by the second phrase in a different key. He needed to get Lucy to dream up some lyrics. He daydreamed about recording it, hearing it played on the radio, and becoming a professional pop star. Soon he got bored sitting on his own, he needed some company. He thought maybe he could busk in the main square, maybe take a bit of money. When he got to the square, he saw that the bar was filled with a crowd of travellers. He gave up the idea of busking so decided to join them. He bought a beer and sat down with them.

'Hey! Ringo, give a tune,' One of the guys shouted, seeing his guitar, obviously a bit drunk.

'Stupid! Ringo plays the drums. This guy has a guitar. What's your name?'

'Harry.' He strummed a few notes and launched a favourite and easy to play number by Ray Charles.

'I can't remember all the words. This is the last verse.'

He noted that many of the crowd were listening, so he

went straight into a fast version of "*I'm a Believer*", by the Monkees.

'That's fantastic, man. Give us some more, some Beatles. Hey Jude or something!'

A man in his 60s came up to the table. 'Stop making that racket. Some of us have come all the way here to get away from this sort of noise.' He had a grey military moustache, and red puffed out cheeks. 'You all need to get your hair cut and washed. Why do you want to look like girls?' One of the girls giggled, the blokes shifted around in their seats.

'You all look like those Nancy-boys.'

A woman, probably related, with fixed, sculpted hair and half the crown jewels round her turkey neck, joined in. 'Those awful Rolling Stones have long hair, just like you, and they make so much ghastly noise. They are a disgrace to our country.'

'A couple of years in the National Service in my regiment with the Sergeant Major would soon make men of you. What you do is not music, it's just a horrible racket. '*Stranger in the Night*', by Frank Sinatra is music. '*Land of Hope and Glory.*' A tune you can stand up to. That's the proper stuff.'

The guy sitting next to Harry spoke up, he had an educated accent. 'To Edward Elgar '*Stranger in the Night*' might have sounded a horrible racket. Things move on. People move on. Tastes move on. Come on,' he looked around the table, 'Let's move on, get away from these dinosaurs.'

As a group, with a clattering of chairs, they all finished their drinks and left. Harry wondered what to do with his guitar. 'I'll just ask the guy behind the bar if he can look after it.'

With an assurance, it would be safe. 'Pick it up later, till about midnight, or tomorrow after we open in the afternoon.' He joined the group outside in the cobbled square.

'Hey man, let's all go and explore, we've been here a few days and never got past that bar.'

Harry had just learnt that his name was Griff, he was a leader and a joker, but not very worldly. 'Let's go and look in some of those chimneys this place is famous for, are you two girls up for a bit of sightseeing?' There was general agreement.

'We have been riding on pills ever since our bus left Calais.'

'Here have some, we have scored plenty, or better still let's do some acid. I have got a tab for you.' Harry hesitated.

'You done much?'.

'No, just the once, I think it was fake, cost me a tenner, I just sat around waiting for the light to come on.'

'Yeh! Sometimes happens, these are real, come on have two, it's mild, good and clean.' Without thinking Harry popped a sugar cube in his mouth. His thoughts went to Lucy, she was having fun at the full moon party, with Donna, in Love Valley. He hoped there was none of that going on, Love! Should he have taken a psychedelic without her next to him?

Griff was obviously used to a lot of drugs, 'Dope from the same location always hits the same, ten lines of coke from the same source is the same hit, but do acid, every trip is to a different galaxy.'

Harry knew it would take a short time for the acid to hit, he felt quite calm, but buzzing after two beers on an empty stomach.

A short, round man wearing a long black cloak approached them. 'Halo, halo, you boyos, are you tidy, are you?' It was a very Welsh accent. Griff, always first with a quip, replied, 'Yaki-da.' He obviously knew a bit of Welsh.

'You follow me, now, I'll take you to my church. You can fill out my audience. We are starting in just one minute. We keep it simple, just sing praises to our Lord.'

Griff looked around at his new friends. 'I can't see anyone here who wants to go to church, we are just going to find another boozer, come and join us.'

'It's the liquid of the devil! You will be led to damnation.' The Welsh minister's voice was gradually rising. 'It's the pathway you walk with Satan.' His ginger beard, which projected at a curious angle from his face, bounced and wobbled. 'I am from Bangor, Wales, that is, Bangor. I left there to find a new path. The people in Bangor were all miners, all sinners. They drank the beer every day. They even drank the beer on the Sabbath Day. They took drugs, they had long hair, they were like girls, just like you, all homosexuals. Listen to the words of the Book,' he had stood up on a raised platform, spittle and foam were dribbling onto his beard. *"...do not fear those who kill the body but cannot kill the soul. Rather fear him who can destroy both soul and body in hell."*

'And from Revelation, 21:8 the book says *"...the cowardly, the unbelieving, the vile, the murderers, the sexually immoral, those who practice magic arts, the idolaters and liars – they will be consigned to the fiery lake of burning sulphur…"'*

Harry listened to him in amazement, wondering if the acid had already hit. Griff was bending over, hands on knees, almost crying with laughter. 'Listen, Vic, if you want an audience closer to spirituality, go over there,' he indicated the bar, 'Colonel Bloodknock and his missus are on the whiskeys and gin and tonics, they are into real spirits. They can lead you on the road to Revelation.' There was laughter all round.

'Come on guys and dolls, let's go explore. Are we all pilled up? Where we are going into weird *'Fairville,'* we are going to need it.'

No one knew which way to go, so they wandered aimlessly. Once away from the dolmus, taxis, bars and lights they entered a world of conical rocks, growing out of the earth like stone fungi. High cliff faces were carved with terraces, caves, and ancient decorations in relief in the white tufa rock. They climbed up and along a narrow walkway, little more than a shelf in the rock. There were several openings into huge caves, impossible to see around until one of the girls pulled out a little pen light, she pointed the beam over a wall of faded, peeling paintings of religious figures. Bishops in tall mitres, angels with silver wings, fanged, fire breathing monsters from the underworld. They moved on to other caves, some decorated with Byzantine religious paintings, some with modern graffiti, some plain, smoke crusted walls. They wandered on through a vineyard, the full moon rose above the cliff surrounding the valley, the silver light brought into relief the weird shapes and chimneys that surrounded them. They all climbed up steep, rough-cut steps to another cave. Every surface of the walls and roof was covered with well preserved paintings. The crucifixion, God surrounded by cherubs and angels. Griff called everyone over to a painting of the Last Supper. The moonlight fell on it from a tiny window high up near the roof. 'Look, all the apostles look just like us, like hippies. Long hair, stoned look in their eyes, bright coloured clothes, even Jesus sandals on their feet.'

'They're a rock and roll group,' said John. 'Matthew, Mark, Luke and John. Like the Fab Four. And all the others are roadies, gofers and groupies. Looks like fish and chips for supper. Get that huge fish on the table.'

For Harry, the magic carpet of acid arrived slowly and landed safely. The sky was black, the moon white. A girl in their group walked by, leaving a slipstream of an exotic scent. Harry asked himself if acid cures colour blindness. He thought he must have been colourblind since birth. The colours in the paintings were bright, oscillating through the rainbow colours. He wonders if he had ever seen anything in his life, or just listened to a description. He found it difficult to speak, to find words. Somewhere there were bells ringing, tiny bells chirping in the gentle breeze. He feels the breeze, he must be outside in the vineyard again. He needs to find a place to sit, maybe sleep, and dream. He sits on a rock under an apple tree, there are more bells ringing, and the sound of a gentle breeze in the trees. He looks up, there are silver clouds moving across the black sky. They pass over the moon. It goes dark, then light again leaving stark shadows of the rocks on the ground. He could taste the air. A mixture of earth and apple. The taste of body scent, musk and strong aftershave.

Then he was back home, back in the cave. Had he been led there? Had he climbed up the narrow steps, through the low doorway? A lit candle was on the floor. Who has done this for him? The candle threw coloured lights on the wall. They moved, so many colours. He could see a road, black tarmac through a rainbow, going into the distance, going so far away it looked like a pencil line. Where does it go? It moves, racing towards him whilst he is stationary, there is a sharp bend, should he go round to see what is there? Nothing, the road goes towards infinity. It starts moving up and down, heaving up, dropping down. A steep hill, he waits till he reaches the brow of the hill. Looks over, no road, just hills and moors. He was rolling down a steep grass slope. Falling, rolling, laughing. Tries to grab a tussock of grass. Misses. The branch of a shrub, misses again. He stops, and bangs against a rough stone wall. He can feel the sharp Yorkshire stone cutting into his back. Where is he? Is he at home? He can hear Rolly laughing on the other side of the wall. He must have fallen down the slope as well. He calls to his friend, no reply, he calls again to ask if he is OK, no reply. There is a scent of heather, ferns and gorse. There is a large flat slab above him. The fish is on it, still alive, mouth opening and closing with a slurpy, popping sound. It morphs into an erect penis, liquid dribbling onto the rock. His mind tells him this is a dream, a terrible dream, how can he stop it? His hands are ridged like claws. His fingernails dig into the stone floor. There is pain. Eyes looking into his eyes, close. Lips moving, but no words. A face he does not recognise. His mind drifts into nothingness. Now driving the camper van. In the driver's seat, but no controls, no steering wheel. In front of him are big bunches of flowers, a sweet smell. What are they? Forget-me-nots. The colour is different, yellow, the same as the candle flame. A new candle, big flame. Another candle across the cave. A woman by the candle, next to the window. A stranger, in our room. He didn't recognise her, different smell, but there is something in the silhouette. So many pictures flit across the screen at the back of his mind. Places, small towns, water, rivers, people, many, many different people, voices, different voices, some he understands, some not. A policeman in a tin shed. Through the door, he sees piles of passports. Each one is empty, with no paper. Psychedelic patterns, and swirling colours on the side of a long bus. Smoke, mist, it is gone. Again nothingness, his head drops onto his chest. A cat climbs onto his lap, Aagh! A tiger, he pushes it away, a claw catches in the blanket, not a tiger, too small, a cat. He hears prayers, speaking in his head in a Welsh accent, "Follow God, your salvation, avoid damnation." Is it thought-speak? Music far away, good jazz. "Sodom and Gomorrah are in eternal fire." There was a face close by, eyes looking into his eyes. A mouth, lips moving in speech, no sound. Who is this woman? Something familiar, a different smell. He pushes away, away from the candle, back against the wall. A beam of moonlight shines through the window. Tiny motes of dust illuminate, there is Lucy in the motes, a distinctive profile. She looks good. He moves closer. Waves at her, the motes rush around in confusion, she disappears. His head drops, he slips sideways onto the floor. A deep, long dreamless sleep engulfs him, confused thoughts disappear.

It was daylight. He felt a shaft of hot sun on his back. The candle had gone, replaced with a glass of water. He was desperately thirsty. The water was fresh and cold. He looked around the room, a figure approached him.

'Hello, my darling, how are you?'

He recognised the voice, but the face was different, the smell was different.

'Wh', … who are you?'

'It's Lucy, of course, your lover! Where are you, Harry? Are you still tripping?'

Harry searched his mind. Still, so many confusing thoughts and ideas whirled around.

He looked at her, she looked into his eyes. His pupils still dilated to tiny black dots. 'You have been on a big trip, was it coke or acid?'

'A guy gave me some acid. I should have never done it, especially without you. Some things were good, but many things were bad.'

'I'm here to look after you now, as I was for most of the night. You were very strange, far, far away.'

Lucy was still looking hard at his face.

'I just don't recognise you. What have you done? You look so different, you smell different. I think I saw you by the window in the night, I didn't know who you were.' She was sitting on the floor close by. Her wrists were covered in dozens of glass and plastic bangles that jangled with every movement.

'Those were the bells I could hear in the night.'

Lucy shook her wrist, the glass bangles rang.

'What have you done to your hair? It is different. And what's that all over your arms and shoulders?'

'Donna made me have a makeover at the party. She said

157

I didn't look the part, living with you. So, she had my hair dyed all the different colours and cut much shorter. There were lots of people, artists doing things there. It started off as a great party.' She stretched out her arms. 'This is henna, very traditional designs, that girl was brilliant, she did over my shoulders, the palms of my hands.' She turned both hands over. 'Just like the bride at the wedding we went to last week, and she did the soles of my feet.'

Harry sat staring, he found it difficult to take it all in. 'And your smell, what is that?'

'It is some special Turkish perfume I had put on me.'

'Donna did all this for you, she paid for it all?'

'She was fantastic, what a party goer!' Lucy paused. 'There are a few things I must tell you, but first I bought this from the market this morning, freshly made.' It was a small tray of *baklava*, sweet, sticky and filled with roasted almonds.

Harry drank another glass of water and ate six portions of *baklava*. The sweetness and texture started to revive him.

'What time is it? What day is it?'

'It's late afternoon, getting dark, and it's the day after yesterday. You have been out all day,' said Lucy. 'I have to explain a few things to you first before you start telling me about where you went on your trip.' Lucy moved away and sat on the blankets that made up their bed.

'Donna is great, such a good friend. She did all this for me.' Lucy, with jangling bangles, waved her hand over her hair and shoulders. 'But there was a problem, we were hungry, so she bought a pizza, a mushroom pizza. You know I hate mushrooms, but I had already had a beer, and a couple of very strong *Raki*. So, I ate just a quarter slice, Donna ate a lot of the rest. We were both sick, badly sick. Which was not a bad thing because it turned out they were magic mushrooms on the pizza. I got confused, didn't know if there were any toilets around, didn't know which way to get back here. Donna was even worse. She was falling over, giddy and giggling, but also panicking and anxious, anxious about me more than herself. I could see people as strange shapes, square heads, triangular arms. Trees moved and waved branches although I could feel no wind. It was horrible, I just hung onto a park bench, shouting at people to not sit on it. Anything I touched felt funny, and there were sounds coming from all over the place. Some of them just in my head.' She took a deep breath, paused before continuing. 'We didn't know how we were going to leave the party, it was already quite late, we could see the full moon, it could have guided us here, but we didn't know which way. Anyway, a couple of guys hooked onto us, more onto Donna than me. I think they were Turkish. Donna grabbed hold of the handsome one and hung on. I was left with the one with bad teeth, and even though my smelling was off, he stank of BO. Fortunately, there was a girl with them, I got her to show me part of the way home, to a place where I could remember the rest of the route. When I got here you were sitting just where you are now, staring at the wall, chanting strange words in a strange language. I lit candles and hoped I could look after you. Donna, meanwhile, had gone off with this Turkish fellow, about half her age. I'm sure she had fun!'

Chapter 13

Geome, Cappridocia, central Turkey. April 1971

"The journey, not the arrival matters."

Lucy asked if Harry wanted to eat, but he had nodded off to sleep again. She decided to leave him for a short while to go to the market. She soon returned with some fresh bread, yellow cheese, some apricots and a bag of '*Su boregi*', a sweet filo pastry filled with white cheese. She had already eaten two *dolma*, stuffed vine leaves, on the steps back to the cave.

She lit two candles, tucked a blanket around Harry and went to sleep herself.

They both woke up as the dawn light spread across the white rocks and vineyard outside their window. They could hear the sounds of the small town setting up for another day. They made a flask of coffee, neither wanting to talk about their trips. They were uncertain of what day it was. When were the trips? One, two or even three days previously? They were both a little ashamed of their actions. Eventually, Harry said he was really hungry and wanted some boiled eggs and toast.

The cafes and bars had already filled up with local men sipping strong, black coffee, and colourful travellers who had yet to move on to a new destination after the full moon party. They ordered soft boiled eggs and toast. Harry looked at the eggs when they arrived, they were bright red. He had never seen red eggs before. He called over the waiter to ask. 'Oh! They are dyed red, so we know that they have been cooked.' Harry was relieved, he was worried he was still tripping.

Lucy was concerned about Donna. After eating her eggs she said to Harry, 'I'm going to find Donna, make sure she is OK, then come back here. Don't take any pills or drugs, promise!'

He nodded, fully understanding, and went across the road to collect his guitar from behind the bar where it had been carefully looked after.

Very soon Lucy returned arm in arm with Donna. They had discussed the adventures at the Full Moon Party. Donna looked radiant but denied having any lasting relationship with her new Turkish lover.

'Yolculuk iyi miydu?' she asked Harry, who looked mystified.

'I don't understand'.

Lucy said. 'She's gone all native now, talking in Turkish, since she has a new Turkish boyfriend!'

Donna had a small smile and a slight blush on her cheeks. 'He is not my boyfriend. I asked you if you had a good journey, trip.'

'It was different, I don't think you could call it a good trip.'

'Don't do it again. Especially without Lucy next to you. Now I am having a coffee, a Turkish coffee. You will join me. Then we can go on a tour of my town. I will show you some secret places the tourists don't go to.'

Thick, black, sweet tiny cups of coffee came, with a glass of water each. 'Yesterday, I heard from a taxi driver that your Irish friend who went to the clinic after an overdose is OK, she is recovering.'

'That's good news, I doubt whether we will ever see those two again.'

'You never know, the journey is in the same direction, and the road is narrow.' Harry sounded almost poetic.

After drinking their coffee, Donna led them through the town, down some narrow paths and up steep steps into a dark cave.

'We came here last night. I remember all these paintings. One of the guys reckoned the painting of the Last Supper looked like a bunch of hippies, and four of them would make a rock band. He looked at the painting of a fish in a tray. There was something at the back of his mind he found disturbing but couldn't remember what it was.

In one remote cave, they met two nuns from France. The cave had been an early Christian church. It had no religious paintings on the walls, it was simple and spartan, there was an elaborate cross carved into the stone, possibly Byzantine thought Lucy. Marie was the leader, Charlotte, the second nun was very quiet, not speaking any English. Marie spoke in a quiet, soft voice. They had both been brought up in a convent since childhood, now they were on a pilgrimage, going to an ashram first then joining a nunnery in Sikkim, the far northeast of India, close to Bhutan. They reported back to the Mother Superior in their convent with daily stories of where they were and who they met. Charlotte had the habit of carrying small titbits of food to give to the wild street dogs. She was sensitive to all animals and got upset if anyone chased or hit them.

Marie was an older, handsome woman with a well shaped nose, bright eyes and a rosebud mouth. She wore elegant clothes, obviously bought in France and carefully looked after. Surprisingly, because of her religious order, she wore jewellery, a coral bracelet, and a green Aventurine bead necklace. On her dress, there was an unusual gold brooch, with a Latin inscription *"Love conquers all"*. Charlotte was always in the shadow of Marie. She rarely raised her eyes, always fussing around and tidying up.

They were offered refreshment by the nuns, a sweet, refreshing juice made from berries collected in the hills they had travelled through. As they sat talking about the ancient Christian church they were sitting in, and speculating on the characters who had lived there, priests and bishops, and some of the adventures that had occurred in the church, an English man came in, knelt on the hard stone floor and said some prayers. When finished, Marie gave him a blessing, long and in Latin, he held his hands together, bowed his head and thanked her. He spoke in a soft, quiet voice explaining he was from England, he was trying to travel to Calcutta in India to join a Christian community. He was hitching rides, taking local, cheap buses in short steps and staying in the cheapest places because he had little money. Lucy suggested he stayed in a cave, it wouldn't cost him anything.

She called to Donna for help as she had wandered to another cave down a narrow path for help. She suggested meeting up with him in the square in the early evening, she would find him the right place to stay.

For most of the day, Donna led them exploring the fields of 'fairy' chimneys and white rock cliffs of caves, tunnels, passageways, orchards and vineyards.

Harry started to feel very tired and confused. 'I need to go back to bed, and sleep some of this off.'

Back in their cave, Lucy asked. 'Tell me about what you did, it will probably make you feel better to talk about it. Who gave you the acid?'

'I met up with some guys in the bar. I was going to busk, but a beer seemed a better idea. There were some awful posh tourists there who complained we were making too much noise, so we left. We bumped into this weird Welsh priest. This was before any trip but now seems very much like all part of it. One of the guys gave me a couple of tabs. I know I shouldn't have but I was missing you.' He looked at Lucy with plaintive puppy dog eyes.

'The trip was not good, I was really confused. I promise I won't do it again.'

He lay back on the bed and immediately fell into a deep sleep. Lucy soon followed.

The next day they woke full of energy and ideas. 'I think we should stay here a few more days,' said Lucy.

'Not too long, we still have a long way to go. All

through Iran, Afghanistan, Pakistan and India. We are not even halfway there. If we had Rolly with us he would know exactly how many miles.'

'We must contact Rolly, send him a card or letter. And I must contact Mother and Papa, I will write them a letter this morning, and you must do one to your mum and dad.'

Another two or three days passed. They met many travellers, some going east and some returning to Europe. Many bits of advice were passed on, places to visit, places to stay, and things to avoid. Lucy met this guy who said he came from New Zealand, he was going to London, taking public transport all the way. She was fascinated by the geometric tattoos on his arms. She compared them to the henna patterns on her arms and shoulders. 'My tattoos are traditional Mauri. The men have most of their bodies covered with these patterns. Each one tells a story. It is the same with the Aboriginal tribes from Australia. They have not had any written tradition, they have storylines, and stories are told in their tattoos.'

Lucy said she was told the henna patterns were very traditional from Turkey but didn't know what they meant. Next time she saw Donna she would try to find out.

The New Zealander, called Butch, had many friends he had joined up with on their travels back to the West. They were full of stories of experiences in India, Afghanistan and Iran. One of the group had learnt to play the *sitar* from a well know player in Delhi, he was sad he could not buy one whilst in India, they were expensive, and he only had enough money for the journey back to France. He was determined to get a job and buy one with his first savings.

Others talked of the music in India and Pakistan, dominated by Hindi films, but occasionally they found a single musician busking. Sometimes two or three in a group with a Kutchi dancer. A friend of Butch said that they had met up with a wedding band in Paktia, south Afghanistan. The band had been asked to play at a wedding in a remote village that would probably last for three days. For a short while, as the band rehearsed, they sat with them to learn about playing the *rabab*, a multi string lute inlaid with intricate patterns of mother of pearl, the *tabla drums* and *doyra*, a type of tambourine. Their instruments were decorated with tassels and amulets.

Harry was interested in these stories. 'I hope we can meet with people like that. It would be great to learn to play local music. And the *sitar* is now very trendy, George Harrison plays it on several of his tracks.'

Lucy asked if any of them found on their travels what they were looking for. Did they satisfy their quest? The answers were varied. They talked mainly about the poverty, health and food, but also the satisfaction of travelling, meeting people and discovering different cultures.

Two couples had been living in The Rishikesh Ashram in the foothills north of Delhi. They initially went for a two week meditation and yoga course but stayed for a year until their Indian visas ran out. They said they had had a spiritual transformation, it completely changed their lives. They were returning to London to set up their own ashram.

Lucy noticed the further they travelled east, the more colourful and exotic the clothes were worn by travellers. She decided it was time to buy some new clothes, now that her hair was short and she had henna decorations on her hands and arms.

There were always a lot of travellers sitting in cafes drinking coffee and smoking, strong Turkish cigarettes or hashish.

Harry, when he was asked to take a puff off a reefer or chillum, replied, 'We're abstainers, this world is magical enough.' Looking for a glance of approval from Lucy.

Harry spotted two guys he had met a few nights before, Griff and John.

'Hey! You guys are still here, I thought you would have gone off in your bus several days ago,' said Harry.

'No, still here, no one wants to get back onto that death trap of the bus, they like it here too much. But we are probably leaving tomorrow. How was the acid trip? You just disappeared, we wondered where you had gone.'

'I had to go back to our cave, it was too scary out amongst all those weird shapes.

'This is Lucy, my girlfriend.' She had just come up to stand by Harry. 'We will also be leaving tomorrow with many miles to go. We need to get away from these touristy places.'

Griff said, 'I met the mad Welsh bishop again the other day. Still preaching and shouting out passages from the Bible.'

Lucy wanted to know why they were travelling to India. There was a chorus of answers from the group of travellers that had gathered.

'I had to get away from family, all those silly family traditions and routines.'

'I am on my way to find the perfect mind-bending drugs, Afghan Gold from the north of the country. I am reading *'Politics of Ecstasy'* by Timothy Leary. I guess he found it.'

'I just want to travel, feel freedom, meet people, learn new languages and customs. I come from a boring little town in the middle of nowhere. Nothing happens. Then you find a place like this, wow! It's wonderful.'

'I am looking for some life changing experience, probably religion. I don't know which, Buddhism, Hinduism, Hari Krishna. I will know when I find it.'

'My bucket list is this: Kathmandu, Lhasa, Mount Kailash, the Swat Valley and Chitral.'

Harry picked out that comment from the noise of chatter, he said, 'You've got a lot of travelling to do, it will take you years.'

'As long as the money lasts, I am a habitual nomad!'

The talk, questions and conversation moved around, they ended up talking about the place they were staying at.

'Are we destroying the very places we visit? Because of the beauty and simplicity of the culture?' questioned one traveller, wearing an unusual black cloak and a pointed hat. He looked like a magician.

'You know, this place is on the meeting point of many lay lines. And there is a deflection in the magnetic lines here.'

'It's not a portal to another dimension, is it? With all these fairies around it could be.'

'That's just a load of mumbo-jumbo.'

Harry turned to Lucy, breaking away from the chatter. 'If we are leaving tomorrow, we had better start packing up and go to see Donna.'

On the way past her cave, they called up to Donna, they could hear her quietly singing.

'We are leaving tomorrow, we must get together tonight for a meal.'

A time was agreed. Harry and Lucy went to their cave to start packing.

Donna was downcast when they met up in the bar, the same one they had their beers in when they first arrived.

'I have some sad news, your Irish friend has died. The clinic told me she escaped, found some opium, and took an overdose.'

Harry and Lucy went very quiet, taking in this news.

Lucy gave her a big hug, they didn't say anything.

The meal was without the usual flow of conversation, each reflecting on the news of Saki's friend dying.

Part of Donna's Diary

I am going to find Suki, help her however I can. And I have decided to start working at the clinic. I feel I can help, I have some expertise and can offer them help in some way.

This is going to be a big change in my life, but I now need to do something. I have sat around for too long dreaming, not doing anything all day.

I love my cave, all my cats and collection of textiles. There are so many good people here in this town, some stay but most pass through. My new friends Lucy and

Harry are such good people. We must keep in touch and hopefully meet again. Their quest and approach to life is very true. They know what they want, I am sure they will find it. Their friendship and their journey has inspired me to start living again.

My help at the clinic will be for travellers with drug problems, of which there are many, I am in a good position here in the middle of town to find them and help.

Lucy said, 'I think we should wait a day or two before leaving, I want to go into the chimney fields to do some drawing. I need to create a special memory of this place.'

Harry agreed, 'I will write a long essay in my diary, this is not a place we will forget, we need to remember every detail.'

When they finally left after two more days, they carried their possessions to *Forget-me-not* and said goodbye to Donna, and others they had met. It was difficult to leave so many friends and adventures behind, but happy to keep all the memories.

It was unfamiliar to them to pack the camper, they had been away for over two weeks, but it seemed like months.

When they had looked at the map and decided to go towards Sivas, some miles to the east, Harry turned on the ignition. The battery in the camper van was dead. He dug out the jump leads he knew Rolly had packed away and hitched them to an old saloon driven by a German to get started.

Just as they were pulling out of the camp site a couple waved them to stop.

'We are hitching, have you got room for the two of us?'

Chapter 14

Sivas and Erzurum, central Turkey. May 1971

*"Live life with no excuses,
travel with no regrets"*

They were happy to be on the road again. The cassette music was turned up high, the hot sun shining onto desiccated fields and dusty road.

The two hitchhikers, sitting in the back were Danish. 'My name is Jensen, and this is Hanne. We are going to explore India.'

Lucy introduced themselves, they seemed quite polite and correct, different from the usual casual initial greetings. The Danish couple were neatly dressed in clean laundered clothes.

'We are hitchhiking today, just to meet new people, but usually we take a coach ride, we always stay in small clean hotels. Hanne does not like little insects.'

'That must be costing a lot of money,' said Harry. 'We usually camp when we are on the road. We have just lived for a week in a cave. That was cool.'

'No, that would not be good for us,' said Jensen.

'If you are going to India, we have been told it is very dirty, very poor. You are followed by beggars wherever you go. It may be difficult for you,' Lucy said.

'Yes, we understand that, but we will find a clean place to live.'

'That will cost a hell of a lot, best of luck. We are exploring, finding places to get away from the tourist trail, so we can learn about the local culture and people', Lucy said.

It was obvious the Danish couple had different objectives to her. They wanted to visit the tourist places, visit ruins. 'The archaeological museum in Kayseri was good, and of course the museum in Cappadocia is excellent. Sivas has many exciting remains from the old times. Many invaders stopped there to build mosques and castles. There are also many, many in India we must visit.'

Lucy wondered why they didn't just fly to Delhi, rather than travel overland.

Harry said, 'First we're going to Sivas, maybe stop before the town to camp. Then we're going north toward Erzurum, the mountains, and to look at *Agri Dagi*, Mount Ararat. I doubt if we will go looking for Noah, too many people have already tried. Also, we are not equipped to go mountain climbing. Mount Ararat is very high.

'If it is good with you, we can leave you at Sivas. We will offer you a little money for your fuel,' said Jensen in a halted Danish accent.

Later in the day, Lucy spotted a shallow valley to the side of the road. 'That's a great place for us to stop.'

Harry who was driving said, 'It is only five kilometres to the town, we will take you two and drop you off. We need some fuel and food so it is no trouble.'

After they had dropped them off, Lucy sighed with relief. 'That was hard going, they were so straight, I couldn't think of anything to talk about.' Harry agreed. They filled up with fuel and filled two jerry cans to carry on the roof rack together with a plastic can of water. They collected fruit from the market, some fresh meat and went to the supermarket for tins of food, before returning to the camping site Lucy had spotted earlier.

It was off to the side of the road in a small glade of eucalyptus trees, providing shade and a sweet oily smell. There were no buildings or farms nearby, the hills were sun burnt to a dull brown colour, dotted with shrubs similar colour to the earth. They were both happy to be away from other tourists, people, and towns.

After a simple meal, Lucy gave Harry a big hug. 'I love you to the moon and back.'

Harry said, 'I don't think we have any Turkish Delight left in the box, we will have to get a big supply before we leave Turkey.' He lifted her up and carried her to the bed. They made passionate love.

The next morning the sun woke them up early. Harry was trying to work out an interesting route towards the remote areas they were hoping for. Lucy was making coffee and omelettes.

She said, 'Wherever we go, I want time to do some more drawing and painting. I have only done a few recently, I was hoping to fill my sketchbook every week. I did some rough sketches of faces when we were with the Hog Farmers and some good ones of the fairy castles, but I need time to finish them off.'

Harry nodded in agreement. 'I think it will be best to carry on through Erzincan towards Erzurum. It will be cold in this area at night, it's very high altitude, lots of mountains and wiggly roads, so going will be slow.'

'If there are mountains the scenery will be great, and we like wiggles, there will be no need to hurry, just take our time.'

'Yep, we have seen a lot of people, now let's see lots of beautiful scenery. We've got enough fuel to get us to Kars, and plenty of food. If it's cold, we cuddle up under blankets. And we can stop anywhere for sketching.'

'Whilst I'm sketching you can always go fishing or catch one of those goats,' Lucy joked.

They chatted on. 'I was told a story by a couple driving back to Europe from India. That was before we stayed in the cave. They went right up into the mountains, they said that the roads were terrible and that bandits were roaming the hills. They told me to be very careful.'

They soon set off, the road climbed steadily, then suddenly dropped down into deep gorges. It was slow going, with lots of twists and turns, but very little traffic. After passing through Erzincan the road went into a narrow gorge, steep mountains towering up either side of the road. They stopped in a small passing place to stretch their legs.

'I think all the ancient raiders, armies and travellers came down this route. People like Genghis Khan, and

Alexander the Great. Maybe this narrow pass is the place they called the 'Persian Gate' or 'Camel's Neck', said Harry.

The distances between villages increased, the size and loneliness of the landscape, the bleak uncultivated fields made time stretch out like the narrow, unmade road ahead.

'I hope it is not going to be too far till we find somewhere safe to stop for the night'. Lucy was worried about the lack of any village or town. They had driven for many miles and the going was slow.

They arrived in Erzurum as the darkness of night approached. It appeared a harsh city set on a red plateau, surrounded by dark hills. The history of travellers, traders and armies gave the impression that much of the life had been sucked out of the city. However, after the desolate dried out countryside that surrounded the town, a tree-lined boulevard was a surprising welcome relief.

They tried to find a hotel or hostel to stay the night. Harry was worried about security for the camper van, so they looked for a place that had a lock up space close by. Lucy was tired from the exhausting day on the road. The only place they could find had a drooping sign outside with peeling paint announcing it was a 'hotal of excallance', spelt wrong, in curling Persian script.

Harry, using all the Turkish language he had struggled to learn over the past two months, asked for a room for two. For the first time in many weeks, they had to dig out their passports to register with the apparent owner. He was a jolly round fellow with a moon-shaped face. He was wearing traditional clothes, a waistcoat over a white collarless shirt, baggy pantaloons and a red felt hat. He triumphantly showed them a room with a large double bed and a grubby window overlooking the rear parking lot where *'Forget-me-not'* was parked. Under the eaves, there were swallows nesting, swirling off in the hot air, searching for insects.

When the owner left, Harry said. 'You didn't see in the register. The last person who stayed here was over two months ago, a Belgian. He had written a comment, *'concrete and cockroaches!'* I can see the concrete, hopefully the cockroaches have gone to bed.'

Lucy looked doubtful.

'I have booked us in for two nights as it is cheap. We can explore the town tomorrow.'

There was a gentle tap, tap on their door. A well-dressed man also in traditional Turkish dress announced that he was a cousin to the hotel owner, he was called Ozcan, a common Turkish name. He unusually had no beard, a smooth complexion. He said, in good English, he was instructed by the police to look after the visitors during their stay.

Lucy objected. 'We like to explore places on foot by ourselves, we don't need a guide.'

'I have to accompany you when you walk out of the hotel. It is the regulation. It can be a dangerous place for foreigners here. There are bandits.'

They agreed, there seemed to be no option. Harry asked, 'Can you show us a good, cheap place to eat, we like traditional Turkish food, not tourist Western food.'

Ozcan replied that when they were ready, he would show them the best place to eat, where the locals go. He waited for them outside under the drooping hotel sign.

He led them through narrow lanes in the old city to a brightly lit café.

'Here you eat *mantarh guvec*, it is traditional to this town. It is made from a casserole of lamb, pimientos, onions, tomatoes, mushrooms and cheese. You will like it. My mother makes it, she lives in this kitchen.'

He led them to a small table and disappeared through a door to the kitchen.

Harry noted that all the other customers were drinking water or tea, no alcohol, so he asked for tea for both of them.

Two big dishes of casserole were brought to them by a rotund woman. She said nothing, carefully arranging a spoon for each of them. It was obvious she was Ozcan's mother, and very proud to be serving two foreigners.

The meal was delicious, beyond any expectations. When finished they were led back to the hotel. Ozcan said he would meet them after breakfast to show them round the town.

The breakfast was not exceptional, the usual omelette, bread and tea. Ozcan was waiting for them by the door. He greeted them, 'I can show you the usual sights in the town, or I can accompany you to visit some of the old areas, the narrow streets and old houses.'

Lucy said, 'We don't like looking at old ruins, we like seeing how people live, what they eat, how they work. However, I'm sure there are some big historical buildings you want to show us first.'

'OK, first we go to the Madrassa. You can see the two minarets from here, towering over all the other buildings. They are on either side of the entrance. The entrance gate is built in the traditional Seljuk style with superb, coloured tiles. It was built in the 1200s, and like many places in this region has been partly destroyed by earthquakes and raiders such as the Mongols. But then most of the armies and great warriors from the past have visited our town. This is a religious teaching school, but there is little sign of that now.'

They went into the main courtyard which was gradually being taken over by handicraft stalls.

'You will find much better craft shops in the old town. These are just for the few tourists who visit Erzurum, so are expensive,' said Ozcan. 'I will take you there later. You look around for a while, I will then take you for a coffee.'

After exploring for a short while, Lucy looked at the small gift market, then they were led along the main street of the town.

'My brother has a coffee shop just here, we have proper Turkish coffee.'

'Do you have a big family here in Erzurum?' Asked Lucy.

'I have four brothers and four sisters. You have met my mother last night. My father is well, he has a small farm he keeps on the side of the town. We are all healthy and happy.'

The brothers greeted each other with warm hugs. The coffee came in small copper pots, with a wooden handle, heated individually over a charcoal fire. Served with tiny, patterned glasses, a lump of sugar and a glass of water. It was of course excellent.

Ozcan said, 'I will now take you to *Uc Kumbetler*, the three tombs. These are also Seljuk designs, from the twelfth century. It is believed they are built to look like the conical tents used in Central Asia, the sides are carved to look like tapestry.'

Harry and Lucy soon finished looking at old buildings. They wanted to go into the old town to explore the narrow lanes and old houses.

'First, we must post our letters home, to our parents and our friend Rolly, and go to a bank for some money, we have traveller's cheques.'

'We will stop on the way, we go past the main bank and post office.'

The old town was everything they hoped for. Tiny wooden houses, almost touching across the narrow lanes, steep, tiled roofs designed to discard the heavy winter snowfalls. It did not take long for Lucy to discover the jewellery bazaar. With the help of Ozcan and much bargaining she bought two silver bracelets.

Ozcan was always hungry and soon suggested a stop for lunch. 'We will go to a café next to my home, but first I would like to show you inside my home.'

It was a two-story stone house, the main room on the first floor. It was decorated with a big rug hanging on the wall, comfortable seating deeply carved in dark wood and furnished with patterned brocade fabric. There were several handwritten, framed Islamic scripts hanging on the walls, alongside a photo of Ataturk, a collection of beautiful woven baskets and a small chiming clock. In the corner was a large metal chest, heavily locked, decorated with hand-painted flowers. There was another carpet covering the floor, with an intricately carved metal table on a folding wooden stand.

The impression was one of warmth and a happy home.

Ozcan led them to a café. 'This also belongs to one of my family, a cousin. Please let me choose your food, and pay for it. We will have *Pide*, a common Turkish food, I am sure you have already had it during your travels, but here it is a little different. It is a flatbread made from local grains, baked in a stone oven. It is shaped like a small boat and filled with cheese, onions, peppers and tomatoes. All the ingredients are grown near here and are very fresh.'

'That sounds delicious,' said Harry. 'I must ask you, how do you make a living, and how do you speak such good English?'

'I learnt English and history at school. I now earn some money from the town council for looking after the safety of travellers like you. There are tour buses that come from Ankara several times a week, for all nationalities. They stay in one of the expensive hotels, and I and my colleague keep them safe. But I like to be with travellers like you. You are very interesting.'

'It is very different from other parts of Turkey here,' Lucy said. 'The women cover up, some cover even their faces. Is that a tradition here?'

'Yes, we are conservative and Islamic. We are close to Iran where all the women must cover up. We also do not have alcohol here, like Iran. Many of the people are from Persian and Kurdish tribes so we have different traditions.'

In the afternoon Lucy found another bazaar. Harry had to persuade her not to spend any of the money they had just collected from the bank.

As they walked back to the hotel, Lucy questioned about returning home, once they had explored Iran, Afghanistan and reached Nepal. Would they sell Forget-me-not or drive back to England? This immediately worried Harry.

He was disappointed Rolly had got homesick and left, he hoped Lucy was not feeling the same.

'Don't worry,' she said, 'just be cool. We are both happy, doing what we want to do now. I was just thinking about what we could do in the future. Maybe when we have done all the exploring, I was wondering what we could do back in England. I thought maybe I could open a shop, selling stuff from Turkey, Afghanistan and India. Most of the stuff I see in the UK is ugly, and horrible. You look around a bazaar here the designs are just brilliant, look at those textiles Donna had, they were beautiful. There is so much that is old, even antique, but is so cheap. We could use people we meet like Donna to collect for us.'

Harry was reflective. 'It's an idea, but let's do what we set out to do first.'

Ozcan said, 'I have a plan for us this evening, first we go to a music festival here in the main square, then I take you to the same café for dinner. My mother is cooking for you. The music festival is not like you have in America with big bands and thousands of people.'

'Sounds cool, as you know, we like to learn about your culture.'

The dance entailed about six men in a circle. They were each wearing frogged waistcoats, wide red, striped sashes around their waists, white baggy trousers, ornate gold slippers with up-turned toes and tall colourful, striped fez on their heads. They danced at first slowly, holding a white handkerchief in the air. The rhythm of the music increased until in the end, they were whirling dizzily round and round, to stop suddenly and collapse into laughter, hugging and arm wrestling.

Harry wanted to know about the instruments that were played. Ozcan introduced him to the two musicians. Dressed the same as the dancers, one held an oriental clarinet, not dissimilar to those Harry was familiar with. This he was told was called a *Zurna*. The other musician played a bass drum called a *Daval*.

The musicians then marched away down the road holding banners above their heads with photos of Ataturk. Ozcan said that Ataturk, the former leader of Turkey was still an important figurehead in their town.

The meal that evening was similar to the day before except the casserole cooked by Mamma was a different recipe. Ozcan explained she had made it especially for the two visitors. It was followed by *sutlac,* sweet rice pudding baked till a light brown crust on top. Initially, Lucy refused to eat any, she said it was just like pudding at school. Eventually, she was persuaded to try a little spoonful. She ended up eating the whole bowl full and asking for more.

Ozcan had joined them at their table. He asked if he could find out more about why they were travelling, he was always trying to learn. Lucy said that in Europe and America, there was a big change, especially among young people. There was freedom, education, security of good employment. Her generation had independence never found before. They had the freedom to have an intimate relationship like she had with Harry. There were huge changes in fashion and music since the end of the war. Many people of her age wanted to find new ideas, explore, discover the world and different people. She and Harry didn't want to just follow the trail across the world that had grown over the past ten years but wanted to learn about people. They wanted to explore places where travellers did not usually go.

Ozcan was impressed. 'I wish I could meet more young people like you. A few weeks ago, I met three young Americans who had just been fighting in Vietnam, they had left the army, happy to be still alive but they did not want to say much about that experience, I think it upset them a lot. They were on a tour with many others, and I believe they wanted to escape the memory.'

He paused, looked at the two visitors. 'Why are the Americans fighting?'

Harry said, 'We are totally against any war, in Europe our parents had a terrible five years of fighting. We studied a bit about the Vietnam War at school and college. From what I remember is that originally many, many Americans supported the war.'

Lucy joined in. 'The Americans are worried about communism, they are still worried about Russia taking over everywhere with communism.'

Ozcan said, 'We have communists in Turkey, they are quite a strong party, people don't see much against them.'

Harry said, 'The Americans are afraid that if they give in at Vietnam, communism and Russia will soon spread to other countries in Asia. But now, just in the past year or two, there has been a big mood change. We understand that many Americans are opposed to the war on moral grounds, appalled by the devastation and violence of it. Others claim the conflict is a war against Vietnamese independence, or an intervention in a foreign civil war to claim more world territory. Others oppose it because they feel it lacks clear objectives and appears to be unwinnable.'

'Both Harry and I have been on demonstrations against the war. But there seems little we can do. A lot of the problems are with television and reporters. We see first-hand the devastation of villages, people, the jungle.'

Ozcan said, 'They show it sometimes on our television. It looks terrible. You get taught very well at your schools. Here it's all so far away they don't teach it."

Harry said, 'It has divided people into two camps, those that see the Viet Cong killing their sons, and those that must stop Russia and communism taking over. They are conscripting young men, who don't want to be killed, forcing them to a place that is alien to them, from an open farmland in the middle of America to a dense, hot jungle, to fight for something they don't understand.'

Lucy said, 'We talk about how bad it is and discuss it like now, but we will never fully understand it, we demonstrate but there is nothing we can do.

'There are times when we just don't like to talk about it, especially sitting in a lovely place like this.'

Harry brought the conservation to an end. They thanked Ozcan for his hospitality, exchanged addresses, promised to keep in touch, said good night, it had been a great experience and that tomorrow they were leaving to go to Yusufeli, to the north into the mountains.

Chapter 15

Yusufeli, Kars and Dogubeyazit, east Turkey. June 1971

"Travel opens your heart, broadens your mind, and fills your life with stories to tell."

The drive to Yusufeli was relatively easy, the road was in reasonable condition. It wound up hills, high up close to the clouds, then down into deep valleys alongside rivers that boiled with fast flowing water.

They arrived at midday, soon contacting a group of men enjoying sitting in the sun outside a café. They were instructed the best place to camp was to follow the road, cross a narrow bridge into a small park with poplar trees and surrounded on three sides by the river and its tributes. It was a clear, sunny day, the mountain peaks to the north were confused, jagged, and covered with patches of snow. In the clear light they looked very close.

It was the perfect spot to camp. Initially, Harry

was worried about the river flooding as it had done in Yugoslavia, he was assured by a householder nearby that it was safe, the river never rose above its banks except in snowmelt in the spring.

Once they had set up camp, Lucy said, 'I'm going to do some painting today, why don't you go off and explore?' She soon set up her folding stool, looking across the river to the mountains.

Harry wandered into the town, he joined the men sitting in the café they had talked to earlier. He ordered a beer and attempted to join in the conversation using his limited vocabulary of Turkish. It was difficult because the men were discussing football, Harry did not know the different teams, so he was cautious not to upset any they supported. The conversation moved on to politics and local politics, this was even more difficult to follow. One of the men questioned him about why they were visiting Yusufeli. He haltingly tried to describe their journey from home to this corner of Turkey, and where they planned to move on to. The men, who had probably never travelled further than in the district they were born in and now lived in, could not comprehend their journey and the reasons for doing it.

He soon left the café to walk up the valley, passing past well-maintained small holdings of vegetables and farm animals. Each plot was surrounded by beautifully built stone walls.

He returned to their campsite hungry for some lunch. Lucy had finished one sketch and had started on a painting.

During the afternoon she carried on with her artwork. They listened to the birds in the trees and the roar of the river. Harry caught up with writing his diary.

Lucy was impressed by Ozcan, their guide when staying in Erzurum. She said, 'It was a pity we could not talk more with him. But we know very little about the war in Vietnam, we demonstrate against things we object to, but do we really understand what is going on?'

'I agree, but I do feel relieved that I have never had to be involved in a war, I'm not sure whether I would need to defend our country, or be a conscientious objector.'

'Whilst we are here doing what we want and deciding on, we must learn from it and enjoy it. Are we moving on tomorrow or stopping here?'

'I think we must move on, there is still so far to go. I want to leave Turkey 'cos we have been here a long time and get into Iran.'

The sun was still shining the next morning when they left their riverside campsite. The views, the mountains and the attractive town filled them with good feelings and well-being.

Harry said, 'We'll have to stop in Kars, and maybe somewhere else before the border crossing into Iran. I think Kars is about four hour's drive. I hope we can camp there, it's so much easier than dealing with a hotel or homestay. We can always eat out and meet some of the local people.'

On the approach to Kars, the road climbed out of lush valleys and evergreen forests, then high above the tree line into vast rolling steps, a sea of grass with high mountains in the distance.

They found a good safe place to set up camp. It was not exposed to a howling wind, so Forget-me-not did not rock on the springs, like a boat. In the distance, over the mountains, black thunder clouds built up, and soon there was a deluge of rain whipping across the town horizontally, with flashes of lightning and rumbles of thunder.

'We are not going out in this,' said Lucy.

'No, we may well end up cooking here and going to bed early.' However, the storm passed quickly, Harry and Lucy ventured out into the town. It appeared different from the familiar sights of western Turkey. Many of the men had henna dyed beards, and instead of the usual fez headdress they wore a turban. Both the men and women had large black eyes and clear olive complexions. There were very few cars or lorries, the men mostly riding on horseback. They had to stand aside when a heavy cart with solid wood wheels passed by, loaded with firewood.

Wandering down a narrow lane they saw that the women, many wearing veils, were sitting on the front step of their house, churning butter in sheep skin churns suspended from poles, being jerked back and forth. They were baking bread in individual ovens inside the house, not in a central bakery. There was a lot of activity sorting, spinning and preparing wool for weaving carpets.

They decided to cook and eat in Forget-me-not, rather than in one of the bleak looking cafes, and to go to bed early. They had a disturbed night with the wind still howling hard and the wild dogs roaming the town, barking. The thunderstorm rolled around the valley, thunder echoing off the mountains.

It was still windy and raining heavily in the morning, so they set off immediately after a cup of coffee.

They had decided to head south towards the border crossing with Iran.

Harry said, 'We must follow the road a short way back to Erzurum then find the turning to Agri. It's going to be a very twisty road through mountains, then it's a busy road through some town I can't pronounce, then to the border. It's a long way, too far for one day, so we will stop somewhere for the night.'

'That's OK, I'm always happy to camp, and we can take our time.'

They were getting on well, but the road was rough stones and sand, so slow going. As they were going down a steep hill, into a valley there was a loud bang from the rear of the camper, a crunching rattling sound.

'Shit, shit, shit, we've got a puncture, the first one.' There was nowhere to pull off the narrow road, so they had to stop in the middle.

Harry climbed onto the roof to get the spare tyre, he found the jack and other tools.

Lucy said. 'Do take care, jam a rock under the other wheels so we don't move. I've seen others do it beside the road when changing a wheel.'

It took a long time to jack up the wheel, and even longer to undo all the bolts, they were impossibly tight. Finally the wheel was replaced.

'A good job no one came by and wanted to get past, there is no room.'

'I'm sure if someone did come by, they would have helped you.'

Harry washed his hands and face which were covered in grease and sand. He took a long drink to quench his thirst.

'We are soon going to have to camp somewhere along

the road, it is too late and too far to get to the next town before dark. We are not driving on this road at nighttime.'

'That would be so cool! It will be exciting camping here in the mountains. It's so wild.'

They found a place after a short while. Harry was exhausted after the stress of having to change the tyre, so he climbed onto the bed. Lucy got out her paints to draw a picture of the desolate landscape. Rolling mountains fading into a misty mauve in the distance.

It was peaceful, just the sound of a distant river and waterfall, the wind in the shrubs and heather. Suddenly there was the noise of motorbike engines. Lucy stood up. She could see two motorbikes coming over the hill and down towards them. They stopped, switched off their engines.

'Hello, are you here on your own?'

'No, I'm here with my man.' She indicated over her shoulder to the door of the camper. At that moment Harry poked his head out, having been woken by the noise.

'Are you stopping here for the night? It's a wild place.'

'Yeh, we decided to stop, we had a flat tyre which took a long time to fix. We felt it was better to stop here than to drive to the next village in the dark. The road is terrible, and we are not sure where the next place is.'

'Yep, we were getting worried, we are also not sure, but we reckon the next habitation could be miles away, maybe several hours. If it is OK, can we stop with you? Better safety in numbers.'

The other biker said, 'We must be on the lookout, we heard there were rumours of bandits in this area.'

Lucy looked really concerned.

'Yep, come and join us, we will be cooking some food soon. Probably another bean stew, we have plenty of fresh vegetables.'

'That's cool! I am Billy, this is Bert.'

Harry introduced himself and Lucy.

They moved their bikes in closer and lifted them on the rests. They unpacked some of their panniers and sat down on a rug with Harry and Lucy.

'We were in this area three weeks ago, on our way to Iran. We got to Erzurum to get our visas and papers for the bikes. Only to be told they don't do them there. Go back to Ankara.'

'A while ago we had seen an official looking notice in the Pudding Shop in Istanbul saying it was much easier to get the papers in Erzurum. But it was obviously out of date,' said Bert.

'Yeh! It was a real bummer, we went back to Ankara, to the Iran Embassy. They took our details and passports. It took two weeks before we got them back. We had booked into a hotel near the Embassy, quite expensive.'

'No, very expensive.'

'We couldn't change hotel, 'cos the Iranians had our passports, we couldn't go anywhere, just hang around waiting.'

'They dated the passes for one week ahead, so we have to get to the border the day after tomorrow. That's 3rd of June', said Bert.

A thought struck Harry. 'Jesus, I haven't looked at our visas.' He jumped up and fished out their passports from the safe box under the seats. He found the page with the visas for Iran stamps.

'It gives us the date 05/06/71. What's today's date?'

'End of May, maybe 1st of June, I think.' No one had thought of dates, they were just travelling from one day to the next.

'That, I think gives us four days, no more.'

She felt more relaxed, now understanding they had four or five more days. But there was a feeling of worry amongst all of them, time and dates had suddenly entered their lives for the first time in three months.

'What route have you come to here?' Asked Bert. Harry listed some of the places they had been through.

Bert said, 'We came along the north road, by the Black Sea. It was good.'

'Where in England are you two from?' asked Harry.

'We are both from East Ham. East End of London.'

You don't speak with any East End accents.'

'No,' replied Billy. 'I went to Hackney Grammar, the English teacher, Mr Marshall, didn't do much in the way of grammar and spelling. He just gave us elocution lessons. He said you'll never get a decent job if you speak like a barrow boy. He wasn't posh, just spoke with a good accent. He even took us all to 'My Fair Lady' once. That was a laugh.'

Bert said, 'I was sent to a grammar school in Hampstead. My dad didn't want me to go to school with all these losers.' He poked Billy in the ribs. 'My name is Herbert Marshall. My dad is the English teacher, Mr Marshall, at Hackney Grammar. We met up at the boy's club in East Ham and been mates ever since.'

'That's some story,' said Lucy, laughing.

'Where are you two from? I can't work out your accents.'

'Lucy comes from Sussex, that's why she's posh. I come from mid Yorkshire, I used to have a Yorkshire accent but since I have been bedding with her, I seem to have lost it.' It was Lucy's turn to dig him in the ribs.

'Those are good looking bikes.' Harry nodded towards the two colourful motorbikes.

Billy said, 'The yellow one with raised handlebars and dropped seat is Bert's. It's called the yellow submarine, not just because of its colour, but because he always seems to be driving around in torrential rain! He thinks he is in 'East Rider,' playing both Dennis Hopper and Peter Fonda.'

Harry took a closer look at the bikes. They looked impressive and powerful. ' 'Easy Rider' was a cool film. My mate Rolly would have liked to look over those bikes.'

Bert said. 'Mind you, it's the only way to travel. Riding on a motorbike you are aware of everything around you, not just sun, temperature, and rain, but smells and sounds. Those senses are a big part of what you get in the countryside and towns. In a car you see everything just through a window frame, on a bike you are part of it, it's all around you.'

It was starting to get dark. Harry got up to prepare some food. The conversation drifted around the usual subjects. A reefer of tobacco, hash, and dried apple crumbs was passed around.

Suddenly Bert sat up with a jerk. He stood up. 'There are five or six blokes just coming over the hill over there.'

They all turned to look. About a five hundred meters away six men were silhouetted against the last light in the sky, they appeared to be carrying sticks, or were they guns?

'Quick, pack everything up. They may be bandits.' Lucy looked in horror, a terrified expression on her face.

'Billy and I will drive towards them with all our lights on, make a lot of noise. You get the camper going, sound your horn long and loud. We will come back and join you.'

Harry packed up the *gaz* stove, stored it in its safe place in the back of the camper. Lucy piled all the plates, food and cutlery into the middle of the rug. She threw it into the camper, closed the door, and climbed into the cab, followed by Harry.

They started down the track, sounding the horn, lights on full beam, indicators all flashing. After a few moments they could see the lights of the two bikes behind them. Harry drove recklessly, bouncing off stones and rocks, swerving side to side trying to keep on the track. After about five minutes they pulled up. The two bikes pulled up next to them.

'Pheew! That was dodgy, I think a couple of them had guns, but they looked like old flint lock *jezails*. Very inaccurate, I heard a shot as we left, but it missed.'

'So what will we do now?' Harry asked. 'Carry on in the dark 'till we get to a village or something?'

'I dun 'know. I looked at a map a while ago, but I remember on this road there was nothing. Next town is a good two hundred kilometres away, about three or four hours, after that there is a good road to '*doggy biscuit*'.'

'*Doggy Biscuit*'? There can't be a place called that!'

'No it is an unpronounceable name, travellers and truckers call it that.'

'OK, we best just carry on 'till we find somewhere safe

to stop,' said Harry. 'We can keep close together in convoy, but just keep moving, whatever.'

Bert said, 'I am not sure how much petrol I have left, probably used a lot roaring around on that hill. I will have to stop somewhere.'

'We have a can of diesel on the roof, but that won't be any good to you. With that, we will be able to get to the next place. If you run out, we can get some for you and come back up the road.'

They carried on down the track, watching for rocks and sudden bends. The bikers rode ahead, helping to point out deep potholes and the edges of the track. It was exhausting driving.

After about an hour they stopped for a rest. Lucy quickly made coffees to pass round. After another hour they came into a very small village. Bert indicated they should stop there until daybreak. At first light they set off again. To their relief, they soon arrived in a small town. They were all able to fill up with fuel, get an omelette from a café, and continue to a good, but busy road towards the east. Everyone was very tired, ready for a break. Bert and Billy wanted to get on to the border crossing before their visa date ran out.

Lucy went up to the two bikers. She gave them each a big hug. 'God knows what we would have done without you. You saved us. Thank you. Maybe we'll see you further on.'

Harry and Lucy found a large lorry park to stay the night. Dogubeyazit, the town that was nicknamed 'Doggy Biscuit', was a boring, uninspiring place that was just a transit town for traffic going to and from the border.

The next morning was clear, the view of Mount Arafat was postcard perfect. A tall conical mountain with white snow-capped top. They both thought it would be good to explore the area some more but knew there was not time.

Harry said, 'I reckon it is only thirty miles to the border with Iran.'

'But before we go, we must tidy up, I'll trim your hair, and you do your beard. Put on those plain jeans and a long-sleeved white shirt, no frills. I'll take off all my beads and bangles. Do my hair, we both put on hats. I mustn't forget to always cover my hair with a scarf.'

'It's going to be a bit of a bore, isn't it?'

Chapter 16

Maku, Tabriz and Tehran, Iran June 1971

"Now that I'm here, where am I!"

The road was smooth with flat sun–parched land on either side stretching to the Iranian border. Here and there were fields of cherry and apricot orchards, colourful blooms giving off an exotic scent. The weather was clear, and it was very hot.

The Turkish customs briefly looked through their documents, and then waved them on. They made no mention that the customs post to Iran was closed for a religious holiday. The striped barrier was down, and the offices were unoccupied.

Together with nine or ten other vehicles, they had to camp in no man's land until the Iranian customs opened the next day. They would not be allowed back across the border into Turkey.

Lucy had an uncomfortable night, a griping pain in

her stomach and a bloated feeling. At dawn the checkpoint opened, first by a sleepy soldier, then by officials carrying steaming mugs of coffee and leather briefcases of documents. Cigarettes were lit. *Forget-me-not* was waved forward, the first in the line-up of vehicles and travellers. An official ordered them out of the camper and told them to stand by the newly built and painted customs shed. Two officials, wearing grey boiler suits and plastic gloves proceeded to strip the vehicle. Everything from the cupboards was put outside on the ground. Every drawer was taken and emptied. The bedding, cushions and rug were thrown on top. One official started unscrewing each door panel lining, the other investigated the engine, wheels, and fuel tank with a long probe. It was a very thorough search. Notebooks, instruction manuals and novels were each opened, pages flicked over.

The head customs officer indicated they should go into his office. He had already looked through their passports and examined the documents relating to the camper. He did not search their clothing but gave them both a very detailed look over.

He stacked their documents on his desk and said, 'Come with me,' moving to a door at the back of the office. Harry looked at Lucy with a worried expression.

The customs officer waved his arm across the room. 'This is our smugglers' room, take note, we stop everyone carrying illegal items and drugs. They are put into prison for many years. Some we execute.' The walls of the room were lined with items used for smuggling. Simple bags, complicated cases with false bottoms, clothing with hidden pockets, engine parts, and body work parts.

'Every one of these on display held drugs, and the owners are now in jail.' He put on a phoney American gangster accent. 'Tell your friends not to mess with us!'

Lucy clutched her stomach, her hand clasped over her mouth. 'Toilet, quick'.

Harry, with an understanding nod from the officer, led her from the room and pointed to a metal shed behind the building. A soldier followed them to stand guard next to Harry. After a long time, there was a muffled shout from Lucy.

'There is no paper, get me some paper!' Harry ran back to the pile of their possessions, now just abandoned, grabbed a toilet roll to hand to Lucy.

After another long time, Lucy appeared, looking distraught, shaky, and pale.

'There's no fucking water! I've got to wash my hands.'

There was a stand tap across the yard. Harry noticed the soldier pointing to his head. He grabbed the scarf from over Lucy's shoulders to put it on her hair. 'You must remember to cover your head.' The soldier gave a nod of approval.

Lucy muttered under her breath., 'This is a shit place. Literally shit!' She gave a quiet, snicker laugh. 'I don't want to stay in this gross country for any longer than we need to.'

Harry led her back to *Forget-me-not*. All their gear was still spread out on the pavement. Lucy climbed onto the bed, Harry started loading their possessions back inside. A customs officer shouted at him to hurry up as several more vehicles were being searched. A German minibus with six passengers and a Citroen 2/CV with two very unkempt

French travellers were being stripped. Harry spent a long time screwing the door linings into place. He retrieved all their documents, found the stomach pain pills, fed two more to Lucy with a sip of water, and with great relief set off down the road.

He didn't have a map, so just followed a tarmac road that seemed to go in the right direction. After about fifteen kilometres he arrived in a small town, Maku. He found a hotel near the centre. Outside was a large modern bus with a logo on both sides, 'OVERLANDERS', and several other vehicles with European registrations. In the reception area was a crowd of travellers, obviously off the bus. They had been held up because the border post had been closed. He tried, in English, asking for a room.

The driver of the bus stepped forward. 'They don't speak English here, only Persian. I can translate for you if you want.' Harry explained he wanted a room, either with a bathroom, or one close by, because his partner was sick. The bus driver, who had already introduced himself as Bob, quickly arranged a room. 'When you have settled in, come and chat with me, I'll be in the lounge.'

Harry made sure Lucy was comfortable, with a bottle of water to keep her hydrated. She was already feeling a little bit better.

He went downstairs to find Bob, the bus driver, who was full of information.

The bus was on the way back to Europe with about twenty seats sold. He talked about Iran, Afghanistan and Pakistan, full of useful advice. Where to stop, best places for tyre repairs, vehicle servicing, where to get Afghan visas in Tehran. Harry exchanged his last Turkish lira into Iranian rials with him and learnt about the black market. Bob explained that there were two rates for rials, the Toma was one tenth of one Rial, it was often quoted as the price, causing confusion. He said many tourists were caught out by this one.

Later he shared a delicious meal of flatbread, chicken kebabs and tea with Bob and several other travellers in a pavement cafe. The conversation was lively. Those who had passed through Iran, had concluded with an impression that the Iranians were consumed by the American culture. They seemed curious but misunderstood it. They followed the latest films, books, magazines, music and fashion with up to the minute devotion. But they adopted the glitter, Coca Cola style that was the worst of American culture in most Europeans' eyes. One of the independent travellers who had joined the group just for a glass of tea said he had stayed with two families. He found there were positive feelings from the older generation. They were warm, welcoming and sophisticated in their lifestyle, but were always looking to the West for good education for their sons and daughters.

Harry left the café on his own, back to their room. He was happy he had heard some positive opinions on Iran. Lucy was asleep.

The next morning, she was still asleep. Harry went to the hotel café for tea, omelette and freshly made bread. The bus had already left for Turkey, so he spent time talking with a few other travellers going towards Tehran. When back in his room, Lucy had woken but still felt delicate.

She took more pills. They decided to stay another day when hopefully she would be ready to travel again.

Harry was restless, having just arrived in a new country. He wanted to explore the town and the surrounding countryside. The town was set in a deep valley with high, treeless mountains around. He loved walking, allowing the landscape into his mind, relaxing him from travel plans and relationships that always worried him. He spent half the day walking and climbing, by midafternoon it was very hot under a cloudless sky, he was thirsty and hungry. Lucy was sitting up in bed when he returned, she was feeling much better and a little hungry. After a meal of tea and plain flatbread she returned to bed, Harry joined her.

The next morning, Harry bought a road map of Iran, a few postcards, and stamps. They were both keen to get on the road again.

Harry said, 'It is a big country, distances seem quite long. We haven't much information, but I suggest we stop near this town called Tabriz, then somewhere near Zanjan and then Tehran. We don't want to go too far in a day with you and your jippy tummy.'

It did not take very long to get to Tabriz, a large, modern town with many hotels. Zanjan was not much further. The roads were good, but crowded with lorries and huge, old American cars. The landscape was featureless with mountains in the distance looking out of focus in the dusty atmosphere. Children sat or stood beside the road begging for small coins or a pen. The elder boys threw stones at any vehicle with great accuracy, probably learnt from guarding flocks of sheep and goats up in the mountains.

They drove past Zanjan and soon found a roadside café, a caravanserai. This they learnt was a traditional stopping place throughout Central Asia. Caravanserai dated back over a millennium as a safe place for travellers, camel trains carrying merchandise and pilgrims to stop, rest and be fed. This one was a typical layout they would find along the trail, a rectangular building surrounding a courtyard. There was a single doorway wide enough to allow heavily laden camels to enter. Around the courtyard were animal stalls and rooms to accommodate travellers. Food was available, and water for washing. A more elaborate caravanserai would have a prayer room, and provision shops.

Harry looked around. 'This is like the one we stopped at in Turkey with the Japanese girl and her friend, but not nearly as decorated. It's perfect, '*Forget-me-not*' will be safe in here.'

The road was good to Tehran, Lucy was feeling well enough to take a turn at driving. It was good to get on the trail again, with a good road and music to sing along to.

It was mid-afternoon when they arrived in Tehran. The traffic was chaotic, the pollution was thick. There were no rules of the road. Taxis sped down bus lanes, scooters went the wrong way up one-way streets, no one stopped at red traffic lights, no one gave way to pedestrians. There was a cacophony of blaring horns.

They found the Amir Kabir Hotel in the south of the city. A white painted building with a semi-circular projection over the road. The ground floor was taken over as a vehicle repair shop, which spread into the street and pavement. Stretching halfway across the tree lined avenue were rolls of sheet metal, replacement doors for old Chevrolets, fuel pumps, water pumps, and complete engine and gearbox assemblies.

Harry had been warned that at the Amir Kabir all the staff were unfriendly and unhelpful. Surprising since most of the guests were foreigners travelling either east or west.

Next to reception was a large sitting lounge that also served eggs and beans on toast. They soon learned there were small kebab shops in the back streets nearby serving chicken or lamb kebabs. Amongst the various notices pinned to the wall, was a big sign in red saying 'No use of drugs anywhere in the hotel.' Along the horseshoe–shaped corridor, their room was clean, with thin well-worn sheets on a narrow iron bed. A small balcony projected over a back street. Lucy was relieved to find the toilet was not far away, and that there was hot water in the showers. Now she felt much better, she was desperate to wash her hair.

They discovered where to apply for visas to Afghanistan. They deposited their passports hoping the visas would be processed quickly. Elsewhere in the city, they found there was not much to do. Even the grand bazaar, famous throughout the world, was not friendly. Backpackers were not welcome as the traders assumed they would have no money to spend. Other travellers in the hotel expressed their desire to move on, it was a place to pass through, just to wait for visas to Afghanistan.

They explored some of the streets of Tehran.

Their first impressions were that although it was a Middle Eastern city, it had the appearance of an American Western boom town. There was new construction on every street, with buildings going up overnight. An international bank faced in marble next to a Persian Wimpy stand built on the pavement.

'This place is way out! I haven't seen anything like it since London.' Lucy had stopped outside the display window of a shop on one of the main streets. 'Look at these fur coats, they must cost thousands. And that hat. It's made from mountain fox fur.

'There appears to be so much difference in wealth here, the poor seem to have nothing, no work, just begging. The workers probably get a few pennies an hour, and then there are these people who drive around in the latest Mercedes, have posh dresses, tailored suits from London's Saville Row and so on.

'And look at those high heels!' Lucy nodded towards a group of women crossing the street. 'They don't seem to cover their heads with a scarf. Here's me looking like a dressage horse rider with my headscarf! There is so much difference. The poorer women wear a head-to-toe sheet, or are they just very religious? It would be good to find out from someone.'

Harry was absorbed in looking at a high performance red sports car parked beside the road.

Back in their room, Harry caught up with writing his diary, whilst Lucy did a series of pencil sketches of roofscapes and television aerials from the balcony.

The next evening, they met up with two travellers going to Afghanistan independently by hitchhiking or by bus and train. Donald, a Canadian, wanted to start a business in Canada selling *Posteens*. These were, he explained, the sheepskin coats, embroidered with flowers that were becoming very fashionable. Lucy said she had seen some in London, and with travellers returning to the west. She said, 'They smell horrible, I don't know why anyone could go out in one.' Donald was obviously on a mission. He wore colourful clothes, a curious beaver hat, a mass of black, curly hair down to his collar and a long, forked beard. He talked nonstop about all the deals he made and the good profits. He also explained what he wanted to buy in Afghanistan: knitted wool gloves and hats for the Canadian winter and eventually expand into going to Jaipur in India for clothing and jewellery.

Harry told him they had met this English couple and an American Peace Corps guy driving back to London with a car loaded with stuff like that.

The other traveller was the opposite in appearance. He introduced himself as Justin, a doctor, who was going first to Afghanistan to volunteer work for an N.G.O. He looked like a doctor, close shaven, with neat hair and clean fingernails. He wore dark trousers, and a matching waistcoat over a white shirt. He quietly said he was helping a traveller staying in the hotel, who had severe hepatitis.

He turned to Lucy, and visually examined her face and hands. 'Are you all right, just a bit run down, or a tummy bug?' Lucy was impressed with the quick diagnosis.

'A tummy bug. My first.'

'Probably not your last,' the doctor replied.

Harry said, 'How are you travelling? We have a couple of seats in our camper if you want to join us.' There was no hesitation, a unanimous 'Yes!'

'It would be cool if you could help with the cost of fuel. We don't want to hang about, as soon as we have got our visas for Afghanistan we are heading out of Tehran.'

'That's wicked, the sooner the better,' Donald said.

Harry found a place in the street where they fixed the tyre and gave the camper van a full service. This made him happy. He thought of Rolly who would have loved this place. Without Rolly beside him, he worried about breaking down and having to find somewhere to fix the problem.

He went with Lucy to the large post restante in the middle of the city. There were piles of envelopes and parcels from almost every country in the world. Fortunately, they were stacked in alphabetical order. There were several envelopes for Harry and Lucy from parents and friends. One envelope had a local stamp on it.

'Hey, look, we've got a letter from Farrokh, you remember that guy from uni who helped us get our visas to here?'

'How could I forget him, he was gorgeous!'

'He has asked us to go and visit him when we get to Tehran. There is an address and phone number. I'll call him in the morning.'

The phone system worked efficiently and well. 'Hey *Rooky*, it's Harry here. We are in Tehran. You remember, we met in Brighton.'

'That's far out,' was the reply. 'Hang on a sec, I want to ask you over, I need to ask my mother what is going on.' A few seconds later, 'Come over any time, how about this evening? We can have some food. You've got my address? Come at sunset.'

During the day Harry and Lucy retrieved their passports and vehicle documents from the Afghan Embassy. They were ready to go the following morning. They changed a traveller's cheque at a bank then did some shopping for essentials for the road ahead.

Farrokh lived with his family in the north of the city, close to the foothills of the Alborz mountains. It was in a new high-density suburban development for the affluent upper-middle class. The neighbours were leading government officials, successful businessmen, senior military officers, and top managers of many oil companies. The tree-lined street was guarded by military personnel. Rather than the risk of driving through rush hour traffic, and getting lost, they hired a taxi. They were dropped off outside large metal gates and a high stone wall. A short time after ringing the doorbell, a servant led them across manicured gardens to a modern house with a deep balcony running across the front. Farrokh was standing in the marble–floored hall. He greeted them warmly and then led them through to the sitting room. The floor was covered by an enormous Persian carpet, highly coloured with patterns of gardens, peacock birds and swirling abstract designs.

Farrokh's father and mother were standing in the centre of the room. He introduced Harry and Lucy to them. There were formal handshakes. His father was tall and distinguished with neat hair going grey at the temples. He had a trimmed moustache, and wore a designer suit, grey with narrow red pinstripes and designer reading glasses. His mother was petite, once pretty, but she had not worn well over the years. Her dress was down to the floor, covered her neck and arms and was adorned with expensive jewellery necklaces of semi-precious stones. She wore gold rings on many of her fingers.

A maid came in carrying a tray of soft drinks: grapefruit, orange, pomegranate, and mango. 'We will have a light dinner soon, but first sit down and tell us about your travels. Farrokh is very envious,' said his father.

The couple described some of the events over the previous months, picking out the more interesting and safer topics. They explained the reasons for taking this journey and countries they planned to go to next.

Farrokh's father explained that he was a senior partner in a large law firm in Tehran. His son, Farrokh, had graduated from university in England and was now training as a lawyer in another company.

'When I retire, he will join my partnership, but in the meantime, we think it is better to work in different places.'

Harry was keen to learn more about Iran. 'Can you tell us more about your country, we learn very little about Iran in England, it seems quite secretive. You have the Shah in charge, he is the King. Is this a democracy?'

The answer was very guarded. 'This is a democracy, a dictatorship and a kingdom. The Shah rules by repressing and restricting political freedoms. After the Shah came to rule, about thirty years ago, he upended the wealth and influence of the traditional landowning classes, altered rural economies, and this led to rapid urbanization and westernisation. He tried to incorporate all the various nomadic tribes into the country's rule. The changes made to the landowning classes changed this country.' Harry was not sure whether Farrokh's father approved or disapproved of these changes.

'We are going through a rapid transformation of wealth from oil and industrialisation. Many young people now move to the cities from the countryside, leaving villages almost deserted.'

Lucy wanted to move away from the political discussions, so she turned to Farrokh's mother. 'I am a bit confused about what women are allowed to wear. Before we arrived in Iran, we were told women must cover their arms, legs and heads all the time. Also, men should wear long sleeves and not shorts. Yesterday in downtown Tehran we saw many fashionably dressed women in the streets.'

Again the reply was guarded. 'Women are free to wear what they want, there is no law against it. But many women still cover their hair, either as a statement against the monarchy or because their choices are restricted by patriarchal values such as honour and the strict control of male members of the family. I think there are religious implications as well. The white-bearded clerics want to have laws that make all women cover themselves completely, from head to toe in a chador, with even the face covered.'

'The clerics make my job difficult, they believe lawyers have too much power,' added Farrokh's father.

'I think this is the time we go to eat,' Farrokh said with relief, hoping to move away from difficult topics about the influence of clerics in Iran to a more relaxed conversation.

The dining room was another grand room, a long, shiny table with enough chairs to seat at least twelve people. There was another huge Persian carpet on the floor, and heavy drapes over the windows.

Farrokh's mother said. 'We have simple food here. The cook makes traditional food. We have *'fesenjun,'* which is chicken roasted with pomegranate, walnuts and cardamom. With it we have *'dolme bademjan'*, that is stuffed eggplant.'

The food was served, there was no conversation whilst it was being eaten. Soft drinks were served. There was fruit and sweet pistachio nougat to follow. After the meal was eaten, Farrokh invited them back to the sitting room for tea, black and served with a lump of sugar. The evening stretched on with idle chitchat about customs in their respective countries, until Harry said Lucy was still very tired after her brief illness and they should go. A taxi was called to take them back to the Amir Kabir Hotel.

'That was a bit formal,' Harry said quietly when in the back of the cab. 'Poor *Rooky,* he seems to be squashed by his family.'

'I'm glad I don't have to do that again, it was like a dinner party with PaPa and Mother.'

It was still early when they arrived at the hotel. Harry rolled a joint and smoked it on the balcony outside their room, he needed something to relax with and look ahead to the journeys ahead. Lucy found Donald, the Canadian, to tell him they were leaving the next morning before she went early to bed.

Part of Lucy's Diary.

Every country we go to is so different. Now in Iran, I find the contrast between the rich and poor outstanding, and difficult to understand. Why can the women be made to wear burqas that cover their whole body and faces. Is it just a religious thing or is it a male domination? I see them always walking two steps behind their man. Never in front or alongside. I certainly could not suffer peeking through a little net window over my eyes and covering from head to toe in what can look like a sack. Do they wear colourful clothes underneath, have pretty underwear? It must be so hot. Then the rich women wear the latest fashions from Paris and have expensive furs. They all seem to have a hankering after America, and all things American, which is odd since they have such a fantastic ancient culture.

It was good meeting up with Farrokh, and his parents. Good to see another side of the Iranian culture. Poor Farrokh, I feel so sorry for him. He obviously has very little freedom away from his father and mother. I could see he was envious of us and wanted freedom. I am so lucky to be travelling like we are, with my Harry, we are free.

The tummy bug I have just had was as everyone described, horrible. So often the toilets are disgusting, there is never any water. Now I am feeling better, and it is good to be able to wash my hair, get all the dust and grime off.

Billy and Bert were great characters, thank God they were with us when those bandits came over the hill.

I don't know what would have happened if it was just Harry and me. They would have robbed us, taken us as hostages, even killed us. I can't even think about it. I was so scared.

Harry must never take hallucinogenic drugs again. It was so scary, he didn't know where he was, what was going on. Was he trying to say something to me, about our relationship? I do love him but having a close relationship and living together all the time, day and night can be difficult.

I have got some quite good sketches and paintings now. I must remember to get some more white and silver paint. I've used it all up. Cappridocia was brilliant, and to meet with Donna, she is such a good person, I know we will always be close friends. The letter she gave to us was obviously written from her heart.

I am happy she feels inspired to take up working again, she will make a good nurse. She is always helping others.

It inspired us to bond with someone who has the same approach to life as we do.

Tehran and Mashhad.
East Iran June 1971

"It always seems impossible, until it is done"

After omelette and tea, they found Donald had packed his rucksack and was waiting in the lobby for them.

He said, 'The doctor won't be coming with us. Two other travellers have come down with some infection. They are in a homestay just nearby. He wants to treat them.'

'That's a shame, we can't wait. We'll have to go without him.'

The pollution in the city was even worse that morning. The sky was a grey, yellow colour, the fog so thick the sun wasn't shining through. The cloud of smog had spread beyond the city into the suburbs.

Harry found it difficult to find the road going east, even with Donald sitting next to him with a street map of the city. Eventually, at a junction, they saw a sign in Persian:

'روشم روشم'. Donald jumped down from the camper, with the map in his hand. There was a small garage workshop across the road. With gesticulation, arm waving and pointing he returned.

'They say that is the road to Mashhad, and it is nine hundred and ten kilometres. They asked if we had good tyres. I imagine they wanted to sell us a spare set.'

'I hope that doesn't mean the road is terrible. On the map it shows one road going round to the north, and one going more direct. I have no idea which one this is.'

'It looks as if it goes to the east, that's where we are going, isn't it? So, we take this one.' Donald seemed to dictate which route they took, not having a clue that this was the ancient, rough road.

They set off, rough tarmac surface for the first ten miles, then sand and stones. The landscape was a flat wild desert, with misty, blue mountains in the distance. Brown sand stretched to the horizon. The only signs of habitation they saw until the midafternoon were black Kurdish tents. Lucy thought it was reminiscent of the Arabian nights. The sand, gravel and rock road was corrugated by heavy lorries, that travelled at a fast steady speed from the top of each corrugation without dropping into the dip between. Harry, who was still at the wheel found that matching their speed shook the camper to pieces. 'We will just wreck the vehicle in no time, I have to go much slower.'

He found the right speed, much slower, between twenty and thirty miles an hour, but it was still very rough. The suspension was banging and squeaking. They were all worried if the camper could take the rough beating. At times the only way they judged where the road ran across the desert was the slight difference in the texture of the dust and the truck tyre marks.

They came to a group of buildings, mud bricks the same colour as the desert, and flat roofs.

'This is a caravanserai,' said Donald. 'There are a number of them at even distances along the road. It shows on the map as a 'c'. Looking now at the map, I think we are taking the road that goes along the '*Dasht-e-Kavir*,' the salt desert.' He was trying to understand the key to the map that was written in Persian. 'The map shows it as a vague dotted white line, not a red one like a highway. It does show it going all the way to Mashhad.' He was trying to justify his earlier decision that they should take this road.

Lucy said, 'We've got to stop here, at his caravanserai. I've had enough for one day.'

The caravanserai was the usual square courtyard inside high walls. There was evidence of a charcoal fire where kebabs were daily to be cooked.

Once they had settled down, Harry said, 'I suppose we have to carry on this road, rather than now turn back to Tehran to find the smooth one.'

Donald said, 'Never turn back, just keep on truckin'!' He found an alcove to lay out his sleeping bag. Harry and Lucy settled down in the camper after a simple meal of kebabs they cooked themselves, and bread.

They were on the road again before sunrise. The music was at full volume.

'Here Comes the Sun.' They sang along to the familiar words as the sun rose in front of them through the early morning mist.

The road was still rough, with stones, rocks, gravel and sand. It was hot and very dusty. They hit a swarm of locusts or flies that splattered the windscreen. It was an excuse to stop, scrape them off, have drinks of water and stretch their legs. There was nothing around, no other passenger vehicles, just occasional passing lorries kicking up a cloud of dust that followed them for a mile or more.

It was in the heat of the day that they had the first puncture. It was not as difficult to change as the previous one in the mountains of Turkey, Harry had had practice and now had experience on how to do it. But now they had no spare. It was very hot, the white sun burned from a bleached sky. Mirages wavered and hovered in the distance. Dust devils chased and twisted across the sand and rocks. Donald said, 'This is called the salt desert, I think it is more like the desert of death.' That comment was not well received.

Harry quoted 'Only fools and English men go out in the midday sun.'

'Yeh! You are the English men, I am the fool,' was Donald's response.

'There is a mark here on the map that is another serai. It is quite close.' It was just a few miles away, in a small village called Semnan. There was a repair shop attached to a filling station and a very busy tyre dealer. They were not the only ones to have a blowout. There were three other vehicles having repairs done. They were persuaded to buy a second spare wheel and tyre by the repair man. He explained that the road ahead was even worse and they would probably need both before the next stop.

Lucy said, 'We have to stop here, I can't take any more of the dust and heat this afternoon.' They set up camp in the caravanserai as before. They found a place in the shade. It was a fraction cooler than out on the road. Lucy prepared lunch of tinned sardines and fresh unleavened flatbread. As it cooled in the late afternoon, Donald and Lucy went off walking around the serai and the small village, looking for some fresh food.

'I saw a little shop with local craft looking things as we drove into the village. Maybe I can buy a few things to sell later on.' Said Lucy when they got back to '*Forget-me-not*'.

Harry was sceptical. 'Best wait till we are in a bigger market.'

Donald, showing off his expertise said, 'Don't buy stuff here, no way, it is too expensive.'

Again the next morning they were on the road early. They had been told it was no better further on, in fact much worse. They wanted to make as much progress to Mashhad.

There were steep drops down into gullies where they presumed flood waters from snowmelt ran. They were now dry but littered with very large boulders. It was difficult to find a route through, and to climb up the side back to the road. They approached some buildings that were not marked on the map. The rough road bumped up onto smooth tarmac, obviously recently laid, there was a roundabout, with green grass, street lamps and newly laid roads leading off the roundabout. The houses lining the road were newly built, but unoccupied. After a hundred or so meters the tarmac stopped, and they bumped down onto the unmade road.

'What's that all about?' exclaimed Harry. 'That's so weird just stuck out here in the middle of nowhere.'

The others agreed, it was very confusing.

An hour or two later, they came to another roundabout, with the same new roads and buildings. Lucy, whose turn it was to drive, stopped. 'We just have to have a look around, this is more than weird.'

They wandered around the false and phoney village, not understanding why it was there. It looked just like an abandoned film set.

Before they carried on Lucy made some more sardine sandwiches. She insisted they all took a long drink of water from their bottled supply.

It was in the mid-afternoon when they had the next tyre blow out. Harry could see the tyre was ruined, it had a split across the inside wall. The routine of fitting a new wheel was now familiar to them, but this time the jack just sank into the soft sand. They made a small mountain of sand under the wheel, but it sank again, and this time slid to one side, trapping it and making it impossible to lift out. The full weight of the rear of the camper was resting on the jack. It could easily bend creating a dangerous and impossible situation. They had no way of lifting the camper to safely remove the jack.

Harry sat in the sand to light a cigarette, Lucy brought out more water for them to drink, and Donald stood alongside the road, looking in both directions for a lorry.

After about an hour in the hot sun, he shouted that he could see the dust trail of one approaching. The lorry pulled up near them in a cloud of dust and a hiss of air brakes.

A short man with a round, smiling face, and a round belly jumped down. He was dressed in Western sports clothes, an outsized blue polo shirt with an American football logo blazed across the front, oily grey jogging pants and an embroidered pillbox hat. He had black hair, greying at the temples, an apology for a moustache and no beard. He wore an unusually tight necklace of tiny cowry beads on a red cord.

'OK! Looks like you have a problem,' he said, without introductions, as he got on his hands and knees to look under the camper. 'This happens many times, especially around here. The sand is very soft. I will help you.' With no more comments, he went back to the lorry and returned with two wooden planks and a long metal pole.

'What we do is we three men lift the back of the van. This young lady lies on the ground with the metal pole to carefully push the jack away. We can put the van down, rescue the jack, and place the wood boards with the jack on top. We can then change the wheel without sinking.' He looked around to check if his instructions were understood. 'If the jack is bent or broken, we have a real problem, I only have one for lifting big lorry wheels.

'Now I am going to teach you some Persian. One, Two, Three, Four: *yek, do, se, charah.*

'We three men lift the back when I count to *charah*, the young lady pushes the jack away. She must be very careful to keep clear of our work, it is dangerous for her.'

The whole operation went without a hitch.

As they rested and got their breath back, Lucy opened the small kitchen in the rear of *Forget-me-not* to get some drinking water. The lorry driver looked in. 'That is very neat, did you make it?' He turned to Donald.

'No, this is not mine, it belongs to Lucy and Harold, I'm just hitching a ride.'

Harry introduced them all. The lorry driver said his name was Rashid. 'I am a Turkoman, my country is north from here. But I was born in Iran.'

'How do you speak such good English?' Lucy asked.

'I also speak good German. When I was younger, I drove international lorries from Hamburg to south Iran for a German company supplying equipment to the oil fields. After some years, when I had made enough money I bought this lorry, got married and now stay in Iran. I do short deliveries all over this country.'

They eventually changed the wheel, using the wooden planks so the jack did not sink into the ground.

'This is finished.' Rashid indicated the split tyre. 'But I see you have an extra spare. You may well need it, this road is a killer for small vehicles like yours. May I suggest you stop here for the night. It is a few hours to the next village and will soon be dark. I am stopping here now for the night, it is quite safe. We can look after each other.'

The three travellers agreed to stay.

They sat in a circle on the sand in the shade of Rashid's lorry. Lucy said, 'I have a couple of questions to ask you. The tents in that gipsy camp over there.' She indicated a group of black tents about a mile away in a dip in the dunes. 'They are round, all the other tents we have seen before here are a different shape. Also, what are those new villages we have passed, with a short section of new road leading to them, a grassy roundabout and street lights? Are they film sets?'

'Ha, ha! They were a fantasy of our king, Mohammad Reza Shah. He built those villages believing he could take world leaders in his helicopter to visit remote villages in the desert to tell them how advanced his country was. He would take them from Tehran and drop them into one of these places for a short time. I hope world leaders are more clever than that to believe him!' Rashid laughed so his face and belly wobbled.

'The tents over there are with gipsy or herders from my country. They are Turkoman. The tent is called *'Shāh-nāmah khargāh'* in my language. It is called a *'Yurt'* in Afghanistan, and I believe it is called *'Ger'* in Mongolian. In this part of our world, many people live in these, more people than in houses.'

Harry asked, 'What do these gypsies do? Do they just herd animals? I can see a lot of sheep or goats near their camp. Do they take them to market to sell?'

'Sometimes, it depends on the time of the year. Come, follow me, I will show you a bit closer.'

They left their vehicles, unlocked and unattended, and walked in a distant circle from the gypsy camp.

'We mustn't go close, they have big fierce dogs. That is why I know it is safe to stop on the road near them. If you look, you can now see the door to the tent, the *'Shāh-nāmah khargāh'*. They always face it away from the wind. Hanging over the door is a patterned felt. This is the name of the family. It is like in Europe you people sometimes have your name on the door.

'I am from a different family. I will show you on my lorry.'

They returned to their vehicles. 'See I have our family pattern painted on the door. No, no! Not on the rear door, that is my beautiful lady who always follows me!'

There was a good painting by airbrush of an Indian starlet, clad in a revealing sari covering the rear doors of the lorry.

On the driver's door, there was a painting of a pattern of a felt hanging, it looked similar to the ones on the tents, but a different pattern.

'OK, I am going to leave you people for the night, you will be very safe. It is good weather, no clouds and tonight no moon. The stars will be good.' Rashid gave a little bow, put his palms together, and said, looking at the setting sun. 'I must make prayers to my God. '*Shab Be Kheir*': Good night.'

Donald took control of the food for the evening. He rummaged through lockers and bags and found a fresh cabbage and some carrots. 'I will cook some mixed vegetables to have with this cold meat.' He held up a tin of ham.

'You are very practical,' said Lucy, do you cook back at home?'

'Yeh, since my girlfriend left me, I have been living on my own. One of the reasons I am out here travelling, is I got lonely.'

Whilst the food was cooking, he sat down next to Harry and rolled a joint. Harry noticed he smoked holding the reefer in a different way.

'You hold it between your second and third finger,

make a fist and pull in from the end of the fist. I just smoke it like a cigarette.'

'Yeh! This is the way we do it back home, you get a better hit, without taking in too much smoke. Try it.'

Harry did and passed the reefer back. 'That's good, more air less smoke, you take it deeper down.'

Lucy, making a pointed gesture against the smokers, took a large bottle of water to pour herself a glass full. They had supper sitting outside, away from the awning.

Harry said, 'It is such a beautiful evening, I'm going to sleep outside.' Lucy said she would as well.

'You can sleep in the camper if you wish, or we can all sleep under the stars. I know it is going to be safe if Rashid says so. What a nice fellow! He is so calm and helpful and knows so much about Iran and the world. Maybe we will get a chance to talk tomorrow morning.'

They settled down under rugs and blankets. It was already getting dark. 'Wow! Just look at all those stars, I have never seen so many.'

They gazed at the sky, transfixed by the beauty above them. Harry rolled another reefer, and he passed it to Donald.

'Are they always there? I don't see any when I'm in a city,' said Lucy.

'Yep! They are there all the time, day and night. We move through space and so do they, so they appear at different places in the sky on different months, and in different countries. I used to know the names of lots of these galaxies, I think that one like an upside 'W' is Cassiopeia,' said Donald.

Harrold filled them in with his knowledge. 'That one

is the Big Dipper, the saucepan with a handle, and two of the stars point directly to the north star, but I don't know which two. The north star always stays in the same place, that is how you find which direction to go.'

Donald finished the reefer, and lit another one, about twice the size. They were getting happily stoned.

'Look, look, there's a shooting star,' said Lucy.

'I think it's a spaceship circling the earth. It is moving quite slowly, and going directly north from south. Shooting stars are just a flash across the sky.'

Lucy said, yawning, 'My God! You two are so stoned.' She got up and climbed into a sleeping bag.

Soon Harry rolled up in a blanket, he cuddled up to Lucy, she was already asleep.

She woke up early, just before sunrise. She saw Rashid had just finished his prayers. He waved to her to come over to his lorry.

'You had good sleep?'

'Yes, great, the others are still asleep. I think they had a lot of hashish last night, looking at the stars and talking.'

'It was a good night for that, I can see you are happy travellers. I am leaving now, I have to reach my destination today. Say goodbye to your friends. Drive with care, the road is bad. We will meet again.' He put the palms of his hands together and made a small bow. Lucy did the same.

The sun woke Harry and Donald at the same time. 'Has the lorry gone?'

'Yes, he has to make the delivery today. I am surprised it didn't wake you, he left a couple of hours ago. I have made you both some tea, we have run out of coffee. And we just have some stale bread.'

'It looks as if we will have to get on the road to Mashhad then. I don't think it is too far, we should make it today so long as we don't have any more flatties.'

It didn't take too long, but because of the late start, it was mid-afternoon when they arrived.

Chapter 18

Mashhad, East Iran June 1971

"To travel is to live"

The three travellers did not know Mashhad was a religious pilgrim centre.

All the roads led in a star formation to the centre of the Holy Shrine complex. They were worried, seeing so many pilgrims on the streets, that there may not be suitable accommodation. Lucy had demanded as they entered the city, that they must find a hotel or accommodation with washing facilities. She desperately needed to wash her hair, wash all the dust, sand and grit off her body, and wash some clothes.

Donald had a note about the Hotel Nadiri. It was recommended by another traveller. It was close to the centre and one of the few places said to take in Western travellers. It did not take time to find, next to a religious artefact emporium, and several floors above a textile shop and a mini market. Behind it was a large garden, cleared for development, but newly planted with flowers and shrubs. There were two Persian ironwood trees, tulips, fritillaria, and crocus, all adding colour to the surroundings.

Attached to the back of the five-storey concrete hotel building was a small stone–built cottage. It looked old, maybe survived the recent clearing of the site of other old buildings. It had small windows and a green painted door. It was partially covered by a jasmine climber.

Harry and Lucy checked into a double room, close to the bathroom. Donald moved into a small, cheap single room. He said he would only stay one night as he wanted to push onto Afghanistan. He kindly gave Harry a fist full of notes in payment for his ride. 'That was a deal more adventure than I was expecting, pretty hairy in places.' He said, 'I guess your truck will be OK. It is a tough beast.'

They decided to find somewhere later to eat, a goodbye dinner.

They both felt relaxed having finally reached Mashhad. They discussed the past few days, hoping they would not experience more roads as bad as the one across the desert.

The evening came quickly. They still had not become used to night falling like a dark curtain, as it does the further east and south you go. They looked out across and down the street towards the Holy Shrine. It was decorated with strings of coloured fairy lights that swung in the breeze. There were fluorescent tubes hung vertically on lamp posts, bright red and green spotlights picking out parts of tall minarets, blue mosaic tiles on an entrance and golden domes over the main areas of the shrine. They could see men and women moving in the distance over marble paving. Some of the women, dressed from head to toe in black chador were sweeping courtyards with reed brooms.

Donald had spent the early evening exploring some of the bazaars. He was excited. 'There's a shop in the next street full of posteens, beautiful, embroidered sheepskin coats. Obviously from Afghanistan. And loads of jewellery with cornelians, lapis lazuli and turquoise stones. The prices looked quite high, but I know I can get stuff like that for a fraction in Kabul. The Americans just love turquoise. The native Americans have always valued them. Any cool dude in the cities now has to have a heavy turquoise ring. One of the shopkeepers trying to sell me a necklace said all the turquoise comes from Mashhad. It is the best in the world. I told him I would get some in Afghanistan.' He handed me a business card of an address in Kabul. 'This is my cousin. He will help you.'

They had an enjoyable meal of kebabs and fruit. They went over the trip across the desert once again. It was still very fresh in their minds, and they talked about Afghanistan, where to go and what to expect.

Harry and Lucy had decided to stay a few days, to recover, to have a mechanic check over *Forget-me-not,* and to look around the town of Mashhad.

Several other travellers were staying in the Hotel Nadiri, all travelling to Afghanistan. They were a lively, happy crowd who congregated in the garden for a smoke, conversation and maybe a few songs each evening. Lucy and Harry joined them. They introduced themselves, they were keen to find out more about the other travellers.

One was a large, broad shouldered man in his late twenties. He said his name was Mike. He had a squashed nose with a wart, and red tufts of hair from each nostril, black reddish bushy eyebrows, carroty straight hair. He had no beard or moustache, but mutton chop sideburns down his cheeks. His body lent forward with a slight hunchback. They soon learnt he smoked continuously on strong roll-ups when not smoking a chillum or reefer. He introduced the two girls sitting beside him.

Sue was English, she wanted to travel to Rajasthan in India to join a weaving school. 'I've just spent a year at the West Dean College in Sussex doing a weaving course.'

Lucy said. 'That's quite close to where my parents live, I did apply to go there but decided to do an art course at Brighton. It was a good decision 'cos I met my Harry there.'

'I am also interested in carpet making in Iran and Afghanistan. I've seen some here in west Iran, I particularly like kilims. They are flat-woven rugs. One shopkeeper in Zanjan said they were more original than knotted carpets. Kilims are traditionally made for the family by the women. Persian knotted carpets have been changed by big Western buyers for a hundred years or more. They demand colours and sizes to fit in with the latest interior fashions, not so kilims, they have kept traditional.'

She was dressed in a colourful jacket with different patterns in tapestry weave.

'I did this for my finals at college.' She gave a short turn showing off her jacket.

Lucy immediately went to sit beside the two girls. Harry felt a bit abandoned, and shy to talk to any of the other guests, he was very attracted to the two girls. The one that had not yet spoken was perhaps the prettiest looking girl he had seen in all the time on the trail.

Sue greeted Lucy warmly. 'I'm travelling with Gillian.' She indicated the girl sitting next to her.

'Hi, everyone calls me Gill.' She had a strong American or Canadian accent. 'I'm into dying and travelling to Jaipur in India to study the art of dyeing. I have already been to the John Thomas Dye School in LA. I then spent two years in the Philippines studying the language and some of the traditional handicrafts. I lived with the family of our home help back in my hometown. It's sort of a back-to-back reversal. Their daughter lives in LA, and I live in the Philippines. I now want to learn about indigo dyeing, and I am going on the trail with Sue to India.'

Lucy soon realised she was a big talker and liked to dominate any conversation, but she knew she could quickly get to like these two girls.

'I want to set up a business dyeing natural sheep wool in the US.' Gill had henna–dyed hair to a bright yellow orange colour, piled up in curls and plaited with beads. She was wearing a short-sleeved top made from a patchwork of many bits of denim, with shorts to match. She had well shaped, tanned legs.

Harry studied the three girls sitting close together on a bench, he wished he could join them. One of his frequent glances in their direction was met by Sue, who flashed a dazzling smile at him.

His attention was then distracted by two French men who were travelling together. Hugo had thin straggly blond hair down to his shoulders, he was clean-shaven. He had a deep bass voice.

Harry asked, 'Do you sing? you have a good sounding voice.'

'Oui, Basso,' was the reply. He had a string of beads, stones and little bones like fiddle beads a Greek would have used. He flicked them around his palm. It was obviously a talisman he believed would bring good luck and keep him safe from harm.

Harry said, 'We must get together, I play the guitar, Lucy, my girlfriend, sitting over there with those two beautiful girls can sing. We'll sit down one evening soon and have a gig.'

'Oui. A good idea, I like to sing.'

His friend introduced himself in a good English accent. 'My name is Jaque. I am with Hugo to help translate, he is French, he likes to speak only French. That can be difficult. He does understand a lot of English, but he is typically French so makes a point of speaking only French, if you understand my meaning.' He gave a Gallic shrug. 'I'm also from France, but I learned English working in a London office of lawyers as part of my degree training. I am now taking a gap year and travelling to the Far East before settling down. If you need any help with passports or visas, just ask. I'm getting good at those local laws.'

'I reckon we are OK, we have a visa stamp for Afghanistan, we don't need them for Pakistan or India.'

'Ah, yes, old colonies!' He continued, 'We travelled here in our Citroen Deux Chevaux.'

'What! In that little French car parked outside?'

'Oui, yes! It was at times difficult, on some of the steep roads. One of us had to get out and help push. But it is fun. Many people laugh at us. The problem is it has a very small engine and small tyres. Not good for rough roads. The customs men at the borders can't believe we travel like this. They never search us.'

Justin, the doctor, who they had met in Tehran came into the garden, still carrying his travel bag.

'Hi, Justin, come and join us. So, you have managed to get away from Tehran?' Harry introduced him to the others. 'Hugo and Jaque are French, they drive that little Citroen that is outside, my Lucy is over there chatting with those two gorgeous girls, you remember we met Donald in Tehran, at the same time as you. He came with us across the desert to get here. This is Mike, we all seem to be moving towards Afghanistan. We now have a whole team of professionals to help us. Justin is a doctor and Jaque is a lawyer.'

'I have just arrived by bus, this looks like a nice town. I have managed to get a tiny room here. There aren't many places to stay, are there? I would like to have a look around tomorrow, visit some of the sites.'

'That's a good idea, said Harry. 'We arrived today and want to stay here a few days. Maybe we could get a party together, get a guide to show us the best bits. We could do that tomorrow.'

'How are your patients in Tehran, have you made them better?'

'Yeh, just the usual tummy bugs, they're OK now.'

Mike said, 'I've been here for almost a week now, I haven't had much of a look around. Nor have I yet to meet the illusive, mystery gipsy palm reader who lives over there in the little cottage. There were loads of stories about her from travellers who were staying here when I arrived and have now moved on.'

'A palm reader! I would like to know what's going to happen to me!'

'Yeh! She does fortune telling, palm reading and tarot cards. She also tries to get into everyone's pants. She is sex mad! Old, but very attractive though.'

'Sounds like someone just for you, Harry.' Donald poked him in the ribs.

Mike continued, 'The story has also gone around, and there were plenty of stories, that she is a world traveller. She had travelled around South America for two years, Brazil, Argentina, Bolivia, and Chile. It is said she likes places with lots of ancient cultures, but now lives here in Mashhad. She has been on many pilgrimages, to Santiago de Compostela in Spain. She said she walked from the French border right across Spain, a long way. Apparently, if you carry a conch, a type of shell, people will give you food and lodging for free. She has also been to Syria and the Dead Sea, and of course the pyramids in Egypt.'

'But she doesn't come out to join in with us travellers?' said Harry.

'No, she doesn't, no one who is staying here now has ever seen her. Maybe she will pop out one day soon.'

Harry changed the subject. 'It's still early, we can have some music, I'll go inside and get my guitar.'

So the evening continued, some good singing, storytelling, and smoking hashish from Mike's chillum. It was quite late when they packed up and went off to bed.

The next morning, Mike was in the garden. 'I've got a guide to come with us, he speaks good English, and he is free. He doesn't charge anything. He is paid by the council to guide tourists. We may need to buy him lunch, or just tea. We'll see. He'll be ready in about an hour.'

They met up with Ishmael outside the tourist office. He was a charming young Persian. He explained that he had done his compulsory time in the army and got this job with the help of his uncle who had something to do with the town council.

Ishmael started by telling some of the history of the city. It grew from the legend of Emam Reza who was poisoned in 817 and buried in the *Haram-e Motahhar-e Emam Reza*. 'Quite a mouthful, but it is the Holy Shrine of Mashhad. The Shrine is a city in itself. Two mosques, over ten *Eivans,* they are the high arched doorways that are covered in elaborate, coloured mosaics, two of them are gold. There are learning colleges, libraries, a post office, museums and a guest house. All visitors are welcome, including infidels, like you, but you must dress properly, and show great respect.' He looked around the six tourists. 'Not bad, but the girls must cover their shoulders and arms. I can guide you to most of the buildings, there are some that non-muslims must not enter, but I will direct you. You can take photos but be discrete and sensible. This is a very holy place.'

They continued as a crocodile, with Ishmael leading into the shrine complex. He explained the development of the shrine over the centuries, how it had been destroyed in religious wars, by invading armies, and then rebuilt.

Once they had admired the amazing blue mosaics, the towering gold domes and the intricate decorations of the mosque's interiors, Mike raised the question of lunch.

Ishmael agreed to take them to the best, cheap restaurant. He was happy to be treated by the visitors.

The group sat round a low table covered in a carpet. Harry managed to sit between the two girls, Gill and Sue. He quickly launched into his chat up mode. He was sparkling, remembering his one liner jokes. Then he felt a sharp kick on his ankle. Mike, sitting opposite him made a small nod to down the table. Lucy looked daggers in his direction. He stopped mid–joke. To his relief, Justin asked a question. 'You said there are learning colleges by the shrine, are there any for medical learning and research?'

Ishmael replied, 'Yes, many of the famous Iranian doctors have studied here over several centuries.'

Jacque asked a question. 'This shrine is Shiite, what is the difference between Shiite and Sunni Muslims?'

Ishmael looked up at the ceiling. 'How long have you got? Any Muslim will talk to you for days about our religion. It started almost two thousand years ago, there were murders amongst the descendants of Mohammad. This led to a major split. Here in Iran, the Shiites form the majority, especially here in Mashhad where the tomb of *Emam Reza* lies. However, throughout the world Sunni Muslims are the majority. Shiites follow the descendants of *Ali,* the Prophet's son-in-law.'

The group were satisfied with this brief history lesson. They left the shrine and straggled back to the hotel. Lucy kept her distance from Harry showing she was angry with his approach to the two girls.

Chapter 19

Mashhad, East Iran June 1971

"We have nothing to lose, and the world to see"

When the evening came, they once again gathered in the garden. Harry was very keen to play some music. He asked Hugo to sing along to some deep south blues ballads that suited his bass voice.

Harry knew a wide range, and with the strike of the first few chords, Hugo drew a deep breath to start singing, first Janis Joplin's *"Cry Baby"*, then they launched into Jimi Hendrix's *"Red House"*, finally Muddy Waters, *"Got My Mojo Working"*. That got everyone on their feet, dancing and singing along to a few of the words that they knew.

A local merchant, dressed in baggy pantaloons, white shirt, with a colourful sash across his shoulders and a matching turban wheeled in a cart supported on three bicycle wheels. He carried trays of local mezze to sell. All local Iranian food, yellow split peas, cardamom and cumin, tiny glass bowls of cinnamon tea. Limes, rose water and orange blossom water. Tempting bowls of nuts and seeds, a platter of fresh fruit, a tray of tiny chickpeas and sweet cookies. He did a roaring trade.

There were grumbles from some that there was no beer, but that was made up with a good supply of excellent hashish.

Several new travellers arrived in the garden, it became a great party. Some of the new arrivals were in a group travelling on a minibus who had found accommodation in another homestay on the edge of the town.

A tall Scandinavian man with locks of corn–coloured hair plaited with beads joined in the music with a harmonica. His girlfriend, Astra, also Scandinavian had a beautiful voice that melded well with Hugo's bass. Lucy joined in, at first shyly, but then brought in new harmonies with the Scandinavian girl, Astra.

Later, the travellers were having a break from the music, sitting, lying, and lounging on wooden benches covered with rugs, cushions, and embroidered textiles under the trees in the shadows around candles and lamps. The green door to the cottage opened, they all turned in unison towards the figure that approached.

She carried a stick, a long staff, carved with twisting mythical beasts and snakes with an ornate silver top, which she gripped with long fingers, each one decorated with three or four rings.

She stopped in the centre of the circle. Her hair was bound into a knot with a long velvet ribbon, a shade of purple that matched the sash around her waist. It cascaded down her back, some curled tendrils framing her face. It was black with streaks of silver running through it.

She wore a full-length velvet dress of deep burgundy and purple, over which she had a long waistcoat embroidered in coloured sequin beads. There were patterns of elaborate mythical beasts that glinted in the light with red eyes.

She stood in the middle of the circle, commanding, like an actor on stage about to deliver a soliloquy, supporting her straight, upright posture with the ornate staff. The light from the one electric light bulb illuminated her sharp chin and sculptured cheekbones. Her eyes, shadowed with deep purple mascara, slowly swept around the gathering, picking up on each individual. All the conversations stopped as each person was drawn in and absorbed by her commanding presence. Some met her gaze, some looking away timidly.

Her dark grey eyes looked into the very soul of each person individually. Time seemed to have stopped.

Without speaking a word, she turned, and walked like a statue supported by her staff, tapping the ground to the green door. There she stopped and again surveyed the group with piercing eyes, she turned and went into her cottage.

The travellers sat or stood in dumb silence, each trying to understand the event.

Eventually, someone said, trying to break the mood, 'Will she say anything if she reads your palm, or are you supposed to guess?'

'Looks more like a witch than a palm reader, I certainly won't go to visit her.'

Harry looked towards the closed green door with a certain longing in his eye. Still holding his guitar, fingers ready to play a cord he declared, 'Some more music, I think.' He strummed a few cords. 'This was written by Aretha Franklin, a great blues singer. You will not have heard this version by Carol King, "*You make me feel like a natural woman*". It is just out, Lucy and I have been rehearsing over the past few weeks. I am going to ask Lucy to sing, but please join in.'

Lucy was joined by Astra, together they wove in and out of successful harmonies. The Scandinavian tuned in with his mouth organ, another beat the rhythm on a wooden chair.

It ended up as another late night, with plenty of smoking, music, chatting and laughter. All the while in the back of Harry's mind was the look Alison had given him when she stood amongst them. There was a mystery, an excitement, an unknown!

The next morning Lucy said she was going out with Astra, Sue and Gillian. They wanted to go to a bazaar on the edge of the town to look at indigo dyeing and a weaving school for carpets and kilims.

She said they should be back in the afternoon, so told Harry to look after himself.

He moped in his room for a while, then decided the inevitable. He would pluck up courage to visit the palm reader, Alison, in her cottage in the garden. He was curious but also unexpectedly quite afraid and concerned about what she would foretell.

He dressed in a clean white cotton shirt, an Indian style with no collar, and clean shorts.

He went to the garden and nervously tapped on the green door. It was opened by Alison. She was wearing different clothes from the evening before. A voluminous

240

kaftan printed with multi-coloured stars and a moon. She wore colourful shawls around her waist, with a matching bandana on her head.

'I was expecting you to call today.' She indicated for Harry to come into her cottage, smiled showing a small gap in her front teeth.

The room was highly decorated with printed cloths of Hindu deities, three strings of Tibetan prayer flags across the room, and a strong smell of musk and patchouli from smoking joss sticks in every corner. Harry paused, looking at the details in the room. It was very exotic, very crowded. An ornate parasol hung upside down from the ceiling.

'Come in and sit down, I've been observing you since the day you arrived.' She looked up with a glance to the bed loft in the corner of the room. 'I see you are a charismatic and powerful person. The other travellers all look towards you. I observe all the travellers through my secret window'.

Harry looked up to the bed loft, it looked comfortable, covered in more exotic textiles. There was a small window, partly covered by a creeper, with a view across the garden.

In the middle of the room there was a circular table, covered with a cloth decorated with a large compass and astrological symbols. Two chairs were facing each other.

'Please sit down.' Harry took one of the seats, Alison sat opposite.

'First, I'm going to read your palm, if I feel there are any idiosyncrasies or variants from the path, I will study the Tarot cards. Are you happy?'

Harry was still in a state of confusion, he nodded 'yes.'

Alison gently took both his hands. Hers were warm and

soft. She started caressing his palms and wrists, exploratory to start with, soon with a sensual touch. Her caresses moved up to his forearms. Harry became aware that this was more than looking at the lines of his hands as he had expected. He withdrew them to his side of the table.

'Please don't be shy, don't be afraid.' She spoke in a quiet husky voice, hardly more than a whisper. She rolled her 'R's' with a slight West Country accent. She reached to take his hands again and traced the palm of each with the tip of a fingernail. It tickled, Harry felt excited, sexually. Alison looked deep into his eyes, hers unblinking with grey centres circled by deep purple. Harry's mood intensified, he noticed how attractive she was and despite the difference in their ages, he became sexually aroused.

'I feel you have *Air Hands*, they are rectangular palms with long fingers. Dry skin.' She dug a little harder with her fingernail. 'This confirms the impression I have already gathered of you. You are sociable, sometimes talkative and witty but you can easily turn cold and withdrawn. You are comfortable with solving problems that are intangible and difficult. You like to do things in different ways to the normal.'

She looked intensively at each hand in turn. 'I can tell you are right-handed. Your dominant hand reveals how your personality and character are actualised in practice, together your hands reveal how you are utilising these potentials in this lifetime.

'However, it is important to remember there is no proven scientific basis for palm reading. It is how you believe in the interpretation, and keep in mind that both palm lines and your life will change with time.

'I will study your dominant hand first. This top line, your lifeline, is long and slightly curved. It means you freely express your emotions and feelings and at the moment you are content with your love life. The length of your lifeline has no relationship with how long you will live. It reflects your health and physical vitality.'

Alison's other hand moved away from the table, slipped onto Harry's knee and started a gentle caress. He did not stop her.

'You have a long headline which joins onto your lifeline. It is also curved which means you have a lot of enthusiasm. However, it looks as if you have had an accident with your hand. A deep cut across the palm. Did you once cut yourself?'

'No, never, I have other cuts but never there.'

She took his left hand. 'This is interesting, you don't have this same line on both hands. On your dominant hand it cuts through your life line, head line and your love line. They all become broken and a little twisted towards the end of the line. But there are no little circles in the line. Those always mean there is a serious illness. I need to read more, it could mean that at some stage you meet a disaster that will change the direction of your life. It could be an accident or illness. But if there is a problem, I will discover more soon.'

Harry looked shocked, he withdrew his hands and looked closely at them trying to understand what she had seen. Alison's hand caressed more and advanced to his thigh above his knee.

'I will read more, don't worry, this is not a direct science.' She repeated and took his hand back into one of hers, again caressing and touching the back, palm and wrists, as well as his thigh.

'Your fate line is strong and deep, this confirms to me that it is the character of your life, but on both your left and right hands it does divide. That can mean your life will change through no force from yourself. Do not worry, this is seen in many people. It is the natural way of life and how we move through it.'

She closed his hand into a fist to look at the lines on the side by his little finger. She did not comment, she could see no marriage or love lines. She knew each line or groove is thought to represent a different marriage, and deeper and longer grooves represent stronger or longer-lasting relationships. There were none. She opened his hand looking at his palm again. 'The heart line here,' she traced the line below his fingers with a fingernail, 'simply shows your love style. How you like to relate to other people, and how you wish they'd relate to you. Ideally, everyone learns from their heart line that it's not about how they are accepted, but how you accept yourself.'

Her hand crept further up his leg, to under his shorts. He felt an inevitable hard coming on. He felt embarrassed.

Alison continued, 'Your Venus mount, that is this one under your thumb, indicates a predisposition for hedonism, promiscuity and the need for instant gratification.' Her hand slid further up into his shorts. She could feel his erect penis.

'Come, I can read you are a great lover. My bed is waiting for both of us.'

Harry's mind was racing around in circles, he sensed it would be an unforgettable experience. To have sex with an older, experienced woman. With both hands, she helped him from the chair and started moving towards the sleeping loft. Was he going to resist or follow? He was following, his hand reached around her waist, up to one pendulous breast. On the bottom step of the loft, an image of Lucy crossed his mind. He was so confused. It was her he loved so deeply. He could not do this, be so unfaithful. He turned away. He had such a hard-on he could hardly walk out through the green door, he sat outside on a bench to wait for things to quieten down. Alison did not say a word, she gently closed the door behind him.

Harry was confused, his mind raced through the events that had just happened. What was it all about? What did it mean?

He needed time to catch up. To think it through, quietly.

He sat in the garden. He took off his shirt. It was a beautiful clear sunny day. He sat in the partial shade of a mulberry tree and tried to relax. He was all the time nervously aware that he was being watched by Alison through the tiny window, partially covered with the jasmine climber.

He rolled a large reefer, his best hashish. He decided to write in his diary.

Part of Harry's Diary

Oh! My God. What's going on? My mind is racing around like I don't know what. I can hardly write my hand is shaking so much.

What was that woman about? Does she do that with everyone who comes into her room? Try to get laid by them? Is her palm reading just an excuse?

I am not sure she seemed that genuine. She was more interested in getting me going than reading my future. And what did she mean by what she said about all my lines? She said I'm going to have some sort of disaster. But then she said don't believe in any of it, it's never exact.

I can feel her eyes on me now. Looking through that little window. If I move round this tree a bit, she won't be able to watch me.

He reflected for a long time, just looking into the distance.

I must make sure I am especially nice and loving with Lucy. She means everything to me.

We've been getting on well, especially well since we are together most of the time in Forget-me-not. We agree on where to go, when to stop, what to eat.

I'm not going to tell her about Alison, but she is clever enough to guess. I'll just have to blag it.

I reckon the trip is going well. We are doing most things that we wanted to do before leaving England. We are meeting lots of great people. Finding exciting places to stay. We should try to get off the trail more and explore more. Get to remote places.

In the next few days, we will be travelling in Afghanistan. A new country, with new people, new language, new currency, and new places, and I am sure we will find some very remote places there.

I can't wait. It's going to be the most exciting bit of our journey up to now. Everybody we meet coming the other way, from India, say it's a fantastic place, fantastic people.

Looking back over the past few weeks we have done so much. Ever since we left the cave in Cappadocia, which was fantastic, we have done so much. Everything has been good except for the mistake I made with taking some acid. Not a good trip!

The mountains in east Turkey were spectacular. Seeing Mount Arafat, it looked such a perfect shape with snow on the top.

Oh yes! Lucy got sick. Not good. I am amazed I haven't had a bad tummy bug yet. Tehran was strange. So much of it trying to be American. I feel sorry for Farrokh, stuck with his parents in that secure compound, being driven into a job he doesn't want to do.

The mistake of taking the road across the desert was a good mistake, it was tough, but we made it. And now in Mashhad. Good crowd of people here, but that woman! I must get her out of my head. It's not good!

So, what next? The big thing is going to Afghanistan, but before that, we need to have Forget-me-not checked over by a mechanic. I'll organise that this afternoon. We need to check our money is OK. I don't know how much we are spending, but I reckon we are good for where we are, and how much there is to go. We must be over halfway to Kathmandu now. Rolly would know exactly. I'll send him a card as soon as we get to Herat.

It's Lucy's money. She must know how much we have. It's depressing when we see travellers like us begging on the streets. Trying to get money from the locals, and from tourists. I've heard that some travellers sell some of their valuables, like cameras and watches. I don't want to do that, anyway, I haven't got a camera. Also, some guys sell their blood. That seems dodgy with hygiene and stuff.

The most important thing of all is Lucy. Keep us close together. Keep our love going. I must work harder on it. Perhaps think up some ideas.

Ideas are jumping around in my head. Maybe I should go to see another fortune teller and get a different viewpoint. I'll wait until we get to India, there are supposed to be plenty there. The Indians have their fortunes told all the time. In fact, most important decisions are made after seeing a fortune teller.

Chapter 20

Mashhad, East Iran June 1971

"Life is short, but the world is wide."

Harry was still sitting under the mulberry tree, thinking about the events of the morning, his diary open at the last page he wrote, when Lucy came back in the middle of the afternoon.

Excited and enthusiastic after her visit to the bazaar with the other three girls, she said a quick 'Hi' and then straight away went out for lunch in the street with her new friends.

He realised he had not eaten, just smoked a couple of strong reefers throughout the morning. He went out into the street to buy a samosa pastry, and a fizzy drink, then went to the little store next to the hotel to buy a small box of Turkish delight as a treat for Lucy.

When she came back later, she was bubbling with enthusiasm. Harry sat under the mulberry tree, still feeling confused and morose. He was on his own, none of the other travellers were around, and he thought some of them had already moved on towards Afghanistan. He was hoping to ask one or two of them to share a ride in *Forget-me-not*. Maybe help with the cost of fuel.

He decided now was the time to have a heart-to-heart talk with Lucy. Sort out a few things in his muddled mind.

He gave her the box of Turkish Delight, wrapped in a stripy paper bag. She picked out one of the small sugary cubes and popped it into her mouth. She licked the fine grains of sugar off her lips.

Harry stood up, clasped both her hands and said, out of the blue, completely unrehearsed, 'Will you marry me?'

Lucy looked at him askance for several moments. 'No. No!'

Harry sat down in disbelief. What did she mean, 'NO?' He was convinced the palm reader had implied he would marry soon, and to Lucy. How could she just bluntly say 'NO?'

He buried his head in his hands. What did it all mean? Surely, she loved him? They had been together now for over two years.

Maybe she was just being clever, using her posh Sussex school education. A Mr. Collins moment. *It is usual with young ladies to reject the addresses of the man whom they secretly mean to accept.* He remembered the phrase from *Pride and Prejudice.* It was the book he had to study at school for his English exam, years before.

Why was he thinking of that? He could not understand what was happening. The whole day had been one of confusion.

Lucy stood looking at him for a long moment, shrugged her shoulders, then turned on her heel to go back to their room, carrying the box of Turkish delight.

It was about an hour later she returned to the garden. She sat down next to Harry, gave him a big hug, and rested her head on his shoulder. They said nothing for a long while. Eventually, she whispered in his ear, 'I love you'. They fell silent again. It was very quiet in the garden, just the distant noise of traffic in the town. Harry could feel the eyes of Alison watching them through the small window. It made him shudder. At the set hour the muezzin started calling from the top of minuets for the early evening prayers.

Lucy stood up, 'I really do love you. But it is too soon for us to get married. Anyway, where can we get married in this town? There are no churches, not even an embassy. And what would Mother say? She has already got the hat, I guess. They wouldn't allow it.'

Harry shuffled his feet in the dust. 'I suppose so. It was silly of me to ask.'

Lucy looked across the garden at the green door of the cottage. 'I know you went to see the palm reader, this morning. I can see it all over your face. I suppose she said she could read in your love line or lifeline you would marry very soon.'

Harry glanced again up at the little window, certain they were being watched. He didn't deny his visit, nor did he say what had happened.

Lucy announced, 'I'm going to see her now. Have my fortune told.' She started to walk to the green door.

'Do be careful. She is not what she appears. Don't take any notice of what she says.' Harry called to her retreating figure.

Lucy knocked on the green door. It was instantly opened. Alison was no doubt watching the garden and saw Lucy approach. 'Come in, I was expecting you to call.'

Her reaction to the decorated room was very similar to Harry's, she glanced around noting the ethnic hangings and a strong smell of joss sticks burning.

'Please sit down. I know you have come to me to have your palm read.' She didn't mention that Harry had visited her earlier that day.

Alison went through a similar routine of examining Lucy's hands, without the sensual touching.

She described each line, the shape of her hands, and the importance of each. She talked about Harry and how much they loved each other, how close their relationship appeared to be. She stopped talking when she found the line cutting across Lucy's hand, similar to the one on Harry's hand. She noted it cut through the life line, head line and love line in the same way. She studied this for a long time, without saying a word only remarking, 'This is most interesting.'

She pushed Lucy's hands back across the table, giving the impression the palm reading session was over.

'Well, what about my fortune, my future? What is going to happen to me?'

Alison repeated what she had told Harry. 'The art of palm reading is not an exact science. It is just possible suggestions. I can see that you are very happy and enjoying life. You are enjoying travelling. But there may be changes ahead. That is the natural course of every life.'

Lucy left the cottage, she straight away found Harry. 'That was a load of nonsense, she just made up rubbish, and then said more or less none of it was true. She is no palm reader, she just lives in that sweet little cottage in a make-believe world.'

'Yep,' Harry replied, still feeling some emotions but hiding them well. 'I think we need to leave this place, find our feet, get on the road again and forget about her. There are so many other good people around, we don't need to mix with the likes of her.

'Let's go to get some of those nice kebabs in yoghurt from that place just round the corner and do some planning.'

They sat at a greasy plastic table on plastic chairs balanced on the narrow pavement outside the kebab shop.

Harry opened up the road map of eastern Iran and a notebook. 'It looks quite easy to get to the Afghan border, then to Herat. But it will be more than one day. We've to get *Forget-me-not* checked over by a mechanic. That won't take long, there is a guy just around the corner. We just need to get a bit of food and water for one night. Sort out paying for the hotel. If there are any of the travellers we've got to know, say good-bye, or ask them if they want a lift. I guess the border will be closed at night, but open every day, unless it's a holiday, like it was getting into Iran. I know we still have plenty of time left on our visas for here, and we're all fixed up for Afghanistan. So that'll be OK.'

'I'll be happy to be on the road again.'

'We need to look at all our money. I have no idea how much we have spent, or how much we have left. Afghanistan will be cheap, but we're spending a lot staying in places like this. We've got *Forget-me-not* to live in. We need to do more camping and looking after ourselves.'

Lucy opened a new page in the notebook. She started listing columns of figures. 'This is a very rough guess of how much money we still have with us in cash and traveller cheques. It certainly should see us for a month, especially if we camp most of the time. I've still got about two grand in my bank account back in England. When we get to Kabul, I can ask Papa to send some of it to us.'

'OK! We still have a few rials of Iranian money left, we can pay the hotel with those, pay a mechanic, and get a bit of food and fuel. Any left we hope we can change it into Afghan currency, whatever that is, when we cross the border. It would be good if we could get a couple of guys to come with us to help with the costs of fuel.

'That's a plan. I'll go to pay for our room, you go to the mechanic and book him for first thing tomorrow morning. Hopefully, we can get off by midday.'

Harry came back to their room after just a few minutes to pick up the keys to the camper. 'He says he can do it now. These places never seem to shut, they work all hours. I'll stay with him to make sure he does a proper job and doesn't nick anything.'

The next morning breakfast was the usual omelette with flat bread and a pot of tea. The owner of the hotel, Mohammed, said he was sad to see them leave, they had helped make it a good place with the parties they had each evening in the garden. He asked them to recommend his hotel to other travellers. When asked, he told them most of the crowd that had been staying there had left the previous afternoon on the public bus to Taybad, close to the border.

They were finishing their tea, talking about getting provisions and packing their stuff. They noticed a guy sitting outside alone on the terrace, having a pot of tea, and reading a book. Lucy thought she recognised him from somewhere. She went over to him and introduced herself.

'Yes, we've met before, my name is Colin. We met in a cave in Cappadocia, you were talking to two nuns. You very kindly introduced me to your friend who found me a cave to live in for free. It saved me a lot of money. If you remember I'm travelling to Calcutta to join a Christian group.'

Lucy then remembered him, she called Harry over. 'We are leaving this morning to go to Herat in Afghanistan. If you would like a lift, we have space in our camper van. We'll be camping for one night somewhere off the road.'

'Oh! That would be great, I have no money. I was robbed a few weeks ago. They took almost everything I had. I have been trying to contact my church in England to send me some money but no luck yet.'

'We want to get on the road soon, I'm sure you haven't got much luggage. Can we meet here in about an hour's time?'

'No problem, this is going to be such a help, you are both such good people. Bless you!'

It took a long time to get organised and on the road. Finally, when they got going, it was easy driving with clear road signs to the border, and the road condition was good. The landscape was a flat, sandy desert with little vegetation, just small, scrubby trees. Harry and Lucy felt happy to be on the road again, away from the problems they encountered in Mashhad. The music was turned up loud, a couple of bootleg cassettes bought in Mashhad, *Good as Gone by The Incredible String Band* and *Kathmandu by Cat Stevens*. 'That is very appropriate,' said Colin, comfortably sitting in the back surrounded by the luggage and provisions. 'I would love to go to Nepal, but my money will not go that far, I just need to go to Calcutta, find my feet there, and then maybe be able to explore more.'

'You are a vicar in England?' asked Lucy.

'I like to call myself a parson, it is a bit pedantic, just me being old fashioned. A parson was someone in the old days who did marriages and funerals originally, so it's a "*working preacher.*" A priest is a claim to theological hierarchy. Most protestants won't use that. A parson is really a vicar in the Anglican church which means "leader of a parish" but historically it meant someone appointed by a bishop. I have been working with our local bishop, not in any parish church. It's all quite complicated, but irrelevant these days.'

'Does that mean you could marry us?' asked Harry, not even catching Lucy's eye.

'Yes, I suppose I could, if we could find a Christian church.'

'No such luck Harry! Good try but first you have to get me to say '*Yes*''.

'I love you Lucy, I'll keep trying!'

This conversation was quickly and cleverly diverted

by Colin. They were passing a group of nomads with a caravan of camels on the edge of the road.

'I think they are Turkomen. We met a really nice guy who helped us with a puncture in the desert. He was from one of their tribes. He was not driving a camel, but a big lorry.'

Later in the afternoon they stopped at a firm, flat area away from the road to set up camp for the night. They fixed up Colin with a spare sleeping bag, his was stolen. Supper was a simple meal of tinned fish, bread and fruit, followed by a lot of talk, and some long silences as they gazed up at the star-filled sky.

Chapter 21

Herat, West Afghanistan June 1971

*"You can shake the sand from your shoes,
but it will never leave your soul"*

The morning was warm and sunny. There was no wind. Colin was sitting on a small camping stool reading. He had already prepared a large pot of tea.

'This is so beautiful and peaceful. I have sat here since before sunrise just looking out at the desert. There is no one to be seen. I always like to spend time to meditate each morning, say my prayers and read a bit of the bible.'

'Are you going to India as a missionary?' asked Lucy.

'No,' he laughed, 'We don't go around converting wild natives to the ideology they would never understand. We just gently preach the word of God.'

'I don't think you are going to convert either of us, we are not married, and we live in sin, we swear a lot and take illegal drugs.'

'That's not a problem, I can see you are good, honest people who are on this adventure to find your place in life. Maybe you will find God later. I give you my blessing this beautiful morning.'

'Thanks, time for a cup of tea, do you want some eggs, or an omelette?'

'Tea is ready, you do the omelette, cooking is not one of my best subjects,' admitted Colin.

Harry came out of the camper van in just his boxer shorts. 'Morning all.' He stretched, and looked across the desert. 'That was a quiet night! It's going to be a good day.' He turned to Colin. 'I always get a bit nervous crossing a border, having to deal with the officials, listening to a new language, different money, different ways things are done.'

'This border is going to be fine, we have got visas, we know where we are going, and everyone says the Afghans are really cool.'

'Yeh! I know, but where are we going?' Harry joked. Lucy flicked a tea towel at his boxer shorts.

After an omelette with naan bread, they packed up their few belongings and set off towards Afghanistan.

Everyone seemed to be in a good mood this morning. The Iranian customs and immigration briefly looked at their passports and waved them onto the Afghan border crossing. There they were asked if they had any cigarettes. Harry, now getting wise to how things worked in this part of Asia, handed over two packs of strong Turkish cigarettes, and they were waved through after a quick stamping of passports.

'Well! Here we are in Afghanistan. I have been dreaming of this moment for two years now. Finally, we are getting into a really foreign place. It looks different, smells different,' Lucy exclaimed.

Harry looked out of the dusty windows, 'It looks very much like the last bit of a country we were in. Flat and burned out.'

Colin suddenly pointed, 'Look at that weird building over there. It looks all collapsed, it is not a mosque or house, it is the wrong shape.'

'Let's stop and have a look, I need to stretch my legs,' said Harry. They investigated the ruined building, trying to guess what it once was.

Colin said, 'I think it was a kind of windmill. Those are grinding stones down there on the ground. I reckon it was a vertical windmill, those woven bits were the sails that drove the grinding wheels through that wooden gear. All very ethnic and crude.' The others agreed, they got back onto the road. 'It's all very basic farming here, over there I can see a farmer ploughing with a wooden plough that looks like it had come from the Old Testament. He has got a bullock pulling it.'

The traffic on the road increased, not of cars or lorries, but carts pulled by donkeys, trains of camels, bullocks wandering aimlessly.

Gradually the landscape changed as they drove along. They could see the city of Herat in the distance through the clouds of dust, tall minarets, and domed roofs. It emerged like a green jewel in a fertile, green valley watered by the river Hari Rud. Fields and orchards were bounded by irrigation canals, edged with lines of tall poplar trees. Farmers in white turbans worked in the fields of barley and wheat, spices such as cumin and saffron.

'We will try to find a place to park and stay not too far from the city centre,' said Harry, without a clue of the local geography. 'Maybe first we should go to a tourist place, or hotel with foreigners to ask, we've usually succeeded in doing this before.'

They soon discovered that it was a very different town than they had experienced before.

There were avenues of trees dividing the traffic lanes. The traffic was of donkeys pulling carts with wooden wheels stacked high with impossible piles of goods. There were men on bicycles, some ancient and rusty, some more modern imported from India and China. There were small horse-drawn carriages for two passengers, the horses decorated with a multitude of coloured ribbons, amulets and tassels, bells jangling with the rhythm of the horses. Many people were walking in the dusty road with bare feet or heavy sandals with car tyre soles. Any motor traffic appeared to be from a different decade. Ancient wrecks were held together by faith and some string. Old Bedford lorries, rebuilt in timber, higher and wider, decorated with hand-painted scenes of mosques, mountains, and occasionally a movie starlet. Every surface covered with shining metal embellishments, tassels and bells. The inside of the cabs were likewise decorated with paintings and hangings over the windscreen. Texts from the Koran to give protection to the fearless driver, who would find it difficult to see out through all the hangings.

The three travellers quickly realised this easy-going, relaxed, proud ancient country would absorb them totally and be unforgettable forever.

They stopped outside a police station. 'Is this wise?' asked Lucy. 'We have usually tried to avoid the police wherever possible.'

'I dun 'know. I've got a good feeling about this place. I'll go in with Colin. He looks very respectable.'

The chief of police was sitting behind a large desk, empty of anything except a layer of dust. He looked up. 'Good morning,' said Harry. 'We have just arrived in a camper van, we are looking for a safe place to camp for a few days near the city.'

"*Sobh Bakhair*". That is how we greet in Afghanistan or "*Salam alaikum*", which means "Peace be upon you", that is more formal. So, you want somewhere safe to stop. That is very important in this country, to find somewhere safe. Afghanistan is a most dangerous country. There are brigands and scoundrels everywhere.'

He looked from one boy to the other, 'Just remember playing sex with other boys is illegal, and traffic laws are non-existent. Do not travel after it is dark and respect the police. Those are the only laws I know of.' He roared with laughter, his large belly which hung over his trousers and belt wobbled like an earthquake. His two minions, sitting at another desk were well rehearsed in the reaction he expected from them.

'I will get my driver to guide you the way, it is the respect I can show you for coming to ask me first.' He stood up, gave both the boys a big handshake, clicked his fingers and waved his hand to tell his driver to show the way.

'Is it just you two friends travelling together?' Was there a suspicion of illegal homosexuality in his voice?

'No, no!' explained Colin. 'I am just riding with them from Mashhad. I am going straight on to Calcutta, my friend here has a lovely lady with him, Lucy.'

'Very good,' replied the police chief, 'have a good visit to my city. My name is Sarif, please contact me if you have any problems.'

They followed the police car in convoy. Fortunately, there were no sirens or blue lights. They were led into a large field on the edge of the city, it was surrounded by a high mud, stone and brushwood wall, with an arched stone gateway at the entrance. Grape vines hung down, loaded with delicious looking black, juicy fruit. The policeman vaguely waved his arm through the car window, presumably indicating they could go anywhere, and then drove off. They continued around and chose to set up camp under a mulberry tree.

Colin quickly announced that he was not going to take any more of their hospitality, and that he would find somewhere to stay in the city. Both the others protested vehemently, insisting he continued staying with them. As soon as they got settled in, a neighbour, who was camping in several tents close by came over and said, 'I suggest you park the other way round, there is a strong wind that blows later in the day that carries a lot of dust and sand, it will blow straight into your door.'

'Thanks,' replied Lucy, 'that's useful to know. Have you stayed here long?'

'About a week, it is a cool place, everyone is so friendly. I'm Jo, my friends have all gone off exploring, to minarets, castles and stuff. I have stayed behind because I had a very gimpy tummy last night. I couldn't risk being far from a toilet.'

'I'm Lucy, this is Harry, and this is Colin. He is just riding with us at the moment. We are on the way to Kathmandu, Colin is going to Calcutta.'

'There are about five or six of us travelling together, some go, some join. Just a loose group. We camp all the time, none of us have much money, and we are probably going to end up in different places.'

'When we have turned around, got sorted, come and have some tea with us. I've got some special herbal tea, great for the trotting tummy.'

'Thanks, that would be great. Were you brought here by the police? I saw a car. Have you been in trouble?'

'No, no! we asked for directions to a camping place, and they brought us here.'

'That's cool, they are all friendly here. But make sure you put all your gear away and lock up. The toilets are over there, not too bad, seen worse.' He grimaced. 'There is a wash place, stand tap, I shouldn't drink it, and a cold shower. A guy comes round each day, just looking and checking, there are no charges, it's free!'

'Wow, free! That's great. We'll see you in a bit when the kettle is on.'

A lot of storytelling continued until late afternoon, when the rest of Jo's group arrived back.

A strong, hot wind was blowing, making it uncomfortable sitting outside in an exposed place.

'This is the 120-day wind,' Jo explained. 'It can be quite cooling, but also a pain 'cos of all the sand. It is called that 'cos it blows for four months from May to September. It comes from the south and east. The locals celebrate it because it cools. They even design their houses in the right orientation, and some have air conditioning from specially shaped chimneys to take in the wind. It is also used by farmers to clean the chaff off their corn, and to drive the windmills.'

'We stopped by some of those windmills just across the border, on our way here,' Lucy said.

Jo's friends, who had just arrived at the camping field, introduced themselves. Only Colin could memorise their names, so that evening when they all went out for some kebabs, and the next day, he helped Harry and Lucy get to know them. Later in the evening, when the wind had dropped a bit, they lit a small fire to sit around. Stories rolled around, Harry got out his guitar and songs were sung.

That night Harry did not sleep well, he tossed and turned. It was very hot in the camper, the wind rattled the awning outside. His mind kept turning over and over the meeting with Alison, the palm reader. What did she mean that there would be a big change in his life? And she said the same to Lucy. Perhaps he shouldn't believe anything she said. He finally dismissed her for what he had experienced of her, a frustrated older woman.

The next morning was sunny and very hot, there was no wind. It was the usual breakfast of coffee, omelettes, and local flatbread.

There were five of them gathered later by the gate. 'We are planning on going to look at the citadel, and four

265

minarets on the edge of town. We usually take a *Gaadis*, which is one of the pony trap taxis. They are really cheap, if you bargain a bit, and great fun.'

'Yeh! We saw lots of them when we arrived here yesterday,' said Harry.

'What are all the red tassels and baubles for?

'They are just traditional, on all horses pulling *Gaadis*. They are called *Popak*,' answered Carlos, in a Southern American accent.

'If these are taxis, they are just great. It's so good to just hear the bells after all the noise of horns and chaos of traffic in Iranian cities,' said Lucy.

There were several *Gaadis* parked outside the gate, they all piled into them, and one of the party gave instructions in Farsi to the drivers.

'Do you speak the local language?' asked Lucy.

'I am Sid, I am living with a family here in Herat. I am teaching English at one of the schools here for about six months. Farsi Dari, the local language is quite easy, the other main language in Afghanistan is Pashto. That is spoken over in the east. There are so many languages here, every tribe, even every village seems to have a different one.

'I know your names, we talked about you last night in our tent. Johnie, who is part of the group travelling together, said he heard tales of you two in Turkey. You helped with the earthquake that happened a few months ago. He saw you on TV.'

Lucy shyly demurred.

They went around the city, avoiding the crowded markets. 'We must explore this place later. Those markets and bazaars look great.' Said Lucy. A moment later they were covered in dust from a passing lorry.

'Those are called *"jingle trucks"*' A camper explained. Harry had forgotten his name 'It's slang that probably goes back to the very first motorised lorries. They are called that because of the jingling sound that the trucks make due to the chains and pendants hanging from the bumpers of the vehicles. They are usually highly customized and decorated by their owners. It can cost thousands. The decoration often contains elements that remind the truck drivers of home, since they may be away from home for months at a time. It is a form of art. The lorries and buses are completely rebuilt, higher and wider in carved wood, which is then decorated with metal and paintings of scenes and quotes from the Quran. On the tail they have phrases like *"Blow Horn"* and *"Use Dipper at Night"*'.

The Citadel was close to the city. It towered over all the surroundings, a huge crumbling mud brick pile. They scrambled up the surrounding walls and battlements. Sid knew some of the history, of course. 'This is the oldest building in Herat, it is believed to stand on the foundations of a fort built by Alexander the Great. It has served as a seat of power for centuries, used by every invading army. It was rebuilt by Shah Rukh in 1415, after Timur trashed what little Genghis Khan had left standing. At this time, the exterior was covered with the monumental Kufic script of a poem proclaiming the castle's grandeur, *'never to be altered by the tremors of encircling time'*. Sadly, most of this tiling has been lost, bar a small section on the northwest wall, the so-called 'Timurid Tower'. Repeated conquerors pillaged the Citadel, with locals taking the valuable roof beams and baked bricks for their own projects.

'There is an extensive renovation programme just started. For a few years there have been occasional archaeological excavations in the main courtyard. But they always seem to run out of money. Over to the left, there is a small *hammam* with beautifully painted but damaged walls, showing flowers and peacocks. The biggest attraction is the Citadel's huge curtain wall topped with battlements that we are now standing on. These offer tremendous views over Herat, looking south towards Chahar Su, and north to the minarets of the Musalla Complex. It's also possible to make out the last remains of the Old City walls. We have a great view of the city. All mud flat roofs the same colour as the surrounding desert.'

One of the campers jumped on top of the highest wall. 'I am the king of the castle. This is my castle.' He was dancing around in a very stoned manner. 'My name is Alex, so this was built by my ancestors, Alexander the Great,' he sang. The other hauled him down to the ground in case he fell down the long drop.

When they had finished looking around the Citadel, they moved on to the four minarets. Sid again knew a lot of the history.

The travellers decided to carry on in the *Gaadis* to explore a couple of the small villages outside Herat. Lucy and Harry decided to go their own way to explore the bazaars of the city. Colin joined the group of travellers. He had decided to join their group when they leave to go to Kandahar.

'It's been great to meet you and travel from Iran, but I must keep moving on. I hope I shall have some money sent to me in Kabul. May God bless you, take care.'

It was only a short distance to the bazaars, so Lucy and Harry walked.

They were immediately overwhelmed by the busy markets. There was everything for sale, including a lot of Chinese and Indian imported goods that covered every need of a household or small holding. The men were usually dressed the same, a colourful, embroidered waistcoat over a white shirt that stretched to below the knees, loose baggy trousers and either bare feet or heavy sandals. On their heads, they wore either huge turbans of varied coloured cloth, wound round and round a small, heavily embroidered skull cap, or a flat felt hat with the rim rolled up. The women either wore a floating blue burqa, covering from head to toe, with a netted visa to see through, or more western blouse and trousers that covered arms and legs, and a scarf covering their hair. There was an occasional glimpse of femininity with red pained toenails and fashionable slip-on shoes.

Without delay, Lucy went into a shop that was dark and dusty. The window was filthy with dust and grime, as was the jewellery on display. The shopkeeper, an old man dressed in a *chapan*, a type of striped coat worn over the shoulders, got to his feet from a squatting position in the corner to turn on the one light bulb. This illuminated more dust and more cobwebs. Whist Lucy looked at the jewellery, necklaces, bracelets, and rings made from cheap metal, but decorated with cornelian and lapis lazuli stones,

Harry picked up an ancient *jezail* from a pile of weapons in the corner. He reckoned it must be several centuries old, decorated with inlaid patterns of mother of pearl. The firing mechanism was an old flintlock, that seemed to still work, there was a long metal ramrod that fitted under the barrel. He toyed with it for a while, then turned to another pile of ethnic artefacts, the use was mostly impossible to identify.

They moved on to several other shops. A rug and kilim dealer who had shoulder high piles of rugs around the sides of his shop. Here there was even more dust in the air, mixed in with several clothes moths flying around. Next was a shop that dealt in embroideries, from large shawls to tiny purses, each intricately embroidered with coloured silks. Around the corner, in another bazaar, there were three baker shops in a row. As well as the traditional *Naan* bread, one was making small, sweet pastries, filled with a choice of almonds, figs or dates. Lucy bought a paper bag full of them, which was their lunch whilst sitting on a low wall watching everyone go by on their business.

They moved on to another bazaar to find a tea shop.

The owner beckoned them to sit on a carpet-covered table. They removed their shoes at the doorway. He asked them *'Chai Sabz?'* Not sure what that meant but knowing *'chai'* was the word for tea, they both nodded in agreement. From the large steaming, copper samovar boiling water was poured into a decorated teapot with a handful of green tea leaves. Small glasses were half filled with sugar and the teapot was put in from of them. They already knew from Iran that this was the usual way. Pour a bit of tea onto the sugar, take a sip, then pour more until eventually all the sugar has gone. The tea, with a taste of cardamom, fully refreshed them so they continued exploring past a shoe mender, working on the pavement outside a dentist advertising his shop with a window painting of a gruesome, huge pair of tweezers and a set of bright white false teeth with very red gums. Further shop signs were hand painted in psychedelic colours and flowing Islamic script. Harry took a mental note of them to copy into his note book later.

Further on they came across the famous glass makers. For several hundreds of years glass had been made in this street by the same extended family. Harry was fascinated by the way they created the blue drinking glasses, candle sticks, and dishes. He went inside the shop and squatted down next to a small furnace made from a dome of mud. It was fiercely hot.

Two owners were working at the kiln. They were happy to demonstrate their skills. Harry was surprised to learn they were making the glass from raw materials, not melting down scrap glass. The maker heated a portion of mixed powder they had prepared in the kiln until it was red hot and melting. He then shaped the glass on a smooth stone, swung it around his head to extend it and using a metal tube blew it into the right shape. It took only a few moments to make a drinking vessel which was left to cool next to the kiln.

The owner offered the metal tube to Harry to have a go, he declined but stayed watching whilst several more pieces were made.

Lucy waited outside, it was too hot and smoky to be in the shop. She was distracted by an old man on the pavement further along. He was holding parts of a broken teapot between his two feet. A young man, dressed in a football shirt and jeans stopped beside her. 'This a *'Patrangar'*. He is a mender of pottery, my grandfather had this job, I always watched him when I was a boy. As you see he holds the pot between his feet. The broken shards of the teapot are tied around with thread. He saws away with a drill. Just a metal point winding back and forth with string. This makes a hole in the ceramic. He then makes small clips from wire and fits them into holes he has drilled. He uses glue from animal hoofs to fasten the broken pieces together to make a usable teapot.'

Lucy continued watching until the teapot was restored. She turned round but the helpful young man had disappeared into the crowds. When Harry returned, they both decided they had seen enough for one day. They found a *Gaddis* to take them back to the campsite.

Chapter 22

Herat, West Afghanistan. June 1971

"Tourists don't know where they've been,
travellers don't know where there're going"

The city of Herat cast a spell over the two travellers. After two days exploring, they realised they had not yet got to know the city as they really should. It was a warm, sunny day. The wind had dropped to a gentle breeze. They decided to stay several more days. The camp site was free, quiet and there were always groups of interesting people passing through.

Herat was built of mud and earth, some buildings with domed roofs, most with flat roofs the same colour as the desert. Splashes of colour came from the many trees, golden leaves of the plane trees, tall, emerald poplars that rose above the roofs, mulberry trees, soon coming into fruit with black or white berries. There were patches of bright colours from centuries old mosaics, cannibalised from collapsed mosques and forts, now used in newer buildings.

Lucy said she wanted to spend at least a day drawing and painting in and around the city. Harry was fascinated by the various bazaars, he wanted to find the glass makers again, and hopefully talk to the graphic designers who hand painted the shop signs and the huge posters for up-and-coming Indian films.

They went their different ways. Lucy found a quiet corner in a small tea shop, opposite the police station and Tourist Information Centre. She thought this would be safe for a Western girl on her own to sit to paint. She soon became totally absorbed in her work. There were ruined buildings in this street, bazaar stalls and a few shops with conventional, but very dusty front windows. There was also a stream of men, and occasionally a woman, walking, cycling or riding along the street. Most of the men dressed very traditionally with white turbans, some of the women in faded blue *burqa*, or *chador,* struggling to hold the pleats together in the breeze and peering through the *musharabieh*, the fine net face mask. She was told by one of the men who stopped when visiting the tea room that the women dressed in that way *"just to make men dream!"*

She could see further down the street the entrance to a mosque. In pencil, she drew the forecourt with two old, turbaned men, squatting, with knees drawn up to under their chins, guarding sandals slipped off at the entrance by worshippers. All watched by grey doves searching for crumbs in the dust.

She did a few rapid sketches in pencil to capture their clothes, faces and postures for finishing later.

Harry quickly found the glass maker's shop. He squatted down on the floor to watch their skilled work. He was invited, by sign language to try his hand. His attempts at making a goblet were a disaster and caused much laughter amongst the glass makers and those watching. His goblet had collapsed into a heap of molten glass with no discernible form.

He moved on to find the shop of graphic designers. The owner spoke good English, he explained how and why they worked with exaggerated, oversized images, bright colours and sections of Islamic script. He looked at his notebook of sketches from the previous day, hoping for inspiration. The owner suggested he tried his hand at doing a design for a pharmacy selling bottles of lotions and packets of pills. He did several large outline sketches. The owner thought they were great and promised to paint them onto a sheet of metal to hang outside the shop.

By late morning it was getting hot. The sun brought out the powerful smell of dung, people and animals. It hung heavily in the narrow streets. He went to seek out Lucy. She was very excited, the man in charge of the Tourist Office had come over to her sitting in the shade, seen her paintings, and taken one to hang in the office. She said he might get it copied and printed in the latest tourist brochure.

'Did you charge him?' asked Harry.

'No!'

'You should have, we need money to live on.' But Lucy was proud of having her work recognised, the thought of having it shown in Herat thrilled her. Harry wanted to see the painting that he had chosen.

They crossed the road. The manager, Sahid Mohammed, was pleased to see them both, and thrilled with the painting. He had not decided where to hang it but thought it would look best on the wall behind his desk. By then it was too embarrassing to ask for some money.

They spent the afternoon exploring more bazaars. In mid-afternoon the schools emptied children in the streets. The noise of shouting increased. The afternoon breeze had picked up, the pale blue sky was soon filled with homemade kites of all colours. Just tissue paper or plastic with a thin bamboo frame. Harry was reminded of making one of these as a boy. Getting the strings caught up with Rolly's.

Here, in Herat, flying a kite was more than just fun, it was war. The children, all boys, coated the strings with ground glass, with the objective to cross with another line and cut it through so the kite would float away. There was always a team of shouting, younger boys to chase and capture the lost kite.

Back at the campsite Lucy started to finish off one of her drawings of a group of men, with white beards, long flowing turbans, colourful caps and waistcoats, cycling and weaving through the bazaar. Harry had procured a large lump of hashish. He rolled a spliff and relaxed in the shade.

They chatted and thought up ideas of where to go next, and when to move on towards Kabul. They had explored most of the recognised landmarks of Herat. They had been to the citadel, the Musalla complex, the five standing minarets and various tombs, walked in the flower and tree filled gardens, met with poets walking the paths, reading aloud traditional works by famous Herati literary writers.

Herat was a city of culture, history and exciting bazaars. With good reason.

They learned it had been called the Pearl of Khorasan for centuries.

Harry was lying flat on his back watching clouds float by. 'We can't stay here for ever. We need to explore some more. Why don't we go into one of the remote areas to the north of here. I can see some mountains not far away from where I'm lying. They look interesting.'

'We haven't got any maps or guides. We will just get lost.'

'We will go to find your friend, Sahid, and ask him. He's the tourist guide, he should know and help us.'

'OK, we will go tomorrow, I'm dog-tired right now, just want to eat something, then go to bed.'

They found Sahid the next morning in his office, they asked him for suggestions of where they could go. He said, 'Most travellers like you just go on the new paved road to Kandahar, Ghazni and Kabul, why don't you just follow them?'

Lucy said, 'We are travelling to Asia to find out about the countries and people. We are interested in meeting different people, to learn about their lives, and tell them something of our lives.'

Sahid thought for a while, he looked at a large map of the area pinned to the wall. 'The Minaret of Jam?' He pointed at a remote spot on the map, to the east of Herat, surrounded by mountains, in a river valley. 'There is nothing there, no chaikhana, no hostel, no electricity, no village, very few people. Maybe a small farm nearby on the track. I have not visited there, just a few people have.'

'Sounds perfect,' said Lucy. 'I'll do another painting of the minaret for you to hang in the office.'

'Oh, yes! But first I must ask my friend in the police house next door what the situation is, whether it is safe for you to go.'

A few moments later he returned with the chief of police. 'This is Sarif.'

'Yes we have met before'. Harry and Sarif shook hands, he nodded his head to Lucy. 'I understand you want to visit the minaret of Jam. It is not dangerous from brigands now it is summer time, they are busy dealing with their crops. In the winter it is impossible because of snow. The road is not good. In places it is just a rough donkey trail, very often washed away by rivers. But now it has been dry for some months so maybe OK. I warn you, there is nothing there except the monument.'

'We have been told that by your friend here, that is what we like. Do you have a road map, and any details of the area?'

'I can give you a map, it is drawn by hand by an American scholar who visited,' Said Sahid, digging in a desk drawer full of papers.

'I will send a message to our police post that is on the route. He will expect you, and maybe want papers from you. I will write my permission for you to travel on official police papers. Are you leaving tomorrow? It will take two or three days drive to get to Jam, the track is bad.'

'We will leave after tomorrow, first we must get some provisions.'

'Yes, very important. I have told you there are no restaurants or chaikhana, or places to stay.'

'We will get food and water tomorrow in the morning, it is Thursday, your weekend, so I presume the bazaar closes,' said Lucy, already planning a list in her head.

'That is all good,' Sarif said. 'Take care, it is a difficult and wild area. You may meet three horse riders who I was told left Bamiyan, in the east about four weeks ago. Nothing has been heard from them. If you meet, report back to me so we can watch out here for their arrival.'

So, with a rough map, lists of shopping to do, they went back into the bazaar to find fruit and vegetables. They would go to the mini market on the edge of the city in the morning. Lucy had already decided they would not take any fresh meat. It would soon go off in the heat.

'It's lunch time, let's celebrate by going to the tea shop where I did my drawing yesterday,' suggested Lucy. 'It's very friendly.'

They entered the *chaikhana*, once again knowing to remove their shoes before sitting cross legged on a table covered by a carpet. There were many dusty carpets laid overlapping on mud floor. There was a buzz of conversation, at one table a game of carom was in progress. They watched it for a while, trying to understand the rules and how it was played. It was like finger billiards on a square board played with coloured discs. That they understood but did not understand the way the game was scored.

They had a meal of lamb kababs, cooked over charcoal next to the large, steaming copper samovar. The kababs were spicy and served with several slabs of fresh naan bread.

'I saw a bakery this morning, in the bazaar,' said Harry. 'There were three men working, rolling out the flour then putting it on the wall of an oven sunken into the ground. It smelt fantastic. There was a constant stream of women coming for fresh bread.'

Back at the camp in the early evening, still with lots of preparation for their trip to do, a man approached them.

'Hi, y'all, how are you doing?' He had a very strong American accent. I am Jack, from the United States. I know your names, Lucy and Harry. I was told by the guy in the tourist office I would find you here.'

He was dressed in a short sleeved, button-down shirt, khaki chinos, and traditional sandals. His blond hair was cut short, he had a well trimmed beard, almost white in colour. He looked to be in his early forties, and very different from any of the other travellers they were accustomed to meeting.

'This is your van?' He stated the obvious. 'I was told by the tourist office you are going to Jam.'

'That's right,' replied Harry.

'I am looking for a ride that way, I hope you can help me. There are no buses that go there,' Jack said. 'I can help you with the driving, and pay for fuel.'

Harry looked at Lucy, they nodded heads to each other. 'I guess we could take you. We may only stay there for a day or two, and it will take up to three days drive each way. If you want to stay longer you will have to find your own way back here to Herat, or you could find a way to carry on to Bamiyan.'

'I will want to stay there for several weeks. I am an archaeologist working with a group up in the north, near a place called Balkh, outside Mazar-i-Sharif. They sent me to find this minaret at Jam to see if it mixes in with any of the stuff we find up there.

'I am self-contained, got all the camping gear. So, I won't interfere with you guys.'

It seemed a good idea to Harry and Lucy, they always liked to meet new people, and if they are willing to pay for the fuel even better.

'So, yep! That's a deal. We're leaving tomorrow, not early. We still have some shopping to do, and to pack up the camper. She is called *Forget-me-Not*.'

'That's neat. I'll tell you what, come to my hotel this evening. I'll treat you to a meal, we can get to know each other and we can talk some more. I stay at the *Mowafaq Hotel*. You can get one of those horse *Surrey gigs*, the driver will know the way.'

So, it was agreed, a travelling companion, and a free hotel meal.

They caught a Gaadis just after sunset, not being sure at what time a hotel served dinner. They had both dressed in their smartest clothes, Harry in his long off-white trousers and a traditional white collarless shirt, down almost to his knees. Lucy wore her long new dress she bought in the bazaar the previous day, sleeves covering her arms, an embroidered square panel on the front. She wore a head scarf.

The *Mowafaq* was smart, with a bellboy at reception, air-conditioning and large potted palms in the reception. Jack was sitting at a table laid with cutlery and glasses, and a white embroidered tablecloth. He greeted them warmly.

Lucy sat down, immediately examined the edge of the tablecloth.

'This is traditional embroidery from Kandahar,' Jack said.' I saw some when I passed through. They do great tee-shirts with very fine stitching on the front, I bought one to send back home.

'So what do yah all want to eat, there's a big menu, Western, Arabic, Afghan, Chinese, you choose, I am going to have a good old US burger.'

They studied the four pages of the menu, all printed in English.

'I'm going to have a *Kabuli Pillou.*' Said Lucy. 'It sounds very Afghani.'

' I will have a *Dolmay Murch-E-Sheereen.* I don't know how to pronounce it, or what it is,' said Harry.

Jack gestured to the waiter standing nearby. He pointed to Harry's choice. The waiter replied in fluent English, 'It is green pepper that is filled with lamb, onion, tomatoes and spices. It is very spicy, hot, I can ask the cook to make it less.'

'No, no, I like spices,' said Harry.

Jack gave the waiter their orders, 'They always start with soup and flat bread here. What do yah want to drink? They have beer, whisky, some sort of wine and the usual soft drinks.'

They all chose to have a beer.

Some small dishes of almonds, walnuts and raisins were put on the table.

'So, tell me about your travels, you've obviously been

all across Europe and West Asia to get this far. Where are you heading for?'

Together, Harry and Lucy told some of the stories of their trip, some of the people they had met, some of the adventures they had had.

'Where are you heading for and why?'

Lucy replied. 'Our destination is Kathmandu in Nepal. Maybe go further if our money doesn't run out. And why! To find out about people, places, cultures. A kind of advanced education. And what about you?' She looked directly at him. 'You said you were an archaeologist.'

'Yeh that's right. Not very expert yet. Not much is known about Jam, I'm on my way there to catch it before it is blown up by some fundamentalists or collapses into the river.'

The meal was delicious, and the beers went down well. It was relaxing sitting in cool air conditioning in comfortable surroundings. It took Harry somewhile to persuade Lucy to leave and say goodbye to Jack. She finally got up and told Jack, 'We'll see you tomorrow morning at the campsite.'

Part of Lucy's Diary.

Herat is a lovely city, one of the best places we have been to. There are so many interesting people here, and the city, with the bazaars is fantastic. And it is going to be interesting going to Jam. I am not sure about Jack. Things don't all ring true, some of the things he says don't fit in with being an archaeologist. But no doubt it will all come clear in the next few days.

Are we getting blinkered – just looking ahead and not seeing anything on the sides? What is it ahead that we see? Jut a trail to a destination, and what is there at that destination? Are we doing the right thing? I have asked myself so many questions this past week. I am sure Harry loves me, really loves me. Do I return it? I could see his love in his reaction to my delayed period. He was lost, devastated. He did not know what to do, how to react. I just could not believe him when he asked me to marry him, I am not sure he knew what he was saying. I am sure I was right to say NO.

Do I really love him that much? Love him more than just having good sex? Love him more than just a great friend? How do I find out? Maybe just carry on and wait and see.

Maybe that is what love is? A roller coaster of ups and downs, that eventually everything just drops back into place, then carries on.

I think of what Yildiz said to me, a long time ago back in Turkey, such reassuring words. That family is so sound, lovely people. I should learn from them, and from some of the other beautiful people we have met.

I have got a good collection of sketches now. In this diary I need to write longer descriptions of places and people. There are so many things happening, it is easy to move on too quickly, and without writing, things get forgotten.

Chapter 23

Herat and Jam West Afghanistan June 1971

"Take only memories, leave only footprints."

Their final morning in Herat was chaotic, Lucy went to the local mini market to get last provisions, Harry checked the water and diesel in the metal cans on the roof rack. He studied the map the police had given him of the route to Jam. It appeared that they just needed to follow the River Hari for most of the way. There were no villages, caravanserai or interesting places along the road.

Jack arrived mid morning in a Gaadis, carrying a small soft case and a roll of bedding. He handed Harry two bottles of Jack Daniels whisky. 'This is to keep us on the road.'

Harry quickly stowed them away before Lucy saw them.

They said goodbye to the travellers who were in the camp, they were wished good luck and good travels. Two of the travellers in in old American pick-up truck said they would probably see them on the road to Kabul in a week or so. They went to a filling station on the road out of the city, Jack pulled out a large bundle of Afghan cash, still wrapped in a paper band from the bank, to pay for the fuel.

They left Herat on the road going east. Lucy said, 'We follow the road that goes up to the north and after a few miles we turn off it to the right to a place called Chishti, it has it written in Persian.' She handed the map to Jack who was riding in the front. After a few minutes he saw a sign and pointed it out to Harry. They turned off the badly made tarmac road onto an even worse dusty, narrow track.

Harry said, 'I think we have done the most important bit of navigating now. We just follow this track and the river for many miles until we reach Jam.' The track was little more than a donkey path, loose sands, stones and rocks and a lot of tight bends. There was little evidence of other vehicles passing that way since the last rains, several months before. On the wide level plain either side there were small villages of mud houses, some with domed roofs the same colour as the landscape. Fertile fields lined the river. Further north they could see the land was a waterless wasteland. There were irrigation canals running a short distance from the river until the land started to rise into the low hills and then a mountain range. The canals were bordered by tall, spindly poplar trees. They saw high rectangular towers in the fields.

Lucy said, 'I was told by Sahid, in the Tourist Office that there are pigeon towers. They form an essential function in the vineyards. The thousands of pigeons that roost at the top of the towers produce fertilizer which is spread around the vines. That means the best grapes in the whole of Asia are produced by pigeon poo!'

They had to pause to wait for two boys, waving sticks and throwing stones, to move a large herd of sheep off the track. The track climbed over to high passes away from the banks of the river, far below. There were some weird geological formations close to the top of a hill looking like ruins of a building. They took a break to examine them. 'These are just very old rocks that have been eroded by the wind and sand,' said Jack.

They eventually arrived at a small group of mud buildings, that was probably Obey, there was no village sign, and no people in the street. 'They are probably all working in the fields,' Jack announced again. Lucy thought to herself he was trying to give the impression to them of a studied knowledge of that part of Afghanistan. Obey showed as just a small dot on their map. They decided to stop and camp near the river for the night. Before a meal was prepared Jack walked off into the low hill. He soon came back saying there was the remains of an ancient archway, that was probably part of some historic mosque or fort, built centuries before. They all walked back up to it. There wasn't much remaining, it was big and tall, the top inside covered with decorative ceramic tiles. Lucy asked Jack what he thought it was. Surprisingly, being an archaeologist, they assumed he would quickly identify it. He replied he vaguely thought it was probably about the same age as the minarets in Herat.

The night was quiet, just the gentle noise of the river, a few calls from night birds and the mysterious barking of a fox or a wolf.

The next day was similar, no people around apart from in the distance working in the fields and orchards, small villages, just farms of one or two mud buildings. The track got worse and worse, in places it was not wide enough to take the camper van, wheels on one side running in very rough ground with large stones and rocks. It was slow progress. After several hours they came across two oil drums in the middle of the track. They thought this must be Chishti-i-Sharif, another small dot on the map. To one side, on a small hillock was a mud building with a flat roof. It didn't look lived in, it was partially collapsed, with cardboard instead of glass in most of the windows. Jack, who was driving, sounded the horn. Nothing happened. As Harry got out to move the drums so they could pass, a man wandered round from the back of the building. It was the policeman. He was not dressed in a police uniform, but in a dirty shirt down to his knees and a cotton shawl round his waist, like a sarong. He wore no shoes. Jack handed him the paper written by the police officer, Sarif, in Herat. It was obvious the policeman could not read or write, he held the letter upside down and peered at it as though he was very short-sighted. After a long pause he handed the letter back and moved the oil drums. He did not say anything. As the camper van pulled away, Jack called from the window, '*Tashakkor, Khoda Hafez*. Thank you, goodbye!'

Lucy was disappointed not to see or meet anyone. Jack and Harry took turns driving, carefully studying the map. They had to ford the river in two places. One of the crossings looked difficult, the water was running fast and deep, but a short way up the river they found a better place to cross. Harry got out to guide Jack where to drive across. The water was up to his knees, and surprisingly cold. Fortunately, he spotted a hidden bolder under the water, if they had hit that they wound have got stuck. There was not much chance of getting any help as there was no one around. They took a long break in the middle of the day, Harry refilled the diesel tank from one of the spare cans. They all took long drinks of water, it was very hot. 'This is worse than that road through the desert in Iran,' Harry said. Lucy, who was quiet and disheartened, said, 'I hope we don't have a puncture.' Both Harry and Jack gave her a look that said, 'Don't even think about it!' In mid afternoon they stopped again by the river to camp. Jack made a big vegetable stew on the little *gaz* stove to eat later. Across the river they could see a small village of mud houses with domed roofs. They were relaxing, reading and watching a large predatory bird hunting from high up in the sky, when a tall man crossed the river on horseback. He wished them all good evening in good English.

'I live in the village over there, it is called Karmenj. Here we are from a different tribe, Taimani, and live quite separately from other tribes.' The three travellers were astounded, they didn't know what to say. Here in the middle of nowhere was an elegant, middle aged man who spoke English. 'I can see you are surprised that I speak your language. I was in the army in India for many years, many of the squadron spoke English, and I learnt more from a good family who lived there.

'My father was part Indian, he died many years ago, my mother is from this region. I now live with my mother.

Would you like to visit my house? It is traditional in Afghanistan to welcome travellers for refreshment.'

They hesitated, then Harry said, 'Thank you, that would be great, very interesting.'

'Ok, you won't be able to drive your vehicle, there has been a big landslip that has blocked the road. I will go to get some horses to help you cross the river. It won't take long.'

He galloped off, across the river and returned a short while later leading two horses.

'I could only borrow two, one of you ride my horse, I will walk.' Jack declined. 'I don't want to go, I can't ride. Just you two go, I'll be fine here.'

Harry and Lucy, with help, mounted the two ponies, crossed the river and entered the village.

'My mother does not speak English, but I can translate.' Harry introduced themselves. 'My name is Gul. Gul is a flower in Pashto. My mother is called Bibi, that means mother of the house, or grandmother. We are Taimani Aimaq tribe from these mountains. Aimaq means nomads, but we are settled in our village. The men are away in the summer with their flocks of sheep and goats, a big distance away in the mountains finding the best grazing. They come back to the village in winter. It is very cold here. Here in our village, we grow many crops of fruit, apricots, pears, apples and juicy pomegranates. In the autumn we collect walnuts, almonds and pistachio nuts. We sometimes take these to the market in Herat.'

He stopped in front of a small mud house with a single domed roof. 'This is my house, please enter.'

It was very dark inside, they both slipped off their shoes, Lucy ensured her head was covered with a scarf.

Bibi, his mother was sitting on a colourful blanket printed with large roses. She welcomed them in Pashto. They sat in a circle on the floor, tea was soon served in tiny glasses. Lucy asked some questions about the few decorative possessions that were in the room, Gul explained their significance to the family with some stories of the history behind them.

Any conversation was soon exhausted. They left, saying a warm farewell and thank you to his mother. They mounted on the ponies again. Gul handed Lucy a carrier bag filled with fruit and nuts. She was so grateful, it was a great gift. When they got back to *Forget-me-not* Lucy rummaged in a bag and gave Babi Gul two pairs of ankle socks as a gift for his mother. He galloped back to the village.

'Wow! That was fantastic. What lovely people! So kind and generous. What an experience to be invited into a house like that,' said Lucy.

Harry said, 'Riding those ponies, even just such a short way, makes me want to go on a trek for several days. You would see so much more than driving.'

Jack was not very interested, he just wanted to have supper, go to bed and get to their destination. It was still hot, so they all slept on the ground under the stars.

The next morning, they studied the map carefully. Harry said, 'It can't be much further, I think we are just here where the track goes away from the river. I reckon we can be at the minaret by the middle of the day.'

Lucy, not happy with the trip and fed up with the ride on the rough track, said, 'It is only a very rough map, we could be miles away still.'

However, by the middle of the day the sides of the valley closed in, they drove along side of the river again. It was a rugged gorge, with vertical cliffs climbing up several thousand feet, jagged and broken, with no vegetation. Above the cliffs they could see the peaks of craggy mountains, naked of any vegetation. Then, on a sharp bend, where the water was cutting into the bank, was the Minaret of Jam.

They were all exulted, they had made it! Possibly just a few westerners had ever seen this historic place. The Minaret was very tall and leant off the vertical. Harry observed that the river would soon undercut the foundations and that it maybe would fall over. They explored all around the minaret and surrounding area, Jack examined some of the beautiful, colourful tiles, and bricks in detail. There were three sections of tapering cylindrical storeys rising from an octagonal base, the whole completely covered in intricate café-au-lait coloured brick decoration. Interlocking chains, polygons and medallions wound delicately around the shaft, interspersed with text from the Quran. Jack knew some of the history. 'It was built at the end of the eleven hundreds, that is over seven hundred years ago, when in Europe you were just starting to build cathedrals. It was built by a Sultan of the Ghurid rulers. His name is written in ancient text in those coloured, glazed tiles.'

They explored some more and found a narrow entrance hole that led to the interior. There were two staircases that wound each other. It was very tricky to climb the worn, narrow steps. Halfway up the tower was an open chamber which looked onto the two rivers, Hari-Rud and Jam and amazing views along the valley. They found another staircase that led to the tiny lantern. Lucy didn't go, she thought it was too scary.

After the initial explorations, Harry decided to look further up the valley, Jack spent some more time looking at the various ruins in the vicinity and Lucy sat on her camping stool with her sketch and drawing pads. The day wore on, the light changed to a golden colour leaving long shadows and the narrow gorge deep in a dark gloom. Harry soon returned and made a pot of tea. 'Is that for the tourist office in Herat?' He was looking at Lucy's drawing. 'Yes, I'm working on two, we'll choose the best. Have you seen Jack? It's getting late.' Harry told Lucy he had seen him amongst some of the ruins at the base of the Minaret some while ago.

An hour later, Jack still hadn't turned up. Harry said, I will go searching for him. But first I had better look in *Forget-me-not* in case he has crashed out on the bed.' Harry soon returned. 'He's not there, and I can't find his sleeping bag, rucksack or case. Do you think he has gone off for the night?'

'That's dangerous, the police said we should stick together, there may be bandits around.' Her thoughts went back to the lonely mountain in Turkey when the group of bandits appeared over the hillside, they were with the two motorbike boys.

There was nothing they could do, it was already nearly dark, they knew nightfall came very quickly in the part of the world they were in. After a quick meal, they sat watching the moon rise, the light changed to silver, and they listened to the river and occasional wild animal calling.

The next morning they had to decide what to do. Go searching in the valley for Jack, just wait by *Forget-me-not* or to start the journey back to Herat.

Harry had spent part of the night deciding which was the balanced decision. He said, 'If we go searching it will be easy if he has stayed by the river, but he may have found a path out of the gorge and up into the mountains. We would never find him. I think it is better to stay here, then if he hasn't turned up, we leave for Herat tomorrow. He did say he was going to stay for several days and would make his own way back.'

The next day, Jack still had not turned up, so Lucy and Harry packed up their gear and set off along the track. Lucy was quiet, thoughtful and worried. After a while she said, 'I'm not sure about Jack, he didn't fit in with my idea of an archaeologist. He didn't look the part, I'm not sure how an archaeologist dresses, but it wouldn't be like him. He had no tools, no little hammer, no trowel, camera or sketch book.' Harry thought for a while. 'What do you think he was doing? He wasn't a tourist, competing to find things that are not on anyone else's list. I've got no idea, but I agree he wasn't an archaeologist.'

'When we went to that arch, early on, just off the track, he vaguely said they were probably the same age as the minarets in Herat, and the bit he said about the age of this minaret could have been in any book or tourist guide. And another thing, he said he was working with a group in the north of Afghanistan, at a place called Balkh. The ruins there, I'm sure are much older, probably a thousand years older than this minaret.'

I think maybe he is something to do with the Afghan or US Government. Maybe searching for a drug baron, a fundamentalist leader or maybe he is a spy with the CIA.'

Neither of them had a clue. 'We will tell the police back in Herat that he went off camping on his own, and was making his own way back, as he had already said he would do before we left. We will also tell them that we have not seen any sign of the horsemen he asked us to look out for.'

The return trip back to Herat was much the same, along the same route. They waved to the village, Karmenj, but there was no one to see. There was no police man at Chishti. Harry wondered when Jack returned, he would be stopped by the policeman because they still had the letter giving him permission to pass. It took less time to drive back to Herat, they were now familiar with the route. They drove straight to the same park, collapsed with tiredness from the difficult journey. Lucy stated she didn't want to do that sort of thing again. She wanted to meet people, not just go into the wilds where there was no one.

Harry reminded her of the visit to the Tamiami village. 'That was just what we want to do, find out about local people.' Lucy agreed. They both thought it was great to see how wild and remote it was away from roads and towns.

They woke next morning by noise of people talking just outside the camper. It was a group of travellers who had arrived the night before. All in independent vehicles. Harry stood in the doorway of *Forget-me-not* looking at them. The largest vehicle was a minibus with about seven seats. It was highly decorated with ban the bomb symbols, words of peace, lists of countries visited and those still to come. There were a couple of small vehicles: a VW bug, a

Ford saloon, and surprisingly an Enfield motorbike with sidecar. It was obvious which couple were riding it, they were dressed in leather helmets and goggles, looking like second world war fighter pilots. One of them noticed Harry and came over to the camper van.

'You been here long? We just arrived late last night, we are going to Kandahar in a few days, then Kabul. Would you like to join us? We are just a loose group travelling together for fun and security.'

Harry replied, 'We are going towards Kabul, probably tomorrow. We have been in Herat for some time, we have just been on a great trip to the Minaret of Jam.'

'Is that one of those towers just over there?'

No! It is about three days drive into the desert along this river, and then three days drive back, all along a very rough track.'

'No, not for us, we like smooth roads straight from one town to another,' was the reply. 'What is there to see here in this place?'

'Well, in addition to some good monuments that are very historic, there are fantastic bazaars full of small industries, shops selling antiques and new things. There is plenty to do for several days.'

The motorbike rider saluted his thanks and rejoined his group.

Lucy had got up. 'Let's have breakfast out, a nice omelette and coffee, then we go to the Tourist Office to tell Sarif I'll bring a finished painting for him tomorrow before we leave. And tell the police, Safid, we are back, we have left Jack behind and no sign of the three horse riders.'

After breakfast, they changed their minds, deciding to relax and deal with the tourist office and police the next day. The rest of that day was spent reading, writing diaries and Lucy putting finishing touches to the painting of the minaret. In the evening, they had a quick meal of chicken kababs and collapsed for a long sleep.

Chapter 24

Kandahar, Central Afghanistan. June 1971

"Have a story to tell, not stuff to show"

Part of Harry's Diary.

Things seem to be going well. Forget-me-not is working well. Maybe I shouldn't say that, tempting fate! Lucy and I are getting on fine. It can be a bit difficult and stressful living so close together, doing everything together. That's probably what married life is like. Maybe we should try to do more on our own. But that can be difficult for Lucy now we are in Central Asia, such a male dominated country.

The trip to the Minaret of Jam was terrific, one to remember for always. I know Lucy said it was a bit boring, not meeting many people or other travellers, but that was made up by the guy who rode up to us and took us to his village to see his house and meet his mother. Just what we want.

I am worried about Jack, the way he just left with all his stuff without saying anything. A bit odd. I think Lucy was right thinking he was not all that he said he was. He certainly didn't look or act like an archaeologist. He was definitely doing something else, maybe something secret. But isn't that just what you read in spy novels?

We told the police, so they will hopefully sort it out.

Riding a horse across the river was fun. I think we should do some more. When we get to Kabul, we could hire a couple of horses to go on a little trip. I am sure we can do things like that. We should have asked Sarif if they organise stuff like that whilst we were in Herat. There were a lot of horses there.

Herat was just great, as Lucy said the best place we have stopped in up till now. "The pearl of Khurasan." So interesting and friendly. I found the bazaars very interesting. The glass blowers. The same family doing that work for hundreds of years. And the design and posters shop. I hope they use my design for the pharmacy.

We must look after our money, I am not sure how much we have spent and how much we have left. We are going all the way to Kathmandu, and maybe further. We must do a big reckoning in Kabul and send for more if we need it.

Now we just go east and find what happens next. More interesting adventures, places to visit and people to meet. It has got very hot, I suppose it is the middle of the summer, difficult to tell which season it is here because of the different trees and vegetation.

Sarif, at the tourist office was thrilled with Lucy's painting. She had wrapped it in handmade paper and tied a colourful ribbon round it. He looked at the wall of the office and decided to move a map of Afghanistan to hang the picture under a framed picture of the king, next to her earlier picture of the bazaar from outside his office.

'I will get both your pictures framed in the bazaar, they deserve the best presentation.'

They described the journey to Jam, some of the problems with the road and river crossings, the invitation to the Taimani village. Harry told him they thought the minaret was in close danger of falling over. Sarif added notes to the map which they returned.

Next door, Harry told Safid, the police officer about the fact that Jack had not returned with them and that they saw no sign of the horsemen he had asked them to look out for.

'That's four people missing in the middle of nowhere. I shall have to ask the army to set up a search. They won't like that. They don't like doing anything, especially for the police.'

They were tempted to have another look around the bazaar, everything was so tempting, but they resisted and took a gaadis back to the camp site.

'I suppose we had better get back on the road, we have been in Herat for weeks now.'

'I know', replied Lucy, 'but it has been the best place yet. The whole area is lovely, and the people are just so friendly.'

They left with a sadness in their hearts, not sure if they would ever come back. Harry had decided they would stop on the way to Kandahar, to camp for one night. The road was the smoothest they had experienced for many months, since the early days in west Turkey.

'It was built by the Americans just a few years ago, from Herat to Kabul. The Russians competed by building one to the north of Kabul to their border.'

The countryside was a wide, flat desert plain. Mirages shimmered and shone like smooth lakes, tempting but vanishing when they got close. There was very little vegetation, except where there was obviously a small water shed in the winter. There the farmers grew pistachio nut trees, and in places huge watermelons. Even though they still had some of the fruit given to them on the way to Jam, they stopped at a roadside stall to buy one. It was so cheap they had to search for small coins to pay for it. They made good progress and decided to stop by the trickle of a river past a village called Delaram. They found a level area under some poplar trees. There was some farming next to the river, a vineyard, orange trees, and a field of yellow sunflowers. It was a peaceful spot so they knew they would not be disturbed. It was exceedingly hot, even under the awning. In the late afternoon and early evening, a gentle, cooling breeze sprung up.

Later with the campfire lit, the darkness closed in on them, they were a tiny island in the huge landscape. Just two people drawn together by the need of some company, a close relationship and the urge to travel to the destination they dreamed of.

As they approached the centre of Kandahar the next morning, they searched for the Kandahar Hotel, it had the reputation on the grapevine amongst travellers that you could camp there. They found it close to the centre, on the very busy road, with no apparent security. They drove to the central crossroads in the middle of the town. There they saw a small sign for a hotel, with the symbol of a tent and a caravan. It was along a narrow lane and looked secure and just the right place to park for a couple of days whilst they explored the area. The owner, a middle aged man, wearing the traditional clothes of the area, an embroidered, long shirt, loose pantaloons and a white turban on his head. They could not understand a word he said. Through a toothless grin, he made a piercing whistle. A teenage boy, in a football shirt and cut off jeans appeared at the door to the small hotel.

In poor, schoolboy English he said, 'My father only speaks Pashto, he is very traditional. Do you want to park here or stay in our house?'

They confirmed they wanted to stay in *Forget-me-not* for maybe two nights.

'You stay for as long as you wish, it is just twenty-five Afghani each night. If you wish you can eat in our restaurant, tell me, I'll arrange food.'

Harry and Lucy nodded agreement. 'That's only a few pennies each night,' Lucy said.

The parking for the camper was in the shade under several big tamarisk trees.

In one corner there was the remains of a transit van, stripped of its tyres, wheels and most probably all the engine parts. There was no one else staying there. It was very hot, mid afternoon, so they sat in the shade waiting for sunset.

Kandahar was an easy city to explore. It was laid out in a grid within the remains of a tall city wall, much of it destroyed over the centuries by invading armies and earthquakes. The original gateways into the city remained in restored condition. Harry and Lucy walked to the centre, where there were several bazaars. The first stall they came across sold grapes, brought in from the surrounding area. Piled into neat displays there were small, round green bunches and artistic mounds of big, juicy red grapes.

Lucy said, 'We have so much fruit now, we can't buy any more. We still have some left from the guy on the way to Jam.'

They moved on into the *Char Suq,* the four bazaars. There was a small area of beads, silks and mirrors the women use in embroidering turban hats and the famous Kandahar shirts. Fine, intricate embroidery in white silk on white cotton.

Lucy remarked, 'That's just like the table cloth in the hotel we were invited to by Jack. He said he had passed through Kandahar. He bought one of these embroidered t-shirts to send home.' She was still worried and mystified by his disappearance.

Next was the area where the local *hakim,* doctors prescribed herbal medicines to their patients. Beyond there was the silver and goldsmiths' bazaar. Young, enthusiastic rug sellers were overlooked by their elders, white bearded merchants, who had for generations dealt in carpets and kilims.

There were beaded and embroidered skull caps, for the men to wear under their turbans. Velvet waistcoats embroidered with gold cord in patterns that were reminiscent of soldiers' uniforms from the previous century.

Most handicrafts were made by women, working at home, their finished items brought to market by the men. Harry could not resist buying a red velvet waistcoat, Lucy chose an embroidered skull cap.

They went to another area to find some food. One stall on the pavement specialised in ribs of lamb, *ghora-i-angur*, sprinkled in cumin and crushed grape seeds. They bought a rack, wrapped in an old newspaper, they both got very greasy fingers and faces. There was a fountain with just a dribble of water near by to clean off some of the grease.

They soon found themselves sitting in a chaikhana, with a cracked tea pot and two glasses in front of them.

Harry was interested in the small green–coloured tins, with a mirror lid that many of the men had. He soon found out the contents were called *naswar*, a mixture of tobacco, slaked lime and ashes. He was offered a pinch and shown how to put it under his tongue. Initially the taste was not good, but with some saliva it became sweet. He waited for a hit but was told you need to take it for a lifetime before you became addicted and then feel the effects. He spat it out, against the wall as shown. He could see now why many walls were stained red close to the floor. The men fiddled with the small tin, admiring their features, adjusting the curl of their moustache in the mirror.

The next two days were spent wandering around Kandahar, once venturing out into the surrounding farmland. They tried talking to a farmer who was working in a field of watermelons, but couldn't understand anything that was said. The language was different from that of Herat, it was Pashto, a soft form of the language spoken over most of east Afghanistan.

It was time for them to move on towards Kabul.

'The road is good, there shouldn't be a problem in getting to Ghazni by this afternoon, Harry said. 'I think this is the same road Alexander the Great took when he was going to India nearly two thousand years ago.'

Lucy was not impressed with this bit of history. She was looking at a large group of nomads close to the side of the road. She looked at their camp of low black tents, camels, sheep, dogs and children, as they drove by.

'I wish we could stop, talk to them and make a few sketches. Look at those women. Their coloured skirts and all the jewellery.'

Harry slowed down and pulled onto the side of the road in a cloud of dust.

'OK, let's give it a try. But be really careful of those dogs, they look vicious.'

As they walked across the road, a man dressed in big pantaloons and a coloured shawl over his head, held up his hand, palm facing them. He shouted at them, but in a language they did not understand. He was telling them to stop. He walked towards them, first picking up two stones to throw at the nearest dogs.

He greeted them in Pashto, *"Assalam-o-alaikum"* (peace be on you.) His hand across his chest towards his heart. He signalled behind him for one of the women to approach.

There followed a dialogue that Harry and Lucy could not possibly understand. The dialect was guttural and sharp. They politely responded in the few words of Farsi Dari they had picked up in Herat.

Lucy looked closely at the jewellery the woman wore, the henna tattoos on her face, and the bright colourful clothes she wore, voluminous skirts and an intricately embroidered shawl over her head.

Likewise, the woman examined Lucy's clothes and particularly her blond hair. She came close enough to feel the texture of her blouse. She had a strong, earthy smell of curds and fire smoke.

A small girl ran up, hid in her mother's shirts. It was presumably her daughter. She also had tattoos on her cheeks and wild unkempt hair. She was wearing a necklace of black cloth covered with tiny white glass beads.

They could not walk any closer, the dogs were guarding the tents in the distance, snarling and dribbling. They did not know how to follow up the meeting. Shake hands, continue talking in different languages or enact some of the words. They guessed they were *Kutchi* nomads. The wandering tinkers found all over Afghanistan. From the huge flocks of sheep around the tents and over the hillside it was obvious they were traders in livestock. The meeting spoke of the difference between cultures, their languages and the way of life. There was little more Harry and Lucy could do but wave goodbye and return back to the camper.

'Wow! Oh wow! They were amazing,' exclaimed Lucy. 'The woman was so beautiful, so open and unafraid. Unlike most of the women covered head to foot in a *burka hijab*. I must try to do a sketch from memory. Don't drive yet, I must get something onto paper.'

Harry also got out his note book to write of the experience and descriptions.

The road onwards was smooth, flat desert on each side, purple, hazy mountains in the distance.

Chapter 25

Ghazni Afghanistan July 1971

"At the end of the day your feet should be dirty,
your hair messy and your eyes sparkling."

There was not a lot to see from the road further on. It was marked by the ruined remains of forts about every ten miles, Harry thought it was about as far a camel train could go in one day back in the olden days, now lorries drove past at speed to the next town or serai.

'I can imagine this was a rough and dangerous place back in history with all the various tribes fighting over whose land it was, and of course highwaymen and bandits.'

'Don't stop,' said Lucy, looking nervously at the bleak, desert surroundings, thinking back to the motorcycle bandits in East Turkey.

There were villages, small groups of houses, each with a domed roof. To the south was the river Tarnak that supported small farms with orchards and crops of watermelons, grape vines and wheat fields.

They stopped about halfway to Ghazni at a typical caravanserai with a large chaikhana. They had long soft drinks and a plate of rice with lumps of tough goats' meat. Further on, past the village named Moqor they were mystified by circular mounds of earth looking like lines of bomb craters. They learned later these were *karez*, a specialised irrigation system found in southern Afghanistan. They consisted of underground tunnels, often several miles long, taking water from the mountains to the fields. The mounds were earth dug from shafts, at regular intervals, to maintain the canals of water.

The road went closer to a high range of jagged mountains to the north. These were the lowlands that led to the high mountain range of the Hindu Kush.

As they approached Ghazni, the road climbed a barren, desert pass. There was a toll booth near the top. They had to find 30 Afghani in coins to pay the lonesome man in the booth. They could see the city of Ghazni on a hill a short distance away, but stopped beside the road to investigate a large, well maintained house. It looked like a mansion of a wealthy landowner. Again, they were told later it was a *qala*, a classic Afghan dwelling.

Surrounded by high, forbidding mud walls on all sides, pierced in one place by one large studded, wooden doorway. The walls enclosed a rectangular courtyard where animals and fodder were stored. The living quarters were arranged alongside the courtyard, with all openings and windows looking inwards. Sometimes they had towers in the corners, with a balcony looking out over the countryside.

In Ghazni it was the usual problem of finding a secure place to park *Forget-me-not*. Conveniently, close to the centre they saw a number of tents, and a few campers in a small park, next to a large chaikhana.

The tearoom was crowded with some local men, and a few travellers and tourists. There were four large tables, covered with carpets that had been pushed together into the middle of the room.

Harry and Lucy removed their shoes and sat amongst the others. They were immediately drawn into the conversation, spoken in English, some with strong foreign accents.

A man, in his mid forties, asked where they had come from that day. Harry told him they had driven from Kandahar. The discussion moved to how hot it was in Kandahar at this time of the year.

'Are you hotelling, camping or caravanning?' he asked.

'We are travelling in a camper van, on our way to Nepal. But we like to stop at many places on the way, not just follow the quickest route.'

'So, where have you been in Afghanistan?' By his expression he presumably knew the country well.

'We obviously went to Herat, and as I said, Kandahar,' replied Harry, 'but we took a side trip to the Minaret of Jam.'

There was an instant focus of attention from all those round the table.

'The Minaret of Jam! I didn't think anyone went there, I didn't know if you could even get there.' A woman siting opposite said. 'I live and work here at an NGO, in Kabul, you are very adventurous.'

She was also a little older than most of the travellers they usually met. She was dressed in flamboyant clothes, with an embroidered head scarf. 'My name is Margaret.' She pointed around the table. 'This is James, Edwin, Sue and Natalie. We are all working in Kabul. We work in different government departments and NGOs, and we come from different countries in Europe, Germany, France and America. I don't know the names of the other people.' She indicated the four young travellers that were sitting on the table.

Harry introduced himself and Lucy.

'Is the minaret still standing? I have seen reports that it has collapsed.'

'Yes, it is still there but is leaning a lot. Unless it is rescued soon it will fall into the river.'

The group fell silent, thinking that another precious monument would be lost.

One of the girls who was sitting with the young travellers said, 'I am not travelling around, I am staying here in Afghanistan for as long as possible. I am studying embroidery and amulets. They are the triangular items you see attached to clothing. I come to Ghazni a lot because the Hazara tribe, who are just north of here are amazing embroiderers. I have a good Hazara friend in the bazaar who collects pieces for me.' She added, 'My name is Julie.' She was wearing a tight fitting jerkin, covered in embroidery, over a plain white t-shirt. She had an amulet sewn to the top of each sleeve.

Margaret said, 'I've seen those triangular things sewn on children's clothes, and hanging round camels' necks, and horses' trappings. Are they the same?'

'Yes, they are just the same, the ones for animals are carved out of wood. Amulets are good luck charms, you see them on clothes, especially on babies and young children. They are embroidered, decorated with coral stones, metal discs and small coins. They protect against disease and ill health. The Mullah will write on a scrap of paper, for a small fee of course, a paragraph from the Koran which is sewn inside. The wooden ones for a camel have a small space in the back for the prayer, then it is covered with a piece of wood or a smear of glue.'

There was a pause as a young boy brought ten small tea pots followed by tiny glasses, each with a lump of sugar. Small bowls of sugar-coated almonds were put on the table. Then there was a hubbub of decision as choices for food were made.

Five more travellers arrived. Room was made around the table. It was becoming crowded in the tearoom. They were presumably travelling together as a group. The men all had long hair and beards, the women wearing a variety of ethnic clothes and hats. The leader looked quite different. He greeted everyone in Pashto, then continued in English. 'I am a Native American. I come from a tribe on the west coast, far north in BC. I am travelling overland to the east. And have joined up with these guys.' His hand swept around the group, he continued in English, without hesitation, and no embarrassment in telling some of his life story.

'My mother gave birth to me in the middle of winter, high in the mountains. She told me it was it was by a big river in a wood of spindly trees. That is why I am called White River.'

More pots of tea were brought to the new arrivals.

He continued. 'When I was tiny, we travelled across the plains into French Canada. It took a long time. When

I was about five years old we all settled in Quebec. I had had no schooling. My father then left to go on travelling. I taught myself the rules of life, how to read, write, do sums, then drifted onto streets of Quebec. I taught myself English and French. I never got a job. I lived off street scams, doing a bit of thieving. Later, when I was about twenty, wandering was in my blood, so my itchy feet took me across the Atlantic as a stowaway on a cargo boat. I then travelled, like everyone else towards the east. And now I am in this place. I have no objective, just need to keep moving.'

It took a while for this life story to be absorbed. Sue, who had not yet spoken, said, 'That's quite a story.'

River asked, 'Can I ask two things since there is a crowd of us all together this evening? Question one, from those who are working here in Afghanistan, what do you think of us travellers, passing through on the way to some other country? And question two, those who are travellers, why are you travelling? Do you have a destination and an objective?'

Edwin replied without hesitation, 'You are all hippies, following each other along the Hippy Trail.' From his cultured accent he was very English, dressed in a checked shirt, white shorts and white socks pulled up to the top of his calves, and sandals. 'I have seen the likes of you in town begging, sleeping in the streets, probably thieving. Filthy dirty, no shoes, just bare feet, and smoking hashish openly.'

One of the recent arrivals interrupted, 'I am from the States, I lived in San Francisco for some years, including the summer of flowers, 1967. I can't believe that was only four years ago. The word "Hippie Trail" was invented by a journalist. It didn't last long, at that time most of the flower people rejected all news and journalism, in fact they were anti all things conventional. So, the title Hippie and Hippie Trail died immediately.

'My name is Ronald, Ron. I think the words used now for travellers and those who like alternative lifestyles are freaks, heads, shoe-stringers. Names like that. I think the word for those on the Trail is *Travellers*.'

There were nods and mutterings of agreement.

'And why I am travelling, it is to find a new place to live, away from the war in Vietnam, a place that is away from politicians, a place that is calm and beautiful.'

A small, quiet man, who was sitting in the background, spoke up. 'My name is Abi. I am from Belgium, and was living in a small village, working as a clerk in a local office. I have joined this small group a few days ago to try to reach India. I have very little money. I have never been sure why I am travelling, but I am looking for some religion that will help and guide me. I have read many books, I am always studying. I have read about Islam, Christianity, Hinduism, Sikhism, Judaism, Jainism, Zoroastrianism. I don't think there is a religion I have not studied. I just hope I can find the right one.'

Natalie, who was sitting amongst the group who were holidaying for the weekend from Kabul, said, 'That is a lot of studying. What is Zoroastrianism? I have heard of it but never found out anything about it.'

James, who was sitting next to her, said, 'It is the ancient pre-Islamic religion of Iran that survives there in isolated areas and, are more prosperous in India. There, the descendants of Zoroastrian Persian immigrants are known as Parsis, or Parsees. The Iranian prophet and religious reformer Zarathushtra was more widely known outside Iran as Zoroaster. Zoroastrianism contains both monotheistic and dualistic features. It likely influenced the other major western religions such as Judaism, Christianity, and Islam.'

Julie said, with a laugh in her voice, 'I hope you know what all that means! It sounds as if you have just read it from an encyclopaedia.'

'I have studied some religions of this area as part of my job in Kabul. I'm at Kabul University.'

Lucy said why she and Harry were on the trail. 'We want to learn about the places we are visiting, we like to meet with the local people, find out about their families, what they do, how they live, stuff like that. We have stayed in some very interesting and remote places and met some fantastic generous people.'

Edwin stood up. 'This is all poppycock, you are just sponging off people and your parents so you can have a long holiday rather than working. I am going to have my food outside in the garden.'

There was a long silence. Margaret, with an embarrassed voice, 'I apologise for my colleague, he can be very opinionated.'

River persisted in finding out the travellers' quests and desires. Jim who was wearing a large leather hat, dark, round sunglasses and a sleeveless tee-shirt stated he wanted to find the best dope in the world.

Ruben, who was bare chested, added that his quest was to visit the north of Pakistan, Swat and Gilgit, take the very high pass over the Karakoram mountains into Tibet

315

and China, walk three times round Mount Kailas, then travel to Lhasa and back south to Nepal.

'That's a long, long trip,' River said. 'It will take years, and loads of cash.'

'Yep! I know, I plan to work sometimes on the way.'

The conversation, arguments, eating and drinking tea went on a long time into the night.

They were woken up late in the morning by Julie. 'I live in the caravan just next to yours. Would you like to come on a short walk with me? It is my favourite. And then I can introduce you to my Hazara friend, Abdul.' They agreed and set off immediately.

Lucy asked, 'You live in that caravan, but you don't appear to have a car.'

'No, I keep it here all the time, I travel from Kabul by bus. I have a small room in Kabul.'

They passed two minarets, both capped by corrugated iron. 'They have been damaged over the past nine hundred years by just about every marauding army passing through. I think they served as models for the Minaret of Jam you visited.'

The walk followed through orchards of almond trees, citrus fruits and pomegranates. The meadows were full of summer, wildflowers. They returned to the streets of Ghazni. Julie took them to meet Abdul in a small dusty shop filled with embroideries of every pattern, colour, shape and size.

'Abdul has an outstanding knowledge of all these embroideries. I want to write a book with him before all that knowledge is lost.'

Harry and Lucy spent two more days in Ghazni. Soon they needed to get to Kabul, sort out money, post and decide where to go next.

Chapter 26

Kabul, Afghanistan. July 1971

"Remember that happiness is a way of travel,
not a destination"

Harry and Lucy's first impressions of Kabul was an ugly, busy city filled with pollution, streams of old vehicles, large, new Russian Volga saloons, horse-drawn carts and man-drawn barrows, all blocking the narrow streets that had no side pavements. They saw the handsome faces of many tribesmen in flowing turbans, striped *chapans*, the popular silk coats worn by men over their shoulders. Women in body-covering blue burqas and colourful shalwar kameez. There were tourists and travellers in every street.

The city was ringed by mountains, misty purple, brown and green with a shimmering silver, white necklace of snow on the high peaks. This was a strong temptation to draw them into the surrounding countryside without delay.

They found a suitable parking space for them to camp in the garden behind the Mohammed Guest House in Flower Street, close to the centre of Shahr-e-Naw. This they soon discovered was one of the main tourist shopping areas.

After setting up *Forget-me-not* with the awning, they went exploring. Close by was Chicken Street. They had heard from travellers the reputation that it was the best place to find gifts, that many of the business people and buyers of ethnic goods gravitated there. There were several interesting restaurants close by, not just Afghani, but Italian and Chinese.

In the first afternoon they located the main Post Office in Pushtunistan Square and the Bank Mille where they could arrange for transfer of money from England. They picked up letters for both of them from parents and friends. It had been more than a month since they had had any news from home. They sat in a quiet park close by to read their news.

Harry looked at one of the flimsy blue airmail envelopes 'Hey, here is one from Rolly!'

He carefully opened it, and started reading.

'Read it out aloud, I want to know what he is up to,' said Lucy.

Harry turned back to the beginning, *'Dear Lucy and Harry,'* I see he puts you first now! *'How are you? if you are reading this you must be in Kabul, I haven't heard from you for ages. All is good here, I have got plenty of news for you.*

The trip back across Europe was good and quick. Hans is such a nice guy, we hit it off well. It took only six days back to Holland, then one day all the way to Yorkshire. It was great to see Mum and Dad, they were so surprised, they didn't know I was coming home. I saw your mum and dad who are both well. We met up at the pub and I gave them all the news.

The big news from here is that I have got a new job. My boss got another garage, it's in the city, and has asked me to be the manager. I start in about four weeks' time. It is going to be a big responsibility. I don't know how many mechanics will be working with me, maybe two. It means I get more money, but I will have to move from home to a flat in the city. Your dad, Harry, said he will help me find one.

My boss said I had learnt so much travelling with you, he has given me a lot of responsibility. I was planning on going on holiday to Spain, now I know about travelling, but that will have to wait now until next summer when I can get time off work.

I hope the lovely lady, Forget-me-not is behaving. Keep looking after her, oil and grease, and check the tyres. You have gone a long away, about 5000 miles, with still over 2000 to go.

Stay safe, Love Rolly.

Harry looked at Lucy, 'Wow! he is going up in the world.' He wiped a small tear from his eyes. 'I'm so happy, he is such a good mate.' Lucy gave him a big hug.

By the time they had caught up on family news, they realised it was too late to go to the bank. Lucy had previously worked out how much money they still had, in cash and travellers' cheques. She had concluded they need to send home for some more of her savings to finance travelling on.

They returned to Shar-i-Naw to have an early meal. They chose, for a change in diet, an Italian restaurant, Tritonis. The restaurant was busy with tourists and travellers. Before they found a table, they heard a loud shout. 'Hey! You guys, come over here.' It was Donald, who they had met back in Tehran.

'How are you doing? Welcome to Kabul.'

They sat down at the table. 'This is my girlfriend, Adina,' Donald said. 'She is from Israel and is just gorgeous. We are so in love.' She was very beautiful, with olive coloured skin, dark, almond–shaped eyes and long black, shiny hair knotted into a plait and wound on the top of her head.

'I met these two guys in Tehran more than a month ago. They gave me lift to Mashhad, but we took the wrong road. It was three days of dust, rocks, burst tyres. I won't say it was scary, but it was hairy.'

Adina smiled, looking at Harry and Lucy. 'I have heard that story several times now. It is good to meet you.'

'OK! Let's have another beer, and you guys choose what to eat.' Donald pushed a menu in front of them and called for four beers.

The thought of not having another plate of rice with tough lumps of goat thrilled Harry and Lucy. They ordered a pizza, and a spaghetti carbonara.

'So, you have made it across Afghanistan to Kabul without too many burst tyres.'

'Yeh! We just arrived today, all we have done is park up behind the Mohammed Guest House, round the corner, and gone to collect our post. We hoped to go to the bank to transfer some savings to here, but it was closed.'

'I stay at Greens', just along from here. If you want to transfer money it will take five days. It always does, that takes you to the weekend, so the earliest you will get your hands on it will be Sunday.'

Lucy looked at Harry with a downcast expression. 'That's such a long time to hang around here. Maybe we should go to the bank tomorrow, then head off to the north, come back here next week to collect it.'

They both thought about that idea. Donald interrupted. 'I have an even better idea, why don't we hire four horses and ride up to Istalif. It will take about two days each way, and we can have a few days there. I need to get to Istalif very soon to organise some new embroidery for the *Posteen* they are making for me.'

It took them no time to make that decision, and so the planning started with Donald taking charge.

Early the next day, Harry and Lucy got to the bank just as it was opening. After filling in many forms, showing their identities and sitting in a dismal room for about an hour, the official handed them the confirmation of the transfer, telling them it would take five days.

They went to find Donald in the Greens' Guest House. He had booked four reliable ponies, a man to help with the ponies, and the language. They were leaving the next day.

It was very exciting, a new venture. They didn't want to look at any old monuments, castles or mausoleums in or around the city, so they wandered around the bazaars, buying a few essentials Donald had told them they would need. They packed them into the two double saddle bags that were supplied by the horseman who was guiding them.

The weather was fine, clear blue sky and a gentle breeze. They met up with the quiet, well-trained ponies and their guide in a small park on the edge of Shahr-e-Naw. Harry was the only one who had no experience of riding. He had only once been on horseback at the seaside when a small boy and briefly on the way to Jam. The horseman and guide, called Badam, spoke good English. He proudly claimed he was a *Chapandaz*, a Buzkashi horseman. He described himself as "the king among horsemen", he could ride a horse at full gallop for two days without stopping. He then said there would be no galloping, just gentle riding.

He instructed them on mounting, a few words to use to direct the ponies, and an outline of the route they would take. He then led them off in single file through the outskirts of the city. Soon they were following a narrow path alongside fields and orchards, and a canal lined with tall, spindly poplar trees. The fields were busy with men and women taking in an early harvest, separating the chaff from the wheat by tossing it up into the air, letting the wind blow the chaff away, leaving the wheat grains to fall into big flat baskets. They were surrounded by chickens picking up any stray grains. It was a biblical scene, no technology, no electricity. The next field was being turned over by a bullock pulling a wooded plough, the famer struggling to keep the furrows straight.

In the early afternoon, they stopped for lunch of goat's cheese bought from a group of nomads camping by the path in black, wool tents. Fresh water was taken from the small well. Soon the path was joined by a river, sparkling in the sunshine as it bubbled over pebbles and small rocks. They were shaded by huge walnut trees, wildflowers grew in colourful profusion, orchards of almond and pistachio nut trees. Badman, their guide explained he was named after these trees, his name meant almonds in Pashto. In the spring, when the blossom was out, many residents came from the city to picnic in these fields.

By mid-afternoon they were all getting sore from riding in the traditional Afghan saddles. They stopped, with aching muscles at a chaikhana in a village called Kalakan.

From the terrace in front of the chaikhana they could see the houses of Istalif in the distance, climbing up the hill in terraces towards the distant Hindu Kush mountains. The village was surrounded by lush, green fields. There were bunches of grapes hanging from the eaves of most houses and from branches in the trees. Badman told them the grapes from this region were famous throughout the world. Many dried into sweet raisins.

He took the ponies away, to feed them, and settle them for the night in adjacent stables, a rough wooden lean-to with a grass and heather roof.

Donald had spotted some pottery in a shop opposite the chaikhana. Before even sitting to have some tea, he was talking to the owner, negotiating to send a wooden case of it to Kabul for him to export to Canada. He told them later he had found out it was very traditional work to just this area, it was all handmade and decorated the same way it had been for hundreds of years.

He said, 'I came here for embroidered *Posteen* coats, but I have a gut feeling those bowls will sell well, I already know several stores that will love them. However I am going to have to find out about shipping them, they are far too heavy to airfreight.' Donald was obviously very involved in his trading now.

They sat in the late afternoon sun, drinking tea and chatting. Adina looked at Harry, 'You must wear a hat, your face and head are red from the sun. It is very strong here.' Lucy also noted the burn on his face and neck.

'Perhaps I need a bigger one that shades my neck.'

Before the evening meal was served, Lucy said, 'I could do with a long hot bath, soak some of the pain in my thighs away.'

'Not much hope of that, it will be a cold wash in the river, then sleeping on the tables with several snoring, grumbling old men around you.'

They mounted their ponies the next morning, feeling surprisingly refreshed after a long sleep, the fresh air and exercise had exhausted them. They made their way following the river, uphill to the village. It was very picturesque. Wooden houses built on top of each other, the roof of the lower one forming the terrace for the one above. They were surrounded by lush gardens of flowers and vegetables. Women and children, if not working in the fields, watched them from intricately carved wooded upstairs windows, calling out friendly greetings. They stayed for two nights in a comfortable chaikhana, each sleeping on a *charpoy*, a simple bed strung with rope. Donald and Adina conducted their business buying in several shops and workshops, the others explored the alleys and paths around the village.

All too quickly it was time to mount the ponies again and head back to Kabul, they followed the same path most of the way, taking small diversions to look at some historic remains, just mounds in the fields that were expected to be surveyed by archaeologists sometime in the future.

They decided to meet for a meal at Tritonis' again that evening, to talk and go over the adventures they had just experienced.

It was a riotous party with another group of travellers joining them. Plenty of Italian imported beer was drunk.

Harry and Lucy called at the bank to collect their bank drafts, early the following day. Donald, using his experience, told them to get the money in dollar bank drafts. It would cost a bit more, with the exchange from UK pounds, but he would take them to meet Mr. Singh in the money market who would buy them at a good exchange rate.

'Is that just a black market? Which is illegal in Turkey and Iran.'

'No, it is an official black market. There is a street of money changers who do this, sort of legally, but compared with the bank you will be about twenty percent better off.'

On the walk back to *Shar-i-Naw*, Harry spotted a barber sitting cross–legged in the dust shaving the head of an old man.

'That is what I want. To have my head shaved and have a head massage.'

He sat down near the barber on a paving stone to wait his turn. Lucy stood nearby wanting to watch. The barber had a full, white beard and long sideburns. He wore a clean, white turban and had wire rimmed reading glasses perched on the end of his nose. When his turn came, the barber waved his razor for Harry to move forward. He studied his long hair for some time, perhaps never having the opportunity to cut blond hair. He reached out with two fingers to feel it. With his limited vocabulary, Harry instructed the barber to cut all his hair, but not his beard. The barber, with long sharp scissors that were similar to ones they had seen being made in a metal workshop in the bazaar, carefully cut off the locks, placing them on a mat beside him.

'I know he is going to sell those in the market as soon as he has finished,' said Lucy.

The barber with great skill shaved Harry's head with a cutthroat razor, then with an evil smelling lotion massaged it with strong, bony fingers.

Harry was not sure how much a hair cut would cost, after a pantomime of hand signals, the barber showed two small coins in a basket next to him. Harry produced three from his pocket to put in the basket. The old man was thrilled. He was going to make plenty of money off this traveller, after selling his blond hair.

Lucy had become bored waiting, she had found some clothing stalls further down the street, with trestle tables piled high with second hand western clothes.

'These presumably all come from various charities in Europe. They look really clean and in good condition,' Lucy said. 'It's topsy turvy that we have ethnic clothes made here, using local materials and embroideries, and the locals buy western charity clothes.' She looked at Harry's shaven head. 'You need to get a hat now, otherwise your head will burn in this strong sun. I'll choose one for you in a shop in Chicken Street.'

They soon made their way back to *Forget-me-not,* Harry wearing a new embroidered skull cap like those seen under men's turbans. They spent the rest of the day writing letters home, including a long one to Rolly, then posting them. They were not sure whether they would find any post offices outside Kabul.

They had decided to leave the next morning and soon were packing *Forget-me-not* to head to the north of the country. They had originally planned to drive to Mazar-i-Shaif and Balkh but were easily persuaded by Donald to go more slowly, to visit Bamiyan, Band-e–Amir and places on the way.

The traffic on the road out of Kabul was at a standstill. There was a police barrier checking every lorry, taxi and car going in both directions. This was the first holdup they had experienced in many hundreds, in fact possibly thousands of miles. When they finally reached the red and white painted barrier, a police officer politely asked them for passports and vehicle papers. Once they were checked, they passed through the barrier with no problem, but it had delayed them sufficiently so they would not get to Bamiyan in day light. Lucy, looking at the map said it would take about four hours, maybe much longer because the road from the highway to Bamiyan was shown as unmade. She pointed to the dotted line from a small village, Charikar that led west towards Bamiyan.

They found a suitable place to stop near a farm on the outskirts of the village. They had a good supply of food from the bazaars in Kabul, and plenty of fruit, so Harry chose to cook that evening. After the hubbub of the city and, the unusual experience of horse riding it was a quiet night with a long sleep.

Chapter 27

Bamiyan and Band-e-Amir, Central Afghanistan. July 1971

*"The world is a book, and those who do
not travel read only one page."*

The road to Bamiyan was not as bad as the map showed.
It had been recently graded in preparation for blacktop.
They drove slowly without stopping, except for the
occasions they had to give way to buses and a lorry
going towards Kabul. When they arrived at the edge of
the valley of Bamiyan they stopped in amazement. The
valley was a flat area of land, intensively farmed with
the river meandering through. On each side there were
cliffs, pale sand and tan–coloured, towering on each side
of the valley to over one thousand feet. They gazed in
amazement at the spectacular view, their eyes travelled
along the cliffs, picking out many small caves in deep
shadow. Initially they did not notice the two huge niches,

each holding a sculptured, carved Buddha in the same coloured stone as the cliffs behind.

They learned more later, from a guide who persistently told them they must go with him to explore the honeycomb of caves and tunnels in the cliffs. He told them Bamiyan lay on the ancient Silk Road, which ran through the Hindu Kush mountain region to this Valley. Historically the Silk Road had been a caravan route linking the markets of China with those of the western world. This stopping place was the site of several Buddhist monasteries, and a thriving centre for religion, philosophy, and art. Monks at the monasteries lived as hermits in small caves carved into the side of the Bamiyan cliffs. Most of these monks embellished their caves with religious statuary and elaborate, brightly coloured frescoes, sharing the culture of Gandhara, to the north and east of Afghanistan. The caves resembled the Troglodyte caves of France, but here Buddhist monks and hermits had lived many centuries before.

An area directly in front of the Buddhas was kept clear of traffic, buildings, chaikhana, and guest houses so the view was not disrupted. It was, however, a good football pitch for the local boys. They found a space to park to one side amongst some other travellers in tents and camper vans.

Lucy declared they must stay there for at least three days. They knew it was going to take days to explore the valley and surroundings.

Harry agreed. 'It would be cool to hang out here for a while, then we could then go to Band-e-Amir for two days. It's further along this road. You can go swimming in the lakes, then come back to Bamiyan, before we travel to the north.'

They went to a chaikhana for a meal, they now thought they could afford it, as they had just got a load of money from the bank, with a good exchange rate, thanks to Donald. The chaikhana was filled with travellers. There was a loud buzz of personal adventures, full of stories of travelling, excitement about arriving in such a beautiful spot, a highlight for many of the young people.

One couple related the story of how they refused to pay the small fare of about two dollars for the bus from Kabul because they thought they would never reach the valley. 'The bus had no glass in the windows, it broke down twice on the steep climb up the pass near here. The engine overheated. Everything was covered in smoke and steam. The driver and *batcha,* he was the boy who puts a log or stone under the wheels to stop the bus rolling away, sorted the problem by pouring endless buckets of water from the river over the red hot engine.

'We were sitting next to two cages of chickens, and there was a piglet tied to the leg of one of the seats. The seats were, in fact just two planks of wood, incredibly uncomfortable. When we got here, we did pay the fare, much to amusement of the driver, the *batcha* and most of the passengers.'

In the morning the Buddha sculptures were in shadow, it was difficult to discern the carving in the niche. Without the help of a guide, they climbed up twisting steps to stand on top of the head of the giant Buddha. The view across the valley, to the cliffs on the south side filled them with awe. Men, women and children were working in the fields, a long way below them. The river, a vivid blue, sparkled in the sunlight. At the top of the niche, above the Buddha's head, they could see the remains of coloured paintings. Lucy took her sketch pad from her bag and did a rapid drawing of the view, and details of the painting above them. They explored the maze of tunnels and caves built into the cliffs. Although some of the caves were filled with rubbish, many of them were decorated with religious images of the likes of Buddha.

'It's a bit like those caves in the fairy town, where there were white shining pillars and religious paintings in the caves' said Harry.

'Different religion, different time,' Lucy said, thoughtfully. 'I wonder how Donna is, I would love to hear from her. She was such a loving person.'

When they climbed down to the valley, the sunlight shone directly onto the Buddhas, revealing the intricate carving of the folds in the shawls worn by the Buddha.

After two days of exploring the cliffs, they walked through the fields in the valley, passing through a couple of villages. The people living there were all from the Hazara tribe. The women did not aways cover their faces, they looked, openly with curiosity, at the visitors. They wore full skirts over flower printed pantaloons, the hems and cuffs of the skirts were embroidered with neat, cross stitch patterns. Every woman and girl had either a plain or embroidered shawl over their head and shoulders. Round their necks, they wore the family wealth in weighty silver necklaces of coins, silver and coral earrings, and heavy silver bangles and ankle bracelets. There was some activity, helping with the harvest, collecting water, weaving or cooking on a charcoal fire by their small mud house. Lucy watched as they spun wool using an egg-shaped stone as weight, spinning as they walked along a path. The weaving was done on a loom stretched along the ground, making narrow strips for donkey sacks or baggage ties. These were also sewn together to make colourful kilims used on the ground to sit on.

Several times they were invited to enter a house to share some food or have a pot of tea. Harry said to Lucy, 'That guy we met last night, I can't remember his name, he told me about the code of *pukthunwali*. He knew a lot about customs and the tribes in Afghanistan. I would like to chat with him again, get some more knowledge from him. He said there are two principles within all the tribes. One is the obligation to show hospitality to a stranger, without hope of a return favour. That is called *malmastiya*: the other is the duty to fight to the death to protect the life of a stranger who had taken refuge among them called n*anawat*i.

'He said he is often invited to have a drink, or take a meal with Afghan people, often very poor people who have little or no food for themselves. He also said that Afghanistan was a country deeply fragmented by ethnic, linguistic and regional differences. If there was one thing that could be said to unite the Afghans, it was religion: virtually all Afghans are Muslims and the overwhelming majority of them are Sunni Muslims. Travellers often remark upon the simple piety of the people. All activity stops whenever the call to prayer sounded from the local mosque.'

'Yes, we've both noticed these things.'

A woman, with a face as wrinkled and the colour of a walnut sitting on the doorstep of her tiny house beckoned them to come in.

With the correct greeting they joined her, her farmer husband and two children first for a pot of tea, sitting outside their house in the late sunshine. Then the older daughter beckoned them into the house. A meal of dhal and rice, with small individual bowls of spicy greens, was laid out on the rough wooden table. They were invited to sit down, a jug of warm water was passed round for them to wash their hands. There were no knives and forks, the plates were fresh banana leaves. They had become accustomed to eating with their fingers. They had no common language, but with hand signals, and a certain amount of pantomime acting they exchanged some information about the food, which country they came from and how much they were enjoying visiting Afghanistan.

Their thanks to the family for the meal, inviting them into their home was dismissed by the woman with generous smiles from all the family. Even though they had recently learned about the normal hospitality to complete strangers, Harry and Lucy were both deeply moved. It was obvious to them this was a poor household, a simple farming family.

Along the side of the house was a horizontal, traditional loom, set up with warps and wefts to complete a fine cotton shawl, the woman and her daughter showed Lucy the basics of simple weaving.

They knew they would return to Bamiyan, there was so much more to see in the valley, but they decided to go to the next destination in the morning, the lakes of Band-e-Amir. It was only a short day's drive further along the valley. It was very hot, in the mid-afternoon when they arrived, the clear, sparkling water looked tempting. Lucy immediately put on her costume and jumped into the freezing cold, vivid blue water.

'My God, this is cold, why?'

'Probably because we are three thousand feet up, and it gets pretty cold here at night. I should imagine they are all frozen over for the winter.'

'Come in, you should go skinny dipping, there is no one around for miles. It's great once you are in.'

Harry stripped off his shorts and leaped in next to Lucy. They splashed and ducked each other, their laughter and shouts echoing off the cliffs. The cold water eventually drove them out. They stretched out in the sun to dry off.

There were six lakes, the lowest one being the biggest and deepest. They were formed by natural dams built up over a long period of time by natural salts in the water. Where the water cascaded over the dam, small mills had been built, grinding the grains grown further down the valley. Later they investigated one of the mills, but it was not in use and vacant.

The rock formations, the sky and high cliffs over the water were reflected in the clear, vivid blue water.

'These are just like those swimming lakes you took me to in Turkey,' said Lucy.

Harry thought, 'yes, and we are in a much better mood now, much better than we both were back then.'

They spent two days by the lakes, relaxing quietly without seeing any other visitors or wandering shepherds. They drove back down to Bamiyan, to park in the same place as earlier in the week.

Lucy said she just wanted to go to the village to buy a

few things, and some fruit. Harry sat in the sun, smoking a joint, looking at the cliffs with so many caves carved into them, the Buddha sculptures, so awe inspiring. He wrote a few lines in his diary, trying to describe the view and the atmosphere of the place.

Lucy returned and placed a small, wrapped parcel in Harry's hands. It was wrapped in sheets of a local newspaper, tied with a rough piece of string.

'The answer is YES.' Lucy said.

'What do you mean, YES. I don't understand. What is the question?'

'The question was made many weeks ago, and I said "NO". Now I say "YES!"' Harry was still mystified.

'Come on, thick…oh, get a grip, you asked me back in Iran, in Mashhad if I would marry you. I said "NO", but now I say "YES!"'

Harry leapt up, 'What! You will marry me!' He gave Lucy the biggest hug he had ever given her.

'Well, look at your engagement present then.'

He tore the wrapping away, it was a fine, cotton shawl, deep purple with two fine lines of red running lengthways down the middle.

'You got it from that old lady who invited us in for tea and food several days ago, didn't you?'

'Yes, I saw it then and knew it was just for you.'

Harry gave her another huge hug. 'I must get you a ring. I'll go now.'

He ran off but was back in two minutes because he had forgotten his money. He jumped up and down, gave Lucy another big kiss.

It did not take him long to find a ring in the bazaar.

'The man said it was silver, and these red stones are rubies. I'm not sure because it wasn't expensive.' He carefully put it on Lucy's finger. 'There, you are my fianceé.'

Lucy looked at the ring, her eyes sparkling. 'I don't think it is silver, not the right colour, and I think the rubies are tiny bits of red glass. But it means a million pounds to me.'

The couple were overjoyed, they could not stop grinning at each other.

Next to them, parked close was an old Land Rover, with army decals from the second world war still attached to the bodywork, and Irish registration plates. They soon got to meet the four Irish travellers, who had watched the excitement of the engagement activity earlier. They were rehearsing playing on three violins and the girl playing a Bodhrán, a handheld drum. Gren, the leader introduced himself. 'We are putting on a small gig tonight, just the four of us, we hope we can get a ceilidh going. We'll do it just to celebrate you two love birds.'

'That's fantastic, we'll definitely join in. First, come and join us in the chaikhana.'

The chaikhana was busy, a lot of expectation for an exciting evening ahead. The Irish were easy to get on with, conversation flowed without pauses. They quickly introduced themselves as Fin, Rohan, Gren and Caitlin, then launched into various stories of their travels across Europe, Asia to Afghanistan.

The Irish jig started without introduction, without endless tuning, just the scraping of bows, the sudden screeching of three violins played with any syncopation and harmony lost within the first chords, drowning out the beat of the Bodhrán. It was frenetic, fast, and totally Irish. And it didn't stop, they played for fifteen or more minutes without a hesitation or break.

Next, they moved into a slower routine, tempting couples to join in groups of six or eight people into squares, the dancers swapping sides, swapping partners in a chaotic mix up that ended with the dancers collapsing in a heap on the ground, filled with hilarious laughter.

Fin and Rohan called to see if anyone could dance the traditional step routines. There were two brave girls who stepped forward, to join the two males and Caitlin in the stylish, formal and regimented routines with little upper body movement, precise and quick foot movement and a strict number of steps.

The gig went on until very late. The travellers watched as the full moon rose over the cliffs, to illuminate the carved Buddhas in a silver light. There were chillums and reefers passed from hand to hand, groups gathered in the darkness as others continued to dance. The music did not slow down.

It was a late start the next morning. Harry and Lucy told their new friends they wanted to go to Mazar-i-Sharif. Glen said they were planning to head that way, but looking at the map it was more than one day's drive, over a very high pass and difficult roads. He said that they had decided to stop at Tashkurghan, a village before Mazar. They did not like big cities. Lucy immediately agreed. 'I don't want any more big, polluted cities for a long time. Not when we have such amazing countryside to go to.'

After further examining the map, it was decided they

should go for about three or four hours, then stop by the road before they got to the busy highway from Kabul to the north.

Chapter 28

Tashkurghan, North Afghanistan
July 1971

"A good traveller has no fixed plans and
is not intent on arriving."

They gathered together beside a small river, under the spread of huge walnut trees. Harry played his guitar with the Irish violins, Caitlin sang the words of a west Ireland poem. Later they settled down for a peaceful night.

The road onwards climbed steadily to the Salang pass. It was bitterly cold at the top of the pass. A sharp wind was blowing down from the Hindu Kush. There were fields of snow still in corries on the north face of the peaks. There was a painted sign beside the road, *11,030 feet, the highest road tunnel in the world. Built in 1965.* The tunnel dived through the mountain, driving through it felt like dropping down a dark well. There were dim lights at infrequent intervals, not enough to illuminate the concrete walls dripping with water.

The road from the tunnel followed hair-pin bends, dropping rapidly through surrounding crags and above a rushing river. At one point, coming round a tight bend, it appeared as though they were confronted by a sheer wall of rock, reaching the sky. For millions of years the river had carved a narrow cleft through the rock, so narrow it felt as if you could touch both sides with outstretched hands. Suddenly, having passed through the narrow gorge the landscape opened to an enormous pancake flat plain, the Steppes, that stretch far north into Russia and follow the River Oxus through fertile land of cotton, mulberries, corn and fruits. Behind were the peaks of the Hindu Kush.

'This is the most incredible road we have travelled on, anywhere.'

A short way in the distance they could see the domed roofs, the same colour as the earth, of the village of Tashkurghan. They met up with the Irish Land Rover and found a suitable place to park on the edge of the village.

'This looks such a cool place, I want to go now to explore,' said Lucy. There was general agreement from all of the group.

The bazaar was a number of narrow, covered streets. The roofs constructed of a series of domes, pierced with small windows of brightly coloured glass. The atmosphere was one of eastern promise, of exciting finds, of unexpected beautiful handcrafted artifacts. The tiny stalls on raised platforms lined each side of the narrow bazaar. The traders chose their most interesting products to place in a shaft of light from the coloured glass in the roof. A surprisingly clean small stream ran down the centre, cooling the air and absorbing the dust.

The four men went straight for the chaikhana, to order fizzy soft drinks, Caitlin and Lucy went down a side bazaar to look at shoes. The cobblers had handmade embroidered slip-on ballerina type designs, long knee length boots with tooled leather or covered with intricate embroidery. There were long riding boots, with high heels, no difference between the left and right foot. The stall holder explained these were boots for Buzkashi riders. He said that he was the maker for the very best riders and told them there was an important match the next day. Another part of the bazaar was given over to copper pots and utensils, next to an area where four paths joined devoted to traditional skull caps worn by the men under their turbans, similar to the one Harry had bought earlier in Kabul. Each pattern from different locations, villages and districts.

It was overwhelming, Caitlin tried asking each stall holder in her broad County Kerry accent the price of items. There was confusion and not much understanding. They followed on down the bazaar, to come across the partridge cage makers. Dome shaped cages woven from willow with special covers that were made by the tailors. Died indigo blue with special markings in white for each owner. They were told to go to the camel market later to watch some partridge fighting. They returned to the chaikhana, Fin and Rohan had borrowed a small leaflet distributed by a local hotel describing some of the facts about Mazar and Tashkurghan. Fin read out a passage. 'It says here that Alexander the Great of Macedonia passed through here, and married Roxan on a hill just over there.' He pointed down the street to the open countryside.

Harry reflected, 'That guy, Alex, who we met in Herat, should come here. He was dead keen on Alexander, he thought he was some distant relation.'

Lucy said, 'I remember him, he was jumping off the walls of the Citadel, I thought he was stoned out of his mind and would probably kill himself.'

Caitlin passed on the information about a local Buzkashi game that was on the next day. They decided they would have to go to watch, not having any idea about Buzkashi or what it involved.

As they returned to their camp site, they saw crowds of people, all men, heading down the road to where it was obvious some game was to be held. They followed them.

They reached a dusty square, where the camel market was held. A circle of men were watching a partridge fight. The birds are caught in the spring, then trained and strengthened by the owner. Two birds were released from their cages, two judges ensure there is fair play, and that no bird is injured. They push them to face each other. The winning bird dominates or frightens off the opponent. The men in the crowd gamble loudly, exchanging handfuls of bank notes.

Lucy was relieved that no blood was spilt, that it was well organised, and appeared only an excuse for the men to gamble.

The next day, in the late afternoon, it was obvious the buzkashi game was soon beginning. A large crowd had gathered at the edge of the village. In the distance they could see furiously galloping horses, creating a dust storm in the late sunlight. The horses were suddenly approaching. The crowd parted, the riders stormed past, short whip in hand, sometimes between teeth. They looked like a horde of conquesting warriors. The horses, foaming at the mouth, wide eyed, nostrils dilated, were being driven by the riders, knee to knee, whipping their mounts, and their opponent riders. The thunder of hooves disappeared across the sand, out of sight.

'Where have they gone? Is it over now?' exclaimed Gren. A young man standing next to them, dressed in a white turban almost to the ground and a black beard down to his waist explained to them. 'Buzkashi is played with a dead goat. They killed it yesterday, in a ceremony, then filled the skin with wet sand. It's very heavy. There's no playing field, like you have in your football games, there's no limit to where they go. Now they may be beyond that hill.' He indicated a distant rise. 'If you carry the goat, other players will want to take it from you. A goal is scored by passing round that post you see over there, then returning to the circle marked in the ground. That is called *hallal,* the circle of justice. There are two teams, but the rider who scores a goal is so praised, he is like a *Khan,* a king, so many times his own team will fight for the goat to be the *khan.* Look,' he said, 'they come back.' The riders galloped back, as a tight horde. One man, in the middle, held the goat between his thigh and his saddle. The rider next to him, hit him fiercely across the cheek, blood ran down his face. With just one boot on the saddle, he rode his horse into deliberate crash, his two hands stretched to grab the goat. A wild cheer rises from the crowd, he had firm hold of the dead goat as he charged to the final circle.

The riders dismounted, their attendants start brushing down the mounts, adding a nose bag of sweet hay, and a drink of fresh water. The winning *chopendoz* was carried on shoulders through the cheering crowd. The heat and tension of the game soon dissipated.

The six travellers return to their camp, exhilarated but exhausted. They decide on a quiet meal cooked by their vans.

In the morning, still enthusiastic to explore more of the bazaar, and the village, Harry, Lucy and Caitlin left early to find a change in the market stalls. It was clearly market day, there were donkeys, carts and farmers arriving from all directions, bearing farm produce to sell during the morning.

Outside the covered bazaar there were fenced off areas filled with sheep, goats, horses and camels. The atmosphere in the village had changed from the quiet bazaars when they first arrived. There was noise of women bargaining for groceries, men haggling over the price of a piglet, and the excited cries of children running through the legs of the adults.

They gathered together in the early afternoon to discuss where to go next. Lucy was keen to follow their Irish friends to Balkh, a town past Mazar that they knew was a centre of the ancient Gandhara dynasty. Harry was indifferent, willing to go where everyone else wanted.

Then they saw about five police vehicles approach their camp, parking in a semi-circle facing the campers. About ten policemen in uniform gathered in front, the officer in charge was dressed in a western suit, worn at the cuffs and elbows, with food stains on the lapels.

He spoke in good clear English, 'We have come to inspect you, we are searching for illegal items. You must stand without moving in a line here.' He indicated with his boot a line in the sand. 'Now please empty your pockets of all possessions onto the ground in front of you.' There was an immediate reaction of questioning, and refusal.

'I have the full authority of the ministry to examine your possessions.' He waved a type written piece of paper. He indicated for four of the police to stand behind the travellers. 'Do not try to throw anything away. My men are watching you, and do not touch any of the items on the ground.' The reaction from the five travellers was one of disbelief.

'Hey, man! You can't just do this, we are visitors to your country, we've done nothing wrong.'

'Silence. And stand still. I will start with you,' pointing at Fin who had voiced the objection.

Two of the policemen started a finger search of the few possessions he had put on the ground.

They then moved one by one along the line, carefully searching. The found no criminal evidence.

The officer then instructed the police team to search the camper vans, to bring out all the bags. 'Please identify your own bags, they will be placed in front of you.'

This was developing into a very efficient, well organised operation.

The police spent a long time rummaging in the camper vans, the line of travellers was becoming irritated and impatient.

Harry called out, 'We've nothing to hide, this is crazy.'

The officer indicated to one of the men to look in Harry's bag first, a small rucksack. He tipped the contents onto the ground, and immediately seized upon a lump of hashish. He handed it to the officer, who picked a small piece off with his fingernail, put it in his mouth. Looked hard at Harry, with raised eyebrows.

The officer indicated to the men to continue searching each bag, emptying the contents onto the ground.

Lucy's bag was full of cosmetics, some coins, a packet of pills and some tissues.

The policeman pulled up a cellophane bag and handed it to the officer.

He looked at it carefully, tried to open it, then took it to the back of his car. With a sharp blade he made a small slit, touched the white grains with his fingertip, and tasted it.

'What is this?' he demanded of Lucy.

'I've no idea, it's not mine. I've never seen it before' she said, her voice had some panic in it.

'It appears to be an illegal substance.' He clicked his fingers, two policemen took Lucy firmly by the elbows. 'You will have to come to the station in Mazar, and this will be sent to Kabul to our laboratory for full examination.'

Caitlin exploded, 'Jesus Christ and Holy Mary. What the fuck is going on?' She marched forwards towards the officer, flame red hair cascading in waves over her shoulders, face flushed with anger, wild green Irish eyes, pointing a finger at his face.

He had never been confronted by a woman in this way.

There was an instant outcry from everybody. Harry shouted, lurching forward, 'You can't do that, it's nothing to do with her. That bag has been planted on her. She never takes any drugs.' He was apoplectic, sweating, red in the face.

'Quiet! everyone stays by their possessions, or I'll take you all to jail' the officer shouted.

The officer calmly took the lump of hashish he had found in Harry's possession. 'This is yours? Where did you get it?

Harry muttered, 'Kabul.' The officer handed it back to him, with a small smile on his lips. 'It is good quality, enjoy it.'

Lucy was dragged, her feet digging a furrow in the sand, to the nearest police vehicle. The convoy drove off.

Harry was so distressed and angry, he lurched towards *Forget-me-not*. 'I've got to follow them, I can't leave Lucy.'

Gren reached out a restraining hand. 'You can't drive, man. Too uptight. I'll drive you.' They piled into the Land Rover. Glen drove fast, they soon caught up with the convoy outside the local police station. There was a guard outside the closed door, with an ancient rifle. He would not let them pass, they tried to push pass, the guard pointed the rifle at them, so threatening they had to back off.

After a long time, a note was passed out through the door.

'The suspect will be escorted to Kabul in the morning. The suspected substance, now locked in a safe box, will be taken to the laboratory in Kabul for testing.'

Chapter 29

Tashkurghan, North Afghanistan – Kabul. July 1971

"In times of stress, the best thing we can do for each other is to listen with our ears and our hearts and to be assured that our questions are just as important as our answers."

Glen and Harry stood in stunned silence. The armed guard had marched away, the door was firmly bolted with two large padlocks, all the lights were switched off.

'What can we do?' muttered Harry totally distressed.

'We can do nothing now, not till tomorrow, morning. It is dark now.' He paused in thought. 'I suggest we book a taxi to come to pick you up first thing tomorrow and take you to Kabul. You can't drive, it would be too dangerous. You are stressed out. It's about eight hours drive, you will have an accident or run off the road. You would drive too fast and dangerously.'

They went back to the square in front of the Blue Mosque. They asked at a rank of taxis, parked waiting for late tourists to leave a restaurant. One of the drivers agreed to a deal. Harry passed over a handful of bank notes. Glen made a note of the driver's name and the registration number of his taxi.

It was a sleepless night. Glen arranged with his friends to keep a watch over Harry, each taking one hour in turn. He noted that their possessions had been gathered up and packed away and locked into *Forget-me-not*.

Harry sat on the ground, staring into the dark, seeing nothing, his mind numb, not able to collect any thoughts.

There was a glow of morning light on the horizon when he saw the headlights of the taxi bouncing along the track. He climbed into the back seat. The driver wore a long white turban and had a long black beard. He spoke no English, so the long journey back to Kabul was in silence. They stopped briefly for tea and a bowl of pilau. It was mid-afternoon when they arrived in the centre of Kabul. The taxi driver had never been to the city. Harry stopped a traffic policeman to ask the way to the police station. The directions were given to the driver.

After a very long wait in the dismal police station, a junior officer asked Harry to come forward.

He explained, slowly in great details of all that happened in Tashkurghan. The officer took notes of every word. He turned and showed them to a senior officer sitting at a desk at the back of the room, who came forward and said to Harry, 'Your friend will be in *Pul-e-Charkhi* jail.'

'Can I see her now?'

'No, you may visit her on Thursday afternoon, that is the visiting time.'

Harry worked out it was in two days' time. He was still in deep shock.

He left and sat on a low wall, alongside three small boys, typical ragamuffins dressed in filthy torn clothes and no shoes. One of them was holding the string to a paper kite, flying high above the roof tops in a clear azure, blue sky. The boy offered the string to Harry, inviting him to fly the kite, he shook his head in refusal. All his dreams, hopes and desires for the future had collapsed and crashed. Tears filled his eyes, he buried his head in his arms. The three boys were mystified, they muttered amongst themselves and left to enjoy their kite flying.

A short while later, he was still sitting on the wall, unable to think straight, the junior police officer he spoke to earlier came up to him.

'Excuse me, sir, may I sit with you?' He sat on the low wall. 'I have just come off duty, I see you are still here. You are very stressed, it is a difficult time. May I suggest you go to the embassy of your country? They will help you.'

'Oh! Thank you! Thank you! I can't think, I'm so confused. Yes, I will do that now.'

'It would be better in the morning, your embassy will be closed now. Take a taxi to your hotel. You can visit them in the morning.'

The young officer left, Harry found a taxi to take him to Sharh-i-Naw. He checked into Greens' Guest House. He didn't want to go back to the Mohammed, where they had stayed in *Forget-me-not*.

He collapsed on the charpoy, unable to eat or to get to sleep for the second night, until the early hours when complete exhaustion took over.

As soon he thought the embassy may be open, he caught a taxi to the area north of Sharh-i-Naw. The embassy was a classic old building set in well maintained gardens.

The high metal gates were guarded by the *chowkidar,* wearing a coloured turban with one end raised stiffly above his head like a cockerel comb.

The *chowkidar* listened to Harry's request to speak to the Ambassador. He retreated to his guard room next to the gates, Harry could see him talking on the telephone. After a few moments he opened a small gate and indicated for Harry to pass through, pointing ahead across the gravel drive to the entrance.

He was met halfway by a smartly dressed man who introduced himself as Charles Wright-Smith, the first secretary to the Ambassador. He explained that the Ambassador would see Harry as soon as possible, but in preparation could he explain the circumstances for him to wish to speak to him? Charles was a personable thirty–five year old, his hair was neatly trimmed and parted. He wore dark trousers, button down white shirt and shining polished shoes.

They went into a small, well furnished office. Harry explained the best he could the whole situation, getting confused about the sequence of events in his anxiety and stress. Charles calmly made notes on a large pad, repeatedly asking for clarification on many points so he could understand all that had happened.

Cups of coffee were served on a tray, with an elegant

coffee pot, an item Harry had not seen since he left England. He felt reassured that the situation would soon be in hand and sorted out by top professionals.

It was mid morning when the telephone rang, Charles answered it briefly.

'The Ambassador will see you now, he is called Sir Richard Thorpe. I suggest you address him as 'Sir', but don't worry, he is very easy to talk to.'

Harry was led to the Ambassador's office. It was large, well lit by floor to ceiling windows that opened onto the garden. The Ambassador sat behind a highly polished desk, empty except for two silver framed photos, there was the smell of expensive cigarettes. Harry suddenly felt he was back at school in the headmaster's room in school being disciplined for some minor infringement.

'I am Richard Thorpe, I see your name is Harry, what is your full name?'

'Harry Braithwaite,' he replied nervously.

'Do you have your passport with you? It is just a formality to establish your nationality.'

Harry took his passport from his money belt, hidden under his shirt. It was the only possession he had brought with him from Tashkurghan.

'I have read the notes from Charles, here.' He indicated the note pad pages filled by Charles. 'I can see there is a big problem. Please fill in with your story.'

'My girlfriend ... My fiancée ... was taken three days ago. The police put a suspect packet in her bag. It was planted by them. She never does any drugs.'

'I see.' He looked over his half rim glasses, steepling his

fingers. 'I note that your fiancée is called Lucy. Have you contacted her parents?'

That was something that had not crossed Harry's mind. 'No, but I know it would take days to make a phone call from here.'

'Maybe we can help, what is your fiancée's full name, and her parents' names if you know them.'

She is called Lucy Ann Commins, her papa, is …er… Mr Cummins. It may help, but I think he works for some ministry in London.'

'Ah ha! That would be very useful.' He clicked his fingers to Charles, who had already pulled a large directory from a shelf and put it on the desk. He flicked over some pages.

'Here we are, Sir, Dominic Cummings. He is in the Finance Ministry at HMG.'

'That's excellent.' He looked at a wall clock that showed the time in London. 'It is too early now, I'll call him at 10:00 London time. It's easy from here, we have a direct line to London from the embassy,' he explained to Harry.

'At least that is some positive news. The rest is not so good.' He leant forward with a concerned expression on his face. 'Lucy, I understand is in *Pul-e-Charkhi* jail. That is a terrible place. Certainly not the place for a woman. We come across situations similar to this occasionally, it takes a long time and is expensive to sort out.

'We will get a lawyer, we have several we know, and we will make representations to the judge.' He paused. 'Do not take this information outside this room, in the experiences we have had, the police who placed the substance in Lucy's possession do it so they can earn money from any settlement in court. It is extortion, *baksheesh,* and takes a long time to sort out and is expensive as I have already suggested. We know visiting to the jail is restricted to Thursday afternoon. I will write a note to the Governor, and Charles here will accompany you. Hopefully it may make access a little easier.

'In the meantime I suggest you stay in our guest lodge, you will find it less stressful that staying in town. Best of luck!'

Harry was led across the lawns to a small cottage in the grounds. 'You will be comfortable here. Do you have any luggage at your hotel?'

Harry almost felt like laughing. 'No! I have nothing. This is all I've got.' He spread his arms.

'No problem, we will find you some clean clothes. I'll arrange for cook to bring you some lunch.'

The wait until the next day seemed to last for ever. Food was brought to his room, he manged to eat some of it, and Charles kept looking in, asking if everything was OK.

An embassy car took them to the outskirts of the city. Charles explained that the *Pul-e-Charkhi* jail was new, still being built. The accommodation was very basic, in fact non-existent. Occupants are forced to buy their food from a guard. The food supplied by the jail was just not edible.

'I have an Indian film star magazine here. I have done this before with another inmate. I suggest you put some cash into the folds of the paper for Lucy to buy some food. Hand it to her concealing the cash. She must be so careful, never let any of the other occupants see it, or it will be stolen. Also here is a bag of oranges. The same, keep it secret.'

Charles spoke to the guard at the entrance, handed him the note from the Ambassador. They were waved through without delay.

For two hours every Thursday the prisoners were allowed to exercise outside in a small, yard surrounded by steel bars and wire. The prison designed as a giant wagon wheel was still under construction, to a very poor finish. Raw exposed concrete still dripping with water, heavy metal doors and bars on every opening.

Harry soon found Lucy. She looked ill, pale and desperate. She could hardly stand. She hung onto Harry, weeping into his shirt.

'Get me out of here, get me out. It's worse than a hell hole. I have to share a tiny room with other women, who are I'm sure all thieves and prostitutes. They shout and scream day and night. The guards just hit you with their guns. I have nothing, only the clothes I was wearing several days ago. I was given a thin, ragged, lice-infested blanket and have just a rough concrete shelf to lie on.

'Please get me out of here. What is happening, when can I go home?'

'The Ambassador has contacted your Papa. He is coming here immediately. They are getting a lawyer and will soon have you out.'

Harry did everything he could to comfort her. It seemed as though they had been together for only minutes, when the guards were shouting for all the visitors to leave, herding the prisoners back to their cells with long sticks and pointed guns.

Charles made every attempt to be positive on the return trip, but Harry was plunged back into deep depression again.

Chapter 30

Kabul, Afghanistan August 1971

Sir Richard came to visit Harry in the guest cottage later that day.

'I have spoken to Lucy's father, he is flying to Kabul in two days' time. It is taking a little longer than thought, because he is getting a diplomatic passport. That will make things much easier here.

'I have been in contact with a lawyer, the best there is in Afghanistan. He has explained to me the system we have to go through. There are three layers of court rulings, often each one in front of a different judge. At each ruling there will be fees to pay. Usually considerable fees!'

Harry interrupted, 'When can she be released? Made free?'

'It can take a long time, usually months. It will help when her father gets here. He will have the backing of HMG, that will help.'

Harry slumped down on the bed, head buried in his arms.

Lucy's father, Dominic, arrived two days later, he was met by the embassy at the airport, and brought directly to the Ambassadors office.

After a long time, presumably in meetings with Sir Richard, he came to Harry's room.

'This is a real mess you have got my daughter into. I knew nothing good would come of you taking her away to wander around the world.'

He promptly left, Harry was dumbstruck.

It was two days later, in the early morning, Harry was summoned to the Ambassador's office.

Sir Richard, Dominic and Charles were sitting at the desk.

Sir Richard looked concerned and very upset. 'We have just received terrible news from the jail, Lucy died last night of an overdose of heroine. It was obviously a mistake, administered by another prisoner in the cell.'

He looked directly at Harry. 'You have our deepest sympathy. This is a terrible shock to all of us, especially since we understand you became engaged to marry just one week ago. Afghanistan is a beautiful country. It is a tragedy your stay here has ended in this way.'

'There are now certain formalities and arrangements we must make. We will keep you informed. You may now return to the guest cottage, Charles will look after you.'

Later the ambassador instructed Charles to arrange for the Mercedes camper van and the contents to be donated to a local charity.

Charles quietly came into the room. He put down a tray with two cups, a tea pot and plate of digestive biscuits onto a side table. He sat opposite the bed, waiting. Harry was asleep. He found it hard to imagine how the pain and loss of a loved one would feel. His occasional girlfriend was in London, working in a boring job in an insurance office. He is fond of her, but their mutual feelings for each other were divided by the distance between them, his job in Kabul.

After a while Harry woke, he looked up, his eyes were red and swollen from crying, his face pale and drawn. He felt lost. The room was strange, it had a different smell, sound, feel, the ceiling was different.

He got up, pulled back the heavy drapes, it was the noise of the gardener mowing the immaculate lawn that woke him.

He then remembered he was in the guest room at the British Embassy.

Life crashed down around him, he sat on the bed, head on his knees, arms wrapped over his head. Could he cry anymore? Was there a limit to the tears anyone held? His mind was whirling around in circles, what are you supposed to do with all the love you have for somebody, if that person is no longer there? What happens to all that leftover love? He let out a howl, a cry from the very inner soul, a cry from the very basis of humanity.

He then noticed Charles sitting in the corner. 'Your tea has got cold.' He poured some into a fine porcelain cup and offered the plate of biscuits. 'We will have to leave soon, an Embassy car is booked to take us to the airport. Your plane leaves at four. If you remember Lucy's father is here, he will accompany the body back to London in a couple of days. He has assured me there would be a formal funeral at the local church at her home town.'

Harry stares dumbly into the distance, none of the words appear to register with him.

Charles escorted him by the arm to the embassy car. At the airport all the formalities had been previously arranged, he passed through immigration and customs without pause.

Charles saw him walk across the tarmac. He was the last to board, the air steward closed the door, the steps were pulled away. From the departure lounge Charles watched as the aircraft accelerated down the runway, climbed steeply to clear the surrounding mountains. He saw the sunlight shine on the wings as the aeroplane banked to the left. It turned, continued to climb then disappeared to the west.

Chapter 31

Kabul and Kunduz Afghanistan
May 2003

To arrive back in Kabul after over thirty years did not cause Harry problems. He had become very involved in his job at "Farmers Working against Drugs" and had been on the staff for ten years now, finally rising to be the director of the small NGO. (Non-Governmental Organisation). His past life was a distant memory, mostly forgotten.

He had suffered ten years of intense therapy for deep depression that had changed his life. He made many attempts at suicide. He suffered personality, character and physical changes.

Rolly came regularly to visit him in the secluded clinic in Hertfordshire, north of London. His visits helped him to make a slow recovery. Rolly talked without interruption, about his life in Yorkshire, his family, Harry's family, his work in the garage. On one occasion he drove

Harry across London to the church in the small village in Sussex. They visited Lucy's grave. It helped Harry to read the inscription on the tombstone. He was relieved he did not meet her parents.

After a long time he was eventually released from the sanctuary declared fit.

He had obtained sufficient funds and permission to travel to Afghanistan. He sent a telegram to the small office in Kabul, suggesting there was no need to meet him at the airport. He knew that airline schedules to Kabul were vague and unreliable. He took a taxi from outside the Kabul airport terminal to the NGO office. He was proud of his new language skills. He could now communicate well in Farse Dari and Pashto.

The taxi arrived outside the metal gates of the NGO office and house. Harry stepped out of the cab, he paused, looked up to the horizon beyond the city, to the silver necklace of snow covered peaks of the Hindu Kush.

'Yes... Yes... Life does go on!'

He knocked on the gate and after a long wait it was pulled open a crack, then opened fully.

'Welcome, Mr Harold, welcome. *Salam aleikum.*' It was Gulrez, the assistant in charge of communications. He indicated with a wave of fingers for the *chowkidar* to collect his two bags from the taxi. He escorted Harry across a stony and weed covered yard to the two story house that acted as their office and headquarters. The house was rendered white, with metal window frames and a flat roof, very much like the majority of other buildings in the area.

The staff had gathered in the front room, Gulrez introduced them.

He was greeted by each in turn by '*Salam aleikum,* Mr Harold.' The right hand across the heart.

'I will show you your office and your rooms in the house.' Gulrez unlocked the door to the office. Harry noted with a wry smile the brass plaque on the door, '*Mr Harold*'. There was no attempt in spelling his surname. The office was sparse and minimal.

'We have very little equipment. It is often difficult to find supplies. I will now show you to your rooms, Sir.'

'You must never call me Sir, that applies to all of you.' He turned to the other two staff. 'Call me Harry or Mr Harold, I'll always call you by your given name.'

His rooms were a bedroom and adjoining bathroom.

Once left alone he unpacked his bags. One was filled with files of paperwork, the other his few clothes.

He carefully folded his purple shawl with two narrow lines of red woven into the fabric and placed it on the middle shelf of the cupboard.

Harry had followed the news on the civil war in Afghanistan, the Russian invasion, the starvation and killing. With intense sadness for the people of the country, he followed the rise and fall of the Mujaheddin, Al Qaeda, the Taliban, the invasion by the United States and Britain, the long Afghan War, the changes at the head of the governments. After years of stalemate, civil war and factional fighting, it was finally declared safe for the NGO to operate from Kabul as well as London. The UN Combined Joint Task Force attempted to take control of the continuous tribal fighting that waged in all corners of the country.

Under the leadership of Hamid Karzai, large investments poured into the country from the West.

Thousands of refugees returned to their towns and villages from camps in Iran and Pakistan.

He soon settled into life in Kabul, running the office, researching the finances and available opportunities for getting more funding. He obtained a written guarantee that the staff would be paid weekly by stipend from the Afghan government but grants and guarantees from Western countries seemed impossible to get. The income for the NGO barely registered in comparison with the wealth created by the worldwide opium trade.

The drug barons, who controlled the trade from their mansions and estates in remote areas in the south and west of the country, had greater gross income than the national income of many small countries.

Kabul was different from his visits thirty years previously. The younger people had never experienced life in peacetime. The openness, friendship and honesty was replaced by desperate poverty and distrust.

He ventured out into Kabul city on a few occasions. He visited parts of the old city that had not been destroyed by missile attacks and bombing. There were in places rough and ready rebuilding reusing materials from destroyed buildings.

In Shar-i-Naw there was not as much destruction. Chicken Street had changed, most craft and gift shops were different, either closed, sold on or taken over by sons and grandsons of the original owners. Some were still selling similar craft items, in fact selling some of the items that were probably for sale 30 years previously.

He spent a lot of time meeting with government officials, ministers and heads of NGOs busy trying to reestablish their bases in the city. He had long meetings with NATO, US and British advisors. There were discussions with the Afghan Army on safety issues. There were, of course office parties with diplomats and advisors.

Two months later, after a joint meeting with the Agriculture minister, a safety colonel from US, and the British officer in charge of the region north of Salang, his NGO was given permission to travel to the north of the country.

He gathered together the staff for a meeting in the small office.

'Finally,' he said, 'we have been granted permission to travel to an area near Mazar–i–Shaif to negotiate with two farmers.

'Three of us will leave next week in the Toyota pick-up to Kunduz, where we can make a base in an empty house belonging to a British NGO. You, Ariana will remain here to look after this office.' He smiled at Ariana, receiving an accepting nod.

'We will be away for about one week, travelling each day to visit farmers in an area near the village of Qowland. We are told it is fertile and productive, close to a river. We now have sufficient funding for us to offer these farmers compensation to grow watermelons rather than opium poppies. To just persuade one would be a major achievement.

'We will be given maps indicating the only safe routes we can follow, they will be regularly cleared of any IEDs. We have been assured they will be safe.'

It was a week later they travelled up the highway to the Salang pass and then to Kunduz.

They saw the devastation left by years of war. Properties bombed, deserted villages, cannibalised remains of Russian tanks. Close by the road was the burned out wreck of a US military helicopter. There was little work being done in the fields, irrigation canals were destroyed, the farmers were understandably nervous of land mines and unexploded munitions in their fields.

They settled into the house in Kunduz, the following morning they set off in the Toyota pick-up truck for the long drive to the Qowland valley.

****

Bagram Air Force Base outside Kabul and Cheech Air Force Base Nevada USA.
May 2003

The Ground Control Station at Bagram base was a concrete box with no windows positioned close to the main runway. Lieutenant Dale Shenka and Corporal MaryJo Wiseman were on duty. Normally there would be a full team of six on duty, but Predator #2 was in the huge corrugate iron service hangar at the edge of the airfield having a full refit. Predator #1, nicknamed 'Ladybird', was on a routine search grid pattern at 15,000 feet to the north of the air base.

The fragile craft had slender wings, angled double fins at the rear. It was powered by a single two blade variable push-propeller at the rear. Where there should be the cockpit glass for the pilot's cabin, there was unbroken smooth white paint. It looked almost like a paper or cardboard toy made by some enthusiastic school boy. The predator was a pilotless guided drone. It was the latest weapon in the war against terrorism.

It was a routine duty, MaryJo glanced several times at the digital clock on the wall, her bladder was feeling full, she hoped she could last the remaining fifteen minutes before her patrol finished and she could go to the can.

The telephone chirped, Dale lifted the receiver. 'Colonel Rodrigez at Cheech here, we have a movement in zone G65f AS789-2. Go to get visual check.'

The map of Afghanistan was divided into one mile square zones, each individually numbered.

MaryJo, with delicate fingers on the tiller manoeuvred *'Ladybird'* in a sweeping curve. Three minutes later she announced, 'I have visual, patching you through. White Toyota pick-up. Heading east to west at 45 mph. They are following the designated IED track.'

The communication by satellite over 7,500 miles between the two bases was clear.

'I see them. Have you a facial visual of the numbers?'

'No, sir. There is strong light reflecting off the windshield. I will manoeuvre ahead and drop from 15 to 9.5.'

'OK, but stay silent.'

'I now have visual in the cab, two items, each wearing a white turban with cloth across their faces. It is very dusty. No chance of facial ID. Third item in bed of truck. Head covered by purple shawl.'

There was a long pause. 'We have confirmed intel. They are the terrorists. Do you have clear collateral?'

'Affirmative, sir.' Said Lieutenant Shenka. 'We are clear of collateral for over a two mile radius.'

There was another pause. 'We again have confirmed intel. Use Hellfire #1 to destroy'.

Dale looked across to MaryJo. 'OK, Missy, this one is yours. Good luck.'

She felt the temperature in the concrete box rise dramatically, the air conditioning was struggling to cope with the heat off the bank of video screens along the wall. She wiped beads of sweat off her forehead.

'Jesus! I have never fired a live missile.'

'No problem, take it on, your best chance.'

MaryJo pulled the list of actions close to the left of her display pad. She selected a few buttons. 'Laser locked on.' Her eyes follow along the green line, now fixed on the driver's door of the pick-up.

Dale turned a black knob on his display pad 90 degrees. 'Number one lock active.'

MaryJo turned a similar knob on her display pad. 'Number two lock active.' The display showed a row of red lights.

She glanced again at the list of actions. 'Counting down from three... Three... Two...'

At that moment the man in the bed of the pick-up threw back the purple shawl and looked up at the sky. Maybe he had a sixth sense or heard the whisper of the drone.

MaryJo's thumb hovered over the large, illuminated red button.

Quotations

Ch 1.
"In any moment of decision, the best thing to do is the right thing. The worst thing you can do is nothing." Theodore Roosevelt.

Ch 2.
"People were right when they say there is no other place on earth as beautiful looking as Istanbul." Chateaubriand

Ch 3.
"A traveller without observation is a bird without wings." Moslih Eddin Saadi

Ch 4.
"A journey of 1000 miles begins with one step." Laozi

Ch 5.
"A journey is best measured in friends, rather than miles!" Tim Cahill

Ch 6.

"We don't need objects, we need adventures." Unknown

Ch 7.

"In the end, we only regret the chances we didn't take."
Lewis Carroll.

Ch 8.

*"Even if you are on the right track, you will get run over if
you just sit there!"* John Ray

Ch 9.

"Not all who wander are lost." J.R.R. Tolkien

Ch 10.

"It's not what you look at that matters. It's what you see."
Henry David Thoreau

Ch 11.

"We have nothing to lose and a world to see." Rainie Navarro

Ch 12.

"Never go on trips with anyone you do not love!"
Ernest Hemingway

Ch 13.

"The journey not the arrival matters." T.S. Elliot

Ch 14.

"Live life with no excuses, travel with no regrets."
Oscar Wilde

Ch 15.

"Travel opens your heart, broadens your mind, and fills your life with stories to tell." Paula Bendfeldt

Ch 16.

"Now that I'm here, where am I!" Janis Joplin.

Ch 17.

"It always seems impossible, until it is done." Nelson Mandela

Ch.18

"To travel is to live." Hans Christian Andersen

Ch 19.

"We have nothing to lose, and the world to see." Maria Stoyanova

Ch 20.

"Life is short, but the world is wide." Simon Raven

Ch 21.

"You can shake the sand from your shoes, but it will never leave your soul." Lily James

Ch 22.

"Tourists don't know where they've been, travellers don't know where they're going." Paul Theroux

Ch 23.

"Take only memories, leave only footprints." Chief Seattle

Ch 24.

"*Have a story to tell, not stuff to show.*" Abhysdheq Shukla

Ch 25.

"*At the end of the day your feet should be dirty, your hair messy and your eyes sparkling.*" Shanti

Ch 26.

"*Remember that happiness is a way of travel, not a destination.*" Roy M. Goodman

Ch 27.

"*The world is a book, and those who do not travel read only one page.*" Saint Augustine

Ch 28.

"*A good traveller has no fixed plans, and is not intent on arriving.*" Lao Tzu.

Ch 29.

"*In times of stress, the best thing we can do for each other is to listen with our ears and our hearts and to be assured that our questions are just as important as our answers.*" Fred Rogers

About The Author

Alastair Hull has spent five decades travelling and exploring the countries of south Central Asia.

His business of buying the colourful, unusual and unexpected took him to many remote bazaars in unforgiving areas.

His desire to seek and understand the origins, cultural significance and function of domestic items led him to have close relationships and friendships with remote tribal people.